AMERICAN RAGE

Alaska Phase I

N. A. BOTTARI

Wolf Rock Publishing
Juneau, Alaska

Wolf Rock Publishing
P.O. Box 21753
Juneau, Alaska 99802

First Paperback edition published 2014

ISBN: 978-0-9903175-0-0
ISBN: 978-0-9903175-1-7 (ebook)

www.americanrageseries.com.

Printed in the United States of America

For Rachael and Martin...
You are the shining lights in my life
and the source of my joy and strength.

Authors Note

✾✾✾✾✾

AMERICAN RAGE Alaska Phase I is a work of fiction but is tempered with a significant dose of life's prescient nightmares. You may find it is ultimately a dystopian story... and it is. Yet it may seem more real than story to some, especially to those of us who allow our minds the freedom to evaluate the world around us without dragging along preconceptions shaped from what others tell us reality *is* and *is not*. In its truest form Alaska Phase I, book one in the AMERICAN RAGE series, is ultimately about ordinary people and how those people differ in the manner in which they both see and interact with their own reality.

For convenience, I have included a reference section at the end of the text of this book.

N.A. Bottari,
Juneau, Alaska 2014

Prologue

❊❊❊❊❊

I killed the President because he was an enemy of the
good people – the good working people.
I am not sorry for my crime.

Leon Czolgosz, Buffalo, NY
Assassin, 1901

❊❊❊❊❊

*The *__ Mansion on Millionaires' Row, Manhattan,
New York, September 14, 1901*

He shivered as he stepped inside the mansion.

"This way sir," the footman beckoned him. The city
air was unusually crisp for a mid-September evening.
Why in hell he ever agreed to this he would never know.
The old fart better make quick work of this damn
signing business, he thought; he didn't have all night.
He had plenty of other stops to make before he could
unload this thing.

"Please wait here sir," the old butler told him, with a
hint of accent betraying his Scottish roots.

"Thank you," he replied, but the butler had already
left the study. Conall Kesson Duthie sat on the edge of
the button leather chair and set the briefcase down next
to him. The pristine stone fireplace immediately caught
his eye. The white birch logs blazed brightly on the solid
brass andirons, but it seemed to Conall not so much as a
match had ever been struck near this hearth. Yet he

could see the burning logs with his own eyes. This was the type efficient house staff he needed, he mused, not a fleck of dust in the air... fireplace stones scrubbed down as clean as a newborn's bottom.

The warm glow from the fire cast flickering shadows across the hand woven beige carpet, probably imported from India or Africa — expensive as hell he'd bet his life on it. Circling the room on a ledge of wooden molding, ink drawings and framed snippets of odd wisdoms in calligraphy stared back at Conall. These knick-knacks or pictures certainly didn't tickle his fancy but money was money. He supposed with that much wealth a man could put whatever he wanted in his study and call it art — or fermented antelope piss if he chose; who would argue with him?

To Conall's right six oak shelves of an inlaid bookcase displayed leather volumes with vastly eclectic titles. From somewhere outside the study a clock chimed nine times. It was late and Conall heard the grumblings of hunger rise from his stomach as if summoned on cue, gurgling in tempo with the opus of the unseen time piece. He fingered the handle of the briefcase. It was locked and he had no key. He wasn't sure why the contents were so important but he had been instructed to guard it with his life. His uncle had entrusted it to him and Conall knew the man had been dead serious about the consequences should something go wrong. As he scanned the study he decided the owner of this mansion was perhaps not as wealthy as was his uncle. The room was far below the standard Conall himself would maintain in his own house and far less than what his uncle presently sported in his. Of course the butler had ushered him straight into this one room and Conall knew it was likely not the only study in the mansion. Quickly growing bored with his thoughts, he looked down at his feet.

Conall's highly polished shoes were firmly planted on a rich-brown grizzly bear pelt that served as a rug. It stretched the length of the stone fireplace hearth. Conall felt squeamish about setting his feet on the massive hide that had once housed a deadly predator. But then... he knew he must strive to have exactly such a display of virulent opulence in his own elegant brownstone — as soon as he could afford one. Conall sighed. When would he ever hit twenty-five? It wasn't fair to make him wait for the trust fund. Wait, wait, wait... that's all he was ever permitted to do except for distasteful tasks like this one dreamed up by his uncle and his circle of rich old bastard cronies. What if he should die while he was doing all this waiting for money that was rightly his? And he *would* soon die — of boredom — if he didn't have his way with the daughter of his uncle's snippety neighbors. True... Marjorie was two years older than Conall but it wasn't like he didn't have experience in these things. The gilded little bitch with her ruffles and her lacey parasol and her daddy's mansion... yes he could show her something all right. She was just another New York transplant with an accent. To think he'd been hoping to get under those petticoats for two years. She probably wasn't even worth the fuss... the little bitch.

"Mr. Duthie," the master of the house bellowed as he strutted into the den, extending his hand. "How are you this evening?"

"Oh fine sir fine," Conall beamed deferentially, popping up from the chair and shaking the man's hand. "Thank you for asking."

"I'd like to get right down to business," the sixtyish man declared. "I have some emergency meetings to attend."

"Oh certainly sir," Conall replied. "I understand."

"Such a tragedy... this whole business... such a God awful thing," the man grumbled.

"Oh yes it is indeed sir," Conall agreed, frowning, not quite sure what awful tragedy he should be respectfully mourning.

"He passed away this afternoon you know," the man clarified. "I'm not sure if you're aware."

"Who passed away sir?" Conall asked.

"Why the President son," the man told him. "And here we all thought he was going to pull through," he said soulfully, shaking his head.

"Not President McKinley!" Conall exclaimed, shocked to his core.

"Yes indeed," the man continued, "Some infection or such. It's a bloody shame. The bullet damn near killed him, but to survive it only to be snuffed out by an infection eight days later; my God what is this country coming to?"

"I didn't know," Conall mumbled somberly. But he might have known had he not spent most of the afternoon and his generous week's allowance in the back room over at the Yale Club.

"Let's have it son," the man wiggled his fingers impatiently motioning to Conall.

Conall handed over the briefcase. The man laid it flat on the glass-topped conference table and fished in the pocket of his vest. He pulled out a small 18-karat gold ring with one tiny key attached. He opened the attaché and pulled out the top sheet. Conall watched as the man studied the document.

"Well I see your uncle has affixed his name as the very first signatory on the page... excellent!"

"Yes sir," Conall nodded, embarrassed his stomach was growling so loudly. His best hope was that the old man was half-deaf.

"Hmm," the man muttered.

"What is it?" Conall asked.

"Oh nothing," he answered. "I guess that's not a bad name... don't you agree?"

"What's not a bad name sir?" Conall probed.

"What do you say about this," the man queried. "The OPSEIM Directive... it has a ring to it doesn't it? Looks like this is the one we finally selected."

"Oh it sounds impressive," Conall agreed.

"Well," the man explained. "I suppose it doesn't much matter what we call it today; by the time ninety or a hundred years pass they'll probably change the name a thousand times." The man moved around behind his oak desk and sat down. Conall followed him and looked over his shoulder. The man dipped his pen and set to work signing his name under the eighth signature.

"What do the letters stand for?" Conall questioned, scratching his head. "This OPS... OPSA..."

"The OPSEIM Directive," the man clarified for him. "We call it the 'OPP-SUM' Directive. It's supposed to be top secret," he said, smiling and giving Conall a tidy little wink. "But I don't suppose any harm will come of it if I tell you. You'll find out from your uncle soon enough," the man laughed.

"Yes sir," Conall promised. "I would never tell another soul."

"No, this document must never become common knowledge — if you know what I mean," he smirked, planting a soft elbow nudge in Conall's ribcage as if he had just shared a repugnant after dinner joke with the young man. "The unsophisticated classes would misunderstand it. You mustn't breathe a word of this to another soul... er..." he corrected himself, "To another unauthorized soul."

"No sir," Conall vowed.

"Let's see," the man mumbled, holding the paper up toward the light. "Yes here it is," he said, reading from the page, "The Olympus Project Strategic Execution and Implementation Manifesto. Yes *sir*... it's a mouthful; but that's it in a nutshell." The man blew on the sheet and waved it back and forth gently in the air to speed the ink drying process.

"What is the directive for sir?" Conall asked.

"Ah," the man sighed, "Well this document by God is your future son." The man stood and leaned over to whisper to Conall in confidence. "You play your cards right and one day you'll know exactly what this is."

"Yes sir," Conall nodded.

"I can tell you *this* my boy," the man scoffed. "There will come a day when we won't have to worry about rabble rousers like this bastard anarchist Leon Czolgosz running around the streets demanding this and hollering for that... disrupting industry, interfering with a businessman's right to run his company and pay his workers what they deserve — not a penny more. And this shooting of men... the President of the United States by God! No sir," the man snapped before laying the signature page carefully back into the briefcase and closing it, "One day this country will be run properly by men who know what they're doing. Random presidential assassinations will never happen." The man's lip curled as if spitting out a sour lemon. "Uneducated manky bastarts and their idle hands... that's what the problem is. What this country needs are educated, polished, business-savvy men to run things: bankers, coal barons, steel magnates. Those are the men of strength and character; those are the men America needs. No *sir* once this plan is initiated America will purr like an ocean steamer with nothing out of place and no one out of control doing whatever the hell they damn well please. It will be a fine day indeed when this plan is set in motion."

"Yes sir," Conall nodded, feigning eager agreement. But Conall wasn't impressed. As far as he could tell the man was a big bag of wind… all this fuss over a piece of paper.

"Mark my words son," the man slapped Conall fondly on the shoulder. "You keep your eyes open, listen to what your uncle says and pay attention to how he runs his business — the way he motivates people — and one day your great, great grandchildren will praise God they had a forefather like you with such impeccable foresight."

"Yes sir," Conall agreed. But he had other things on his mind. If this directive were so special why had he never heard of it? How could he be expected to become excited about this trivial plan — or whatever this irritating old Scotsman was working so hard to get him to focus on — when his stomach was driving him crazy with its rumblings and Marjorie was dancing around half-naked through his thoughts?

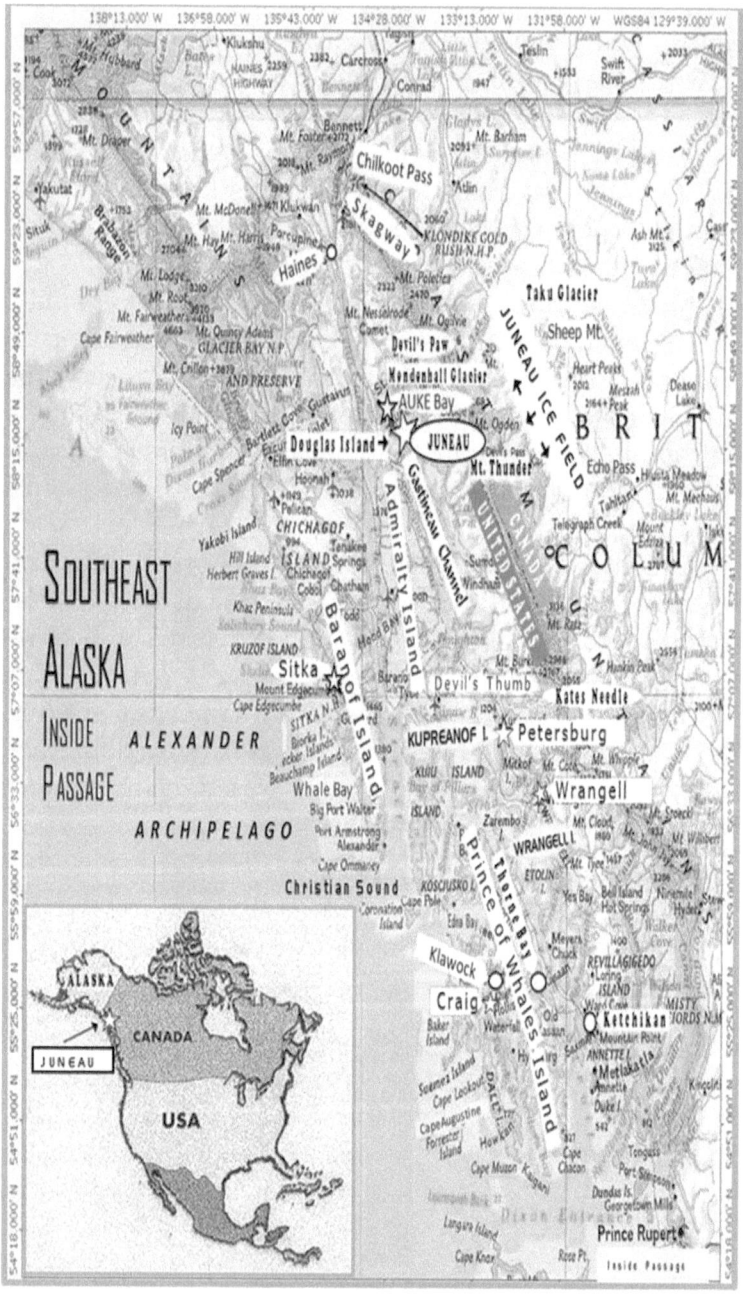

Chapter 1

❄❄❄❄❄

21ˢᵗ Century, Near Future

Juneau, Alaska, August

He struggled against howling ninety mile an hour winds and blinding snow, his chin tucked deep into the collar of his wolf-fur trimmed parka, his shoulder angled downward to the left and slightly forward. Frigid blowing arctic air burrowed deep into his bones. His marrow must be frozen, he thought, his bones felt brittle enough to snap.

"Stop! You can't go on. You're too weak." The voice jabbed at his eardrum like a chipped jagged hunting knife; or was it a thought? *"You can't continue..."* There it was again. But it didn't matter whether it was a voice or a thought. It was trying to poison him... whichever it was. He knew the wretched thing didn't belong to him and he knew he wasn't crazy. If he could only ignore it and focus on the continuous throbbing of blood pounding in his ears he could maintain a constant rhythm — set a steady pace — as he had years before on his cross-country runs at school. If the voice would just leave him alone — stop interrupting his stride — then he could focus.

"Stop... you can't survive this. You MUST rest." The voice taunted.

"No!" Viktor screamed, disoriented. "Show yourself!" He jerked his head to the side. He peered into the swirling snow yet he could see little in the blizzard. He looked again... left and then to the right. "I won't listen! Bastards! Leave me alone!" Viktor demanded. His voice was barely a whisper over the deafening roar of the storm. The wind crammed his words back down into his throat. He gasped. Each inhalation and expulsion of breath was a battle against the terrible force of the arctic blasts. He clenched his eyes shut and pushed himself forward staggering blindly through the snow. He counted to sixty and then opened his eyes but the nightmare was real; so much snow — he had never seen such a vicious storm — and it was only August. He fought to keep moving, straining every frozen muscle to go faster. If only he could run. Yes he had to run... but of course he couldn't. He could not physically run in this deep snow, no human could. Yet if he could convince himself he was running he could move faster. He must trick his own mind into believing he was racing forward, that each agonizing step took him closer. He must convince himself he was nearly there, not let distractions seep into his head. He had to block his mind from the voice — from everything — from everything but Adit 17.

"It's too far, you won't make it," the voice echoed in his head and Viktor cringed. Bile rose into his throat. Wave after wave of nausea gripped his stomach and splayed out across his abdomen. It was so confusing... jumbled thoughts, cramping pain, voices. Which thought, which voice was his own? And the nausea and the pain... were they real? He should speak his own thoughts aloud. If he speaks aloud, if his lips move, then he will know the thoughts are his. He must do this to block the voice.

"No!" Viktor shouted aloud, shaking his head and refusing to slow his momentum. "You're not real. You're the devil. I won't listen." He pushed onward, leaning into the violent arctic wind and using its force to keep himself erect as he trudged through the storm. He plunged his legs into deep snow along the deserted Glacier Highway feeling as if he dragged along the chains of Marley's Christmas ghost with each footfall. Adrenaline spurted wildly throughout his body. His heart pounded so violently he feared it was milliseconds away from bursting inside his ribcage. And the cold... never had he felt such cold.

Viktor Salko, the youngest and last in a line of seven siblings called out to God and his Aukwan Tlingit ancestors for strength... that his long legs would not buckle under the weight of his ice-coated parka and his six foot three inch, two hundred fifteen pound frame. He frantically gulped the arctic air, fighting for each breath, afraid it would be his last. Crystalized ice fog cut, twisted and burned through his lung tissue like tiny shards of glass. He pushed his body to the brink of collapse through the blowing snow. Frenzied thoughts of urgency collided with fears of failure inside his head. Sweat erupted across his brow and slid down to his eyes, now mere narrow slits as he squinted to block out the blizzard's vengeance. The droplets of perspiration froze instantly to his iced lashes in the minus sixty degree temperatures.

It was the worst blizzard in recorded history. It was a roiling ocean of snow that threatened to suck him under, to bury him like the roadway blacktop now entombed — somewhere beneath his size twelve boots — under multiple feet of ice and snow. Viktor battled against the blizzard's vicious fury along this deserted Alaskan highway. His trek had begun almost six miles north of the capital city and he fought for control of his mind every inch of the way.

One hundred mile an hour Taku winds — hurricane force winds rocketing across the Taku Glacier — had driven arctic temperatures, ice, snow and blizzard conditions over and across the mountainous Juneau ice field that had for centuries encircled three sides of a sliver of the southeast Alaska coastline. The strip of coastal land known as Dzántik'i Heeni — 'Base of the Flounder's River' — to the Native Tlingit nation was called Juneau in western civilization's modern day world. But today this world belonged to neither western man nor Tlingit. Today this world belonged to no man.

An eleven-day blizzard had besieged the small Alaskan city and overpowered its residents. The massive super storm had roared across the Juneau glaciers, funneled down from Thunder, Sheep and Bullard Mountains through Echo and Devil's Passes and spilled its rage onto the streets of the state capital. The Taku winds howled through the Mendenhall Valley and Juneau area hammering the entire zone with blinding snow. The violent gusts raced across the Gastineau Channel to Douglas, eye blinks over the one bridge connecting the city of Juneau to Douglas Island.

Viktor lumbered past nature's sentinels standing guard along the highway's edges. These ancient sixty-foot spruces stood like watchmen over this territory on America's clichéd 'last frontier'. The magnificent trees now struggled to maintain their own essence of life, their brittle branches swaying stiffly under the immense weight of snow and thick ice. Somewhere along Viktor's route to the city, Glacier Highway had seamlessly transformed into Egan Drive. As he rounded the small bend where city streets stretched out to transect Egan, the muffled unrelenting sounds of nature's wrath grew even louder, as if screaming an ominous warning not to enter the city.

Weaker and smaller trees moaned, creaked and then snapped... smashing down onto buildings, caving in roofs, and slamming to the ground in fractured death across yards and city roadways in total defeat at the hands of nature's vehemence. He trudged across a desolate intersection. Nonfunctioning traffic lights swayed violently, dangling above his head on frayed cables ready to snap under the weight of the snow and the battering of the Taku winds. He veered left, stepped onto Tenth Street, continued two hundred yards forward and then took the right onto Glacier Avenue. Along his path cars and pickup trucks, nearly totally buried in drifting snow, lay abandoned in the roadway. The simple quarter turn of a key or the one button touch of a key fob could no longer spark vehicles to life. Engine oil had morphed into thick icy sludge. On the corner of Tenth and Glacier Resurrection Lutheran Church sat eerily devoid of God's hand, its windows nailed shut. The recently renovated Sushi Bar on Ninth and Glacier — across from the federal building — lay sliced in two halves by a beefy fallen spruce that had landed squarely in the middle of the newly shingled two-story flat roof. The image was preserved like a petroglyph in testament to the catastrophic moment of impact.

Horrified by the destruction Viktor forced himself to go on. He staggered through piles of virgin white snow, struggling to lift each leg high enough to take the next step forward. He waded in thigh-deep drifts another one hundred fifty yards or so and then he turned left onto Ninth Street. He stumbled his way to the entrance of the Juneau Federal Building...

Then he stopped.

The building was a nine-story federal facility dominating the city skyline and housing numerous government offices: the small Veterans Administration's only Juneau clinic, the Coast Guard's Sector Juneau offices, NOAA — the National Oceanic and Atmospheric Administration — and the USDA Forest Service. The U.S. Post Office — with a discrete bottom floor entrance — was partitioned on the inside of the building from the federal security access point by a set of controlled-entry glass doors. Viktor leaned against this government structure and tried to catch his breath.

He stood under the building's overhang, leaning against the outside wall trying to calm the fire in his lungs and quiet the thundering in his chest. The brittle cold seized every cell in his body. Through the tiny narrow slit between his nearly frozen upper and lower eyelids he could barely distinguish the writing on a placard taped to the inside glass of the door. Viktor mouthed the words on the sign, "Closed until further notice." He peered into the building through the thick double glass doors... into a darkened atrium dimly illuminated by hints of daylight slipping through heavy gray-black skies. The lobby was abandoned. His solitude was complete... oppressive.

Viktor's muscles vibrated inside his body like tight rubber bands as if his inner core remained in motion, as if his ligaments and tendons had been plucked like guitar strings. The sensation of movement inside him was nauseating. He clamped shut his eyes to focus his thoughts and clear his head. Instantly he grew dizzy. *"Yes, that's it... rest. Don't be an idiot... sit... rest."* Damn voice, Viktor thought. He opened his eyes and reached out to the thick glass to steady himself.

"Shut up... I won't listen," Viktor mumbled, thrusting his words out into the storm through chattering teeth and freezing lips. He glanced to his left then his right searching his environment with painful aching eyes. He was desperate to find some form or figure within his narrowing field of vision... some living breathing entity to hear the words he spoke into the wind. He would have settled for any audience: a stray dog, a half-crazed wolf, an angry wounded brown bear. It wouldn't have mattered to Viktor. He would have been comforted by the sight of any living breathing creature to validate his own existence. But he saw nothing except bleakness... the spinning gray-white vortex of unrelenting snow and heavy dense ice that shrouded his world. The unconscionable storm was consuming Viktor and his universe.

If Viktor could have scanned the rest of Juneau in that moment he would have seen the portrait was the same across the capital city of thirty-two thousand. Juneau had become a brittle ice-locked strip of frozen wasteland. The city betrayed only the subtlest hints that man had ever walked its streets pursuing his daily tasks in blessed ignorance of what was to come. Gas stations sat deserted... buried under mounting piles of snow. The fuel pumps encased in massive icicles resembled blown glass replicas of Pterodactyl claws curling around its prey. Fierce winds and heavy snows had battered utility poles and choked off the familiar soft buzzing that sometimes leaked out from electric transformer boxes. Power lines and television cables layered with ice sagged and snapped away from buildings with a *crack*. The few cell phone towers in the Juneau area had waggled, twisted and crumpled dead to the ground. Viktor drew his frozen hands to his temples. He pressed inward against the exposed flesh of his face with his bare fists to squeeze out the demonic voice that resounded inside his skull. "Stop..." Viktor screamed. "Coward! Come out into this damn storm and face me!" But Viktor admonished himself. He had to stay focused.

❆❆❆❆❆

When the cold had first gripped Juneau the media assured the world that it was a fleeting aberration of Mother Nature. *"Yes it was too cold,"* news stations had reported, *"...Too cold for the temperate Juneau climate and far too cold for the month of August."* But Washington politicians told the nation that the hearty residents of Alaska were simply *"... Experiencing a temporary inconvenience... an anomaly of nature."* Viktor had ridiculed these trivializing reassurances. It was damned inconvenient, he had grumbled, even by Alaska standards... but an aberration of nature? Viktor knew otherwise.

When the blizzard began three days after the temperatures had plummeted President Thurmond S. Drew had addressed the nation to calm rising concerns. He had directed part of his speech specifically to Alaskan residents. The President declared:

> Folks, you are strong and spirited, taming our nation's last great frontier. You stand as examples for all Americans. Alaska is vast, it's challenging, and it's thousands of miles distant from the thoroughfares of main street America. As your President, I am asking you to take responsibility for your neighbors who are old or sick and make sure they are warm and safe during this challenging weather.

That was about all Viktor had been able to stomach and he had turned off his radio. The President's sentiment appeared sincere. It was hard to deny that. But this man who had never set foot in Alaska — let alone isolated Juneau — had delivered his speech at the start of the storm. He had given his pep talk prior to the loss of power, prior to the rash of deaths from exposure and injuries from storm-related conditions and before the storm spread across the state like a Texas wildfire.

President Drew had delivered his perfectly timed oratory mere hours before Juneau had gone dark.

City residents lost contact with the rest of the world. Then... like a tumbling stack of cards they were cut off from local shops, supermarkets, the few department stores and the handful of pharmacies located in the small city. Each of these commercial entities had closed its doors one after the other. Juneau inhabitants lost access to air and water transportation and mail deliveries, the lifelines linking this remote strip of southeastern Alaska to the conveniences of the modern world. Critical emergency services stopped responding soon after stores, schools and churches closed. Public works equipment operators found it impossible to stay ahead of accumulating snow. Exhausted drivers abandoned sand trucks, plows and sturdy name brand Front End Loaders on city streets and highways — their heavy equipment depleted of the last available drops of fuel, drivers defeated in the face of unrelenting snow.

"Yes this weather was damned inconvenient," Viktor had repeatedly said in frustration to his colleagues at the SUA Research Facility Southeast — 'SUARS'... an independent research facility with satellite stations located around the state. "So tell me," Viktor had asked his fellow scientists, "What kind of understanding compassionate leader would intentionally misrepresent the severity of the weather and utter such dismissive remarks about 'inconvenience' in the face of such dismal conditions? What kind of government would so quickly and easily write off the people of Alaska?" No one answered Viktor but he wasn't surprised. Most people he knew didn't want to make waves... ruffle feathers... or however they termed it; they simply didn't want to get involved. Washington's indifference toward the state of Alaska was a precursor of things to come to the rest of the nation. Viktor was sure of it. Washington's stance had validated what Viktor already believed.

Americans faced a catastrophic and imminent threat from their own government. Viktor was convinced the threat did not originate with a few rogue politicians. The true menace came from a sole political mechanism that had inch by inch provided itself unfettered power and tossed aside the concerns of those who voted them into office. As far as Viktor could tell, the American system of governance had transformed like a cancerous festering sore into an unpredictable scourge. Powerful American politicians were motivated by one closely guarded ambition and they were focused on a single terrifying objective — control.

Viktor was only twenty-six years old. He wasn't paranoid by nature. He was a scientist. His mind was methodical, his viewpoint reasoned, his opinions based on objective observations and diligent research. He simply refused to go through life with his eyes closed. Blind allegiance to insane government policies and laws infuriated him. He knew his perspective bordered on the unacceptable these days. He had no doubt he was probably on some watch list somewhere as a national security risk. He figured he could easily be labeled any number of things: malcontent, religious fanatic, survivalist, constitutionalist, extremist. But it made no difference to him. He didn't concern himself with contrived 'terrorist' tags. He didn't care how law enforcement or legislators characterized him. Viktor cared only that law enforcement, government agencies and American politicians had provided themselves free reign to trounce on his freedoms and manipulate his thinking to control every minuscule area of daily life. This stuff wasn't theory... a conspiracy vision summoned by paranoid loose cannons with nothing better to do. This stuff was damn real. The federal government had chipped away at liberties that Viktor had been taught were his inherent right under the Constitution. That was as real as anything gets.

When had America surrendered its common sense? The collective American consciousness happily digested and unquestioningly adhered to whatever media-directed themes or issues presently flooded the airwaves. It seemed few objected to anything... accepting everything just as it was dished out to them. Viktor could think of a hundred examples... like the global warming issue.

The government had told the country a new enemy had risen — global warming — and for years the media bombarded America with so-called facts about it and how it must be stopped... in part by the 'greening' of America. This was a noble goal but the plan to achieve this new sustainable utopia became perverted by silent underlying objectives. Yes preserving the environment was a noble agenda. Unfortunately the truth was... global warming wasn't occurring. The platform was an elaborate political hoax. Any rudimentary Internet search would reveal the entire global warming hysteria was based on falsified and purposely distorted assumptions and data. There was simply no truth to the claim. The temperature variation and alteration of the earth's environment was a normally occurring pattern that had been repeating itself for thousands of years.

Viktor had always found it difficult to accept anything without independent analysis and this skepticism drove him to meticulously research the issue. But the truth that global warming wasn't occurring — and most assuredly wasn't caused by any actions of the puny human race — did not fit politicians' schema. The reality was kept out of the mainstream media and the public eye.

The government needed an environmental enemy against which to rally and frighten Americans into accepting new regulations and constraints... so opposing evidence was masterfully obliterated by the media and discredited by government sources. It made no difference whether the government's position was rational or not, whether the evidence proved the government's reasoning flat out wrong or not. It was true... Viktor was the worst type of malcontent — a truth seeker. According to the government Viktor was a prime example of the real enemy who had to be rooted out of society. Viktor would admit he had become cynical in his twenty-six years but his deep sense of integrity demanded he try to persuade Americans to open their eyes — to see what was truly happening around them. Viktor was certain if they did this — truly looked — they would see what he saw.

What Viktor saw was a political machine that had become an entity unto itself, far removed from the people by more than economic disparities or physical distance. As Viktor saw it the country may as well have been managed by Russia, China or some planet light years away. The epic widening of the chasm between the federal government and the common citizen had nothing to do with the abysmal gap between rich and poor or variances in political philosophy. Viktor believed that politicians represented only themselves and worked toward their own veiled purposes. Under the present government it was clear to Viktor that the average American had been deemed nonessential. Yes Viktor had grown cynical, his heart and soul despondent over what he saw around him. What Viktor saw... he simply couldn't let stand.

In his rallying speech to Alaskans when the drastic

change in weather began the President had said Alaska was far from Washington and main street U.S.A... that was the plain truth. From the time Joe Juneau and thirty gold prospectors had put down stakes in Dzántik'i Heeni — around 1880 — the city has been physically isolated. No roads have ever connected the capital to any other location in Alaska or Canada — or to the rest of the world for that matter. Juneau is reachable only by air or sea, neither of which can be accessed when conditions are poor. Saying these present whiteout conditions were poor was somewhat of an understatement. This blizzard was the mother of all storms... most assuredly the mother of all inconveniences as far as Viktor was concerned. Yet it was the source of this weather aberration that troubled him most.

❀❀❀❀❀

Viktor drew his frozen hands away from his temples. The brutal cold depleted his stamina by the minute. His limbs grew heavier, weaker, and he knew his body was beginning the dark downward spiral toward nothingness — a void from which he could not return. He tried to draw from his innate strength as his grandmother had taught him to do when he was a child. If he were going to survive, this could be his best chance. Even now Viktor carried within his soul the secrets his grandmother had shared with him. She had helped him discover his inner force. As a boy he learned of the traditional spiritual unity that bound his Tlingit people with the land and waters of Alaska. His grandmother had taught him to delve within and reach beyond himself to discover clearer straighter paths... to overcome adversity. Yet he wasn't sure he remembered how to do this.

Was this power still alive within him... within this

brittle cold, numb, deteriorating shell of a man that Viktor had become? His body had been battered by this horrifying weather. His robust physique had grown fragile and vulnerable, his visual acuity diminished, his senses impaired. He saw the world with muddled perceptions, as indistinct silhouettes. How could he beat odds like this in his debilitated condition? He had struggled for every millimeter of ground. In his estimation he had barely six blocks more to go. The thought he might fail and freeze to death so close to the end of this insane trek was devastating. He must not let the weakness gripping his body overtake his will. He must not fail to take that next step. "Failure is not an option," Viktor muttered the worn out phrase aloud into the howling Taku winds. Then he grew angry at the other voice... the menacing voice in his head ushering him toward surrender and death.

"I won't do it you bastards. I won't listen!" Viktor cried out against the devil's voice; yet while his lips moved his words were barely whispers. That didn't matter because his lips *had* moved and he knew these thoughts were his own. If Viktor were to die in this wretched blizzard then he would do so on his own terms. He would do so on his hands and knees inching himself forward — if that's what it was going to take. So yes death was probably near. He knew that; and if this should be the end of him then he would accept his fate. But he had come so far — too far — to give in to the evil voice urging him to rest. He pushed his numbed body away from the federal building against which he had been leaning. He took two agonizing steps, maybe three, and then he stumbled.

A powerful one hundred mile an hour gust slammed into Viktor's weakened two hundred fifteen pound frame, rattled him to the bone, dipped him to the left and shook him like an empty potato sack. He staggered. His hands clutched wildly at the air. He tried to grab hold of something — anything — to break his fall; but only the wind and the cold and the whirling snow were there, slipping through his grasp. He swayed, teetering on one numb stiffened leg as the arctic wind spun him around. Icy snow crystals stung his face. His legs buckled. His mind twisted and coiled in circles. The swirling world dizzied him. He toppled to the ground chest deep in a snowdrift. For a moment he sat there stunned... and the despicable voice urged him to remain there. "*Stay... rest...*"

Viktor's impulse was to laugh, to mock the voice as it had mocked him. But he had no strength to laugh. Instead, he thrust his arms forward into the snow and strained to pull his knees up under him. Despite the bitter cold, the snow was heavy... sticking to him and weighing him down; but he stabilized himself on hands and knees. He thrust his upper torso back and pitched himself upward onto his legs. He wobbled on the freezing stumps of flesh beneath him. He leaned his weight into the wind and plunged his foot forward... taking a step, one more... and then another...

❄❄❄❄❄

Chapter 2

❀❀❀❀❀

Takotna, Alaska, August

Two hundred seventy-two miles west of Fairbanks and two hundred twenty-one miles north of Anchorage, McGrath Alaska temperatures had plunged to between minus sixty and minus seventy degrees Fahrenheit. Icy snow crystals whipped across the tundra horizontally in seventy-five mile an hour winds. Seventeen miles from McGrath — in Takotna Alaska — the forty or so residents had hunkered down in their modest homes and stacked extra logs next to their woodstoves to try to wait out the blizzard. They did what they could to discourage the pall of cabin fever from settling over them.

Thirty-five year old Miriam Goodriver and her two children, nine-year-old Kyle and twelve-year-old Kenzie, sat in their small kitchen playing their favorite game, *Melli Moose* — also known as *Myrtle, the Mellifluous Moose* to those who could pronounce it. As Kyle took his turn tossing the dice, soft amber shadows danced across his face under the flickering flame of the kerosene lantern at the end of the thick pine table. While electricity and related modern conveniences had come to Takotna years before, the brutality of the storm had severed links to those amenities. If the blizzard accomplished nothing else, it had allowed families to take pause from the more hurried pace and banal responsibilities of the modern world. Their sole objective became survival: heat, light, water and food.

Since Takotna was a relatively remote Alaskan village, most residents were prepared for such occasions when their survival depended on their ability to provide for their own needs. So while there was no denying the storm was vicious — trapping residents inside their homes for days — the absence of the daily hum of mundane life had not been wholly disheartening. Takotna had been transported back in time to a simpler more reflective and quieter world.

Were it not for the repeated slapping, creaking and groaning of a loose section of siding on the lean-to attached at the back of Miriam's cabin, Kyle's zealous laughter at the pleasure of playing the simple board game might have been heard clear down to Mr. Olani's small general store. As unexpected as the August storm was, Miriam was prepared. She and her children were warm — warm enough anyway. Miriam had cut and split an abundance of logs and Kenzie and Kyle had methodically stacked them in a pile in the woodshed as they had every year. They could easily keep the woodstove burning hot for however long the winter lasted despite this year's early snowfall. She and the children had caught, preserved and smoked plenty of steelhead trout and salmon throughout the spring and early summer and stored them along with a variety of canned vegetables and berries in a small pantry off the kitchen. All of the vegetables she had harvested and canned had come from a small garden plot on her property — a plot which seemed to creep a little farther beyond the previous year's boundaries each spring.

Miriam had also butchered and packaged caribou and moose meat whenever good luck — or caring neighbors — and the living spirits had blessed her with such bounty. She stored these in the aluminum lean-to, a makeshift structure shored-up and reinforced with two-by-fours fastened securely to the cabin at the rear door. In that improvised storage shed she could count on freezing temperatures for seven to eight months of the year. Yes if anyone had asked, Miriam supposed she would say she was *goodly prepared* for this unseasonable weather. She would have been shamed had it been otherwise.

The storm was not so unlike many winters of storms she had lived through in this remote village. Yet while Kyle and Kenzie laughed and teased each other playfully in a festive mood similar to the one Miriam expected from them during the Christmas season, she could not shake the unsettled churning in the pit of her stomach. She would never have admitted it aloud but the magnitude of this premature plunge in temperatures and the August snow piling up outside her ice-glazed window had driven her inherent mother's apprehensiveness into overdrive. It was at times like these that she could not help but question her judgment in raising her children alone in such an isolated settlement as Takotna. Yet this was her home — her children's birthplace — and most days she found thoughts of leaving it preposterous.

Even though the environment could be a venerable foe she normally could not imagine packing up and leaving her home. It was true life in Takotna could be challenging. The small village had a cold continental climate where average summer temperatures ranged from 42 to 80 degrees and winter temperatures fluctuated from -42 to 0 degrees. But Miriam had survived past winters when brutal conditions persistently barred them from safely stepping outside the cabin for more than a minute or two over the span of two to four days. These were the years when their supplies had come closest to dwindling to dangerously low levels. Still, these trials seemed normal to her and she had never believed them to be insurmountable. Yet this blizzard was different. The truth was, she had never seen a storm like this one that had driven them inside for more than ten days... and here it was only August. Today she felt the full weight of the sole responsibility to protect her children and the anxiety that came with that obligation.

Miriam's gaze drifted away from the board game and instinctively settled on Henry Ivan's rack of rifles, shotguns and handguns mounted on the wall near the door. She knew she was capable of protecting the two treasured lives in her care from almost any threat but in severe weather like this her options in times of crisis were drastically reduced. If she faced an adversary like the one that took her Henry Ivan then she might find herself in the same hopeless situation she had endured with her Henry. She hated that feeling of utter helplessness and was terrified by the prospect of having to live through it again. How do you fight an enemy you cannot see?

Beneath Miriam's calm exterior lurked the palpable fear that insidious deadly illness could again invade her home. She had squared off against that enemy six winters back when her life's soul mate Henry Ivan had fallen ill. Miriam had lost the battle with that invisible opponent during a blizzard because the Takotna Medical Clinic did not have the extensive facilities necessary to diagnose and treat her Henry Ivan. He died because Miriam could not transport him out of Takotna where they might have found better equipment and medical services that could have saved his life.

Miriam sighed heavily. As she had done thousands of times she picked through her mind, sifting through her options in anticipation of catastrophes that hopefully would never come. If her invincible fearless Henry Ivan — her loving husband of sixteen years — could not survive his battle with such an enemy, what would she do if an illness were to strike down her much more vulnerable children? How could she save them from a fate like Henry Ivan's if she could not transport them to the medical services they needed?

The seventy-mile long Takotna River is a shallow waterway — approximately thirteen feet or so deep — with a sluggish current. While it was only August the waterway was mostly frozen due to the sustained bitter cold temperatures. The frozen river meant that Miriam could not launch her small aluminum boat and her red cedar canoe was certainly useless — only safe during the two months of summer. It wouldn't matter anyway, the Takotna River leads solely to other small settlements. No... water travel was out.

Miriam's only option for medical services would be to reach an airstrip. Yet she certainly would not be able to carry one, let alone both, of her children all the way to the airport — not in this blizzard. Such a trip would be futile even if she dared attempt it. No planes could fly in this critically diminished ceiling. Even if a private pilot flying the best Cessna, Hellcat, Piper, Beech or de Havilland exercised his own discretion it would be foolhardy to try to take off in this terrain so near the Sunshine Mountains in a blizzard with seventy mile an hour wind shear.

Miriam might have considered the old snow machine behind the shed but she doubted it had sufficient gas to get very far. And whether it would start was another matter. She had not yet had time to winterize it. Traveling on foot by herself she might be able to reach Mr. Olani's small store. She knew without a doubt he would willingly risk his own life to save her children. But what could he do in this blizzard? Even his dog team would be inordinately challenged by the depth of the snow that buried his favorite trails. No... some things could not be changed. If the children became ill she would have no means to get them to medical facilities outside of Takotna in this storm. She decided that Kyle and Kenzie simply must not fall ill during this blizzard and she left it at that for now.

While it had not been easy for her, over the years she had come to terms with human frailty. Miriam knew that no matter how well she planned for the unexpected, bad things sometimes happened in life and she did not have the power to change them. But once the storm died out and the skies became clear serious illness would no longer be the certain death sentence it had been when it had taken Henry Ivan. When the weather broke, one of the bush pilots at the new Takotna airport could fly out Kyle and Kenzie for medical treatment if they needed it. She must take comfort in knowing she could at least protect her children when the power to change their circumstances was within her grasp.

Kenzie and Kyle fidgeted in their seats; Miriam could see they had grown impatient. She briefly studied her children's features and wondered how their faces seemed to have lost that baby roundness without her noticing. Both with chocolate eyes and hair as black and shiny as wet coal, had they been closer in age they could easily have been mistaken for twins. Yes, children grow so fast and time passes so very quickly; had it truly been six years since her Henry Ivan's passing?

"Mama... wake up. It's your turn. Take your turn," Kyle whined. He tugged at her sleeve. She smiled and good-humoredly tussled his hair.

"I'm not asleep. I was only thinking of how you two

have grown," she said. Miriam laughed, picked up the dice — pausing for suspense — and watched Kyle's impatience intensify. "You must learn patience son. Life must not be hurried. Life is meant to be contemplated and taken slowly... never rushed."

"Yes Mama I know. You always say that," Kyle pouted.

"You're such a whining baby Kyle," twelve-year-old Kenzie said.

"I am not a baby," Kyle grumbled, his face growing red at his sister's teasing. "I'm the man of the house."

"The *little* man," Kenzie giggled.

"All right you two... that's enough of that," Miriam told them. "Here goes..." she said, as she dropped the dice on the homemade board, its once bright colors — meticulously painted by Henry Ivan — now fading with age.

"A twelve!" Kyle exclaimed. "How could you throw so many doubles?"

Miriam tittered playfully and picked up the game piece — an intricate wooden eagle long ago carved from soft pine by her Henry Ivan — and moved it twelve spaces forward on the board. When Miriam completed her turn she again studied her children in the fluttering amber glow. She was right, she told herself, to be so vigilant... to think ahead to what she might need to do in this situation or that. She must anticipate potential dangers. In the back of her mind she must be aware that something terrible could happen. She must be ready to protect her children — like a sow bear poised to lunge — as her parents and grandparents had taught her.

Miriam had no doubt her family's safety depended on her ability to think ahead and to think fast. But she also knew her Henry Ivan had been right when he had tried to console her from his deathbed... even in the face of the inevitable and in his weakened state. "Some things are meant to be. You cannot change them," he had told her faintly. She knew he was right. So Miriam refocused her thoughts on Kenzie and Kyle as they sat in the warm kitchen sharing this precious time with her; because Miriam knew how quickly life could take a turn.

For the moment she concentrated solely on playing this simple board game and the joy her children took from it. Perhaps it was safe to set aside more serious considerations. She couldn't alter the blizzard's course, she told herself, but it wouldn't last forever. Soon the storm would end, the winds would die down and bright sunshine would sparkle on the freshly fallen snow like twinkling diamonds. Temperatures would rise toward summer norms under cloudless skies and sunbeams would shimmer across the river and along the back field. Workers would shovel out the Takotna airstrip and the heaps of snow would melt away. The runway would be cleared, planes would take off and land and it would seem as if it had never snowed in Takotna in August.

❋❋❋❋❋

Takotna Airstrip, Takotna Alaska, August

Four feet of new snow had fallen on the twenty million dollar three thousand three hundred foot runway at the Takotna airport and it was still snowing. The U.S. Department of Transportation had built the airport with funds from a federal grant on a preexisting graveled airstrip set into the side of a small hill. Widespread controversy arose from the start at the building of such a costly airstrip to service a community of approximately forty to sixty residents. The media called it Pork Barrel spending; the public called it the airport to nowhere. Many questioned the choice of sites; a longer airstrip existed only seventeen miles away in McGrath. But most residents of Takotna welcomed the costly new facility. It created a crucial lifeline to vital medical services unavailable in the settlement.

While the tiny hamlet could lay claim to approximately eighty miles of local roadway, this network of roads did not link the village to the rest of Alaska. Although it was possible to drive the Tatalina-Sterling road to the Tatalina Air Force Station... a radar site ten miles from Takotna that was equipped with a landing strip... it was not always accessible to civilians. Over the last few years the military had increasingly limited public access. The other nearby airstrip — a five thousand nine hundred thirty-six foot asphalt runway at McGrath airport — just seventeen miles from Takotna, had no control tower. It was privately owned by the Bureau of Land Management. So in the face of the hard question — why build a twenty million dollar airport in a village of forty — and despite the finger pointing and the complaints the federal government went forward with the Takotna airport project.

As with all hot media salvos, before long news sources had steered the public conscience toward more flamboyant and timely controversies. The public debate over the airport to nowhere became old news. When the airstrip was completed the forty or so residents of Takotna and a small handful of airport support personnel pulled on their work boots and heavy flannel shirts and returned to their late summer tasks.

❀❀❀❀❀

ROC Northwest Takotna, Alaska, August

One mile below the Takotna airport to nowhere,

beneath the new airport tarmac under the Alaska permafrost, approximately two kilometers into the heart of the continental crust — where centuries earlier granite-like rock had settled far above the tectonic plates of the lithosphere's upper mantle — the deep earth should have lain undisturbed by mankind. Instead, sequestered in secrecy in full military lock down in a thirty-mile long Forward Operations Laboratory Tunnel — FOLT — Pavel Aleksandrovich Malikov scratched his close-cropped buzz of dark blond hair and yawned. Malikov had been stationed at the FOLT under the Takotna airport for nearly three years.

FOLT military facilities are operated by the Regional Operations Command — ROC — a branch of the armed services within the Department of Defense — DoD. The ROC division was created three years earlier under Presidential Executive Order 1216606, *Immediate Order to Restructure All Military Branches.* In response to certain contingencies or as specifically ordered by the President of the United States, ROC forces will independently assume command of domestic security and the United States FOLT T21 network — a twenty-first century tunnel grid system. The FOLT T21 system consists of a complex secret network of underground military bases, laboratories and research facilities across America. But details like these gave Pavel Aleksandrovich Malikov a headache. He was a soldier in the Russian Federation Army presently attached to a U.N. peacekeeping force in support of ROC troops. He didn't worry about provisos, executive orders, or contingencies. Malikov was concerned about his job, his paycheck, and the quality of his off duty hours.

He glanced impatiently at his watch and tapped his short neatly manicured nails on the long desktop right next to the rigid Shrilk housing of the laptop directly in front of him. Malikov didn't like the Shrilk compound — made from chitin waste extracted from shrimp shells. Of all the biodegradable materials touted as the 'new plastic' this one gave him the creeps. Chitin was a fibrous substance consisting of polysaccharides and forming the major constituent in the exoskeleton of arthropods — an invertebrate animal of the large phylum Arthropoda such as an insect, spider or crustacean, and the cell walls of fungi. Malikov was no expert on the chemical processes used in the manufacture of these laptop housings but he did know some basic facts about the Chitin used in the Shrilk compound. Unfortunately for him the selective knowledge he possessed was sometimes a source of disquiet for him. Each time he touched the laptop he felt like he had dunked his fingers into a bucket of slimy dead insects. He couldn't seem to get the vision out of his head. Of course he wouldn't let on this bothered him. He wouldn't mention it even to his closest friend Sergei. Malikov was a soldier with a reputation to protect.

Malikov, a career military man in what was now the Russian Federation Army, had attained the rank of *Senior Starshiná* — the U.N. equivalent of Chief Master Sergeant. He was far past his military prime and this was obvious to everyone except Malikov himself. It had taken him nearly thirty years to earn the right to sew the *Senior Starshiná* patch on his uniform and in his mind he was entitled to respect. He meant to ensure he received it. He was quick to tell all who crossed his path that he was of the old breed... a real soldier. He had been everywhere, done everything and knew more than any officer he met except — known only to him — perhaps one or two old Soviet generals he secretly idolized. As he sat alone in the FOLT weather lab he stretched out the short sturdy legs that held erect his five foot eight inch frame and sipped from the brown coffee mug he cleaned once a week solely to maintain the appearance of conventionality.

Malikov's computer was connected both wirelessly and via an array of multi-colored cables to a Secret Internet Protocol Router Network — SIPRNet — that displayed data on monitors of varying sizes. The monitors were attached to the walls in a nearly full three hundred sixty degree circle around the limited access control room. Four massive five-foot high enhanced shortwave units in the center of the room wirelessly projected color data readings and graphs on designated LCD wavelength display screens affixed to the lab walls. Multiple additional keyboards, each with a discrete function and each within Malikov's area of responsibility, were placed in sequence along the full length of the thirty by four foot semicircular desktop. His laptop was programmed with a software systems application to manage, analyze and ferry data through a Unique Weather Display & Manipulation Control Component — UnWDMCC — to a mainframe control structure on the Regional FOLT Systems Network — RFSN. Other soldiers with whom Malikov divided his time at the FOLT facility had no idea his job as a button pusher and knob twister could have probably been accomplished by any twelve year old. But as far as Malikov was concerned that was nobody's business.

Malikov was not about to discuss with anyone what he did behind closed lab doors. Security protocols barred him from doing so and that was a good excuse to avoid having to account for his deficient knowledge about the UnWDMCC system. It didn't matter anyway except for the sake of appearances. He knew the purpose of some of the equipment but didn't ask questions. It wasn't the first time he was at the bottom of the need-to-know ladder and it wouldn't be the last. What did he care? He had gotten what he wanted. He was a *Senior Starshiná* and he could retire at any time. Yet he had become intrigued by this U.N. peacekeeping mission and had decided to hang around until he grew bored. Hell... maybe he would retire in America provided the country was still standing when he was ready to leave the army. It would depend on what was in it for him. In the meantime if they wanted to feed, clothe and pay him triple his normal salary to push a few computer buttons that was fine with him.

It hadn't always been like this... where a soldier's main duty consisted of typing a few lines on a workstation keyboard or adjusting the resolution of his LCD monitor. There was once a time where marksmanship and survival skills took precedence over the angle of the creases in a soldier's uniform and the luster of his spit-shined boots. At one time a soldier's primary concern was to stay alive, to dodge enemy bullets and to fight to the death to capture the next hill. That was a time when being a soldier meant something.

Soldiers had been real soldiers at the start of the Afghanistan occupation... before the Soviet Union had crumbled and before the Red Army had hung its head and crawled out of the Afghan countryside like a sniveling dog with its tail between its legs. The Soviets could easily have crushed that backwater dust bowl full of peasants... not that Malikov had anything against a country full of peasants. His motherland had its own share of them but they knew their place. Hell... his grandparents had been Russian peasants. This — Malikov reluctantly admitted to himself — had sealed his own fate as a Russian peasant if only by association.

The Afghanistan invasion had been a disaster from the beginning. Malikov deeply resented Soviet leaders for permitting such a stain on his beloved *rodina* — birth land — a land which he himself would have eagerly defended to his last dying breath. If he had known the Afghan debacle was to mark the beginning of the downfall of the Soviet political system then he might as well have let his angry opinions fly. Maybe he would have become a revered hero, an exalted warrior... another Peter the Great. His courage might have been celebrated by all Russian people, his name shouted aloud from the poorest peasant farmhouse to the most venerable seat of power at the Kremlin. Yet it was communism back then and he knew better. Speaking out would have been equivalent to signing his own death warrant. From the time he was a small boy he had been taught the unspoken Soviet law of survival under communism. Do not mutter aloud disagreement with Soviet ideology, never argue with government officials and never trust anyone... including family members. A free train ride to Siberia or a long painful death would surely follow violations of the unspoken code. Yes Malikov's grandmother Irina had taught him well.

Irina... Malikov's *babushka* — grandmother — was his cherished guardian, his protector. She had reared him with complete unconditional love. In return he had permitted himself to love her. She was the only woman he had ever trusted after his mother deserted him. To Malikov that's what his mother's death had been... the most selfish, despicable kind of abandonment.

In Malikov's young eyes he saw his *babushka* as an angel surrounded by an ethereal majestic aura. He could get lost in her quiet comforting tranquility. Something soft lingered about his *babushka* like a tepid summer breeze. She was the one woman deserving of his respect. Maybe the loose-mouthed gossips in their tiny village mistook Irina for aloof, callous, or even overbearing, but Malikov knew better. She was his *angel-khranitel* — his guardian angel — his only bulwark against life's cruelty.

Malikov's grandmother had sustained him throughout his turbulent youth. She had kept him alive long enough to grow to manhood. She had taught him that his primary goal must be to look out for himself because she had loved him above all else. She had protected him as fiercely as a lioness defends her cubs. With her comforting embrace she had instilled in him how undeniably special he was. His *babushka* had infused him with the belief that he was entitled, that the pain in his young life — dealt to him at such an early age — entitled him to take for himself the best of any option within his grasp. She had never balked at his choices. She had encouraged him to muscle his way to the front of every line no matter who he had to shove out of the way to get there. So while Malikov never fully understood his grandmother's and grandfather's relationship he permitted his *babushka* her one apparent weakness — her only shortcoming. He allowed his *babushka* the inexplicable love she felt for his grandfather. But despite this flaw his grandmother was no less than extraordinary.

In Malikov's mind there were two kinds of women... filthy whores or treacherous black widows. His *babushka* was the exception. His grandmother was wise, saintly, and strong — yet elegant. No other woman was as perfect as his grandmother. She was a woman devoted to her family. She had surrendered herself in total unquestioning loyalty to those she loved. His *babushka* could do no wrong. She was the standard against which Malikov would measure all women. He had spent his life searching for the woman who could live up to those ideals and found himself rebounding in frustration from one brief disastrous relationship to another. He had come to believe he would never find a woman who would devote herself to him as totally and completely as had his *babushka*.

Babushka stood a robust five foot seven inches tall with dense shoulders that some thought were broader than most women ought to have. Her hazel eyes and high cheekbones rendered secret tribute to her family's ancient Mordvinian roots. Yet her features captivated Malikov as a young boy. Her thick silky-white hair accentuated with soft natural random wisps of pale blue fell gently along the edges of her face. Only the bright sunshine betrayed her waning youth when the contours of tiny wrinkles cast diminutive shimmering shadows near her eyes and at the corners of her mouth. Yet in his own youthful mind she would never age.

Babushka's love for Malikov was unconditional. His grandmother would unfailingly smother him in her warm embrace when she was pleased but it was her broad smile of approval — and hers alone — that he had ached to elicit as a boy. Life with his grandparents became the true underpinning of Malikov's adulthood. He did not know what he might have become had circumstances been different — had he been raised by his parents — but he could not have imagined a life without his grandmother.

❄❄❄❄❄

Following the sudden disappearance of Malikov's father and premature death of his young mother shortly after his ninth birthday a confused and frightened Malikov had found himself sitting alone on a wooden bench inside *Moskovskiy militsiya shtab* — Moscow police headquarters — at Petrovka Street, 38, Tverskoy

District. He sat in silence outside the police captain's office on the second floor of a grand six floor sage-colored brick building. The exterior of the structure boasted thick columns and archways that Malikov had admired from the street. He had walked by the station with his parents or at times ridden past the building with them in their *Zhigul'* — a 1970's re-engineered version of the Fiat — that was ultimately exported as the *Lada/Zhigul'*. The three of them had admired the stately ornate building and often wondered aloud what it would be like to walk between the columns and step inside such a grand polished structure. To think that he had been at that moment inside the same building without his parents sitting beside him on that rigid wooden bench was fully beyond his comprehension. Malikov would later think of that terrible day as the day when two thirds of his heart had been ripped from his chest and a huge dark void left in its place. But he would not admit that to himself until later. In those first few hours his mind and his body had simply refused to ponder the situation at all.

Nine-year-old Malikov had stared in silence at the shiny placard above the exit door at the police station. His palms were sweating, his legs swinging nervously. He read the words on the sign over and over until the repetitions in his head synchronized. A droning melody marched through his thoughts in cadence with the swaying of his legs; *serve the law... serve the people; serve the law... serve the people.* He had soon hypnotized himself until nothing remained in his conscious thinking except this newly constructed fantasy world swathed in silent descant. He had plunged himself into a universe comprised only of the imaginary haunting tune with its poster words and the soundless rhythmic swinging of his legs. His mind had fabricated a cosmos where no one and nothing could touch him. This was his sanctuary. This personal universe would shield him from the sudden new reality that he did not understand and refused to contemplate.

Young Malikov may have sat on that bench for hours. His mind silently chanted its monotonous melody until the police captain brought him a drink of water and told him it was time to go. He didn't know how much of the day he had passed waiting on that bench. It didn't concern him. He felt no sense of urgency to be somewhere and felt no particular tug of ambition to leave his spot. He simply felt nothing at all.

The police captain had slipped his hand into Malikov's but the boy may as well have grasped a cold iron pipe. When the captain walked, Malikov walked. When the captain sat in the police car, Malikov sat. He didn't know where they were headed and he paid no mind to his ignorance. It was possible the policeman had told him where he was taking Malikov but if he did Malikov had no memory of it. He was not even certain how he had gotten onto the train. He had no recollection of climbing the three iron steps into the rail car.

The hours he had spent at the *Moskovskiy politseyskiy shtab* were a vague distant blur. He later thought he may have remembered that the captain squatted down, touched his arm gently and spoke to him in a low soothing voice after Malikov took his seat on the train. Yes perhaps he recalled the police captain doing such a thing. Yet Malikov had not understood the words the captain had spoken on that summer day. It had sounded to him more like a distant random tapping all around him like the sharp *clink... clink...* from tapping inside a tin drum. As soon as the train had left the station Malikov fell into a deep sleep... oblivious to everything around him. Had Malikov's mind, soul and heart not been crushed and his awareness of the world fractured by his father's disappearance and his mother's death that morning he would have known the captain had taken him to the train station ticket counter after they left the Petrovka Street police headquarters. He would have known the captain had purchased a third class ticket — *platzcart* — for him for the fourteen-hour train ride to Penza City in the region known as Penza *oblast*. The captain need not have bothered to upgrade the inexpensive fourth-class super economy ticket Malikov's grandfather Aleksi had intended that the *Moskovskaya militsiya* — Moscow police — purchase for Malikov. The boy would have fared just as well with the cheaper *place to sit* ticket that Aleksi had instructed the captain to buy. He had slept through the full fourteen hours all the way to the Penza City railway station.

Malikov awoke only when the tall uniformed *provodnik* — conductor — physically hauled him off the train and passed him off to the elderly couple waiting on the platform. The woman had nodded and thanked the conductor. Malikov watched her pass the man an envelope containing a few kopeks the conductor promptly refused to accept. The lad had then stood — like a stone statue of Lenin — cautiously sizing up the two stoic Russians. He peered at them with a dark vacant boyish glare numbly waiting for some indication of how he should behave and what was expected of him.

The woman had stared back at Malikov for so long he had begun to squirm. Her gaze seemed to crawl all over him — dissecting him, touching him everywhere — without even one of her knobby fingers anywhere close to his flesh. Her eyes appeared sad as if burdened with some terrible pain and she frowned deeply as she studied him. Then her mouth had oddly twisted as if she had felt the sting of an angry female honey bee. Malikov thought she might screech or curse or perhaps cry out but instead she heaved an immense pained sigh. Then all at once she squatted to his level and scooped him into a fierce hug, clenching his body and squeezing the breath from him.

"*Moy malen'kiy vnuk*," — my little grandson — she whispered in his ear, "*Moy dragotsennyy mal'chik*," — my precious little boy. "Your *babushka* is here. Hush now, *bud'te spokoyno vso budet khorosho*," — be at peace... everything will be ok. Malikov's muscles gave way, melting into the warm safe embrace of this woman — this grandmother, this flesh and blood tether enticing him to climb up and out of the terrible gaping hole in his heart. He buried his face in her bosom and drew in her essence. He remained wrapped in her strong fleshy arms and sobbed in silence until his knees had buckled and his emotions were spent. She had refused to release him from her clutches and he did not struggle to free himself. She lifted and carried him all the way to the old rusted truck while the man, Malikov's grandfather Aleksi, traipsed beside them in silent indifference.

Malikov would later come to know his grandmother as a steadfast yet loving woman. She was not a woman predisposed to tears or flagrant displays of emotional vulnerability. Life had plenty of drama all on its own she would say and she had never seen the sense in willingly contributing to the chaos around her. She clung tightly to her grandson throughout the full bumpy fifteen miles of the trip to their modest two-bedroom *dacha* — country home — in Zolotaryovka, a village of one thousand three hundred fourteen. During the ride Malikov had nuzzled his head, eyelids intermittently drooping from exhaustion and relief, against his grandmother's shoulder.

From time to time Malikov had looked up and seen

Aleksi watching them. But each time his eyes met Aleksi's, his grandfather turned his head away and fixed his gaze back on the road. Aleksi said nothing. Yet every now and then when Malikov had seen Aleksi steal a glance at the two of them, Malikov felt his *babushka's* embrace tighten around him as if she were secretly swearing an oath that she would never allow him harm while he was in her care.

※※❈※※

Chapter 3

✿✿✿✿✿

Malikov's Hippocampus... Zolotaryovka, Russia

Malikov's grandfather Aleksi was a burly five foot eleven-inch hulk of a man, every inch a proud inviolate *krest'yanin* — peasant farmer. Aleksi had no rights to purchase the land over which he sweated. Like all Soviet farmers of the day Aleksi held his land in communal ownership within a *mir* — a community acting as a village cooperative government. Land was divided into strips based on soil quality, distance from the village and number of adults in the household. Aleksi devoted himself to working his small plot to keep food on the table and to pay his yearly taxes. Aleksi, it seemed, had little time or impetus left after his work to say much to his nine-year-old grandson.

When Malikov had first arrived at the *kolkhoz* — collective farm — he was a timid wiry young boy unfamiliar with chores or working the fields and uncertain of his new surroundings. He was especially wary of the grandfather who rarely spoke. Malikov had no conscious memory of the one occasion his parents had taken him to the farm when he was a toddler. After that visit he had been left only with a vague sense of awareness of this man... now triggered by a faint scent seeping from Aleksi's pores. Malikov soon came to recognize the scent as the distinct odor of stale vodka.

In those first days after nine-year-old Malikov's arrival the boy had nervously studied Aleksi. He watched his grandfather sweating under a scorching sun, toiling in the rich soil along the *chernozemnaya polosa* — black earth belt (zone) — in the Penza region, three hundred seventy-three miles southeast of Moscow. Malikov had initially served his grandfather as his personal water boy. He timidly carried the tin pail and ladle along the dusty road one-half mile from the farm to the field where Aleksi labored. Malikov grew used to the chore, taking his time filling the container at the nearby Kuvaka Springs — a natural spring with water so sweet it would later be bottled and sold across the region.

Each summer day Malikov would linger at the edge of the natural springs. He would remove his shoes, wiggle his toes in the cooler mud and often pour a ladle or two of refreshing liquid over his head under the hot canopy of the midday sun. He would let the water dribble through his hair and trickle down the sides of his heated cheeks before continuing on his way to bring the water pail to Aleksi. As the days wore on the apprehensive Malikov had slowly grown accustomed to his new environment, finding solace in the soothing chirps of the tiny sparrows and the earthy smell and feel of the moist dirt.

The rich topsoil of the area known as the black earth belt, also called the *fertile triangle* and the *breadbasket of Europe*, comprised only one tenth of the six million five hundred ninety-two thousand eight hundred nineteen square miles of Russian land mass. The *chernozemnhyye* region was nestled between the coniferous and deciduous forests encircling Moscow to the north and the arid steppe to the south that reached down through the grasslands and desert to the northern rim of the Caucasus Mountains. In a short time Malikov grew comfortable in his own tiny piece of that world...

his small private universe comprised of the farm, the dusty road, the small plot of land, the tiny village and his school.

Malikov had watched Aleksi wrestle the environment in a battle for dominance over the soil and the elements. Winters of the Penza *oblast* — Penza region — could be fiercely cold and summers sizzling hot. Powerful sustained winds were frequent. Aleksi clashed with nature daily, determined to tame the earth and coax it to surrender sufficient nutrients to grow enough food for the family. It seemed apparent to Malikov that Aleksi was more interested in the dirt under his fingernails and beneath his feet than in his only grandson. Had his grandfather allowed outsiders to penetrate the small family circle such observers might have seen from the start that Aleksi regarded Malikov with indifference — as an annoyance only slightly less bothersome than the summertime droves of ravenous mosquitos plaguing the *chernozemnhyye*. The skinny youth had dared not cross this man he barely knew and did not understand. After the settling-in period, as Malikov's grandmother referred to the boy's first three months on the farm, Aleksi assigned his grandson greater responsibilities. Malikov struggled to complete his new after-school chores according to his grandfather's unyielding ideals. *Babushka* compensated Malikov for his efforts with her unconditional love but Malikov had reaped no similar remuneration from his grandfather.

Malikov never pulled up the weeds quite properly or cleaned the tools or tidied up the small work shed sufficiently to satisfy Aleksi's impossibly high standards. Yet in his early teens Malikov realized his grandfather's coldness toward him had been a blessing not a shortcoming. Aleksi was as constrained in his demeanor as was Siberia in its seasons. In the unforgiving arctic north it was either summer or winter, hot or cold. With Aleksi it was much the same. By the time Malikov had turned fourteen he knew his grandfather's behavior was limited to either indifference or brutality.

Increasingly severe and unpredictable weather, worsening political and economic trends and poor crop yields across Russia — combined with Aleksi's growing hostility toward his neighbors — had triggered Aleksi's descent into a volatile downward spiral. Malikov's grandfather sank into a profoundly disturbing depression from which he would never recover. Aleksi had begun to spend his waking hours muttering — in a low raspy voice just above a whisper — about conditions beyond his control that he could not possibly expect to change. *"More taxes,"* he complained, *"More money stolen from my pocket. How is a man to live? Curse this weather,"* he swore, *"Let it all go to the devil."* But what Aleksi complained about most was the very system of the *kolkhoz* — often called the *second serfdom.* He grumbled and looked for answers to questions no one in the Soviet Union should dare be asking.

Aleksi was forced to slave over the collectivized land in return for the same minimal crop prices year after year that were provided to all of the farmers no matter what level of effort they invested in the land. The Soviet state dictated what Aleksi would grow, how much he would be paid and prohibited him from leaving the *kolkhoz.* In Aleksi's mind lazy farmers to the right and left of him made the situation worse.

Aleksi complained endlessly about two of his neighbors, both in their seventies. He protested to *Babushka* that he worked three times as hard as did they and yet received the same starvation pay. Aleksi was trapped. If he scaled back his efforts production would decrease and the meager compensation allotted to the *kolkhoz* would exponentially plummet. As his internal torment intensified he withdrew into himself even more, looking to his old companion — the bottle — for solace. Aleksi had begun his final battles.

During his downward spiral Aleksi continued to devote his entire being to carving a living out of his allotted patch of unyielding Russian soil. But as it was with his instinct to survive so it was with everything Aleksi did; he committed himself totally to a sole objective. Aleksi was driven to conquer any challenge before him. In farming he strained each ligament and tendon, sweating and working the land harder than could any other mortal. He was a madman driven by singular purpose, obsessed with dominance. It didn't matter what he was driven to subjugate: the system, the weather, his neighbors, the dirt under his feet or his grandson. When he fell short in his struggle against an opponent Aleksi seemed to feel his only recourse was the transfer of his unyielding resolve to the pursuit of his own self-destruction. The once proud Russian became an explosive unpredictable drunkard.

Aleksi could instantly change from hopelessly depressed when sober, to manically aggressive when intoxicated. In the beginning Malikov's grandmother had successfully reined in Aleksi after each drunken episode of mania but he would then slide into a deep melancholy. From the bottom of his cavernous despair he would all too soon again reach out for the bottle to chase away his demons. The constant merry go round took its toll on them all.

Once, while in a drunken rage, Aleksi had taken his rusted shotgun into the yard and fired on two of the neighbor's dogs. They had burrowed under a broken fence and fixated on consuming Aleksi's small newly harvested potato crop. Aleksi had sweated to gather the potatoes from his strip of land, heaped them into wooden barrels and set the barrels on the front lawn. The temptation was too overpowering for the dogs. After hearing gunshots Malikov and his grandmother had scrambled out the front door of the house and stumbled down the rickety wooden steps in time to witness the last ebbing breaths of two black Labrador retrievers as they lay on the ground pitifully whimpering, twitching and writhing in two small pools of their canine blood. Stunned and speechless, *Babushka* and wide-eyed Malikov watched — their feet frozen to the summer ground — as Aleksi fumbled to reload his shotgun. In his agitated frenzy Aleksi dropped the ammunition in the grass and immediately sunk to his knees to retrieve it. He scooped up the shotgun shells and awkwardly got back to his feet, cramming the shells into the breach. With one hand on the forestock and the other near the trigger guard of the gun he snapped the barrel shut with a sharp *crack...* that seemed to echo. Aleksi then swung on his heels and stormed down the road toward the neighbor's farm, menacingly waving his shotgun and mumbling incoherently.

He stared ahead catatonically as he stumbled and weaved along the dusty road. Malikov and his grandmother raced after him, pleading with him to stop. They caught up to Aleksi and pulled at his shoulders and forearms and grabbed fistfuls of his shirttail, all in a futile attempt to detain him and diffuse the ticking time bomb they had once known as Aleksi. As soon as Aleksi reached the neighbor's farmhouse he bounded clumsily up the five front porch steps dragging both Malikov and his grandmother with him as they clung to his arms, shirt and belt. Aleksi kicked open the front door, breaking the flimsy latch, and stumbled inside. He tramped ahead three huge paces, crossed into the parlor, and stopped to face his gaunt white-haired neighbor of twenty-five years.

The scrawny weathered farmer stood trembling, his mouth agape in shock at the armed demon before him in his parlor. A barely audible squeak slipped passed the farmer's lips. Aleksi grasped a handful of his neighbor's frayed collar and flung the old man violently to the floor. He pressed the cold steel of the shotgun barrel tight to his neighbor's throat. The young Malikov forced his eyes closed and looked away, gritting his teeth and waiting for the thunder of the gun blast to ricochet through the sparsely furnished room.

Malikov never could recall the details of what happened over the next few minutes. He had searched his memory but could not reconstruct in his mind how his grandmother had assuaged the situation, how she had reasoned with the catatonic Aleksi or how she had pried the shotgun from his sweaty hands. Malikov knew only that the horrific screams of the farmer's hysterical wife had slowly faded to whimpers. When Malikov opened his eyes he saw the bobbing head of the farmer's wife vigorously nodding up and down as if in eager agreement with some secret pact. Her chest heaved; her eyes bulged from their sockets. She knelt beside her husband who lay sprawled on the floor in deathlike stillness. She stroked the old man's thinning white hair as robotically as she would the mangy coats of her beloved Labradors after a game of fetch the stick. Her hands shook.

Malikov had been silent during the excruciating walk back home after Aleksi's assault on the farmer. A cooler early evening breeze had fluttered against Malikov's hot cheek as he walked behind his grandparents, his shoes crunching lightly over small stones in the road, his vision still blurred from his own tears that had slid unnoticed down his face. Early the next afternoon the two wary neighbors slipped over to Aleksi's house while he was out tending his strip of earth. Malikov and *Babushka* helped wrap what was left of the two black dogs in old woolen blankets and the neighbors carried the bodies back to their farm. Neither the farmer nor his wife ever called the *militsiya* and not another word was uttered about Aleksi's rampage. *Babushka* did not give up on Aleksi but she became less and less tolerant as his violent outbursts continued.

Life became more difficult after Aleksi shot the dogs. Young Malikov did not share the deep feelings for Aleksi to which *Babushka* seemed to desperately cling. He felt his days on his grandparents' farm were numbered. He knew he would someday soon need to leave the grandmother he loved. If it had not been for his beloved *babushka* Malikov would likely never have become acquainted with his young adult years — not if Aleksi had anything to say about it and *Babushka* had told him in plain terms he did not. But while Malikov hated the beatings he had begun to receive from Aleksi's wretched fists he didn't hate the man... not at first.

Malikov could see Aleksi was most often prompted by vodka to pound his knuckles into Malikov's tender skin. Sometime after his sixteenth birthday he learned more about the source of Aleksi's inner torment. He supposed doctors these days would have diagnosed Aleksi with post-traumatic stress disorder, prescribed him handfuls of colorful pills and rooted around in his psyche for a time to smooth out the rough edges of his rage. Then they would have called it square. Yet back then Aleksi was doomed to fight his own demons and those around him suffered for it.

Aleksi's post-traumatic stress disorder could have been traced back to his World War II service. As a soldier of the Soviet Union's Second Army he was a survivor of the bloody two hundred days of the Battle of Stalingrad. This battle in particular seemed to be the source of the great pain driving Aleksi to the bottle. On June 22, 1941, Nazi Germany launched Operation Barbarossa, invading the Soviet Union and advancing deep within its border. By the spring of 1942 the Germans had established their front line from approximately Leningrad in the north to Rostov in the south. The successful drive into Russia by the German Sixth Army in the early stages of the Russian offensive was attributable to the superiority of German armored divisions and the ability of those forces to mobilize fast. But the German advantages diminished when German troops engaged the Soviet Union in urban battles on the streets of Russian cities.

Hitler's Friedrich Paulus's Sixth Army and Hermann Hoth's Fourth Panzer Army were dispatched to the east toward the Volga River and Stalingrad, a city of approximately four hundred forty-five thousand. The German strategy was to neutralize the supply of oil from the Caucasus area and disrupt Russian industrial output by decimating major cities and cutting off barge transports of grain along the Volga. Once the German army had advanced into Stalingrad the fighting was dominated by short-range firearms. The previous tactical superiority of the mobilized German armored divisions was essentially negated. The ensuing battles were fierce.

Malikov's grandfather Aleksi was conscripted into the Soviet Army in 1940. He spent part of that time serving in the *voyennaya militsiya* — military police. He was rumored to be attached to the secret police — the

Narodnyĭ Kommissariat Vnutrennikh Del... NKVD...
(People's Commissariat of Internal Affairs) — during his
initial and final year of army service. At that time he
was posted to an army unit at the front but he was
positioned behind the Russian line, his orders to identify
undesirables. It was whispered among the troops that
NKVD agents lurked in the shadows at the rear of the
Russian forces to shoot to kill deserters or
counterrevolutionaries. Army officers who made
mistakes could be charged with sabotage or political
dissent. As an NKVD agent Aleksi's official
responsibilities were to apprehend army deserters,
enforce military discipline and recruit new troops.
Babushka never said why Aleksi was transferred as
infantryman to the Eastern Front; but Malikov
suspected his grandfather had committed some real or
imagined minor infraction — minor since he was
returned to the NKVD in his final year in lieu of being
shot himself.

When serving as infantryman Aleksi had faced the
Germans in the streets of Stalingrad — fighting house
to house — for almost seven straight months without
respite; and much of the battle took place in the frigid
depths of winter. As far as the eye could see the Volga
River had become a river of fire and blood. During the
chaos Soviet troops strategically utilized the sewer
system of Stalingrad to travel unseen beneath the city
and to infiltrate the ranks of German soldiers
entrenched on the streets above. On the one hundredth
day of battle after a week in the sewer system a war
weary Aleksi and his two closest companions checked
their gear in preparation to crawl back up the sewer
ladder to rejoin the street level fighting. They huddled
together beneath the street in the quiet moonless
morning hours devising their strategy and preparing to

slide back the lid of the sewer hole as quietly as they could. Aleksi was first up the iron ladder.

He quickly drew fire as he emerged from the hole. He pulled his legs up to the street and rolled to the closest pile of rubble for cover. Prone, he cradled the forestock of his rifle with his left hand and steadied the gun butt against his shoulder. With his weight on both elbows he began shooting toward the silhouette of a bombed out building. He fired at muzzle flashes splaying out from a broken window on an upper floor. He didn't see or hear the German soldier a mere twenty feet from him in the darkness directly to the left of the sewer entrance. But in the midst of the sporadic *pop... pop... pop* of gunfire Aleksi did somehow hear the *click...* of the base cap of a German M24 *Stielhandgranate* — stick grenade — as the German soldier twisted it and moved within fifteen feet of Aleksi in the lingering darkness.

Aleksi swung his body around and fired twice toward the sound of the *click*. He heard the heavy *thud* as the German soldier's body fell to the concrete and the hollow *plunk* as the grenade hit the hard surface. For an instant he heard nothing in the darkness. *One... two... three...* seconds of black silence passed and his mind coerced him to relax... the grenade must be a dud. Then instantly his body was rattled, shaken like a rag doll, and pushed three feet along the street while a violent roar slammed into his head from the explosion of the grenade. Aleksi lay motionless trying to hear amid the ringing in his ears as the blast echoed from down in the sewer; he remained there — on the street where the explosion had pitched him — for what seemed an eternity . When the gunfire ceased and the noise in his ears diminished he had cautiously risen to a crouching position, peering left, right and then behind him into the darkness. When he felt it was safe he duck walked to the sewer hole and lay down.

Smoke was still rising as he leaned over the side of the hole and peaked into the murky darkness. He took his flashlight from his belt. He shielded the dying beam by cupping his hands around it as he aimed the light into the hole. He whispered the names of his two comrades he had left in the sewer but as the smoke dissipated and the beam of his flashlight shimmered on the sewer floor he knew they would not answer him. Both men lay silent... drenched in blood, limbs twisted, mutilated and disarticulated from their bodies. The Nazi stick grenade had rolled to the sewer hole and found its mark just as the round from Aleksi's rifle had snuffed out the final breath of the German soldier.

Malikov's grandmother had related Aleksi's story to her grandson right after Malikov's sixteenth birthday. Yet rather than elicit the empathy his grandmother envisioned Malikov was filled with disdain for Aleksi, regarding Aleksi's World War II experience as additional proof of his grandfather's shortcomings. Far from inciting compassion in Malikov *Babushka's* chronicle only confirmed in Malikov's mind that Aleksi was weak — a pathetic shell of a man for allowing such a thing to torment his mind for the remainder of his life. In Malikov's estimation Aleksi was a coward. It was that simple.

The Battle of Stalingrad had decimated a good portion of humanity with nearly two million deaths. By all reasonable accounts and in light of the psychology of warfare there was no glory, dignity or adventure to be had in that WWII battle or any other. In the wake of war only mayhem, chaos and suffering remained. To Malikov such assessment was *mycop* — trash. He refused to even consider war existed without glory.

Malikov had no compassion for Aleksi the coward, a

man too fearful to even speak of his adventures and too weak to look beyond his tortured soul. After learning of Aleksi's experiences in WWII Malikov's contempt for Aleksi grew. In Malikov's eyes his grandfather remained a drunkard, a bully and a *tpyc* — coward. Aleksi had camouflaged his WWII rage and torment and transferred his fury to his fists, lashing out at his demons by pummeling a defenseless boy. How could Malikov feel anything but contempt? He could summon no respect for a man who could do such a thing.

If Malikov had been in Aleksi's shoes he knew he would have been filled with pride at living through such a critical battle. Aleksi had prevailed hadn't he? So what if lesser men had not. Aleksi had survived the greatest Russian victory of World War II. He had fought for the motherland and overcome the enemy. Yet Aleksi had discarded this defining moment in his life and replaced it with a vodka bottle. Malikov could not stomach the reality of the man his grandfather had become. Malikov knew better than to let on to others how he felt. Exposing inner thoughts or emotions was not acceptable behavior for a strong Russian man. He allowed others in Zolotaryovka to believe what they wanted about Aleksi. Few who knew Malikov as a teen were surprised at the occupation he chose as an adult. Most villagers presumed Aleksi's war experiences had influenced Malikov to devote his life to a career in the military. But it had not been sentimentality or respect for Aleksi that had driven Malikov's decision to pursue a military career. It had been something else entirely.

Aleksi had devoted almost three post war decades of effort perfecting the art of isolating his family from Zolotaryovka and the world. If Aleksi's neighbors and friends had suspected Aleksi was tormented, unstable and violent, no one ever spoke of it... even though at least one neighbor might well have. Malikov was sure whatever the villagers thought they knew about Aleksi was simply an illusion they created in their own minds. No... Malikov bore no deeply rooted proclivity to emulate his grandfather. On the contrary Malikov was ashamed of Aleksi. He was driven to prove he was nothing like his grandfather. That obsession combined with the promise of brotherhood and solidarity within the military mechanism had swayed Malikov to devote his life to the army.

Talk of the military or war had mesmerized Malikov throughout his youth. However he had no desire to hear Aleksi's version of the fighting... not that Aleksi was ever forthcoming anyway. Malikov reserved his attention and respect for real warriors and their accounts. Whenever Malikov was not in school or dragging himself through the routine farm chores he grew to despise he could be found down at the *derevenskiy magazine* — the village shop — in Zolotaryovka. There the *staryye voyennyye veterany* — old military veterans — sipped their strong black tea and waited for the next round of boiling water from the *samovar* — a self-boiling urn — that sat bubbling on the pitted and scratched wooden countertop. Wrinkled toothless old men gathered at the three wobbly tables set up between the scantily stocked shelves to play dominos and rehash their adventures in the Soviet Army. As a boy Malikov listened joyfully to these proud veterans describing their thrilling escapades. Malikov was certain he would be exactly like them in forty or fifty years but he would wear medals on his chest and everyone would want to hear what Malikov had to say. He was not destined to become a despondent broken old man like Aleksi. Malikov was sure he had no yellow stains in his own blood and he meant to prove it.

Malikov did not believe the psychobabble about survivors' guilt and post-traumatic stress. A strong Russian military man — fit and cunning — had no use for such escape routes. Malikov would welcome a battle like Stalingrad. That was where he would find glory. He was nothing like Aleksi. He knew he would never have surrendered to imaginary mental torture after surviving such a glorious encounter with the enemy. At sixteen he resolved he would never permit the vodka bottle to take over his life as Aleksi had done... allowing it to conquer his virility.

Malikov would have welcomed any chance to tell a survival story like Aleksi's. He would have used a great victory like Stalingrad to scratch his way to the top of the modern Russian Federation Army. He would have been promoted, respected and admired. He would not have had to slave thirty years groveling up through the ranks to reach the mediocre pinnacle of *Senior Starshiná*. Malikov would have been so courageous on the battlefield he would have been field promoted. He would be leaning back with his feet up on his thick Russian oak desk mulling over retirement as a *kapitan* or *mayor* right now... not bowing down in submission to a baby faced *mladshiy leytenanty* — junior lieutenant. He would not be playing the ridiculous military *da, tovarishch* — yes, comrade — game with adolescent superior officers. Had things been different Malikov could have traveled an easier path. Afghanistan could have been Malikov's Stalingrad. Glory might have been his for the taking. Instead, the Afghan occupation was a sham. Calling the engagement a war was the same as likening a grain of sand to a tropical beach. Malikov had been cheated.

Whenever Malikov thought about the Afghanistan occupation where he had proudly served as *ryadovoy* —

private — he could not help but shake his head as mournfully as when his *babushka* had died. Malikov had proudly marched into Afghanistan as a young soldier anticipating glorious battles only to be ordered out of the country in shame by a communist government that refused to permit its soldiers to crush the enemy. The Afghanistan action was a political debacle like the Americans' Vietnam. Malikov had simply been one more soldier sent home in undeserved disgrace.

The nine-year Soviet occupation of Afghanistan had been a political game of chess where politicians had orchestrated each chessboard square forward and then pulled back just enough to ensure a stalemate. It seemed it was Soviet intent to guarantee the failure of the overall campaign. To hear Malikov tell it if not for the politicians the Soviets could have marched along the mountainous terrain and mowed down the Afghans in a few days. If the military had been given unfettered power the army would have defeated its enemy, the Soviet system would never have unraveled, and America would have eventually become dominated by his beloved *rodina*. But he had to admit... had the cold war continued he would not be in America now living such a fine life.

Life in the FOLT had been more than he had expected. The army had treated him extremely well... certainly better than he had been treated at any other time in the last thirty years. This treatment was definitely more closely aligned with what he deserved. Perhaps he should hang on another couple of years. Who knew what additional privileges or amenities he might secure? Besides... maybe his own glorious battle — his Stalingrad — was right over the next hill.

❋❋❋❋❋

ROC Training Center Marietta, Georgia, August

Colonel Nick Fizer stood outside Olympus Hall, an ornate great room in the ROC training center as grand as the ballroom in any lavish palace. His eyes were focused on the west corridor of the main training sector. A bead of sweat trickled down his neck. He wasn't looking forward to closing the heavy doors once the graduation ceremony got underway. Four hundred bodies could generate a lot of heat in two hours in a closed room with no windows and little ventilation.

"Good afternoon Colonel," Frank Benton said, sauntering up to Nick's side.

"Good afternoon Major," Nick replied coolly, hoping Benton would continue on his way and keep whatever distasteful remarks he seemed ready to spew out to himself.

"I was wondering Colonel," Benton said, in a low voice as he edged closer to Nick, "If you have any idea where I'm going to be assigned?"

"I'm afraid I don't," Nick answered, taking a half step back and inching away from the major. Benton had an annoying habit of crossing into Nick's personal zone whenever they were speaking. Nick didn't like it. In fact Nick didn't like anything about Benton. He was manipulative and wholly inept. Nick had never ceased wondering how Benton managed to be selected for ROC training in the first place.

"Too bad," Benton said. "I presumed you would have some extra pull with the general. I was looking for a billet to Eastern Division Headquarters."

"Can't help you," Nick told him. "Those decisions are made higher up the chain."

"Well," Benton said. "In case you do have an opportunity maybe you could put in a good word for me. I'm confident I could make a huge contribution to the

Eastern Command."

"I'll keep that in mind," Nick said. "But as I told you I'm not involved in those decisions." This was partially true. He played no role in determining final assignments but General Tucker had asked Nick to provide recommendations for his top ten officers. Benton wasn't on Nick's top ten list. As far as the Eastern Division Headquarters went Nick had already recommended Major Falcon Colby for the position. Nick didn't know what Benton's angle was but he was sure he had one. Benton never did anything unless something was in it for Benton.

"Okay well," Benton sneered, splashing a toothy Cheshire cat grin across his greasy complexion. "I'm sure you're just being modest. I find it hard to believe you have no say in assignments whatsoever." Benton smiled smugly. "So I will appreciate whatever you can do for me," he said, turning and swaggering into the great hall. Nick felt as if the school principal had told him to *run along now*, after a lecture on the shortcomings of his efforts in class. Benton had the knack of leaving a sour taste in Nick's mouth.

Nick gave a quick nod of recognition as two majors hurried past him through the double doors. He checked his watch. He still had ten minutes but the general had an annoying habit of unexpectedly showing up ten minutes either side of the hour. Nick had learned early on to be prepared for this. As Major General Pierce Tucker's Chief of Staff Nick Fizer knew attention to detail and timing were everything. Sloppy protocol was a dead certain career killer... especially these days when Congress and the President seemed determined to downsize the military out of existence. Nick could understand the principle of economizing but he resented the means the Department of Defense used to achieve its objectives. The DoD, like all government agencies, had the authority to determine whether to initiate a Reduction in Force — RIF… pronounced 'riff' — to meet revised quotas for personnel needed to implement mission goals. When contemplating a RIF the agency was required to consider four factors in determining which employees would go and which would be retained: Tenure, Veteran Status, Total Federal Civilian and Military Service, and Performance for each service member. Those were the rules for downsizing personnel. But some generals figured rules were meant to be broken.

Three months earlier the Joint Chiefs of Staff of the combined services had issued a RIF order to scale down the number of military officers… not a frequent occurrence but not in and of itself all that unusual during uncertain economic times such as these. The problem was instead of using established procedures to evaluate each officer fairly against the four mandated criteria the army was using some undisclosed alternative assessment method. The result was nothing less than a massive arbitrary witch-hunt.

The army had implemented an urgent drive to rack and stack — evaluate and prioritize — each career officer based on criteria to which only the highest ranking members of the army's inner circle seemed privy. If a career officer didn't meet the new undisclosed ideal standard he, or she, was urged to retire or resign. Not only was this current RIF blatantly contrary to regulations it was discriminatory and it annihilated morale. Loyal officers were reluctant to support each other since their own jobs were on the line. Because their performance was evaluated against some unknown standard many did all they could to ensure their peers' performance seemed deficient compared to their own.

No one could be sure who might next be thrown under the army bus. Every officer's primary goal was looking out for number one. Nick was sure getting rid of seasoned officers had nothing to do with the fixing of the budget baloney the military was selling the public. Unfortunately real objectives were hard to uncover within the military structure.

The military had long ago perfected the art of compartmentalizing information on a need-to-know basis. That prevented the right hand from knowing what the left hand was doing. Lately it seemed to be the way the military — and government in general — managed every initiative... masking actual objectives under layers of security to keep as many people in the dark about the big picture as possible. Accomplishing little goals one small chunk at a time toward some greater objective was proving quite successful. To Nick's dismay he saw this first hand as the government hacked away at his civil liberties — one liberty at a time — in exchange for 'national security'.

Nick questioned how this trade-off was any different from the neighborhood street thug forcing the mom and pop owners of the corner grocery to surrender protection money. The real threat to mom and pop on the corner was the thug who demanded they pay him for protection against unnamed invisible enemies. If mom and pop didn't pay, that same street thug would be the one assaulting them or burning down their business. Paying for protection amounted to nothing more than a deal with the devil. Was giving up liberty in exchange for national security any different? Nick figured the answer would be clear in an ideal world where reality was exactly as it seemed; if national security were wholly breached all liberty could be in jeopardy. But the problem was it wasn't an ideal world.

Nick had begun to despise the cynicism that had twisted his thinking over the last few years. It was becoming increasingly difficult to blindly carry out his military duties with a clear conscience as he had done as a young officer. This round of massive RIF cuts was the latest fodder for his mental anguish.

While Congress and the Joint Chiefs of Staff persuaded the public to believe the cuts were real and intended to decrease government spending, Nick knew better. It was never about the money. In the last five years Congress had in fact increased allocations to the military. The principle was simple. It was a shell game. Dollars were creatively diverted to classified and special access programs... programs the military specifically designated off limits to public scrutiny — including the prying eyes of ordinary government officials — in the name of national security. These programs were sheltered under classified research and development appropriations. The worker bees employed by these projects were privy to the big picture only to the degree their need-to-know status authorized them. The effect of this current economic downsizing of military officers was a purge all right. It resulted in a new officer corps comprised of inexperienced soldiers programmed since their earliest school days to adhere to a vastly different set of values, mores based on unwavering allegiance to a supreme governing authority devoid of common sense and reason. The goal of the RIF was to root out leaders firmly grounded in tradition, autonomous liberty and national sovereignty.

During his twenty-two years in the military Nick had merely been another average guy trying to make a living and looking for a little relief from daily stress along the way. He had his own family and responsibilities to consider. So he left the job of running the country to his representatives and trusted they would act on the will of the people. He believed that America's best interest was at the top of their priority list. Sure, sometimes the government had issued laws or executive orders that hadn't made much sense to him — even seemed contrary to reason or flat out flew in the face of the facts. Yet he couldn't expect the government to swing his way on every matter. So like a good citizen and a trustworthy loyal soldier he sucked it up and swallowed his cumulative concerns. He went to bed each night never giving a thought to the possibility that the America he knew wouldn't be there in the morning exactly as he had left it the night before. But as his wife had told him a hundred times, his character flaw — if he had one — was his proclivity to be too trusting. It appeared she was right. Somewhere in the night the United States had slipped away from him. America had become a dark place where evil and greed thrived; a place where values, reason and liberty had been so expertly twisted and manipulated that Nick no longer recognized his country... or his role in it. When he realized how utterly his world had changed terrifying questions consumed him as aggressively as flesh-eating bacteria.

When had believing in the Constitution of the United States become an act so depraved that a constitutionalist should now be labeled an extremist — a flat out enemy of the people... a terrorist? Hadn't Nick raised his right hand twenty-two years before and each year thereafter when he extended his service commitment to swear to uphold the U.S. Constitution and its principles? And when had belief in the Bible become so vile that the government had to implement new laws to protect Americans from mere exposure to it? Weren't Americans capable of making up their own minds any longer? Couldn't they determine for themselves whether the Bible or any other book or religion interested them? When had Americans become unable to care for their fellow man based on their own standard of morals — needing government to legislate morals instead — to help Americans know what is acceptable and what isn't... what's right under God and what isn't? When had parents become outlaws unable to rear their own children without government micromanagement?

Nick couldn't reconcile these questions. And it gnawed at him that he could not pinpoint how America had been transformed right under his nose without him noticing. It was no less a mystery to him than Santa Claus or the Sandman had been when he was four years old — or the Tooth Fairy who stole into his room at night to swap a newly lost tooth for cash, sliding a dime under his pillow without him detecting the deed. While questions about the changes in America had distressed him for years he had not once expressed his concerns aloud. He suppressed them. He shoved them deep into the dusty corners of his own thoughts by day and pulled them out of the innermost caverns of his mind when alone at night in a tortuous attempt to process them. The bottom line was... Nick was losing his liberty. Like everyone else he knew he had allowed it to be bartered away by his own failure to object. Maybe Benjamin Franklin had said it best: *"Those that can give up essential liberty to obtain a little temporary safety deserve neither liberty nor safety."*

As far as personal liberties went it seemed to Nick that the latest rules of the game were... you snooze, you lose. He didn't notice too many politicians advocating for Americans to stand up against lawmakers dabbling in the legalized theft of the average American's rights.

Congress and the President made a habit of slipping insane policies through in the middle of the night.

Nick had been living a lie for a lifetime. He was a hypocrite of the worst sort. He was desperately ashamed he had been too weak to stand up and pose the hard questions. He served an indisputably corrupt political-military machine that had grown to massive proportions and he had continued with his daily routine as if nothing had changed. He did this over and over... and he cursed himself for doing it.

The maelstrom occurring inside Nick's mind had intensified one hundred fold almost three years earlier when he was reassigned to the Olympus Project. At that time Nick was designated as General Tucker's Chief of Staff, Regional Operations Command, Field Commander — ROC-FC. As ROC-FC for headquarters, training division, Nick was responsible for preparing the course and training materials for the candidate officers — future leaders of ROC forces — under the Olympus Project. It was during this billet to ROC Training Command while preparing those materials during that first year that Nick stumbled across a horrific document on the general's classified hard drive on the SIPRNet. General Tucker's documents were encrypted but someone, presumably the general, had not followed strict security protocol. A number of the classified e-files had been left open — in plain sight — within the shared software application Nick was responsible for monitoring on the general's behalf. The primary document that had caught Nick's eye, originally drafted in 1901, was the OPSEIM Directive — the Olympus Project Strategic Execution and Implementation Manifesto. The more he read the document the greater his mental torment became. It was at that point that Nick's greatest most terrifying mental anguish began.

Nick fully expected that at some point during his tenure at ROC training someone somewhere in the management circle would mention the OPSEIM Directive — if only in passing. So he listened intently to every ROC briefing provided. But at each of those briefings Nick had been told only what the army determined he needed to know. It seemed the army determined he did not need-to-know about the OPSEIM Directive — or even that it existed. Nick was provided cursory summaries of the project and a vague convoluted sketch of its history. This was a disappointment after the general's initial assurances. During one of his first meetings with General Tucker Nick was promised detailed disclosures of the program.

"What's the significance of the Olympus Project name sir?" Nick asked General Tucker shortly after his arrival at the ROC training facility.

"No significance. The Olympus Project is no different from other army projects," the general told him. "And like some projects it was probably proposed at a late afternoon round table discussion when the brass were more interested in hauling their clubs out to the base golf course. The guy with the biggest mouth or the most hardware on his chest most likely won the honor of naming it. Take the Apollo and Mercury Missions," the general said, biting into a jelly cruller. "Weren't those mission names also based on mythology? No big deal," Tucker said, wiping a dribble of jelly from his chin with his napkin.

"A few of the officers believe the Olympus Project name suggests a metaphor or analogy to the mythology," Nick said.

"My ass," the general chuckled. "You mean like Zeus and a bunch of other gods sitting up in the clouds playing war and moving human beings around a board like chess pieces?"

"Something like that sir," Nick said meekly, breaking apart a plain doughnut and spreading the crumbs around his paper plate.

"What a load of shit," the general laughed. "Someone's yanking your chain Fizer."

Nick laughed to be cordial. "It's just that none of the staff seemed particularly willing to give me much background on Olympus," Nick said, hoping to egg the general on and wrestle some details out of him.

"We have a full round of briefings scheduled starting tomorrow, about a week's worth. You'll get plenty of details Colonel," Tucker said, chewing. "We've got about eight months to shape this into a Class A training program. We need to get busy tactically mapping out this project. You'll find that eight months will pass pretty damn quickly. We have a daunting job ahead of us... building a world-class program for a new Command. We'll need a mission statement, strategic plan, goals, a vision... all the usual stuff. We can get started on that later today. I will be counting on you to draft the curriculum — classwork and field training — the whole shebang."

"Yes sir," Nick acknowledged. Exactly like any other army assignment Nick thought. Give me a list of tasks, due dates and goals and don't tell me a damn thing about how to get them done — or why any of it matters. Oh... and continually say, 'we,' when you mean 'me'.

General Tucker's briefers weren't much help. They provided so few particulars of the project Nick wondered if anyone actually knew the details. The information was fragmented and compartmentalized. Nonetheless, army efforts to deflect serious questions about the project didn't dissuade Nick from sniffing around on his own. He started by familiarizing himself with the basic

Olympus mythology.

A number of variations of the Mount Olympus tale exist but the underlying common thread is that twelve Greek gods and goddesses — the most powerful gods and goddesses — ranging from Ares to Zeus comprised a council of twelve who met on Mount Olympus as the rulers of heaven and earth. There they schemed and planned using their individual strengths and talents to move their earthly pawns around a global game board. Zeus, the most powerful of all gods, had the greatest powers. He could throw his voice and impersonate whomever he chose. He could shape shift and take on different forms. He could transform himself into an animal. Mythology noted that Zeus had a quick temper and could hurl lightning bolts. Nick couldn't help but ask himself who in their right mind would mess with Zeus?

Ares was the son of Zeus and Hera. He was tall and handsome, mean and self-centered. His sidekick Eris — the spirit of disagreement — traveled everywhere with him. Other spirits Ares carried with him were the spirits of Pain, Panic, Famine and Oblivion. Ares, in Greek mythology, didn't care who won or lost a battle; he merely reveled in seeing bloodshed. He caused trouble and most other gods stayed away from him. How appropriate this was Nick had thought... a secret monumental U.S. Army project named after an ancient pagan mythology that included a nasty god who liked to stir up bloody carnage and chaos for the sole pleasure of watching people suffer.

Perfect.

❋❋❋❋❋

Chapter 4

❀❀❀❀❀

ROC Training Center Marietta, Georgia, August

As Colonel Nick Fizer stood outside the great hall staring blankly into space he grew aware of the perspiration that had erupted along his forehead and the hot pink flush that masked his skin. He felt as if he had been caught dozing during a closed session with the Joint Chiefs of Staff and he had forgotten what briefing he was supposed to present. His heart was racing. He rapidly refocused his attention to the west hallway ready to snap into his role. Why should he be so concerned about military protocol when such heavy thoughts weighed him down? As he struggled with the same questions today that he had yesterday he felt his daily dose of self-loathing rising up from his gut. Here he was again... unquestioningly compliant, jamming doubts and legitimate concerns back down into the deep corners of his consciousness to play the army game. Was this how it would be for the rest of his working life... screw everything but do whatever he needed to do to collect that almighty paycheck? Colonel hypocrite, Nick thought, maybe he should have his name legally changed.

General Tucker was nearly on top of him before Nick spotted his ruddy figure thundering down the hall toward him. The general, his boots pounding on the tile floor, was no more than ten steps away. Nick realized the warm air drifting out through the open doors of the meeting hall combined with the soft drone of the crowd's low voices had lulled him into a contemplative daze. He hurled every distracting thought from his head and revved himself up into automatic pilot mode. He thrust one foot, then the other, smartly into Olympus Hall a step ahead of the general and snapped to attention. The heels of his size ten boots *thwacked...* and the room fell silent as Nick bellowed the alert.

"Atten...hutt!" Nick boomed. Hundreds of pairs of shoe and combat boot heels cracked together, echoing for an instant and then fading to stillness as all officers in the room rose to attention. "Major General Pierce Tucker!" Nick roared as he fell in close behind the general and timed his pace with Tucker's quickstep toward the front of the room. The two star general marched down the center aisle swiftly, boots thumping with unchallenged authority. He mounted the steps to the platform and made his way to center stage. Tucker turned, gripped the podium with firm hands and then paused, his brown eyes intently scanning the sea of camouflaged fatigues and black ROC dress uniforms filling the room.

"As you were," the two star ordered.

Nick took up his position at floor level to the left of the stage and motioned the officers to sit. A brief rustling followed as the soldiers took their seats. Tucker then swept his left arm toward an eight foot by twenty-four foot screen behind him. The general nodded to a sergeant stationed at a computer keyboard at the end of the stage and he brought up the first slide, the Regional Operations Command — ROC — logo. It consisted of an all-black background insignia with an oval framed Mount Olympus at the top... below it a color graded square of black and midnight blue with a strip of gold at the bottom. In the center were two embossed red triangles — base of one toward apex of the other, intersecting to create a six-point star — with the letters R... O... C... in the middle of the star in white. Displayed in white lettering above the top point of the star in a curved arc, 'REGIONAL OPERATIONS' appeared. Below the bottom point of the star was the word 'COMMAND'. The six-point star was framed by a lightning bolt on each side. The embossed logo sharply accented the midnight black of the ROC uniform.

While the ROC insignia contained a six-pointed star it had nothing to do with the Star of David — for or against — or religious ideology of any sort according to the army. Accusations of hidden meanings behind the star were summarily dismissed. Senior ROC officers at the highest levels eventually became so angered at ROC trainees' endless speculation that they appealed to the Joint Chiefs of Staff who in turn issued a formal memorandum addressing the issue. Speculation about the ROC unit emblem at the ROC training facility ceased — at least as far as officials could determine.

The next slide depicted two snow-capped mountain peaks, the rugged Mt. Olympus in the foreground towering over a flat oval globe displaying both hemispheres of the world and dividing the earth into thirteen distinct regions. Abundant green foliage with sea and wildlife species surrounded the entire design. Directly below the outer edges of the Mount Olympus image were the words 'T-21 ARES – ZEUS,' in white and red letters representing the entire Olympus Project Command. 'T-21' was shorthand for the 'twenty first century tunnel grid'. According to military officials the use of 'ARES-ZEUS' — referencing the major mythological gods from Ares through Zeus — simply indicated the names of the major tunnel commands and sometimes conference rooms, briefing rooms, and orbiting satellites directly associated with the particular tunnel zones. There was nothing with any rhyme or reason to it... so said officials... although scuttlebutt had it that this too had clandestine significance. Some ROC trainees suggested that by referencing the twelve major pagan gods the intent was to covertly imply a connection between top-secret objectives of the Olympus Project and the pagan gods' struggle to control mankind. Official sources called this adolescent hogwash.

For good measure, in the memo prohibiting assumptions and rumors about hidden implications behind the six-point star of the ROC unit logo, the Chiefs of Staff included a directive banning all suppositions about military projects. It stated in particular that military program names and logos were random and any ROC trainee questioning either the objectives or the propriety of the Olympus Project would be deemed a threat to national security and prosecuted under military law. This of course made no sense to a reasonable mind. If there were nothing secretive about the logo or the program for which it stood why would the army treat an associated rumor mill speculation as an infraction worthy of court martial? That was the army mentality. Nonetheless the memo was apparently sufficient to end candidates' preoccupation with hidden agendas and conspiracy theories. Instead, new whispers began that implied the concept of christening the project 'Olympus' and naming the tunnel commands after mythological pagan gods was meant as a joke. Nick thought upper management could easily dispatch the rumors if they provided these officers with the facts; but this was the army and that would entail complete honesty. That was never going to happen.

The Olympus Project remained shrouded in mystery. It was deliberately kept out of the public and congressional eye by shielding it from scrutiny at the highest levels of national security... no denying that. The specifications, scope and true objectives of the Olympus Project remained expertly tucked away in the shadows under the guise of classified military research and development.

The very existence of the Olympus Project and its sophisticated web of fully engaged and equipped interlocking military tunnels a mile beneath American soil were prime examples of compartmentalizing information at every level. Even Nick had not officially been fully briefed on the entire project and he was supposed to be part of management. As far as ROC officers were concerned it was safer to bury their heads in their own discrete tasks and stifle urges to let their eyes wander too far from their own responsibilities. To the average American, ROC forces and the Olympus Project simply didn't exist.

Efforts to maintain secrecy had been nearly one hundred percent successful. There was good reason for this. Any individual exhibiting the slightest propensity to step over the secrecy line simply disappeared... with a little help. The only thing ROC forces knew for sure was that the military had cooked up something big decades ago and ROC officers were in training to implement it. It was common knowledge by ROC forces that if they wanted to be around to see how the story ended they were expected to keep their mouths shut.

General Tucker, standing at the podium, slid his thumb and forefinger into his top pocket, grabbed hold of his eyeglasses and drew them out of their brown leather case. He wiggled them until the left stem popped out to ninety degrees then slipped them on his face. He momentarily looked up at the ceiling as if deep in thought, then looked at the papers before him on the podium. He shook his head melodramatically before speaking, displaying the same incomprehensibility as if he had witnessed a miraculous triple play wholly executed by a minor league second baseman best known for his bumbling fielding abilities and his 'stone glove' nickname. "Ladies and gentleman," the general began. "Well done," he nodded slowly for emphasis. Well done," he repeated. "You all deserve a round of applause. Congratulating you on this auspicious occasion seems an inadequate confirmation of your accomplishments. You have completed the most advanced, demanding and groundbreaking training available in the world today. No soldiers anywhere on this planet are stronger, more intelligent, more capable, more courageous or more loyal than are you officers."

"The time has come for change, ladies and gentlemen, and you have been chosen to lead that transformation." Nick watched the general's lip curl and his brow narrow. Tucker glared with glassy vacant eyes at the officers. The general seemed to have instantly slipped into some weird catatonic state. Nick edged a step closer to the stage. The general's actions were unsettling. A strange sensation gripped Nick as if a horrific black doom was sliding down over the room. Yet as quickly as the general's odd episode began it ended. He continued with his speech as if he'd had no part in the momentary disruption.

ROC trainee Major Falcon Colby had also observed this brief peculiar expression ripple across the general's face but he had thought little of it. Falcon sat rigidly in his second row seat, head and eyes facing front, shoulders rigid. He focused on General Tucker's every word. This was the moment he had dreamed about for two years. Falcon's skin tingled with a feeling welling up from deep within him... pride maybe... he wasn't sure. How embarrassing, he thought. If anyone knew how he felt at that moment he would be mortified. He was a grown man; yet here he was puffed with pride and as giddy as a schoolboy rounding third base after a grand slam.

❀❀❀❀❀

ROC Northwest Takotna, Alaska, August

At 1602 hours *Senior Starshiná* Malikov consciously straightened his back and sat up taller in his lab chair. He was piqued with anticipation as he prepared to rattle off the standard radio exchange he had spent tedious hours memorizing and practicing when he had first drawn his assignment. He drew in a deep breath and then began.

"T21-ZEUS 006 standing down, request for clearance to proceed." Malikov's Russian accent would be acknowledged at the other end of the connection and accepted without question. The twists to his English pronunciation of simple words were well-recognized vocal inflections normally occurring daily over the airwaves and originating from any one of the more than five hundred thousand U.N. (United Nations) peacekeeping forces stationed in the U.S.A... most all of them in similar FOLT underground facilities. Malikov sat forward at the edge of his chair waiting and listening for confirmation of his request to waft through his computer speakers. He was looking forward to ending his shift and returning to B Sector to join Sergei and possibly some of his fellow Russian peacekeepers for a night of vodka, small talk, cards or maybe some pool. For now he tried to focus on his present task.

The radio crackled. "Roger affirmative, T21-ZEUS 006, stand down; clear to proceed, 1040... out." The reply had lifted his spirits. The shutdown order and validation might not have come for another two hours. He considered himself lucky he had not had to twiddle his thumbs while headquarters pilfered unpaid overtime from him.

Malikov wrapped up his duties, turning three dials counter clockwise from 2.75MHz, 5.25MHz and 8.70MHz to the triple zero mark and flipping three ELF — Extreme Low Frequency — micro switches respectively to the stand down position. Once he had completed the task and noted his actions in the logbook he pushed his chair away from the computer desk, stood, and grabbed the silver plated flask out of his back pocket. He turned it over fondly in his hands, admiring its glossy sheen, and then opened it. He downed the last three hearty gulps of vodka and returned the contraband to his pocket.

He slipped on his parka and grabbed his azure blue U.N. peacekeeping force beret. He hummed as he made his way to the first inner door leading out of the lab. It was a useless regulation... having to wear his parka whenever leaving the common area. It meant he had to drag the heavy thing around with him all day. Fools! He thought to himself. Tunnel walls were ten times as thick as a bank vault and the atmosphere inside the tunnel was temperature controlled, usually hotter than hell. These Americans were *nuzhno kak v zhope zub* — absolutely worthless — as worthless as tits on a boar hog, he thought. They didn't deserve all the freedoms they had and were too stupid and too weak to hang onto them. This ridiculous *parka* rule was simply one more unreasonable directive from a baby-faced officer just out of diapers.

He removed his security card from his top pocket and inserted it into the card reader slot to the right of the inner door. He peered into the pinhead sized biometric iris sensor above the reader, waited for five seconds while the scanner measured his eye fixations and saccades — the rapid eye movements, force of eye muscles, and characteristics of his eye orbit and vitreous fluid. Malikov's lab like many other departments in the FOLT was a Sensitive Compartmented Information Facility — SCIF... pronounced 'skiff.' The lab was enclosed in an area within the FOLT dedicated to processing sensitive classified information and security protocols were high. Because access was limited Malikov was forced to endure additional steps each time he entered or left the lab. Some of these security processes were carried over to the private quarters of ROC and U.N. peacekeeping forces who were assigned to the SCIFs. To Malikov it was the biggest drawback to his job.

Malikov hated the multiple sensors used to screen personnel. This security equipment often spat out false readings based on emotional states. Malikov had failed to trip the sensor at times merely because he was angry or out of sorts. If he had not discovered he could level off his emotions with a few sips of vodka — skewing the sensor readings by distorting the frequency of his eye movements and composition of his vitreous fluid — he might have lost his position a long time ago. There was a three-strike rule... three opportunities to trip the sensor in a twenty-four hour period at any one sensor station. He had been forced to spend a handful of nights at Sergei's apartment because he failed to trigger the sensor at his own door after two tries. Staying the night at Sergei's was the only way to avoid a possible third strike and the ensuing penalty. Fortunately for Malikov he had never exceeded the limit at his lab door — thanks to his handy vodka flask. Three strikes at the lab could have barred him from SCIF areas and provided him a quick ticket back to Russia.

It was contemptible to invade his personal space and use scientific innovations to crawl all over the inside of his body and mind. Why should the government fixate on getting inside his head? He was a warrior not a rocket scientist... give him a rifle and an objective and he would get the job done. But stay out of his goddamn head. Malikov had complained about these technologies once too often and on one occasion it was too late when he realized his platoon leader was not two feet from him. The minute the words had left his mouth he knew he had made a mistake. The lieutenant angrily shut Malikov down before he finished his second sentence.

"Suck it up Malikov. You're not back in the middle ages on a dusty Afghan hilltop. You're in the twenty first century. Deal with it or get the hell out of the army," his CO had chastised him. Malikov had gritted his teeth, angry for his lapse in resolve to never appear vulnerable in the presence of an officer. But there was a point to Malikov's anger over this technology. The concept was as terrifying as life under Soviet communism had been. They might as well have raised communism from the dead and plunged him back in time to a world where he could trust no one — not even family members — where snitches stood at every street corner. But this was worse. The probing snitch inside him, injected there secretly by the sensor to steal his soul and uncover his personal secrets. He didn't care if he sounded paranoid. He would be damned if he was going to let anyone stick a microchip up his nose or shove one in elsewhere in his body. Sensors were bad enough. If it ever came to it they would have to microchip his cold rigid corpse. There was something evil about the whole damn invasive technology thing.

Malikov waited for the red flash from the eye sensor

and quick beep from the I.D. box. He removed his I.D. card and waited. When the door slid open he walked forward and repeated the process at the second door. He waited the five seconds for the iris scanner and card reader to beep and then three seconds more until the door opened. Malikov took in a deep breath as he stepped into the vast tunnel corridor. Two MPs armed with laser sited XM10s were on him like a pair of blowflies on rotting meat as soon as he stepped out of the weather lab. They stood within inches of him waiting impatiently as Malikov made a point of slowly adjusting his U.N. peacekeeping force beret, zipping his parka and checking his watch — twice. Malikov leisurely stretched his arms above his head and yawned. The tall MP stepped closer to the shorter one and they began murmuring to each other in low voices. As soon as their attention was momentarily diverted, Malikov pulled a thick hand-rolled Russian cigarette from his top pocket, lit it and drew in a hurried lungful of smoke.

"Put it out man," the taller MP directed. "You know there's no smoking in the passageway."

Malikov sneered. It was futile to argue with MPs — especially ROC forces MPs. They were all bullies — like Aleksi. MPs were cowards who turned vile when they had an upper hand and they usually had the upper hand because they were armed. When his grandfather Aleksi had been transferred from the NKVD military police to the infantry in WWII, he no longer had the advantage; everyone was armed and Aleksi no longer enjoyed his NKVD bully status. Malikov was sure at that point Aleksi would have altered his behavior. Aleksi would never have bullied anyone until he was sure the odds were in his favor. Clearly that was his modus operandi just as with the elderly peasant farmer. Similarly, the minute Malikov showed up on the farm and Aleksi had a defenseless boy to pummel he quickly found an outlet for his bullying. MPs were all the same. Malikov swore many years ago he would never fail to oblige MPs by serving them up the contempt they deserved whenever he had the chance. This was as good a time as any to adhere to his oath.

Malikov dropped the cigarette to the tunnel floor and ground it out slowly with the toe of his boot. His lip curled and he scowled at the tall MP. For a time he aimlessly lingered at the lab doorway, feigning interest in surveying the tunnel walls, doing his best to delay and annoy the impatient MPs. He patted his pockets, intently, as if he were looking for something particularly important. When he found what he was looking for he slipped it out of his pocket. He took his time peeling back the wrapper. He dropped the foiled paper and popped his last stick of gum into his mouth.

He eyed his armed escorts as they shifted their weight from one foot to the other anxiously waiting to put an end to their monotonous eight-hour post outside of Malikov's lab. Malikov started walking, slowly, toward the transport vehicle pick up point. The MPs walked beside him. Only the distant soft hum of transports, the remote din of voices and the low echoes from the three men's boots disturbed the stillness. Malikov's thoughts drifted back to the cigarette he had ground into the floor.

He had rolled his own cigarettes for decades but Americans were too civilized to stain their spotless fingertips with such things. Americans were arrogant — from what Malikov had seen — and that made them vulnerable. The people believed they were irreproachable. What Americans had done, in Malikov's estimation, was trade in good judgment for American dollars. They allowed themselves to be coerced out of their liberties with promises of protection from invisible enemies. They fell for false government claims that giving up liberty was the path to preserving the American way of life. As long as the dollars kept rolling in Americans willingly surrendered a little liberty here a little autonomy there... all in the name of safety and security.

Malikov knew well such ruses. The American government had taken a page out of the Soviet Union's recipe book on how to condition the people to let down their guard and look the other way. If Malikov could recognize this why couldn't these *Amerikantsy* — Americans? Malikov had watched a world movement transforming the smoking of cigarettes into a nearly criminal act. As Malikov had been quick to argue over the years the issue wasn't smoking. The issue was control. Malikov had been incensed about the loss of his right to choose how he lived his life. He had supposed the army had a right to forbid him to smoke while on duty because after all he was a military man; the government owned his sorry ass. But what right did anyone have to tell him what to do on his own time?

The Soviets had been the masters of propaganda, or so he had thought. Now he wasn't so sure. At least under the Soviet government Malikov understood how the game was played. These days, unreasonable and intrusive restrictions were tossed about freely under the guise of platforms like the greening movement, smart growth, sustainment and conservation. Malikov had nothing against these principled causes until enforcement of these new agendas trampled his own freedoms and suffocated him by confining his own puny life into smaller and smaller boxes; it was the ultimate in micromanagement — mindless, total control.

Malikov saw no difference between punishing a

parent in America for allowing a child to become overweight or drink too many soft drinks... and throwing someone into a Siberian work camp for ripping down a poster of Stalin, uttering an opinion contrary to the politbyuro, or daring to teach a child about freedom. Lethal policing forces and hidden motives lurked everywhere in the twenty first century. Didn't these *Amerikantsy* see the correlation between the new requirements to report suspicious looking people in airports and sports stadiums — or forcing children to report bad parental behavior — and the mandates to inform on suspicious neighbors in Soviet Russia or Nazi Germany? The government had used the benefits of giving up smoking and turned the issue into another exercise in control built on propaganda.

The government had pushed further and further to see how ludicrous and invasive the law could become before the public would stand up and complain. Before he left Russia Malikov had read about an American city that had banned anyone from walking the streets with anything hanging from their mouths because it resembled smoking: smokeless cigarettes, toothpicks, a blade of grass, a lollipop. Malikov had refused to believe the newspaper but he had been wrong. The world had no common sense. What Malikov couldn't understand was why alcohol was still legal. How many deaths and injuries would it take before Americans became outraged at that vice? But... ah... Malikov thought to himself, lawmakers would never criminalize that. They had tried that once and failed and it would fail again because lawmakers liked their liquor. If Aleksi did not have his vodka perhaps Malikov would never have felt the sting of Aleksi's fist in his jaw. Yet Malikov had to admit the war on smoking was a masterful plan — a colossal test to measure boundaries and limitations of governmental ability to influence and control the masses. It was an undeniable success, the magnitude of which had come to Malikov's immediate attention only hours after he had arrived in America.

After Malikov's plane had touched down at Boston's Logan International Airport he had taken the subway from the airport to South Station. When he arrived he had purchased a ticket on an Amtrak train leaving Boston, Massachusetts bound for the west coast of America. All members of his unit had been directed to travel across the United States by train and bus to pick up some of the American language and acclimate themselves to American culture. They were given two additional weeks travel time to accomplish this.

Prior to boarding his train at the Boston station Malikov had stood, smoking, at the far end of an outdoor platform under a twenty-foot high canopy to observe the passengers and his new environment. Four thunderously loud smoke-stained 6200 horsepower commuter engines idled under the rail station's canopy spewing smoke and thick exhaust fumes into the crisp February air. A stream of passengers from both directions went about their business, boarding and alighting from the rail cars. Malikov stood well back of the commuter trains, twenty to thirty feet from the car doors, under the long canopy. He leaned against a cement column under a no smoking sign. He was initially pleased when he had occasionally caught the eye of a beautiful young woman among the passengers hurrying along the platform. Yet although he smiled cordially at one attractive woman she — and most people passing him — did not bother to return his pleasantries. One man who had disembarked from the commuter train yelled at his young son who had jumped down the last iron step of the rail car and scurried ahead of the man. The lad giggled and twirled and eyed his new surroundings with excitement as young children do. The boy had wandered about six feet away from his father's side which was about six feet closer to Malikov.

"Get back here Danny," the crimson-faced man screamed, gesturing angrily toward his feet and frantically jabbing his hand down toward the platform. "That man is smoking a cigarette!" As the boy bounded back to his father's side the man latched onto the boy's shoulder and viciously yanked him closer. "Goddammit! You've been told a thousand times you'll get sick if you breathe that second hand smoke. Don't wander off like that!" The man's loud rebuke caused several people to turn toward the commotion, their gazes falling accusingly on Malikov and the cigarette dangling from his fingers. The boy's father pitched Malikov a despicable glare before grabbing the boy's wrist. The angry father spun on his heels and dragged the boy along beside him, hurriedly hauling him off toward the train station entrance and shrieking profanities at him all the way. Malikov had nearly lost sight of them before they had reached the doors, their figures obscured by the thick haze of diesel exhaust and smoke suspended in the winter air under the outside canopy.

So this was common sense. Malikov had laughed heartily at this absurdity and then quickly stifled himself, snuffing out his cigarette when a conductor scowled at him and motioned to the no smoking sign above Malikov's head. Malikov shrugged at his first American culture lesson. It seemed acceptable to brutalize a small child by yanking the lad's arm and screaming obscenities at him in public but it was not acceptable to smoke a cigarette outside amid a suspended cloud of diesel exhaust. What kind of people were these Americans?

Before Malikov had left Russia for his U.N. peacekeeping assignment to America he had received cursory briefings on a select number of the American government's top-secret programs. 'Thought and Knowledge Management Programs' were high on that select list. But Malikov had hesitated to believe the American government would spend money for something that sounded so utterly ridiculous until he had witnessed the effects of such programs with his own eyes. It had taken Marx, Lenin and Stalin many years of devastating economic manipulation, political oppression and a bloody revolution to accomplish societal control. Yet how long had it taken America to implement these ridiculous 'Thought Management Programs...' all accomplishing the same objective without bloodshed?

It was clear to Malikov from the beginning that the effect of these 'Thought Programs' were the visible components of a bloodless revolution, the components that the public was allowed to witness. The real agenda was to implement every possible method to control and subjugate the workers. Malikov saw the situation for what it was from the minute he stepped foot in America, the effects of a refined sophisticated propaganda machine. Could these Americans be so blind they didn't see it? Well, what did he care? It wasn't his country.

"*Amerikanskaya glupost!*" — American folly! Malikov told his fellow Russian soldiers over pool games and vodka after he arrived at the FOLT facility. "*Amerikanskiy duraki!*" — American fools! — Malikov said to them in colorful Russian as he described in detail all the thoughts swimming around in his head about America. He told them it was true that Americans have no idea Russian troops are in their country right under their noses. Malikov had laughed at the pictures he painted during his diatribes. The more he told his comrades about the arrogant Americans he encountered on his two-week culture trip the more boisterous he became. And as soon as Malikov began comparing Soviet Russia and Nazi Germany to America in a rowdy animated tirade... well it was right about then that Sergei Nikulin — Malikov's dearest comrade — had told him, "Malikov, *Moy khoroshiy drug*," — my good friend — "The vodka say too much."

❋❋❋❋❋

Chapter 5

❉❉❉❉❉

Juneau, Alaska, August

"Move... dammit," Viktor muttered aloud, forcing weak curses to pass between his freezing lips. He slammed an icy fist down onto his thigh as he leaned on the northern corner of the Juneau Federal Building in the alcove under the overhang only yards from where he had last rested. But he hardly felt the blow from his weakened hand against his numbed leg; the force of the impact would not have stunned a mosquito. This area where Viktor now rested was a dangerous place. Powerful seventy to ninety mile an hour arctic blasts drove icy snowflakes over a six-foot berm of drifted snow at the far southern corner of the structure. The full force of the Taku winds funneled the blizzard down through the concourse between the building's entrance and the street side snowbanks. He had huddled there for shelter but it felt like he stood naked at the pinpoint epicenter of a wind tunnel — the incessant gusts spiraling toward his body. He must leave this spot under the roof that he had thought would provide shelter or he would freeze solid where he now stood.

Heavy ice stiffened his eyelids, distorting his world as if a fractured prism of glass had slipped down over his face. His diminishing field of vision, illuminated by the barely discernible glow of daylight filtering through dark purple-gray skies, told him his situation was grim. He knew snow blindness had gripped him... the burning gritty pain in his eyes and dark murky shapes oscillating at the fringes of his peripheral vision affirmed this. Soon his world could be veiled in complete blackness. He tensed the muscles in his back and used his elbows to push his freezing body away from the building. He staggered a step forward. "That's good Viktor," he told himself, mouthing the words... relieved his lips were still working. "At least you're moving."

Hours of official daylight remained. It was Juneau in August and the summer sun — on the infrequent occasions when it wasn't raining in this temperate rainforest — would not dip down below the mountains until nearly ten thirty at night. But it made no difference to Viktor. His world had been a blinding darkened swirl from the very start, from the moment he had found himself alone on Glacier Highway. So with every ounce of strength he could muster he forced his leg to rise and then plunged his foot into the snow a few inches ahead.

"No. Stay here... rest," the voice taunted him. Viktor knew the voice was not his own. He could not silence it but if he could wrench it from his head — crush it, decimate it — if he could convince others the voice was real he could prove its origin was not his own mind. There must be a way to show this demon had been injected into his skull to chip away at his sanity and lure him toward death. If he could only rip it from his head and spread it out on a table for others to examine — to verify it was a vile insidious weapon — but how could he do this? What sane person would believe that Satan himself was stalking Viktor Salko... from inside his very own head? He grimaced in pain as he took another step. His actions seemed like slow motion. The numbness that had gripped his limbs hours before crept deeper into his flesh and sank further into his bones.

Frigid blasts of glacial air raged down from the mountains and continued to spill into the city.

He must not focus on this desolate place he told himself. He must find sanctuary out of the blizzard where he could be safe and warm. But Viktor had only the here and the now and the abhorrent storm whipping around him. Except... one haven did remain. There was one safe place he could go. If he could push the voice aside and look deep into his own soul he could find shelter from the maelstrom. He called out to his grandmother's living spirit. *"Leelk'w"* — Grandmother — "I must find the strength," Viktor mouthed the words, breathless from exertion. *"Leelk'w* ... help me find my inner essence. Take me back to when I was a little boy when you first showed me how to find this power within me. Show me the way *Leelk'w...* guide me."

"No... stop. Rest will not hurt you. Rest... then you can go." Viktor shook his head violently to jar loose the voice, to hurl it from his mind. "I won't listen to you!" He screamed his indomitable resolution aloud but the syllables tumbled out of his mouth through chattering teeth and toppled into the roaring storm as mere whispers, vanishing into the swirling white flakes. His once solid frame wobbled and swayed on weakened knees as he drove his body forward. How had he drawn from his inner strength in the past when he was in trouble? What was the process? He must think back to what his grandmother had taught him.

"Concentrate," he admonished himself. *"Leelk'w* show me," he pleaded, "Help me." Then, suddenly — inexplicably — he knew. There above him he could see it now... nearly silent yet immensely powerful. "Yes that's it," he told himself. He must listen for the *whoosh... whoosh... whoosh...* of its wings as it glides and dips on delicate currents of air as if soaring on a warm Chinook

— a snow eater wind capable of wolfing down a foot of snow in less than a day. Viktor must satiate himself with the potent essence of life flowing out along a seven-foot wingspan and down through sturdy thick legs. Yes he must unite with the spirit of God's natural world and draw into his own body the power of the magnificent bald eagle, his Tlingit Clan's moiety — lineage. He must feel this majestic creature — feel as it feels — when it soars upward toward heaven in a sparkling cobalt sky. Viktor imagined the soles of his mukluks transforming into sharpened eagle claws. In his mind's eye he saw them dig into the black tar of the city street — hidden beneath mounting piles of snow — grabbing hold with the force of thickly muscled talons and this filled him with a renewed potency. It rose up from his soul.

Viktor envisioned the bald eagle's power flowing down through dense muscular legs into the three front curled talons and the longer rear hallux talon... four hundred pounds per square inch of raw vice-like gripping force. And he felt this same strength coursing through his own body. Yes the path to life-saving strength was an inward power. He must not fight *against* nature's wrath. He must respect the energy of this blizzard and unite with it. He must draw nature's force *into* him to strengthen him and propel him onward.

He imagined himself sure-footed and sustained by nature's wrath — not defeated by it. He took a step and then another. Every inch brought him closer to Adit 17 and he knew this was how it must be. He lumbered ahead through the frigid wasteland, his *Tlingit tu kinajek* — guardian spirit — there beside him. His *tu kinajek* will steady his limbs and hold him erect. It didn't matter that he could no longer see or feel his legs through the numbing cold. He must accept that his legs were still beneath him. He must acknowledge this trial could be worse. Yet that thought struck him like madness. It was insane to think anything could be worse than near total blindness and imprisonment in a numb, broken body... death only seconds away from seizing him. He was utterly alone in an incomprehensible blizzard. How could things possibly be worse? Yet he had to be grateful he was still alive... so far. He must give thanks for the warmth of his parka and his fur-trimmed hood and his mukluks and the stamina his *tu kinajek* has provided him. He must appreciate the material gifts his grandmother had fashioned for him that had so far allowed him to cling to life. Most especially he must acknowledge the essence of life these gifts represented.

His handmade sealskin and caribou mukluks were snug against his calves, fastened by leather strips tied below his knees. Their fur lining had bathed him in warmth and protected him from the elements during the first miles of his journey... before the numbness took hold. And while he presumed the boots were of little help now in staving off the frostbite that was most assuredly attacking his distal flesh, muscles, and nerves, he knew the crucial significance of the mukluks. They tethered him to his past, entwining his senses on a spiritual plane with his grandmother's visionary wisdom. It might be incomprehensible to some but Viktor knew his grandmother would feel his pain. He was certain of it. She would sense this terrible danger.

Viktor's Tlingit grandmother Ilya had been nicknamed after a lake in Southwestern Alaska. Like the state itself, the great Iliamna Lake is impressively large. Nestled in a spruce forest seven hundred seventy miles northwest across the Gulf of Alaska from Juneau, Iliamna is seventy-seven miles long, twenty-two miles wide and nearly one thousand feet deep. The Yup'ik, Alutiiq, and Athabascan peoples of the lake have subsistence fished and hunted fresh water seals as far back as the residents can remember. According to folklore, mysterious species of fish swim the cold waters of the Iliamna Lake. Tales of an Iliamna monster not so unlike the cryptid Loch Ness Monster of the Scottish Highlands have been passed down through generations. It was in part the stories of these strange Iliamna Lake creatures that prompted Viktor's great grandparents to call his grandmother 'Ilya'.

Ilya had been so nicknamed to honor all great mysteries of the world and to show respect for the visionary gifts the spirits had bestowed on her. From her early childhood, Ilya's parents had witnessed a profound spirituality in their daughter. She possessed a remarkable prophetic ability to perceive the environment around her, to connect and influence the natural world, and to comprehend the earth's greatest enigmas that others could not begin to understand. From the time Ilya was small her parents saw in her the special abilities of the Tlingit healer and seer. But while Ilya possessed the deep spirituality of the *ichta* — shaman — her parents had nurtured her gifts humbly with quiet humility.

It was well known that the abilities of the *ichta* were often inherited. Ilya had been certain these gifts had been passed to Viktor. She had explained to him how the role of the *ichta* in today's Tlingit culture differed from the role of the *ichta* prior to the encroachment of western society and modern religions. Ilya had told Viktor that while the *ichta* of today was not regarded as the same omnipotent force as in the bygone eras, values of the *ichta* remained deeply woven into Tlingit society and ceremony. Ilya had stressed to Viktor that just as good spirits exist spirits with evil intent exist, and just as well-intentioned *ichtas* exist there are *ichtas* with ill will. Ilya warned Viktor he must never use his *ichta* abilities for dark purposes.

Ilya possessed extraordinary visionary skills. She had an uncanny capacity to expertly mediate any conflict, to bridge the natural and spiritual worlds, and to overcome challenges. His *Leelk'w* was an undeniably exceptional woman and Viktor absorbed all his grandmother had taught him. But he always feared he would not know how to carry forward throughout his own life the good will and purity of his *Leelk'w*.

Viktor's great grandparents were convinced Ilya's special abilities flowed through her fingertips into her crafts as surely as water traveled through a hose and emptied into a bucket. Ilya's parents believed when she fashioned mittens, kelp and abalone baskets, and mukluks they were transformed into items with a much grander purpose. Viktor believed this was true. He felt it. Each gift Ilya had bestowed on Viktor — be it gloves, a parka, mukluks or a simple blessing of good luck — was truly remarkable. The significance of something so simple as one of Ilya's handcrafted mukluks was far greater than its intended material purpose. The great Alaskan land and waters had surrendered the spirits of wildlife and the spotted seal for Ilya's use. "You must never treat these gifts with disrespect," his grandmother had told him.

As a boy Viktor had watched Ilya perform her skin-sewing art. She spoke to the spirits of the seals and the wildlife as she fashioned these items and thanked them for their great sacrifice in providing her those gifts. To Ilya, sealskin and caribou mukluks, gloves and mittens were manifestations of the greater life force where all of nature and mankind were as one. When Viktor's parents had passed on from this life, failing to return one cold spring day from fishing in the roiling waters of Auke Bay, Viktor's grandparents had taken the three youngest children remaining at home and raised them.

When Viktor's grandfather died after Viktor's graduation from the University of Alaska Southeast, he and his siblings had grown increasingly concerned about Ilya living alone in her isolated village. She had no means to travel to Juneau. And so it was after a short time all of the grandchildren had convinced Ilya to move closer to them. For the first few months in her new Juneau home away from Auke Bay, Ilya seemed unsettled... uprooted. Yet as with all other things Ilya would quickly adapt. One rainy October evening Ilya had unwrapped her kelp seaweed and abalone-shell sewing basket and taken up her thick sewing needles once again without further fuss.

The sealskin and caribou mukluks Ilya fashioned for Viktor had protected him from harsh conditions throughout his travels across the Alaskan tundra. Ilya had seemed to know when his boots had begun to wear out even without seeing them. She would then set to work to provide him a new pair. Viktor's mukluks comforted him on a much higher plane than an ordinary pair of boots. He was certain they were the means by which he had maintained his ethereal connection to his grandmother. So yes... his situation could be more dismal. He was still alive. Yet something confused him. His hands were exposed and unbearably frigid. While frozen flesh would be expected after hours in a blizzard without mittens or gloves, it was not having his mittens in the first place that was so disconcerting. Why would he go out in such a vile storm without them?

❄❄❄❄❄

Viktor's Tlingit ancestors had prided themselves on their readiness to adapt to life threatening circumstances. In the nineteenth and early twentieth centuries life in the southeast network of waterways of Alaska had been good... albeit harsh. Availability of game like deer and bear followed unwritten patterns designed and orchestrated by nature. The cycle of life occurred in unpredictable waves. In certain years wild game was just plain scarce. Waterfowl and geese passed overhead during migration periods but they did not always find reason to stop. Tlingit families found it increasingly difficult to obtain enough food even though many had rights to subsistence hunting and fishing. Commercial fishing and trophy hunting seriously diminished the availability of the once abundant salmon, halibut, and Alaskan wild game resources. Yet Viktor's family had adjusted.

In past generations the Tlingits of Juneau and Auke Bay would travel by canoe as far away as San Francisco to trade and fish and sometimes to war with other native tribes. These days Aukwan Tlingits traveled less often for subsistence. Viktor's grandparents had made use of what they had available... most often seaweed, salmon and other species of sea life. They trapped small indigenous game animals for pelts to trade and process to feed and clothe Viktor and his siblings. His grandparents were able to harvest sufficient food to carry them through the winters.

While it was second nature they should never hunt or fish for more than they could use, from the time Viktor was a boy the special art of preparing for the unknown had been instilled into his subconscious mind. He had proved over the years that he could find within himself the seventh sense necessary to survive no matter what he faced. He had consistently demonstrated that he had developed the ancient skills to be prepared, to think in unison with nature and respect it, to recognize the true path and to follow it. So how could he then explain what he had seen when he had looked at his hands during his journey? At the joint of his wrist where the fur trim of his parka sleeve should have rested against the fur border of his sealskin mittens Viktor had seen only white icy flesh. He should have seen his grandmother's rugged hand sewn sealskin mittens. Instead, his gaze had settled on his own clenched bare skin... curled and locked into frozen knobby spheres. Where were his mittens? How could he have forgotten everything he had ever learned and leapt into the center of a violent blizzard unprepared? Clambering out of the research facility and blindly pitching himself into the heart of such vicious arctic conditions with no hand protection was a mistake that could easily kill him. Viktor felt like he was dangling from an icy precipice over the black abyss of death. Had he alone put himself there? Couldn't he have done something different to prevent some of this madness?

❄❄❄❄❄

In the weeks prior to the capital city's seizure by the arctic deep freeze a bizarre dance of colors across the southeastern sky baffled Alaskans. The spectral green and yellow swirl of the Northern Lights is seen infrequently in Juneau during periods of increased solar activity roughly occurring in eleven-year cycles. The unexpected night sky displays caused heads to shake in apprehension that something wicked was coming. Yet it seemed no one in the lower forty-eight — the contiguous United States — had been concerned.

Authorities had made few attempts to disguise their arrogant nonchalance and impudent condescension toward those who dared to present conflicting theories about the unfolding events. The government hastily dismissed contradicting data and metrics that some scientists had accumulated and categorized the Northern Light activity and the unseasonable cold as inconsequential. To discredit conflicting evaluations of collected data the eminent scientific community — those scientists most assuredly on the government's payroll or otherwise beholden to big brother — had pronounced the freakish weather to be a short-term twist of nature attributable to global warming.

To explain wide variants in global temperature and other phenomena the government had worked for years to sell the concept of global warming. As long as scientists confirmed the government's standard theories, authorities advocated for those scientists' popularity. Those *approved* theories noted the glaciers and northern ice packs were receding, adjusting and melting in response to man's early twentieth century industrial blunders. That was the theory the government accepted... the only theory it supported.

Man's unintentional fracturing of the ozone layer had caused the greenhouse effect and according to Washington the greenhouse effect was sufficient explanation for nearly any anomaly. The current severity and aberrations in weather were merely a matter of those types of related consequential events. It was quite simple, the government had repeatedly declared, the greenhouse effect was the result of minor miscalculations that had occurred at the dawn of the twentieth century... miscalculations attributable to great leaps in experimentation and invention previously undetected and little understood. That was the cause of the breach of the ozone layer... period. Yet according to Washington there was hope.

The government had assured the world that over the

last two years the globe's most elite scientists had devised a method to repair these small tears in the ozone. The approach was a vague combination of abstinence of releasing ozone-depleting substances and infusion of oxygen directly under the ozone layer. The catch was that these methods would take time to implement. The President announced that while some abnormalities in weather might temporarily persist due to the compromise of the ozone layer, soon the stratosphere would be restored to normal. President Drew declared:

> We must have faith in these great minds. The world must be patient and face this inconvenience with resolve. We must learn from this lesson, from the mistakes made during these prior decades in our most recent historical period. We have a duty to preserve our planet for our children and for the citizens of tomorrow. We must now embark on a new quest for sustainable practices.

Viktor didn't care what fantasies the government and media were trying to sell the public about the aberration in weather and the environment. He cared only what the data had shown and what he had discovered. His findings had nothing to do with the prevailing greenhouse fable.

In the weeks before the blizzard Viktor and other researchers inside the SUARS facility had grown increasingly concerned when readings from weather stations all along the northern arc were off the charts. These scientists recognized the aberrations in weather and the environment as atypical accelerations of naturally occurring processes. The data they recorded and collected, and their resulting hypotheses, conflicted with the data the government promulgated to explain to the country what was occurring with the weather. Through Viktor's persistence, and supported by the underground media, the government was backed into a corner. Unable to prove its claims that the weather aberrations were caused by the laceration in the ozone layer the government reluctantly — seamlessly — dropped the ozone layer theory. But government scientists didn't skip a beat. They moved to the next contrived hypothesis on their list to explain the dire changes in weather to the American public.

Generally most predictions in seismology — the branch of science concerned with earthquakes and related phenomena — are based on the Dilatancy Theory. That theory provides that when a rock becomes stressed, resulting in fractures and micro cracks, it transmits seismic waves at changing speeds. These fluctuations may alter the rock's magnetic properties and vary its electrical resistance. Scientists analyze these variances along with generalized patterns of activity such as historical data compiled from actual earthquake or volcanic activity for the particular area in question. Government sources reported success with this method for measuring earthquake potentials and volcanic activity. The eruption of Mt. Redoubt in Alaska in 2010 had proved the method useful and validated the government's claim the theory was applicable to predicting such events.

But while the Dilatancy Theory became an accepted method for predicting volcanic eruptions it was not applicable to predicting weather patterns. Yet the distinction was a minor one as far as the government propaganda machine was concerned. In order to conceal the actual cause of the aberrations in weather the government flooded the Internet, airwaves and mainstream media with its hypothesis and conclusions based on application of the Dilatancy Theory. It was an outright misapplication of the theory and a misrepresentation to discredit Viktor, other scientists and conscientious researchers looking for the truth. The intent to confuse and sway public opinion is especially easy when the subject matter is complex and the public has been conditioned for years to doubt the views of dangerous extremists like Viktor.

This misapplication of the Dilatancy Theory successfully skewed the data and resultant conclusions so that the source of the ominous weather could not be traced to government research and testing at the H.A.A.R.P. facility in Gakona Alaska. The High Frequency Active Auroral Research Program — H.A.A.R.P. — is an ionospheric research project reportedly jointly funded by the U.S. Air Force, U.S. Navy, the University of Alaska, and the Defense Advanced Research Projects Agency — DARPA — among others. Certain segments of the research associated with the H.A.A.R.P. project were skillfully hidden away from the scrutiny of Congress and the public under the façade of classified and Special Access Programs — SAP. These programs were veiled in secrecy and justified as imperative for national security... far too classified for auditing or monitoring; so went the rationale for keeping these programs beyond the reach of the government checks and balances. While one of the foremost areas of research at this facility was weather manipulation by ELF — Extreme Low Frequency — electromagnetic radio waves, government sources contended all research at Gakona was benign. Yet if this were true, Viktor wanted to know why certain components of the project were veiled in secrecy and protected by rigorous security measures. If weather manipulation were such a far-fetched concept — merely another laughable conspiracy theory — why would an international treaty have been drafted barring the use of weather manipulation in hostile actions?

Viktor had postulated that if the world were only preparing for implausible events when it had drafted the weather treaty — as the government suggested — shouldn't the international community consider other treaties? How about an international treaty banning flying reindeer with blinking noses — after all flying reindeer are implausible too... aren't they? Viktor thought this analogy a succinct one but the newspaper had refused to print it.

Weather manipulation has been prohibited by international law since 1978. The Environmental Modification Convention — ENMOD, signed and ratified by the United States — is an international treaty prohibiting military or other hostile use of environmental modification techniques having widespread, long-lasting or severe effects as the means of destruction, damage or injury. However, this treaty does not prohibit local, non-permanent changes. It was a convenient oversight... Viktor had noted.

The government approach in its misapplication of the Dilatancy Theory to weather was specifically designed to deceive. The government supported its conclusions by creatively twisting raw data for insertion into a formula that had no application to weather. When Viktor and his colleagues studied these results they proved the government assumptions based on application of the Dilatancy Theory were unquestionably wrong.

Viktor and other scientists had found tremendous unexplained weather disturbances along the northern grid that had never before been documented. They were able to trace the origin of the weather aberrations to a prior surge of radiation in the earth's atmosphere. The surge was tracked to testing of the H.A.A.R.P. system in Gakona, Alaska — a verifiable reality the government refused to acknowledge. Viktor's discovery directly contradicted the government's second hypothesis — the one replacing the greenhouse theory — that weather deviation was a naturally occurring consequence of seismic changes in the earth's crust. The changes were precipitated by underlying geological indicators.

Government sponsored scientists relied on the complexity of the convoluted theory to discourage the average American from attempting to understand it. As for those that did understand, the government quickly set out to discredit them. Newspapers across the nation reported the Washington version of the facts:

> Government officials and world-renowned scientists have discounted independent researchers' conclusions about causes of changing U.S. weather. They expressed outrage that these pseudo scientists have purposely misled the public. According to President Drew, "These questionable researchers are known members of extremist groups with one goal... to undermine the U.S. Government and weaken national security. Their actions have hampered efforts to solve the weather problems affecting thousands of Americans."

The government propaganda machine was oiled and humming, misdirecting the focus of the public. It seemed to Viktor that it no longer mattered whether these so-called eminent scientists actually knew what they were talking about. It only mattered to their egos — and to Uncle Sam — that they were talking. Image and misinformation were everything. No one knew better than Viktor the potential consequences of attempting to expose hidden objectives at Gakona. He now wondered if his own actions could have precipitated the recent aggressive H.A.A.R.P. activity. He hoped this was not the case but it was plausible.

In the months prior to the blizzard strange afflictions surfaced in Alaska: rashes of unknown origin, odd changes in behavior, idiopathic seizures, indeterminate pain and the hearing of voices confounded doctors. No causes and no solutions were found to comfort the victims. Some said it was Gulf War Syndrome. Ah, but Gulf War Syndrome doesn't exist... or does it?

Over the last few months Viktor's body and facial hair had stopped growing. He had developed headaches, mild cognitive difficulties, and vague abdominal distress. He suffered from a peculiar restlessness... an oppressive sense of foreboding that settled over him like a damp woolen blanket. The feeling of deep despair then vanished as quickly as it had appeared. During this period the voice had begun tormenting him. Viktor had found the voice in his head to be most disruptive. Aside from all other symptoms Viktor was compelled to find the origin of this problem. He had left research of the less disturbing disorders to others while he concentrated on the voice.

As soon as the odd symptoms were made public the government initiated a campaign to discount all hypotheses except for those sanctioned by Washington. Authorities dismissed any data or conclusions that didn't reconcile with Washington's agenda. The President told the country:

> Government research has nothing to do with the psychosomatic symptoms experienced by Alaskans. The outrageous notion that the U.S. government is to blame for these recent anomalies is an affront to the foundations of this

country. These groups are trying to split this nation by casting doubt on the integrity of Congress and the Commander in Chief. We will not surrender to attacks on our democracy by extremist groups. It is my solemn promise that I will put an end to such terrorism.

Viktor had listened to this press conference with his colleagues at the SUARS research facility. He had seen the same apathy on their faces before. He watched them with growing despair as the President continued:

I have heightened security and emphasized to my cabinet and heads of the NSA, the FBI, and Homeland Security, that this subversive behavior will not be tolerated in America. We will unify to crush these extremists. I will issue executive orders to remove previous restrictions barring the formation of a federal protective force to safeguard Americans in all states, counties, cities and towns. We will end these blatantly seditious acts aimed at destroying the roots of our democracy. I encourage these agencies I have named to use all means at their disposal in the fight against terror.

It was all Viktor could do to restrain his primordial urge to shake some sense into his indifferent colleagues. But that press conference seemed like years ago. He knew he had no time to replay these chilling events in his head. He had one goal. Adit 17 was his primary mission and right now nothing else mattered.

❊❊❊❊❊

Viktor had never felt such isolation; but it should not have surprised him. Residents had hunkered down in their homes as they had been ordered to do. To Viktor the blizzard was now much like a dream. His mind vacillated as randomly as snowflakes riding the currents of the Taku wind. How wonderful a blazing fire would feel right now... melting away the ice encasing his eyes, the deep biting cold that stiffened his brittle bones, and the snow that stung his flesh. Yes he was alone — as alone as anyone could be. There wasn't going to be any miraculous rescue for him... no majestic eagles swooping down to grasp the collar of his parka with their powerful talons and whisking him off to safety. No one was going to intervene. A new thought had begun to creep into his head. Perhaps this might not end so well for him...

Just then a colossal arctic blast slammed into his body, jarring him back to the reality of the blizzard and pitching him to the ground. He struggled to his hands and knees, crawling ahead through the drifted snow. He used a snowbank for leverage and pulled himself back up to his feet. The wind screamed past his ears, its ferocious power pressing against him as if it were a five hundred pound man leaning on his torso, blocking his way and cutting off his air. Snow whipped across his face, pricking him like hundreds of sharp thorns. He strained to suck air into his lungs. His nostrils stuck together from the cold. He slipped, lost his balance and careened off a solid ice snowbank. He stumbled back onto Willoughby Avenue pleading with his legs to hold him upright. Was he going in circles?

His thoughts grew dark. He might not reach the adit. He could not see; his eyelids were frozen shut. His knee joints were locked. Only the pain in his eyes verified he still lived. It felt as if he were floating above himself looking down on a pitiable vision. He would have looked an abominable sight had anyone been on the cold barren street to witness his final minutes. He staggered and reeled like a drunk, pitched and weaved and clumsily stumbled his way forward in millimeters... not feet. He could easily have been mistaken for one of the regulars leaving the Red Dog Saloon after last call. But the saloon was as deserted as the rest of the city... closed up tight.

Viktor could no longer easily flex his joints so he tried to drag his rigid heavy leg one inch more. He tripped, nosedived and sprawled onto the street face first, his arms flying outward as he slammed to the ground. The arctic wind roared and thrashed him. When he hit the snow-packed roadway his momentum propelled him along a patch of icy slick snow for another six feet. The top of his head rammed hard against the edge of a packed snow berm and his forward motion ceased. He lay stiff and broken... exhausted, frozen. A bleak foreboding gripped him. He tried but failed to conjure even the slightest twitch of movement from his body. If only he could shift his weight. His upper body lay twisted, his arms now somewhere beneath him — so he guessed. If he could only move his hand — if he only knew just where it was. If he could simply figure out what was happening to him.

The freezing snow stung the bare flesh of his face as he lay on the ground. He tried to move his head but sensed no motion from his neck. He could feel death there... beside him... stalking him. Darkness engulfed him. He had come so far... to fail now was more than he could tolerate. His own gasps for breath tortured him, the sound confirming his solitude... and his own end. His only companion was his overwhelming despair. Well that wasn't exactly true. He wasn't wholly alone. The voice was there, wasn't it? He had almost entirely forgotten about the parasitic thing.

So it was true. He had blocked the voice when he

plunged himself deeply into other thoughts. How unfair, he mused, to die now. It made no difference that he had come this far and that he may have overcome the voice, if only in part, because this wasn't the adit. This was not where he needed to go. But perhaps there was another place — not far ahead — where he could find sanctuary... wasn't there? Wasn't there a door less than fifty feet up the street where he could summon help? No... he wasn't sure of anything. He couldn't see, couldn't get his bearings. Here he was... crumpled against a snowbank where his body had crashed to a stop and rebelled against him... refusing to go another inch.

The winds hammered him... the powerful ceaseless winds. Confusion scrambled his thinking... clogging his clarity and obstructing his ability to process one thought from another. It was so cold. "Yes," Viktor attempted to mock the President aloud, "This blizzard was damned inconvenient." He had tried to move his lips yet he wasn't sure he had. But it didn't matter whose thought it was. It was still humorous. It was pretty much the funniest thing he could think of right now. He tried to focus on President Drew's assurances and wanted in the worst way to shoot a hearty laugh into the arctic blasts at the man's idiocy. But he became distracted. Something... something was changing.

He felt... warmth. Someone had poured a stream of luxurious warmth over his legs, dribbled heated water over his frozen body. It was wonderful... ridiculous and wonderful all at the same time. He should give thanks to someone... but to whom? He imagined his lips had curled into a faint smile, his gratitude for the lovely comfort.

Viktor lay motionless, grief-stricken and guilt-ridden by his failure. He thought... if only he could get back onto his feet; but he wasn't sure where he was... aside from knowing his stiff body was wedged snuggly against a rock hard snowbank on a desolate residential street. By his last estimation, he must be only fifty feet from a place he thought he could possibly have reached. Yet in truth Viktor wasn't sure about anything.

This is where I am to die he thought... reluctantly resigning himself to a devastatingly sad probability. He regretted he would be leaving so much yet unfinished. So... isolated, cold and without options, he settled his thoughts down to rest alone with his mind and his soul where it was warmer and safer. He felt himself drifting off to some place that he didn't recognize. It seemed the sky was brightening; or was this brightness he perceived... a light perhaps? He didn't know; but through it all he could hear the dull constant roar of the violent Taku gusts drowning out the low distant yipping and barking, and the mournful call of the wolves. Their woeful song was muffled by the fierce wind and the vast piles of August snow consuming Viktor's tiny corner of the universe...

❄❄❄❄❄

At precisely 1602 hours military time on 7 August the unrelenting voice that had dogged Viktor all afternoon had been silenced. If Viktor had possessed any residual strength — or had he retained some spark of conscious thought — he may have successfully roused himself from his long spiral toward the brink of death as he lay alone atop his icy grave on a deserted Juneau street. He may have been able to steel himself against the odds and plod on as he had done all day during his flight from the research facility to the city. He just might have pulled this off as there was no man of fiercer courage or resolve than Viktor.

Had Viktor been conscious he might have crawled the

remaining twenty-five feet to a place of safety... for an alternative sanctuary was that close and he was a man of unwavering spirit. But even as Viktor's life ebbed away in the midst of the ghastly blizzard he might have at least taken comfort from one important detail. Had his life's essence not been seeping out from every cell in his body, his organs beginning to shut down, his life force spilling onto the virgin snow at that very instant... Viktor still might have attained peace. He might have found solace in knowing he had been right all along... about the weather... and the voices.

❄❄❄❄❄

Chapter 6

❀❀❀❀❀

ROC Training Center Marietta, Georgia, August

Major Falcon Colby swallowed hard and tried not to fidget in his second row seat. He had the oddest sensation that the general's speech had some underlying message — a message Falcon was missing. On one hand the general seemed sincere in congratulating them for their success at ROC training and on the other... his long pauses, gesticulations and scowls were unsettling.

Falcon had the urge to look around the room to see if other officers had noticed anything odd about the general's speech. He wanted to turn to his good friend directly to his left and ask if he had seen, or felt, anything strange but it wouldn't have been appropriate. He was expected to keep his eyes forward and his attention on the general. As a soldier he did what was expected of him. Still, Falcon was disturbed. He had encountered the general many times throughout his two years of training and Falcon had never felt discomfort in his presence.

This larger than life icon standing before them in unchallenged authority, poised on the elevated stage, towered over Falcon and all of the men and women in this great hall who had successfully completed this grueling two-year journey. Falcon watched as General Tucker shifted his weight behind the podium and then ran a hand through his thinning salt and pepper hair. He studied the general, watching as the man drew in a cautious breath as if his only mindful thoughts were on the extra twenty-five pounds straining against his general's beltline. Falcon thought the general was probably relieved the podium was strategically positioned between himself and his audience... a virtual firewall shielding his bulbous midriff from intense scrutiny by onlookers. Perhaps this was the source at least in part of Falcon's uneasiness. Something bothered him about General Tucker.

This general before him was no mythological hero. He was an overweight middle-aged man cutting a once arguably handsome figure that was squeezed into an impressive uniform. He was a man who, it would seem, had little self-control considering his declining physique. The initial mystery and awe of the military that had captivated Falcon from his youth onward had faded away at some point during the last two years. As he now sat eyeing this military icon, he was bothered that this general seemed to lack the self-discipline to live by the standards he demanded of the ROC forces.

Falcon had climbed to the summit of the monumental mountain that had loomed in front of him two years before. He had met the herculean challenges of the ROC program and excelled in ways far beyond what he could ever have imagined. But none of the ROC training challenges had been as terrifying as he had been led to believe and somewhere during that training Falcon's view of the military had changed. Gone were his preconceptions that all military objectives were honorable. Gone were his gullible notions that all superior officers were infallible. He had spent his life reaching for an ideal — the perfect military officer — that he now realized may not even exist.

General Tucker was simply a man. Yet he had the power and authority to make or destroy lives. He could determine that any of the officers sitting before him today were not ROC quality leaders and he could send them home in disgrace. It seemed to Falcon that General Tucker could be one of two types of men. This two-star could be a man who exercised his duties honorably or he could be one who operated only in pursuit of his own agenda. Was this general an honorable man who lived by the standards he demanded from others? Maybe, but viewing the general with a discriminating eye left Falcon with doubts.

General Tucker was a paunch, balding, overly ambitious army guy — general's stars are not usually handed out to soldiers with no ego and no desire to climb the ladder of success. He must be somewhat cunning. Tucker was meticulously choosing his words at this ceremony as judiciously as a fastidious sommelier selecting the best cabernet sauvignon. So if officers were judged solely on their physical appearance and military presence, Falcon was a bit under-impressed with the general's outer packaging. Yet the man was a general. Falcon must at least pay tribute to the uniform and the position. The rank, power and stature that the stars on this man's epaulets represented had to be acknowledged. These were the rules of the military. Yet paying homage to the uniform was not as easy for Falcon as it had once been.

Only a short time ago Falcon could not see beyond the uniform. He would never have questioned any order or underlying rationale for any mission or objective. But at some point during the last two years Falcon had changed. This transformation filled him with both doubt and self-deprecation. It was increasingly difficult for him to play this military game. The army was his chosen career. He alone had made that decision. He had devoted his life to sculpting himself into the ideal soldier. He had worked, sweated and sacrificed everything to achieve his goal. Now that he stood at this milestone in his life and reflected on his achievements he was plagued by questions about the choices he had made. He wondered if his judgment had been clouded all along by some childish perception of honor and duty.

Without his uniform this man at the podium was a man with shortcomings like all men. He was probably as deficient in character and action as was the emperor in the tale of the *Emperor's New Clothes*. This old story seemed more poignant to Falcon than ever. He knew this generation's army was no more an army of perfection than any other force that had gone before it. It was not wholly comprised of soldiers of unquestioned integrity and honor immune from temptation or greed. It was a collection of mere men — fallible men — and women. Yet while Falcon intellectually grasped this concept the boy in him clung to the belief that the army path was a principled one offering a man the opportunity to achieve a more noble purpose in life. Falcon had always thought a higher standard existed — the ideal soldier — and in his stubborn heart he somehow could not let go of the notion that he would be one of the few to achieve it. General Tucker paused, seemed to gather his thoughts and then continued with his speech. The momentary disruption in his oration was enough to tug Falcon's thoughts back to the present. He returned his focus to the general.

"Over the past two years you have made great sacrifices," the general said. "You have been called to step to the forefront of a new army and a new world. You have willingly and valiantly met the multiple professional and personal challenges presented to you and you have prevailed. You can be proud of your success. Today you join an elite group of men and women who will usher in a new world. This world was previously only the substance of dreams. It was reserved for a handful of the highest officials within the ROC organization — as we have all so fondly come to know it." The general's double entendre was not lost on his listeners and soft chortles erupted from the sea of faces. The general grinned. The ROC training program was designed to be brutal, unforgiving and at times... inhuman. Clearly, neither Falcon nor any of the other trainees would have felt anything close to fondness for it.

As Falcon watched the general deliver his pep talk he could not help but admire the general's finesse in accomplishing the job he had to do. It was the general's monumental task to sell the ROC program to these officer candidates as a solemn patriotic mission. He had demanded absolute loyalty to ensure the success of ROC. If only Falcon had been privy to all of the details of the ROC project maybe he would feel more at ease with its purpose. But that was not military protocol and ROC officers speculated a great deal about the underlying objectives.

Without the truth, speculation was all Falcon had. He was too far down toward the bottom of the food chain to be briefed on project details. The army provided him with what he was presumed to need to carry out his own assignment and nothing more. He doubted he would ever know all of the details of the Olympus Project but he expected the army would provide him enough additional information to justify carrying out his orders. Perhaps his best friend Whitehawk had occasional doubts during training — sometimes it seemed so to Falcon — but they never discussed these doubts.

The general droned on. "Your upcoming mission is a solemn one," the general said. "The world can no longer sustain society in the face of our indiscriminate waste, disappearing resources and dwindling energy reserves. The twenty-first century has dawned and every one of you in this room and in this organization must stand strong against the forces that threaten America. You must set an example. Make no mistake. You are tasked with putting the pieces back together in a very, very broken process. You have a serious mission to perform, a shared monumental goal to accomplish. You are charged, ladies and gentlemen, with stopping those who are bent on destroying this country. You will be called upon to rid society of these extremist groups that have threatened our way of life for years. It won't be an easy task. You must carry these new concepts into the world and lead the way to sustainment. You are the one hope for our future. You are crusaders... twenty-first century warfighters who will encourage America — from its tiny villages to its mega cities — to accept these changes that must be implemented. We can no longer do business as usual. We simply won't survive. We all must step up and do our part. You, ladies and gentlemen, will lead the country down this new path." General Tucker paused, wiping his brow with a handkerchief.

"I want you to think about something," Tucker continued. "You have sworn to uphold America's laws, to keep the peace and to implement the innovative solutions you have learned here at ROC training. You will be on the front lines. You are the ones who must encourage Americans to accept the new terms and phrases that signify new government agendas. Memorize these phrases. Go over them in your minds until they become part of you. Phrases like population management, biodiversity, sustainable development, centralized farming, state education, land transfer and conservation, urban smart planning, new anti-terrorist control measures, pandemic management, civilian reeducation centers etc. Remember these phrases and remember them well."

"Some of these concepts will be new to Americans and it is your job to encourage and persuade them to accept these vital new measures by the means and methods you learned here at ROC training. You must work toward ridding America of this recent violent epidemic of extremism sweeping across the country. You must rid our society of these rogue anarchists and conspiracy theorists or we will fail as a nation — and as a world. You are the chosen ones. You, ladies and gentlemen, are here to ensure the future of America." General Tucker looked out over the filled room and took in a deep breath of stale air.

Falcon could see glistening perspiration along the general's brow. Olympus Hall had grown unbearably hot. Tucker scrutinized the audience. The general's piercing glare zeroed in on Falcon. For a split second their gazes collided. Falcon felt as if the general could see deep into his very soul... sense his uneasiness and his doubts about the ROC project. The glower from Tucker's penetrating eyes burrowed into him, seemingly trying to drive him into submission. Falcon shifted his weight. Then... without warning... the oppressive feeling was gone and the general took a drink of water. Had Falcon dozed off? What was that hellish sensation of utter despondency that had crept over him? Had his mind wandered so deeply into thought that he had become confused? He had to have fallen asleep... to have imagined this. No other reasonable explanation could exist for the doom that had settled over him. Falcon's feet were firmly planted in reality. He had no doubt that whatever his mind had experienced... it wasn't reality. Falcon forced himself to shake off the uneasiness and listen as the general resumed his speech.

"Ladies and gentleman," General Tucker said. "The packets you will be handed today contain your orders for the most important jobs you will ever be called on to perform. You will be expected to carry out those orders to the letter." The general paused and looked intently at the officers before him. His voice became lower but his tone more severe, as if he were engaged in a one on one disciplinary session with the miscreant of the month. "We are at war," the general said. "Don't lose sight of that. Never let down your guard. In the last two years our society has changed. You won't recognize it. It has become a quagmire of anarchists, extremists and terrorists. They have infiltrated and infested our country. They are tearing apart our civilization." The general pounded his fist on the podium and several officers, including Falcon, jumped slightly. The general looked to the floor and then punctuated his heavy words and his passion with another thick silence. His face was flushed. His hands had settled into a death grip of the podium. His knuckles were bright white, probably visible from the last row Falcon thought. A slight breeze from an overhead air vent brushed across Falcon's cheek. He was growing tired of the general's theatrics — and a little wary of them. He was ready to take his orders, leave the facility and put this behind him.

"Ladies and gentlemen," the general said. "As you step outside this facility today with your orders in hand, you will take your place as leaders. You will set the pace for the next wave of ROC officer trainees. You can take pride in both your accomplishments here and in your vital contributions to come..." As the general continued to speak — endlessly it seemed to Falcon — of honor and duty and obligations Falcon couldn't help but question his own integrity. In the past few weeks his mind replayed the last conversation he'd had with his Great Uncle Caleb. His uncle's warnings came back to haunt him. Horrific nightmares disturbed what little rest he'd been able to get during training. These nightmares peppered him with guilt about ignoring Caleb and not raising questionable issues with Whitehawk. He was plagued by remorse for his failure to take his concerns to his closest friend. That precipitated self-doubt about his own integrity.

On one hand it was clearly dangerous to openly discuss doubts about the program. All ROC officers were painfully aware of the severe consequences they faced if they questioned any part of the Olympus Project. On the other hand, this was a matter of personal integrity. Falcon had not been honest with Whitehawk. Could he — shouldn't he — have confided in his closest friend? Falcon had begun to dwell on that quandary daily. Whitehawk was a brother to him. Each time he looked at Whitehawk now, he felt like he had deceived him. Where was the honor — the personal integrity — in that?

From the time Falcon and Whitehawk first met at ROTC in college, they had heard it all... hundreds of variations of jokes and puns about their given names: birds of a feather, a bird in hand is worth two in the bush and on and on. They had accepted the endless ribbing from their superior officers and peers with poise and good nature. Yet while it was the friendly teasing that had first thrown them together, their friendship had strengthened exponentially all on its own. Whitehawk, Falcon had quickly learned, was Alaskan born which Falcon figured was certainly an appropriate reason to have a name like 'Whitehawk'. On the other hand the name 'Falcon' for an ordinary New England boy with no apparent Native American roots seemed a stretch.

In the two years since ROC training had begun the trainees had been entirely isolated from the outside world. There had been no time off, no home visits for the holidays and no emergency leaves for family weddings or funerals. They may as well have been cloistered monks. ROC instructors allowed no newspapers, no television, no radio and no access to media of any kind. There had been no correspondence, no phone calls to family or friends. The training command essentially erased these 'special' soldiers from the globe.

It was natural that solid bonds among the trainees had resulted. Yet during that time Falcon had found excuses not to share his concerns with Whitehawk. ROC directives for silence had rammed a wedge between them. Falcon had chosen ROC rules over Whitehawk, allowing the military to alter Falcon's concept of personal integrity. He had sold out to play the army game, sold out by meekly following the ROC 'no questions, no doubts' rule.

What Falcon had done to Caleb was just as bad. The easy way out for Falcon had been to dismiss Caleb's concerns as the ranting and raving of an old man who had nothing better to do than spin wild conspiracies in his spare time… and that's what Falcon had done prior to the start of ROC training. But what if Falcon had been wrong and Caleb's warnings were valid? The worst part was… Falcon now thought about the possibility that his silence may have put Whitehawk in danger. Whitehawk would have no inkling there could be an underlying sinister objective to the Olympus Project. Falcon's guilt gnawed at him. He made up his mind to lay it all out for Whitehawk after the ceremony.

Falcon winced from a Whitehawk elbow-jolt to his ribs. He whipped his head to the left, frowning and eyeing Whitehawk curiously as his friend withdrew his elbow from Falcon's midsection. "Get up to the stage dude," Whitehawk whispered from the corner of his mouth in his low husky voice... all the while leaving his gaze nailed to the podium. "They called your name. Go! Get up there!" he repeated. The six-foot tall Falcon Colby instantly jumped from his seat. As he did this, he heard the general repeat his name. Falcon was on the stage riveted to attention before the general finished the last syllable of 'Colby'. His instinct had kicked in and, though unsure why he had been singled out, he had instantly responded to his trusted friend's direction and propelled his body to the podium. He leaped out of his chair and bounded onto the stage in four astonishingly graceful steps. A smile played across the general's face. Falcon's skin flushed with embarrassment as all eyes focused on him. The audience erupted in laughter and that prompted a deeper crimson hue to inflame Falcon's skin.

The general laid a hand on Falcon's shoulder and addressed the audience with apparent sincerity. "Well after such a graceful demonstration of his physical capabilities I don't think anyone here will challenge the Major's forthcoming presentation," General Tucker said. He removed his hand from Falcon's shoulder and began to read the letter handed to him by one of his aides. *"Major Falcon Colby,"* the general began, *"In recognition of your physical and academic excellence and your achievements in maintaining the highest standards in the noblest traditions of the United States Army, by order of the Commander in Chief, I present you with the Army Regional Operations Command Medal for Meritorious Achievement. This medal bestows on you one of the nation's highest honors under Presidential Executive Order 1216606, Immediate Order to*

Restructure All Branches of the Military Services under the Department of Defense. Through your exemplary leadership, physical prowess and strategic expertise you have provided your fellow officers, this institution and all Americans a true example of leadership, honor, duty and loyalty." General Tucker fumbled slightly as he pinned the medal to Falcon's chest. He shook Falcon's hand and returned the Major's smart salute.

"Thank you general," Falcon said, turning to leave the stage. The general grasped Falcon's shoulder with a firm hand.

"Hold on there Major," the general ordered.

"Yes sir," Falcon said sheepishly. He turned back toward General Tucker and resumed his position of attention, eyes front, torso straight, closed fists at his sides. The general nodded to his assistant and the young officer instantly stepped forward with another presentation cloth and certificate folder.

"Major Colby," the general began, opening the certificate folder and reading aloud, "*A letter from the Secretary of the Army: The Secretary of the Army has reposed special trust and confidence in the patriotism, valor, fidelity and professional excellence of Major Falcon Colby. In view of these qualities and Major Colby's demonstrated leadership potential and dedicated service to the United States Army, he is today and permanently promoted from Major to Full Colonel, Field Commander, Regional Operations Command effective this seventh day of August.*"

The general opened the presentation cloth and grasped the insignias, two silver eagles, wings outspread. Thick silence fell over the grand hall. General Tucker removed Falcon's gold oak leaf cluster insignias from his shoulder boards and pinned a silver eagle to each of Falcon's epaulets. Falcon's knees weakened just the slightest bit. He momentarily wobbled and then steeled himself back to attention. "Congratulations, Colonel Colby," the general beamed, firmly shaking Falcon's hand.

Muffled gasps sprinkled the great hall as the full extent of the promotion sunk in. The audience was stunned with sudden awareness that the Major had been given a double promotion, unheard of in the modern military. Falcon had been promoted from Major over Lt. Colonel straight to full bird Colonel. Any additional promotions for Falcon down the road would thrust him into the elite world of the most powerful of soldiers — the generals.

Thunderous applause exploded in Olympus Hall. The floor vibrated with foot stomps and a few loud *hooahs...* made it to the front of the room. Falcon felt goose flesh prickling his skin and a searing hot blush rise from his neck to his face. He knew he probably looked like a half boiled lobster, but he was too shocked to be concerned about it. Following his salute and one quick photograph taken by a general's aide, Falcon left the stage. This time he alighted from the platform cautiously, aware his knees were milliseconds away from buckling. Crumbling to the floor in a heap was the last thing he wanted to do in front of over four hundred peers and his superior officers.

The new full bird colonel picked his way down the aisle in a daze until he reached his second row seat. A visibly ecstatic Whitehawk stared at him and exuberantly slapped Falcon's shoulder repeatedly. It took another minute or two until the crowd settled down. As the general resumed his speech Whitehawk leaned in and whispered to his friend, "Falcon buddy, I don't know how the hell you managed that... but put in a good word for me with Tucker would you? I think a couple of shiny general's stars would look very handsome on my broad shoulders."

Falcon chuckled softly. Yet while Falcon had to admit part of him was deliriously happy about the unexpected promotion, the other part of him was reserved about it. His good fortune had definitely stunned him; but he found it disconcerting. Why should he who had harbored so many silent vile questions about ROC, the Olympus Project and the military itself, be given such an honor? How honorable was it for a man to accept this promotion when in his heart he was uncertain whether the job he had been trained to do was morally right?

Falcon studied Tucker as the general stood at the podium. Was Falcon on the road to becoming a carbon copy of this general? There he stood... this highly decorated larger than life career military man who spoke so effortlessly about honor and duty and loyalty. Did this general harbor the same questions in his own mind as Falcon did in his?

Tucker was not a stupid man. He would know better than anyone in the room what ROC and the Olympus Project were. Did this general have no misgivings about the very concept of the Olympus Project? The man displayed no outward reservations about what he was doing. Had Tucker made it to the rank of general by compromising his own personal integrity? Falcon couldn't stomach the thought that he himself might one day face a choice between his military career and his own honor. All he ever wanted was to be the best officer he could be... at least that's what he had wanted two years ago.

"I have a few items more as these admin folks finish passing out your sealed order packets," the general said. "But first... I think a toast is in order. I would like each of you to join me in a glass of champagne to celebrate this auspicious occasion." The general scanned the room. "Oh... and folks, you may consider this an order." Falcon expected to see a smile play across the general's face. But the general's expression was cold and rigid. Falcon watched as the administrative officers passed small champagne glasses with factory like precision from graduate to graduate, down each of the rows. When the trainees had been served, the general thrust his arm toward the ceiling in a peculiar Hitler type hail but with his index finger pointing out over the audience like a loaded gun.

The general slowly surveyed the great hall. It appeared to Falcon the general was performing some kind of methodical grid search over the officers. One major in the fourth row had failed to lift his glass. General Tucker seemed annoyed and drew his arm down impatiently. He nodded to one of his aides. The aide quickly made his way to the rogue major's side and whispered something to him. The major nodded vigorously and instantly raised his glass. Whatever objection he had initially thought would absolve him from joining in the toast seemed to have vanished. The general nodded his approval. He thrust his arm once again into the air. Then he lifted his glass to the audience with his free hand and waited.

"Ladies and gentlemen," the general said, casting an eerie glare over the room, "To the future!"

As Falcon lifted the glass toward his mouth to comply with the general's odd mandatory toast Whitehawk roughly gripped Falcon's arm with viselike force. "Colonel Colby," he muttered severely, "Do not let that champagne touch your lips. Let it spill down the front of your shirt." Falcon was startled. He turned to his friend expecting to find a mischievous grin. Instead, the piercing brown eyes and cold resolve staring back stunned him. "Falcon... do as I say dammit." The urgency in Whitehawk's hoarse whisper and his penetrating glare convinced Falcon that his friend was deadly serious. Falcon nodded once to acknowledge Whitehawk's instruction. Bewildered, the new colonel would do as his friend insisted but in doing so he was about to disobey his first direct order as a senior officer. Falcon, glass readied near his lips, watched from the corner of his eye as his good friend lifted his glass. At the general's command Whitehawk tipped back his glass, feigning to drink, and let the champagne dribble down the front of his own uniform.

Chapter 7

❊❊❊❊❊

Takotna, Alaska, August

The August blizzard continued to hammer the exterior of their remote Takotna cabin. As Miriam Goodriver sat down at the edge of Kyle's bed, the *slap... slap...* of loose siding battering against the outer wall distressed her. She should have gone outside earlier and shored up the siding by nailing it to the two by fours but the children teased her to play Melli Moose just a bit longer. She supposed a few more hours would not matter. She would fix the siding in the morning.

She lingered where she sat on the edge of Kyle's bed. For a moment she allowed the warmth from the large living room woodstove to renew her as it drifted into the children's room through the open bedroom door. She smiled at her nine-year-old boy. If only she could rekindle that spark in her children — the particular twinkle in their dark brown eyes that her Henry Ivan had ignited there. If her Henry were here her life would be complete. She reached over to Kyle and used the back of her first two fingers to brush an unruly strand of black hair away from his brow. He giggled and pushed her hand away. He didn't like to be fussed over. She tickled his ribs before she drew her hand back to her lap and he giggled again, drawing his legs up and pulling the covers over his head. As he did, Kenzie came into the bedroom in her pajamas. She kissed Miriam on the cheek and climbed up onto the top bunk.

"You can't find me now!" Kyle muttered from under the covers. Miriam laughed.

"You're so silly Kyle! Of course Mama can find you. You're right there," Kenzie said, "Right where you were a second ago!" The flame from the kerosene lamp cast a soft flickering amber light across the room and Miriam eyed the dance of shadows along the bedroom wall. Kenzie wiggled under her covers on the top bunk and Miriam stood. Kyle pulled the quilt down off his head. Miriam straightened the blankets and tucked Kyle's comforter into the pine frame of his bottom bunk.

"Now you two sleep and tomorrow we will see if this storm hasn't let up enough for us to sled down to Mr. Olani's store for milk and sugar and maybe some news," Miriam said softly.

"But what if it's still snowing?" Kyle questioned. "Can't we go outside anyway?"

Kenzie leaned over the top bunk, tittering with amusement. "Are you crazy?" she asked. "Do you wanna end up like old Sam McGee?"

"Oh that's just a creepy Yukon poem," Kyle whined. "That never happened."

"Doesn't mean it couldn't," Kenzie said. "People die all the time out in the bush."

"All right, that's enough of that kind of talk at this hour," Miriam said in mock annoyance. "We'll see about tomorrow when it comes. Now off to sleep and we'll talk about this in the morning," she said playfully, swatting at Kyle's foot. She gave both children another peck on their foreheads and turned off the kerosene lamp. "Don't forget to say your prayers," Miriam whispered as she turned to leave the room. She left the door fully open so the heat of the woodstove would reach the bedroom and went into the kitchen to make herself a cup of hot tea. She knew the children would lay awake giggling and telling stories before they drifted off to sleep. As long as they remembered to say their prayers and so long as their chatting didn't end up in too vigorous a disagreement, Miriam didn't mind. She took comfort from the soft voices coming from the other room even though tonight's rendition of *The Cremation of Sam McGee* by Robert Service would not have been Miriam's first choice for a bedtime tale. It was too late to change the night's fare however. The cat had already leaped out of the bag when her mischievous daughter had mentioned the old prospector's tale as Miriam tucked them into bed. Kenzie was now reciting the refrain of the old Sourdough poem at Kyle's urging. Miriam could clearly hear Kenzie's soft mischievous dramatization:

> There are strange things done in the midnight sun
> By the men who moil for gold;
> The Arctic trails have their secret tales
> That would make your blood run cold;
> The Northern Lights have seen queer sights,
> But the queerest they ever did see
> Was that night on the marge of Lake Lebarge
> I cremated Sam McGee...

In the summer months after the children had gone to bed Kenzie would read for long stretches of time as the twenty plus hours of daylight cast its brilliance through their bedroom window fanning out across the pages of whatever poem, adventure or romantic tale Kenzie was presently devouring. The sky dipped into a brief twilight each day only for about three and one half hours during the summer. But Miriam found a few hours of rest to be sufficient. Summer was a time for doing, for catching up, for rekindling friendships, and for preparing for the dark winter months when daylight diminished to only three and one half hours or so across the subarctic Takotna community. Bedtime during the winter in the Goodriver cabin was a time for sharing of dreams, imaginary worlds and folk tales passed down from the elders. Miriam supposed it didn't matter that technically winter was not yet upon them. The storm had brought an early winter's bleakness to the village, graying out the summer sky and blanketing the land with piles of unexpected snowfall. The time seemed right to renew that winter closeness no matter if it was a bit early in the year. Kenzie and Kyle were good children. Miriam wanted their home to be a place that would leave them with happy memories to savor when they grew old.

Miriam sat at the kitchen table stirring her tea and watching the steam rise from the cup. If only her Henry Ivan had not died. He was such a loving father. The children had spent so little time with him and he could have added so much to their lives. The long nights were the hardest for Miriam. When the minutes ticked away like hours and the hours passed too slowly... that was when her soul ached for his company the most and her body yearned for his closeness. She missed him terribly. She missed knowing his companionship, strength, and courage were nearby to make her feel complete. So she took her comfort from wherever and whenever she could. Tonight the soft whispers meandering into the kitchen from the children's room comforted her. Miriam was convinced there were few greater pleasures in life than knowing that your children were safe and happy. Still, if she had one wish, it would be that her Henry could share this moment with her.

Miriam's Henry Ivan was unlike the other men in her family. Most of the men including her father and grandfather quietly went about their own business — men's business — and lived more on the fringes of the family than within its emotional circle. But Henry had been so unlike any other man Miriam had known. He had allowed his deepest feelings to rise to the surface and was never afraid to share every bit of himself with her. But when Henry and Miriam married she found her Henry was mysterious in other ways too. Henry Ivan had a secret. Henry Ivan had been an insatiable reader. He consumed everything written as eagerly as most Tlingit men devoured smoked salmon. While she hadn't given a thought to his reading habit at first, she had quickly become almost as fond of a good story as was he. Miriam herself had never been one to pick up a book by choice in her youth but her years with Henry had changed her. While she knitted, darned or worked in the kitchen in the evenings, Henry would read to her. Now that he was gone she was thankful she had the comfort of his small collection of books. Each time she picked up a book they had read together in the past Miriam felt as though Henry were beside her energizing her with his deep love of stories. She felt she owed it to the children to learn as much from his collection as she could since Henry was not around to help them with their schoolwork. She wanted Kenzie and Kyle to have advantages in life. Those books were one way to make sure they had choices. Her Henry had known this.

Miriam turned her head toward the frosted windowpane even though she knew she would not be able to see the blizzard raging beyond the ice-coated glass. The storm had held them hostage for more than ten days but that did not concern her so much. She had never feared cabin fever. She had her knitting, mending and quilting to occupy her time and if she needed something new, she simply picked up one of Henry Ivan's books and lost herself in it.

Miriam loved Jack London's tales of the North, especially the *Call of the Wild* and *White Fang*. She and Henry felt the author portrayed the spirit of the wolf as it should be shown: proud, filled with life's essence, sensitive and devoted to family. The wolf was united with man by its ability to think through challenges and weigh the dangers and risks. Jack London's stories show this side of wolves. Most of the Tlingit elders spoke of the wolf in similar ways but in white man's world wolves were too often regarded as dangerous beasts. This had angered Henry. Tales that portrayed wolves in such manner did not show the wolf's true spirit or acknowledge the feelings that Henry believed wolves and other animals possessed. Henry had warned Miriam. He believed the spirits of the animals that man had disrespected and brought to the brink of extinction — like the wolf, the buffalo and the whale — would rise up in revolt like the pigs in George Orwell's *Animal Farm*. Miriam and Henry had laughed at this and Henry had even provoked chortles from Kenzie when she was little as he acted out the pigs' revolt from Orwell's tale. Deep down Miriam was never quite sure whether her Henry Ivan was serious. She sometimes silently questioned whether he truly believed this animal revolt would someday occur. Perhaps she had not found Henry Ivan's theory so incomprehensible herself.

Miriam had grown up knowing the Tlingit way of understanding the world. She considered the living spirits of the wolves, the yellow and red cedars and the great bears to be as brothers and sisters to mankind. The Tlingit hands that had carved canoes from cedar, drawn salmon from the bay and harvested caribou, bear and moose for life sustaining meat had only been able to do these things because they had been permitted to reap such bounty from the natural world. The spirits of the waters and the fish and the mammals on the land had allowed man to share and to use what natural resources they required to survive. Miriam had learned as a child that disregarding these life forces led to consequences. To discount such spirituality was plain foolishness. Yet she had never known anyone to feel this more deeply or express it more freely than her Henry Ivan — except of course her grandmother.

Miriam was sleepy. She rose slowly from her chair. She took her teacup to the sink, removed the tea bag and wiped the cup clean with the corner of a dishtowel she had dabbed in the water bucket. She knew she would have to go out into the blizzard in the morning to haul water from the creek and the thought of braving the frigid temperatures gave her a chill. While her water tank generally supplied a sufficient volume of water to the cabin, the electricity had been out since the third day of the storm. The pump no longer worked. The water remaining in the tank had dwindled to a few inches and the nearly empty bucket at the sink was all she had left. Retrieving water when the pump was not functioning was generally a chore for the children but she would not send them out in this weather. The creek was barely two hundred feet from the cabin but in this storm, straying ten feet from the house could prove to be a deadly — and final — journey.

Miriam dried her teacup, returned it to the cabinet and turned off the kerosene lamp. She hadn't realized how stiff she had grown from the lack of exercise. At this time of year, in August, she would have typically been outside tending to her small vegetable plot but that had been impossible once the weather had turned. She had gathered what vegetables she could when the first warnings of frost had come through but she had not been able to salvage everything. The plants had not been mature and would have needed an additional two or three weeks of intense subarctic sun. She padded through the living room and retired to her bedroom. She changed into her flannels and crawled under the comforter. Miriam was too drowsy to finish all of her own prayers but managed to complete an abbreviated version before she drifted into a deep sleep.

❈❈❈❈❈

ROC Northwest Takotna, Alaska, August

Dishes, coffee cups and utensils clanked and clattered and about drove Malikov crazy. Raucous laughter, loud voices and the discord of chatter in English — in a form transfigured by multiple accents and varying levels of English proficiency — ricocheted around the B Sector mess hall and bounced off the cluttered tables and antiseptic-white walls. Malikov moved through the mess line selecting his evening meal. He was choosing a dessert when he suddenly recoiled from a jolt to his shoulder. A young American soldier reeking of beer stumbled into him, spilling his coffee.

"*V zhopu p'yanyy dolboyob!*" — drunk ass motherfucker! Malikov blurted out in his native Russian, looking down at his shirt to assay the damage.

"Sor-ry-Chief... I-dint... see-ya," the soldier said, slurring his words. Malikov slammed down his tray on the long metal tray runner. He wiped the spilled coffee from his saucer and then furiously rubbed at the front of his shirt with a clean napkin, his eyes alternating between glances at his uniform and silent glaring rebukes aimed toward the soldier. Malikov ensured he pitched icy stares to the back of the drunken soldier's head as he weaved his way toward the exit. He watched... teeth clenched tightly... as the soldier staggered, bumped into the wall and disappeared through the mess hall door. Slobbering bastard, Malikov thought. He crumpled the damp napkins and tossed them into a trashcan. He breathed slowly — exhaling with deliberateness — to calm himself, picked up his tray and made his way into the dining area.

Malikov and his two armed escorts had returned late to B Sector at the end of his shift. He had then sprinted up to his room to replenish his flask — gulping a few swigs of vodka directly from the bottle as he refilled it — and then hurried to the mess hall. He had finished loading his tray almost an hour after his fellow Russian soldiers had already returned to their rooms.

Malikov's immediate circle of fellow Russian soldiers made a collective decision to avoid the mess hall after eighteen thirty hours — although it wasn't always possible to do so. By that hour too many of the younger troops — American mostly — had overindulged themselves with beer from the vending machines. Rowdy spontaneous poker games frequently broke out and sometimes brawls erupted. The worst of the American enlistees seemed to thrive by the rules of their own game — that nothing was too depraved when off duty as long as officers were not around. Foreign troops were often targets of their aggressiveness. Sergei attributed their unruly behavior to cabin fever — an escalating problem in the FOLT. Malikov argued American forces were simply coddled undisciplined morons.

Experience had taught him and his fellow Russians it was prudent to avoid certain other public areas of the FOLT after hours as well. Their pact to travel in groups of two or more lowered the risk of being marked for harassment. It wasn't that Malikov was a coward. He was ready to fight if he had to, but it didn't hurt to skew the odds with a few extra pairs of fists standing with him. Besides, if the MPs caught him in a scuffle where punches were thrown he would be cited with disorderly conduct and thrown in the SHIDS — Short Term In-

FOLT Detainment Sector, pronounced 'shidz' — and no doubt lose one or two of the stripes he had worked so hard to sew on his sleeve. So even though his first impulse might have been to rearrange the facial bones of the drunk who nearly knocked him down, he wasn't stupid enough to do it in front of a hundred witnesses. He picked his way through the dining room, moving between the eight-foot banquet tables, until he spotted Sergei. Malikov knew Sergei would have hung back waiting for him and he wasn't disappointed. He plunked his tray down on the table and sat across from his friend. Sergei was not alone.

"You late," Sergei said.

"*Da*," Malikov nodded. He eyed Yury Bugak... a tall, lanky, unpleasant Russian sergeant sitting to Sergei's left.

"Chief," Bugak said, nodding to acknowledge Malikov. Malikov paid no attention and began to eat.

"*Vhy* you late?" Sergei asked.

"Drunk American push me." Malikov said, one side of his lip curling with contempt. "*YA khotel bit' yego i v rot, i v sraku*" — I should kick his ass from hell to breakfast.

Bugak laughed.

"*Eece* funny?" Malikov asked testily.

"*Da*," Bugak said. "You talk always to beat up Americans."

"*Da?*" Malikov sneered, not bothering to mask his dislike of Bugak. The man's father was a political minion at the embassy in Moscow. Bugak constantly bragged about his father's importance and the size of his parents' flat. Bugak never shied away from opportunities to goad him into an argument... sliding in snide remarks about Malikov's peasant roots, his unsophisticated ways, his banal military career and his unfortunate orphan status. Bugak seemed to thrive on this baiting game... pushing Malikov's buttons in a bid to incite him to lose his temper. Malikov knew the man was jealous of Malikov's rank. Bugak's goal was to prod him toward the edge of his anger until he did something stupid — stupid enough to get him reprimanded or demoted.

Bugak was the stupid one, Malikov thought. Even if Malikov's CO reprimanded him or he temporarily lost a notch or two of rank, Bugak would never gain anything from it. The army would never promote him. Bugak was in the military only to do his compulsory two years of service. He made it clear he was too good for the army. Soldiers were lower class misfits incapable of contributing to mainstream society. Bugak let everyone know he was counting the days until his return to Moscow where his father would set him up with a plush job at the embassy. Malikov was quite certain Bugak's biggest impetus for pushing his buttons was the sadistic pleasure he derived from seeing other people screw up or suffer.

Bugak was a back stabbing sonofabitch who would lie, cheat or do anything to knock Malikov down a few pegs. Two months ago Bugak ran to the commander and told him he saw Malikov drinking on duty. The little bastard, Malikov thought. Bugak was a snake, a slippery snitch, who would rat out his own mother if it would make him look good. Malikov had been able to talk his way out of a reprimand and a visit to the SHIDS over the drinking incident. He convinced his commander that Bugak had been mistaken; that Malikov had in fact gotten off duty five minutes earlier and he was merely having a few sips of vodka because he was distraught over his grandmother's death. It wasn't exactly a lie... he *was* distraught at losing his *babushka*. He thought about her almost every day since her death six years earlier.

Malikov tried to be more cautious around Bugak now. He watched him closely. When Bugak was nearby, he tensed. One of these days, he would find the right moment, the right secluded area, and he would wipe the smirk from Bugak's face. Malikov would let Bugak know who the misfit was.

The harsh mess hall lighting and the incessant babbling all around them irritated Malikov. The knot in his neck muscles began morphing into a pounding headache. Why did they have to light up the place like an operating room making him feel like a germ under a microscope? Why couldn't these soldiers shut up — for once — shut up and pretend they were civilized? He shoveled corn and mashed potatoes into his mouth like a half-starved soldier in a foxhole. Manners weren't high on Malikov's priority list. Manners were women's creation — their rules not his — and he didn't give a crap if he chewed like a cow. Maybe he did eat a little too fast. Maybe he didn't close his mouth when he chewed. What did he care about manners since his *babushka* died? Right now, he was focused on finishing dinner and getting out of the chaotic mess hall. He wanted to go back upstairs for some peace and quiet. He didn't give a damn about manners. Sharing a few glasses of vodka with Sergei, now that was relaxing... something he looked forward to every night.

Sergei Nikulin was a quiet man, the best friend Malikov had ever had. No one since his *babushka* ever took the time to understand him — except Sergei. Sergei listened to whatever Malikov had on his mind. He didn't judge him, he merely listened. He never nagged him or pointed out Malikov's shortcomings. Sergei never skulked around in the shadows dreaming up ways to trick him. He never crept up on Malikov to snatch something from him when he wasn't looking. Sergei never made him feel like a crude peasant. He could be himself around Sergei. If he ever needed anything, he could count on Sergei to get it for him.

"*Vhen* Malikov retire?" Bugak asked.

Malikov glared at the sergeant. "*Vat eece deece* to you?"

"Malikov hate army much… why Malikov *nyet* go? Go back to *kolkhoz* with Russian peasants, Bugak smirked. "Army *nyet* need Malikov," Bugak goaded him. "Smart Russians like Bugak need *krest'yan,*" — peasants — "For grow food," Bugak laughed.

"*Idi k chortu,*" — go to hell — "Bugak," Malikov scoffed.

"Army *nyet* die if Malikov retire," Bugak said.

"*Da…* Bugak *theenk deece?*" Malikov questioned, chewing on pork that now tasted like an old boot. "*Vhat deece* army do *vit zhopochnik*" — good for nothing ass-kisser — "Like Bugak? Thirty years, Malikov a soldier," Malikov spat. "Malikov know *vhat* army need."

"*Da tochno*" — exactly, Bugak argued. "Malikov old horse. Army change… world change… Malikov *nyet* change."

"*Slushayte menya,*" — listen to me — "*Leetle* bastard," Malikov spat. "Malikov fight Afghan… Bugak *steel vet* bed."

Bugak laughed. "Afghan *var?*" — war. "Malikov say… *deece eece var?*" he mocked.

"*Da… Vy nichego ne znayete,*" — you know nothing, Malikov spat, jamming his fork under his mashed potatoes. He used two fingers to push corn onto it, to stick the kernels to the potatoes. He stuffed the forkful into his mouth.

"Bugak!" Sergei scowled, admonishing the sergeant before turning to Malikov. "Malikov, *ne slushayte yego,*"

— don't listen to him. Malikov shot Bugak a cold glare. Sergei was right. Bugak wasn't worth it. Malikov cut off a large piece of pork and popped it into his mouth.

"Bugak fight Chechens," Bugak announced. "*Deece vas var.*"

"*Var...*" Malikov mocked... chewing intently. "Bugak do radio... *Nyet* gun. Bugak job in *var vas* talk on *deece* radio! Bugak good at *deece* talking."

"*Nyet nyet!*" Bugak roared with laughter. "*Malikov eece* best at *deece* talking. Malikov *theenk* much of Malikov! Malikov *eece* best soldier. Ask Malikov... only Malikov *theenk deece!*"

"*Lyudi uvazhali menya,*" — people had respect for me. Malikov interrupted. "Thirty years a soldier."

"*Nyet!*" Bugak spat. "Malikov best soldier... only Malikov say *deece!*"

"*Idi k chortu,*" Malikov muttered.

Bugak chuckled and reverted to Russian, speaking softly and peering around the mess hall to ensure he would not be overheard. English was mandatory in all common areas of the FOLT. "Soldiers talk about you. They say you are foolish... arrogant. You brag... know everything," Bugak sneered sarcastically. "You are a fool," Bugak smirked. "Why did it take you thirty years to achieve senior chief?" Bugak taunted.

Malikov seethed, his face burned hot. He shoveled in a mouthful of meat and slammed down his fork. He stared at Bugak, chewing purposefully. Bugak was an exasperating, sniveling nobody who would never reach *Senior Starshiná* no matter if he stayed in the army fifty years. "Bugak *leetle zalupa konskaya*" — ass-hole, Malikov said, pointing his knife at Bugak. "Bugak need..."

"Hey Ruskie," shouted an American MP about ten years Malikov's junior and four grades down the food chain from Malikov's rank. "You're shoveling that food in pretty fast," the MP said. "What's the hurry? One of your comrades sneak in a hairy-legged Ruskie prostitute?" The MP yelled from his seat, five chairs down from Malikov.

"See," Bugak whispered across the table to Malikov. "I say even *Amerikantsy* know Malikov a fool!" Bugak laughed heartily. Malikov grew enraged. Bugak was a bastard. The MP was loud and vile. Both of them were laughing at him. His blood churned. Sergei shrugged and nodded his head in empathy with his friend.

"*Nyet*, Malikov no *leesen* drunk *Amerikantsy*," Sergei whispered.

"MP..." Malikov corrected, "Drunk MP!" Malikov said loudly to Sergei, not caring who heard him.

"What's the matter, comrade?" the MP taunted. "You too shy to look me in the eye? You too scared... or maybe you no *speeka goot* English?" Imperialist bastard, Malikov thought. These *Amerikantsy* were contemptuous... mocking foreigners for bad English or thick accents. It was always the American soldiers, he thought, and MPs were the worst. Ignorant scum, Malikov told himself. American soldiers have no respect. They refused to acknowledge his superior rank whenever they got the chance to harass him... whenever officers weren't around. Go ahead, Mr. American Scum, he thought. Mock us; mock our country. You keep telling yourself we're ignorant. How many Americans speak Russian? How many MPs speak Russian! MPs were too stupid to learn Russian. *Ignore them*, Malikov's *babushka* would have told him. Words can't hurt you. Malikov scraped up the rest of the potatoes and corn from his plate and stuffed the last piece of pork into his mouth.

"Look at our little comrade boys," the MP taunted.

"Hey little Ruskie, why don't ya shovel the whole roast into your dirty little red face — all at once — and save yourself some time." The MP elbowed the soldier next to him and motioned to Malikov with his fork. "Look at him shovelin' that food into his gob. Aw gee," the MP continued, "You're all outta food there Red. Hey... I got some for ya. Come on over here and get it."

"Malikov," Sergei pleaded. "Come, *ve* go. *Ve* go room." Malikov felt like someone had pushed his head into a blazing furnace. His heart thumped in his chest. Why didn't the MP shut up? Why couldn't he just stop bullying him? Why wouldn't everyone leave him the hell alone?

"Hey boys," the MP said loudly, "D'ya think little Red could handle one of our *real* American women?" The MP gulped from his beer can and then wiped his mouth with the back of his sleeve. A juicy belch erupted from his mouth, sounding as if he had blown air through a straw into a glass of water. "Hell no what am I thinkin!" the MP bellowed. "He's probly one of them inbred commie's. You know the type boys, bangin' his Ruskie mommy and his dirty old peasant grandma out near the barn 'til he gets the hang of it..."

Malikov balled his fists. He wanted to ignore the MP. He truly did. He wanted to do what his *babushka* would have wanted him to do. He tried to swallow but a lump had grown thick in his throat... a palpable, huge hard lump. His carotid arteries throbbed in his neck, his temples pulsed madly; the pressure in his head was too much. He thought his skull would split in two. Thirty years... he thought... thirty years a soldier and no respect. It wasn't supposed to be like this. He wasn't Aleksi — the bully. He was nothing like his grandfather. He was a soldier and he deserved respect. Malikov was thankful his grandparents were dead. He couldn't have borne the shame if his grandmother or Aleksi had seen him treated like this. He couldn't have tolerated it. He wasn't Aleksi. People had reason to disrespect Aleksi. Aleksi pounded on the weak, on Malikov — the boy. He wasn't a bully thrashing little boys like Aleksi. These ignorant bastard MPs had no right, he told himself.

"Yup that's it boys," the MP persisted. "He didn't disagree now did he! *Tsk... tsk... tsk...*" The MP clicked his tongue on the roof of his mouth and continued his taunts. "Twisted, dirty little commies... hey how tall are you Red... four foot six?" Malikov steamed in silence. "Aw... cat got your tongue? No, wait, I got it. I got it boys! You know what they say about silence; silence is agreement boys! He *is* bangin' his Ruskie mommy and his dirty little bent over peasant grandma!"

"Malikov!" Sergei begged in a hoarse whisper, reaching for his friend's arm but missing. "Stop... *ve* go." But it was too late. Malikov jumped to his feet, steak knife clenched in his right hand. The chair flew back behind him and tipped over with a crash. He spun to his right and stormed in a rage down the wide aisle toward the seated MP. Malikov still had the last hunk of pork in his mouth. But he couldn't swallow, he couldn't work the lump of meat down his throat and he couldn't speak. He almost gagged. Anger burned inside him as hot as the blazing bonfires in Zolotaryovka during the midsummer celebration on St. John's Eve — the Russian tradition from ancient times meant to ward off evil spirits. No evil had been driven from here, Malikov thought. To Malikov the evil in this mess hall was palpable. His heart thundered in his chest. He reached the insolent MP, stopped and stood looking down on the seated impudent moron. Without warning Malikov spat the half-chewed clump of pork onto the soldier's lap.

The MP stared at him in silence. He shook his head

slowly. "*Tsk... tsk... tsk*," snapped the MP's tongue. The MP flicked the gob of pork from his lap onto the floor. Malikov thought back to an old black and white American movie he had seen where Dr. Jekyll transformed into the terrifyingly evil Mr. Hyde. He was reminded of that frightening scene as he watched the MP deliberately rise from his chair excruciatingly slowly, stretching his massive frame up to its full six foot five inches, until he towered menacingly over Malikov.

"What's wrong little commie brother? Don't you know it's bad manners to spit food at your American brothers? Are you trying to start an international incident? *Tsk... tsk*," the MP ridiculed. "And to *waste* food!" the soldier taunted, his lip curling, his brow narrowing. "Isn't your little commie family starving over there in Siberia or somethin'? Here you are spitting out our good American food." The MP folded his arms across his chest. "Or maybe you got a bad case of indigestion? Can't hold your food down? Poor little red bastard."

Malikov's face waxed crimson. He gripped his hand tighter around the knife. "*Kakashka*," Malikov spat aloud. "*Peece* of *sheet*," he repeated in English.

"Aww, ain't that cute," the MP taunted... leaning over from his waist, squinting at Malikov. The MP bent his elbow and wrist and waggled his index finger up and down as he pointed at Malikov's mouth. "Look at that tiny pink Ruskie tongue flappin' in that gourd!" the MP mocked in a squeaky voice. Then he sighed and parked his hands on his hips, frowning at Malikov. "Now you shouldn't be usin' bad words on me. 'Cuz, well, that ain't proper seein' as how you're a guest in my country... and after all we done to make you feel at home!"

Malikov stood right about eye level with the nametag sewed onto the MP's breast pocket. He stared at the tag and then looked up at the soldier. He repeated the MP's name to himself, *Booner... Booner.* He scowled at the vile American, his disdain growing exponentially. It seemed to Malikov the face of this MP standing before him was transforming into an oozing, putrid abscess right before his eyes. Malikov had never before hallucinated... but perhaps he was at this moment. Malikov stood in the middle of the B Sector mess hall. He knew there wasn't much he could do at that moment, short of stabbing the detestable MP with the knife — a flimsy army mess hall poor excuse for a steak knife — he clenched in his fist. A vision of plunging the knife blade into the MP streaked across Malikov's mind like a brilliant flash of lightning.

The air had become too heavy to draw into his lungs. At that moment, Malikov would have given almost anything to end the pain this MP had inflicted on him. Hundreds of eyes were on him in that mess hall. Considering the size of the MP, Malikov had only succeeded in trapping himself in an impossible situation. He was certain multiple blows with the mess hall steak knife would have been necessary to lay this American MP out flat. A hundred soldiers weren't going to simply sit there watching him jab that knife into the MP over and over again. Malikov wasn't even sure if the knife were sharp enough to penetrate the MP's stiffly creased shirt. Clearly, Malikov's back was to the wall and he was angrier than he could ever remember.

Malikov had lost his temper... again. He had reacted in blind rage without a thought to consequences or the odds against him. The instant he had stormed off toward the MP he realized he had nowhere to go but to see it through somehow. He had committed himself to confronting the MP in front of a hundred witnesses. He might as well have been performing center stage in a

N. A. BOTTARI

Chekov play. He couldn't merely change his mind and slip out the side door unnoticed. He would look like an old fool, a coward. Malikov never planned to act rashly but the rage snuck up on him and gripped him before he knew what was happening. Yet no matter how angry Malikov had become in the past, he never crossed the line. He wasn't Aleksi. Malikov could control his own rage — at least until now. Malikov's plasma bubbled like hot boiling oil under his skin. The blood rushed past his ears, pounding inside his head with such force that the sounds in the mess hall grew muffled and dull. This night was so much more infuriating than any other night in his life. Bugak, the MP, the crowd in the mess hall were all laughing at him. How could he ignore this? He had put in thirty hard years to attain the rank of *Senior Starshiná*. In the American Army he was equivalent to a Chief Master Sergeant and they owed him respect.

The MP glared at Malikov. His twisted smile stretched across his face from one pockmarked cheek to the other. The MP's pals, seated around him egging him on, were smiling and elbowing each other like pre-pubescent juveniles.

"Your face is pretty red there comrade," The MP said. "You're lookin' like you might blow a gasket or something... that why they call you guys, reds? Maybe you're gonna have a little temper tantrum... or maybe a stroke!" Malikov's knuckles blanched as he clenched the knife tighter in his hand. His heart began skipping beats, fluttering and pounding against his chest wall. There was no honorable escape from this conflict, no way for Malikov to save face. Without warning his hand flinched forward. Malikov would later swear to Sergei that his arm had twitched under its own power. Malikov jerked his wrist to the side and in the next second he

148

flipped the knife up slightly into the air, catching it again by the handle with the blade pointing to the floor. He flung his arm up above his head, lunged across the soldier's plate and viciously plunged the steak knife down into the soldier's pork roast. The knife blade *pinged...* as it contacted the plate. Gravy splashed up his forearm and droplets of the thick brown liquid sprayed out across the table. Malikov glared at the MP. "Next time," he shouted in clear Russian, "Your bastard heart." Malikov wavered imperceptibly on weak knees and added, "You *peece* of *sheet!*" in English.

"Oh fellas..." Booner gasped, drawing his hands to his face in mock terror. "I'm so *scayerd*! I think this piece of *sheet,*" he taunted, "Threatened me in Russian or somethin'!" Booner roared, doubling over with laughter. Malikov reeled and stomped off toward the exit. Sergei scrambled to his feet.

"*Ve* go," Sergei directed Bugak.

Bugak remained seated. "Sergei go," he said, chuckling. "I come later."

Sergei sneered at Bugak and hurried off after Malikov. As Malikov tramped angrily toward the door, his eyes narrowed, teeth clenched, he cringed at the riotous laughter and sporadic clapping he heard behind him. He quickened his pace. His breaths came like rapid spurts of machine gun fire. In his mind he repeated... *bastard Booner... bastard Booner...* over and over and over, all the way to the elevator. As he rode up to the third floor, he could barely see. His vision was smeared as if he were looking through a full glass of oily water. Sparks and bursts of light flashed in front of his eyes. The pressure in his skull was intolerable. He stumbled out of the elevator as soon as the doors slid open and he staggered down the hallway like a drunk. He reached his apartment and stared into the scanner. Nothing happened. He pounded his fist on the door.

His explosive emotions had flooded the viscous fluid of his eyeball and the iris sensor had denied him entry. Drenched in frustration, he slumped against the door jam and tried to calm himself. He waited a few seconds and tried the scanner. He was denied again. Then he remembered the flask in his back pocket. He grabbed it, opened it and drained it. He waited until he felt the warmth of the vodka coursing through his body. He closed his eyes as he leaned against the door and thought of his village and the cool water from the Kuvaka Springs he had dribbled over his head on hot summer days. Finally, after what seemed an interminable time, he took several long breaths and looked into the sensor for his third and final try. This time the sensor triggered and access was granted.

He lunged into his living room and slammed the door behind him. Mentally spent, hot and sweating, he leaned against the wall, closed his eyes and waited for his heart to regain its normal rhythmic beat. He lingered there for a few moments letting the bite of the vodka overtake his fury and flood his organs with stinging warmth... but the rush was gone all too soon. He moved over to the kitchen counter and opened the cabinet. He grabbed the neck of a fresh vodka bottle and a glass, slammed shut the cabinet door and flopped down hard on a kitchen chair. He poured a full glass and drank half of it. He stared into the emptiness of the room: *Bastard Booner... peece of sheet... Bastard Booner... peece of sheet.* The chant rolled through his thoughts and soothed him like a lullaby. He finished off the glass and refilled it. Malikov didn't move when he heard the knock at the door but the banging grew louder, and then louder still.

"*Da, DA!*" Malikov hollered, annoyed. He stood and

for a moment leaned on the table to steady himself. He went to the door and flung it open. Sergei tromped past him into the apartment.

"Malikov," Sergei said, panting, "Try catch you."

Malikov, distracted, nodded and barely acknowledged his friend. He let the door slam shut. He began pacing, in a stupor, back and forth in the kitchen. The words, *bastard Booner... peece of sheet...* were oddly comforting as they danced repeatedly in his head.

"Sit, sit," Sergei said, pulling out a chair and urging him with an open palm. "Sergei pour vodka." Sergei retrieved a glass for himself from the cupboard and filled both glasses to the rim. Malikov sank into the kitchen chair. He stared at the wall... his face beat red, the throbbing in his neck and at his temples still visible and profound.

"Drink," Sergei urged his friend, sliding the glass across the table to Malikov. Malikov drank half the contents in two swigs. Vodka dribbled from the corner of his mouth and he wiped it with the back of his hand. He stared at the wall, the table and the floor. He drank more vodka and Sergei refilled his glass twice. Malikov started to feel lighter, like a heavy concrete block had been slowly pushed away from his chest. Sergei and Malikov sat for a long while in silence. Sergei sipped his drink and intermittently tapped his finger on the rim of his glass. Malikov languished in silence, drinking, letting the MP's name vacillate through his thoughts in cadence to the steady rhythm of his mind's private opus. The two soldiers sat at the table like this for almost an hour and a half before Malikov began to respond to Sergei's attempts at small talk. Three knocks on the door interrupted the tranquility of Malikov's now settled heart.

"*Da,*" Sergei said in response to the intrusion,

stretching and then walking to the door. Malikov glanced up as Bugak stepped into the apartment.

"*Vhat Bugak vant?*" Malikov scowled, sneering and spitting out Bugak's name. Bugak shrugged, shuffled over to the table and sat down. Malikov's eyes followed him.

Sergei held up one finger to Bugak. "*Vun* vodka... *den* Bugak go." Sergei grabbed a glass and set it down in front of Bugak.

Bugak filled his glass from the vodka bottle. "Malikov *nyet* mad to MP?"

"*Vhat eece deece* to Bugak?" Malikov demanded to know.

"*Da* sometimes I get you mad," Bugak nodded, the conversation reverting to all Russian, "But American bastards treat Russians like gorilla piss... You must stay angry with MP! Bugak, Malikov and Sergei are comrades. We need to stay comrades *Da*?" Bugak swept the room with his arm as he said their names. "Comrades against *Amerikantsy*..."

"That so..." Malikov smirked, following Bugak's lead and muttering dismissively in Russian.

"*Da*," Bugak answered, motioning to Malikov, Sergei and then himself. "Comrades..."

"Bugak is nobody's friend," Malikov grumbled flatly. Bugak looked uncomfortable.

"Why are you here Bugak?" Sergei demanded, his impatience clear in the tone of his native Russian.

Bugak shrugged, "Check on Malikov." Sergei scoffed and leaned back in his chair.

"*Slushayte menya*" — listen to me, Bugak said to Malikov. "You must not take shit from this bastard *Amerikantsy*. You must fight," Bugak said harshly before taking a hefty drink from his vodka glass.

"You would like me to do something stupid," Malikov

answered calmly, continuing the repartee in Russian. "A hundred soldiers in the mess hall," Malikov scowled at Bugak. "*Da... y*ou wanted me to stab the bastard MP. You wanted me to show that I am nothing but a peasant. Then you could say... see me, I am Bugak who would never do such a thing. I'm the *tsvet obshchestva,"* — cream of society.

"*Nyet* — no," Bugak said, letting his forearms drop to the table in front of him. "If you don't fight the *Amerikantsy*, it will be bad for us... it will turn into a war.

"Bugak," Malikov said eloquently in his native dialect. "If you are so afraid of the *Amerikantsy*, then you fight the MP."

Bugak sighed. He tipped his glass back and emptied it. Then he stood and moved toward the door. He rested his hand on the doorknob and turned to face them, shaking his head. Malikov and Sergei eyed him. "*Ya tak dumal"* — I thought so, Bugak glowered. "Malikov *eece* afraid to fight MP *svolotch,"* — scum, he continued, his contempt and exasperation clearly evident in his rapid fire jumble of English and Russian. "Malikov big *zalupa,"* — dickhead. "Malikov *eece krest'yanin,"* — peasant. "Malikov *eece neudachnik,"* — loser, lame duck, nonstarter.

"*Idi k chortu"* — go to hell — "Bugak," Malikov scowled, feeling more fed up with it all than angry. As the door slammed shut behind Bugak, Malikov angled his head toward Sergei and smiled as a new surge of warmth from the vodka flowed through his veins. He tapped the rim of his glass. "Sergei," Malikov said, "More vodka... *tovarishch"* — comrade — "*Nyet?*"

❀❀❀❀❀

Chapter 8

❀❀❀❀❀

Takotna, Alaska, August

Miriam's muscles tensed. It was three a.m. She sat bolt upright in bed from a dead sleep, her heart racing, her palms sweating. Slamming and scraping sliced through what should have been the untainted tranquility of her cabin on a stormy Alaskan night. Her mind scrambled for clarity; metal... tin... no, it was steel or aluminum. This was not the sound of a small corner of the lean-to flapping against the outer wall. This was a two hundred foot Dutch Harbor crab boat creaking and smashing against a wooden wharf in a hurricane. And the thumping... what was that violent pounding? Had the arctic gusts ripped back the entire side of the shed? Her food would be exposed. This was as good as a neon sign from the great spirits inviting the wolves to pillage her cache. The early brutish weather posed a dire threat to the wolves' survival; they would be starving. They would be desperate to feed their pups. Miriam flung back the comforter and swung her legs over the side of the bed. She dove her feet into her slippers and ran through the living room. She yanked her parka from the hook near the kitchen door.

"Mama! Mama!" the voice sounded frantic yet muffled... distant. Miriam instantly cringed. Time froze. She ceased struggling with her coat, left arm outside the sleeve of her parka, the other crammed into the right sleeve. For an instant she listened.

"Kyle!" Miriam yelled, her voice cracking, weaker than she intended, her heart hammering, her stomach twisting into knots. Scraping and slapping from the back of the cabin reverberated through the walls like the screeching of a steel hull peeling away from a forty thousand ton battleship. Then the scream pierced the Alaskan night.

"Kyle! I'm coming." Miriam stuffed her arm into her sleeve and reached for the shotgun. She grabbed twelve-gauge shells, a mixture of buckshot and slugs, from the gun rack and stuffed them into the pocket of her parka.

"Mama!" Kenzie shrieked. She was standing in the doorway to the children's bedroom. "What's wrong? Where's Kyle?"

"Stay in the bedroom and shut the door!" Miriam ordered, hurrying past her terrified daughter. Kenzie moved toward the bedroom as directed. That was the rule in an emergency. The children were to do exactly as told without question... to listen, to wait and follow all of Miriam's commands. Their lives might depend on this. After the crisis faded Miriam would answer their questions. Miriam saw her daughter was visibly shaken and that no doubt adrenaline had set the cells of her body ablaze. Kenzie slammed shut the bedroom door. She was now likely poking her head out from the bed covers, listening to distinguish the sounds of the howling storm, her brother's voice and the next instruction from her mother.

The grating noise of shredding metal grew unbearable as Miriam neared the cabin's back door. These were not the rhythmic patterns of the storm beating the aluminum siding against the cabin. What was Kyle doing back there? Had the shed caved in... crushed him? That lean-to held her cache of food. Without it, they would not have sufficient meat to survive the winter. Kyle would have known that. Had he heard the disturbance and decided to impress her by repairing it? Anyone could see Kyle considered himself a superhero trapped in a little boy's body. Had he done this?

Miriam cringed from the thrashing and terrible thumps shaking the cabin. Oh dear God, she thought, tortured by abysmal visions in her head as she reached the cabin door. It was open, less than a foot, just enough for small Kyle to squeeze through. Miriam peered inside but the door was angled; she saw only a dark miniscule corner of the inner shed wall. She pushed at the door with her shoulder. It was stuck, bound up on something. She pushed harder but it would open no farther.

"Mama, mama... help mama!" Kyle's scream was weaker... more muffled.

"I'm here Kyle! What's blocking the door? Answer me!" But Miriam had no time to wait for a response. She set the shotgun down, lowered her shoulder and ran at the door with all of her might. The impact jarred her bones. Pain shot into her shoulder and down the left side of her body. The door did not move. "Kyle!" she hollered, pounding her fist on the wood. Then... on the tail of a powerful arctic gust funneling into the cabin she caught a dreadful whiff, a slight but unmistakable stench, a rancid odor she had known since childhood. In that instant Miriam heard a soft guttural panting that was barely audible over the howling wind. In one horrific moment of realization a black blinding despair gripped her soul. She knew she was never going to be able to budge that door.

❄❄❄❄❄

ROC Northwest Takotna, Alaska, August

Malikov had awakened with a headache — a blinding

one — and didn't remember any details from the night before. Yet as he now sat harnessed into the morning transport POD on the way to the lab, he was beginning to feel physically better. Occasional blackouts were not new to him — forgotten nights and queasy mornings. On average the price paid on awakening was hardly worth the previous night's overindulgence. In this case he figured his suffering was acceptable. Sergei's attempt to ply him with liquor to forget the humiliation he suffered had not succeeded... although he appreciated Sergei's effort. Over the years vodka had become little more than flavored water to Malikov, as normal a supplement to his daily diet as was a deep breath to his daily respirations. While he enjoyed the buzz from alcohol he rarely drank himself into oblivion as was Aleksi's habit. Malikov's occasional overindulgence resulted only in sporadic forgetfulness.

The vodka did not temper Malikov's rage. Only the vivid images of revenge passing through his mind softened it. He believed in an eye for an eye, pure and simple. Unfortunately, Malikov had concentrated too much on his pleasant visions of retaliation. The MP, Booner, had been Malikov's final thought last night and his first thought in the morning. Now he realized his obsession and preoccupation with Booner had left him with a serious problem. He had forgotten to complete his morning's vodka routine. Realizing his predicament his heart thumped violently against his ribcage. Malikov had not filled his flask or taken his sips of vodka before leaving his apartment. He had stashed the flask in his back pocket but it was empty from last night's face off with the security sensor. All that remained in the small container were a few drops — which might have helped if only psychologically — but he had no opportunity to drink vodka now. The POD driver, the MP escort, or the other passenger would see him. Alcohol was contraband in the tunnel proper.

Malikov knew if the lab sensor locked him out the MP would detain him or throw him in the SHIDS. He didn't know this MP. Malikov would get no free pass based on recognition. The MP could haul him to the security station, search him, interrogate him; Malikov would be humiliated. The CO could demote him simply for having a flask in his possession. They could send him back to his motherland in disgrace... thirty years down the drain. The Russian Army would throw him in prison or send him to Siberia. Russia in the twenty-first century wasn't the Soviet Union of the sixties, but it wasn't Britain or Canada either. Russians would not tolerate having the motherland's name tarnished in an embarrassing political incident involving a lowly Chief Master Sergeant. Malikov had to stop thinking about these possibilities. The more he focused on what *could* happen the more he worked himself up; the more he worked himself up the greater were the chances that the sensor would register his emotional turmoil as danger and lock him out. It was the damn technology. The government had no right to violate him — treating his own natural bodily functions like some kind of indisputable evidence of guilt. How ridiculous... how absolutely inhuman could one government be? The FOLT POD slowed in front of Malikov's lab door, hovered briefly, and then set down on the tunnel floor.

"Let's go Chief," the MP said. The MP swung his legs out of the POD, stood, and waited... one hand resting on the POD roof the other on the holster of his laser-sighted Gen4 .40 caliber Glock 22, with 15 round magazine. "I have another stop before my shift is over," the MP added. Malikov had no choice but to exit the POD. He moved slowly, purging his mind of everything but the thought of better days to try to calm himself. He imagined himself fishing at Lake Pleshcheyevo near his village of Zolotaryovka. Malikov had accompanied his friends and their parents on a handful of fishing trips before he had turned twelve... before Aleksi had completely isolated him. He tried to focus on those pleasant memories. He envisioned the waters of the lake, his friends and their parents who freely welcomed and nurtured him as if he had been their own flesh and blood... as if he were a boy worthy of love. But when he summoned these fond recollections Aleksi barged into his vision as the ogre who put an end to his boyhood innocence and his emotions were only stoked further.

The MP walked beside Malikov. The nearer Malikov got to the sensor box the more enraged he grew at the fools who put him in this position. The damn government put him in jeopardy, relying on technology instead of common sense, imposing unjust punishments for having contraband liquor. Aleksi put him in this position by victimizing him, infusing his entire being with perpetual anger and hate. These were the fools to blame for his present danger. Then there was Booner... the sonofabitch who caused Malikov to lose his focus, to forget his ritual and leave his apartment unequipped to face the ID sensor. Malikov reached the lab door and the impatient MP stood beside him, eager to complete his overnight shift. Malikov would have three tries at the sensor. He was desperate. He saw no way out. If he'd had a gun, he might have shot the MP and then turned the gun on himself. Yes perhaps he would have done this if he had held a gun. His gaze drifted down to the MP's holster but the MP was watching him too closely. Malikov cleared his throat and glared into the sensor box. He began to shake. He waited the five seconds for the beep. Nothing happened.

Malikov turned to the MP, "*Deece theeng no eece* function, *nyet*?"

"Not likely," the MP said, tapping his fingers on his holster. "They tested this sector two days ago. Try again." Malikov swallowed, turned, and again aimed his eye squarely into the box. Five seconds passed... nothing happened.

The MP lifted the snap on his holster. "Do you have access to this lab?" the MP asked.

Malikov nodded. "*Deece* my lab. *Da*, access," he said, defensively. "I say, *deece theeng eece* defect. Tell you, *deece* sensor *eece nyet* work."

"Try it again," the MP directed. "I'm going to have to take you to the SHIDS if that door doesn't open this time." Malikov bit the inside of his mouth — near the corner of his bottom lip where years of practice told him it wouldn't be noticed. He turned and stared down at the box. He tried to swallow but the thick lump was back again, blocking his throat. He stared into the sensor — his third and final chance. Sweat trickled down his neck, his chest and his arms. It was so damn hot in the tunnel, he thought. He marked off the five seconds in his head...

Raz — one...
Dva — two...
Tri — three...
Chetyre — four...

❀❀❀❀❀

ROC Training Center Marietta, Georgia, August

Colonel Nick Fizer stood in the vacant Olympus Hall staring at the chaos left behind in the wake of the final minutes of the ROC graduation ceremony. Chairs lay toppled on their sides — some completely upturned — chair legs reaching toward the ceiling like stiff carcasses of weird cryptid animals in rigor mortis. Small puddles of spilled liquids made walking slippery. Slivers and shards of crystal from broken champagne glasses and scuffmarks covered the floor. Nick saw streaks and droplets of smeared blood on the podium, the stage, the floor and the backs of chairs. He took a few steps forward and nearly walked through what appeared to be vomit. Nick paused, stunned, drained of all reason. His mind was numb, dazed as if jolted by millions of volts of electricity. A thousand thoughts ran through his head, confusing and distressing him all in one incalculable blur. The general's words — the words he had spat out right after the champagne toast — haunted Nick.

Had Nick dreamed it? Or had this army officer indeed delivered those horrible threats? As he thought about Tucker's words Nick's skin crawled... as if a cold, clammy parasite were creeping around inside his body just under his skin. It was a vile sensation he had never before experienced. The events could not possibly have happened the way Nick seemed to be recalling them. Those words... they gripped Nick and stung him at his core, incessantly playing out in his head.

"As all of you have been taught during ROC training," the general had spat out threateningly, *"Never divulge what you know about this program. Do not use the New World Order term. You are to disguise this terminology. You will explain ROC efforts only if you are cornered as simply another support system to foster a stronger, more humane and sustainable government. You will explain ROC as simply another agency created to help with twenty-first century Smart Operations or Smart Growth, or any derivative thereof. You may engage in discussion with the public about U.N. documents already in the public domain... cite Agenda 21, the Earth Charter, or the Kyoto Protocol or any other publicized texts as we*

have already instructed you to do. And I will tell you now ladies and gentlemen, if you disclose specifics or if you spread lies about the purpose of this ROC agency, or publically question the propriety of the Olympus Project, you will be eliminated." The general had punctuated his sentence with a violent pounding of his fist on the podium, his eyes glowing red like the devil himself.

Nick had then looked around the Olympus meeting hall at the vacant faces and the heads nodding in docile agreement and he understood none of it. Nick had tried to catch the general's attention, to search his eyes for an explanation. Was this some kind of joke to which everyone was privy except Nick? How could it be anything else? But Tucker appeared dead serious and Nick had stood frozen in his tracks listening to the despicable threats flowing from Tucker's mouth.

"Your families will be eliminated," the general had again pounded his fist on the podium. *"Every trace of you, your family, your friends, your acquaintances, will be wiped from the face of this earth."*

Nick had not seen it coming. He had not been privy to either the general's words or the swift and bewildering attack triggered by a nod of Tucker's head after the toast at the ROC ceremony. Nick understood none of this. *"Put yourself on leave for a couple of weeks Nick,"* the general had ordered him after the officers had been removed. *"Take some R&R and we'll have a good talk when you get back."* That was it. That's all Tucker had said. That was Nick's debriefing.

Nick walked toward the double doors at the west end of the hall and grabbed his hat from a small table. His boots echoed far up into the rafters as he walked. He took a handkerchief from his pocket and wiped a smear of what looked to be blood from the brim of his hat. When he started to put his handkerchief back into his pocket he thought better of it and tossed it on the floor in a pile of trash. He turned off the lights and closed the double doors behind him. He dialed his wife on his cell phone as he walked toward his office down the dimly lit hallway. His wife picked up the phone on the second ring. "Pack our bags Stephy," Nick told her as soon as she answered. "See if you can book us a flight for tonight. I don't care what time. We'll fly into Dulles and drive to Mom and Pop's. Try to get us an SUV instead of one of those compacts. I hate those small cars. I'll explain when I get home." Nick ended the call and slipped his cell back into his top pocket. He grabbed his briefcase from his office and locked the door when he left. The Georgia night air surprised him, seeming too chilly for this time of year. Yet as he made his way through the parking lot to his car, he felt relieved at leaving the facility and oddly invigorated by the abnormally crisp breezes brushing against his face.

❄❄❄❄❄

Nick stared with vacant eyes into the night sky from the window of the Boeing 737. He sighed, turned his head and looked at his watch under the light of his overhead reading lamp.

"Again?" Nick's wife Stephy remarked.

"You've checked your watch a half a dozen times in the last ten minutes."

Nick looked at her and smiled. "I know. It'll take me a while to power down from the last couple of years."

"Well it better not take too long because you said you only have two weeks. Your leave will be over right when you're ready to start relaxing," Stephy said, laying her hand over his.

"You're right," he said in a low voice, "As always."

Stephy nodded. "I love how perceptive you are," She

laughed softly. "You know..." she began, and then paused before continuing. Nick knew what was coming. It wasn't like him to withhold huge issues in his life from his wife. He knew Stephy would not try to pressure him into talking about something that was on his mind before he was ready to let it out. She might playfully drop subtle hints about whatever elephant was in the room at that moment, but she respected Nick enough to recognize he was on his own schedule and it didn't necessarily coincide with hers.

"You've been home almost three hours," she told him. "Let me know when you're ready to talk about this."

Nick smiled. "Not just yet," he said.

"Okay, whenever you're ready... but for the record," she teased purposefully, "I'm not a clock-watcher so you have plenty of time... at least thirty or forty minutes until we touch down in D.C." She gave his forearm a couple of quick taps and then drew her hand back to her work. Nick watched as she made pencil notations in the margins of her notebook. The small beam from her overhead reading lamp spotlighted the page of what Nick guessed was probably her new book. He would ask her about it once his mind cleared. He closed his eyes and rested his head on the back of his seat. Once they were in the rental car, Nick could not escape the inevitable. He would have to start talking. How in hell would he begin? Maybe he would say something like, "Oh, Stephy, the ceremony was great. Remember that officer I told you about... Major Falcon Colby... the young man I described to you? You know... the brilliant guy with the superhuman physical abilities, the poster boy good looks and the extraordinary mind? Well he won a prestigious award, received a double-jump promotion to full bird colonel... oh, and by the way, after the champagne toast the general gave a quick nod and then the mayhem began?"

It was hardly the right way to start off, Nick thought. Merely because he was angry with General Tucker and incensed that he had been kept out of the loop was no reason to take the focus off the real issue. And what was the real issue? He couldn't seem to wrap his mind around what had happened. How could he explain something to Stephy that he himself didn't understand? Maybe it would be better if he waited and announced it to the family at dinner... or maybe... maybe he should put it out of his head altogether until his leave was over and he had a chance to talk to the general. He was fooling himself. That wouldn't work and Nick knew it. If he didn't get this off his chest his entire leave would be a disaster. His parents and Stephy would start worrying about his brooding. In all the years he had been in the army he had gone out of his way to spare his family the twists and turns of his career. Why should he start worrying them now?

It had been over two years since Nick had been home to his parents' farm in West Virginia. The last time he had seen them was prior to the start of this first ROC officers' training class. No matter where he had been stationed over the years he had never missed the traditional three o'clock Sunday phone call to them. He had begun the custom after his commissioning so many years ago. Only his deployments overseas had modified his Sunday ritual. During some of those assignments he had been limited to writing letters... and write he did. He wrote to them religiously at least once a week. Unlike other soldiers who seemed to let family ties fade away over the years as their own lives had become more and more complicated, Nick had worked hard to maintain his close family connections. He knew he had been raised in an exceptionally loving family and everything he had become in life was due to those early beginnings. He owed his parents everything. Why should he burden them with these terrible doubts and emerging fears that had increasingly swept over him?

On one hand he knew he should spare his parents. Nick had initially refrained from sharing his suspicions about the direction America was taking because he figured no drastic changes would be implemented until long after his parents' deaths. He now realized he might have been wrong. The extrapolations of what he had seen at the ceremony were horrifying. The dangers ahead were real. The general had kept Nick, his right hand man, in total darkness. What else had the general kept from him?

America was being transformed and swept away in broad daylight. American politicians were selling off the country in bits and pieces. For God sakes... a Chinese shipping company bought an American deep-water naval base in California... the U.N. owned American parks — so affectionately dubbed World Heritage Sites. Then, the worst debacle of all as far as Nick was concerned, the damn Mexico to Canada superhighway. The highway is a ten-lane twelve hundred-foot wide superhighway connecting Canada, through the United States, to Mexico, built and operated by a foreign company. Funny, Nick never recalled having had an opportunity to express his opinion or cast a vote on the spending of appropriated funds for design or construction in support of this brainchild. Where were the newspaper articles and news shows debating the building of this superhighway... owned and operated by other countries on American soil? How many Americans know about this project? If there were ever a test case for whether propaganda and government control of the media thrived in the U.S., this would be it.

Mainstream media rarely draws attention to the surrendering of sovereign American soil. They merely gloss over such occurrences and ignore secret backroom agreements. News sources might occasionally interject veiled references to these monstrous deals... like the superhighway and World Heritage Sites... if they note their existence at all. They bury references to these fiascos deep under layers of their normal media speak until Americans are conditioned to ignore the issues and pay no mind to the occasional terminology. How many Americans even know about these deals? Yet the selling of American soil one blade of grass at a time is not the bottom line. These type transactions are only components in a much larger, more sinister plan.

American politicians had been laying the groundwork for the ultimate display of power and subjugation of the American people for decades. This wasn't theory... this was black and white reality and Nick was one of the few people — anywhere in the world — to know it. Should Nick have previously brought this up to his family? Would they even have taken him seriously if he had? It was clear to him after what happened at the ROC ceremony that the nightmare had begun in earnest. The clock was ticking. What choice did he have but to lay it out on the table for his parents and Stephy? Yet there were so many uncertainties... because nothing could be taken at face value.

On the surface, the selling of America had been presented as a logical and reasonable alternative to government overspending. The drive for nuclear disarmament, the moratorium on sustainable development, the increase in environmental protection laws had all been movements to which Nick had initially seen benefit exactly as the public had. These platforms had gathered huge momentum. The basic concepts of these movements had become the impetus for drastic changes in the way the military executed its daily obligations. Passionate allegiance to sovereign America had become a dangerous and openly forbidden path to follow; the rule of the day was political correctness... the order of the day was to run it by the U.N. before the U.S. military acted on just about anything. The days of World War II national pride were out phased. The world conscience had gradually replaced national sovereignty with a collective global agenda that bled over to the U.S. Armed Services, demonizing the old military precepts of loyalty and autonomy of a singular country. The international community demanded an equal share of everything. America was using up the world's dwindling resources and the world demanded Americans curtail consumption. But consumption of resources wasn't the real agenda. The U.N. had determined that all countries were entitled to whatever Americans had earned by the sweat of their brow. The U.N. Agenda 21 proposed a world based on massive redistribution of wealth — a global welfare state where the fruit of an individual's labor would be equally divided among all who felt entitled to take it. The intent was not to raise the standard of living of poorer nations, but to lower the standard of the U.S., to equalize, weaken and control the masses.

The events at the ROC graduation ceremony strongly suggested to Nick that the American government was actively gearing up for the final confrontation. He had initially convinced himself neither he nor his parents would have to face this travesty in their lifetimes. Did he misjudge? He had thought himself more perceptive. Who in hell was he?

✵✵✵✵✵

Nick Fizer, colonel — and by all measures a great success by the standards of his West Virginia family — thought himself a simple down to earth man. His sleek five foot nine inch frame and classic looks — the curly tuft of brown hair accenting his strong jawline, his Roman nose and sparkling blue eyes — did little to betray his surprising strength. He had mastered the Liu Seong System of self-defense and that was a completely adequate foundation of confidence for him in any circumstances. The Liu Seong System is one of the many styles of Kuntao Silat, a hybrid martial arts system derived from the cultures of China and Indonesia. Liu Seong is based on an objective approach, on the principles of physics, anatomy, and psychology. The patterns of movement are designed to be precisely effective and one of its hallmarks is the ability to throw a large volume of attacks very rapidly.

Nick had first been attracted to this branch of the martial arts by its complexity and hybrid nature. He studied the self-defense system during one of his tours in Korea. At the time of his post there, Korea was an unaccompanied billet — spouses not allowed. His mischievous red haired five-foot two inch Ph.D. life companion, Stephy — never Stephanie — was ten thousand miles away. Nick learned she had been eagerly counting the days to his return as passionately as he had been slashing the days off his Korean calendar. While his fellow officers chipped away at their off duty hours by numbing themselves with booze or sordid assignations, he had fought the slow lonely minutes of separation with the study of Liu Seong. He had fully immersed himself in the three-point focus of the art and had sought out the few available Silat instructors to continue his study when he had returned to the states. Nick was proud of his martial arts skills but he had kept his prowess to himself. He had never been a man who felt it necessary to display his assets like a peacock fanning its vibrant array of tail feathers. He found it amusing when men, often times short men, puffed themselves up like Kakapo birds in a mating dance.

According to Stephy — in some measure an expert on such matters with her PhD in psychology — some men were afflicted with what she termed LMS. These shorter men only fit the criteria of the Little Man Syndrome if they were five feet eight and three quarter inches tall or less. Stephy had assured Nick that the height threshold — a product of her own imagination — had no correlation to his five foot nine inches. Of course he believed her. "Men suffering from LMS," Stephy had explained — mimicking the South Carolina burr of her psychology professor — "Struggle with feelings of inadequacy and suffer from an innate need to exaggerate events in their lives. They derive their only comfort from ensuring they are at the center of every conversation. Their life goal is to prove they can one-up everyone else." Stephy had added her final points minus the southern drawl.

"A man suffering from LMS," she had continued, "Is a man whose primary topics of conversation are colored with embellishment, self-aggrandizement and sprinkled with heavy doses of condescension for anyone within range — all toward validating his deep narcissistic sense of himself." Stephy was clearly garnishing reality with a sarcastic twist. Nick thought deep down Stephy might have had some personal experiences leading her to such conclusions. Her observations were particularly poignant and worth contemplating every now and then because according to Stephy, Nick was the antithesis of the LMS character. Knowing this helped to keep him grounded... in case he had any propensities to forget why she married him.

In glaring contrast to the LMS man who spent his days polishing his ego, Nick possessed a keen ability to listen and to empathize with others. He harbored no innate drive to embellish his life or accomplishments to maintain some mythical construct or false perception of himself. He had figured there was no one in the world he needed or wanted to impress.

Nick's study of Liu Seong had helped him connect with his inner self... or maybe the love of his family had instilled him with self-confidence. Either way, Nick was perfectly satisfied with who he was. The only embellishments of Nick's that stood out in a crowd were a few scattered freckles, his curly brown hair, slightly dusted with gray at the temples, and a black ROC forces uniform. Underneath his colonel's insignia was a man of honor standing tall in his deep-seated conviction that integrity was a vital pursuit in life. Without a doubt, Nick was an unpretentious gentleman with firmly engrained values, his feet deeply rooted in the bare earth and his outstretched hands always prepared to steady a friend.

Aside from Nick's laptop and the cell phone assigned him to tether a short umbilical cord to General Tucker, he possessed few of the day's electronic diversions that so many found not only indispensable but indicative of their own worth. The most complex technological gizmos he and Stephy enjoyed in their army post housing unit were a microwave, a television, a DVD player to view documentaries and a short wave radio with which Nick puttered. Leaping into the new technological century was not high on their 'things to do' list. When it came to leisurely distractions, the Fizers had drawn their first and finest comforts from each other's company: a cozy fire, a stimulating discussion and a couple of good books. With these at hand, they considered an evening a success. But it was clear to Nick that above all else, he could only be fully evaluated as a man — no... as a human being — if his wife were appraised in the same breath.

Stephy was a psychologist and an author, although she was vigorously prepared to debate that last point. Faulkner, Zola and Proust were authors, she argued. She was only a writer who caught an astoundingly lucky break by completing and selling the first novel she had ever written. She insisted her accomplishment was a fluke. Yet no matter how zealously she protested her deficiencies as a writer, Nick never ceased to champion her creativity. She in turn found his pragmatism and logic perfect complements. Nick Fizer had been a proud soldier for as long as he could remember. He did as he was directed and, until recently, believed what the military demanded he ought to believe. Shouldn't a good officer believe in what he was doing?

❁❁❁❁❁

Takotna, Alaska, August

This was no wolf on the other side of Miriam's cabin door. Every animal secreted its own odor, each as distinctive as the most refined lady's most exquisite fragrance. This animal's scent was unmistakable. Miriam knew her choices for rescuing Kyle were severely limited now. She had but two options to get to the other side of that back door and find her son. She could approach from outside of the cabin in the pitch-black night where she would be exposed to the arctic wind, the blowing snow, the brutal cold — and whatever else lurked beyond the cabin walls... or pray to God for help and take a terrifying chance.

Miriam Goodriver pleaded with God to steady her hand as she aimed the double barrel twelve-gauge shotgun, loaded with buckshot, at the back door and pulled the trigger. Both barrels discharged in quick succession, the blast echoing in the confined area of the cabin's back hall and jarring Miriam all the way through to her bone marrow. Wood splinters flew everywhere. The blowback from the blast forced the butt of the shotgun deep into Miriam's shoulder joint. Her upper torso and head were jolted backward and then driven forward in whiplash fashion. She fumbled in her parka for extra shells and grabbed two more — buckshot load — from her pocket.

"TALK TO ME, Kyle!" Miriam screamed, as her cold, numb fingers forced the shells into the breach. She didn't wait for Kyle's response. She slammed shut the barrel and fired again, two shells in rapid succession. Her ears were ringing. She blew a hole in the cabin door the size of a compact car's spare tire. The smell of gunpowder stung her nostrils. Splinters of wood splayed out from the gaping hole in the door in a pattern resembling a gigantic spider web. Brown bloody fur poked through the hole. Miriam dug her freezing hand into her parka and fished out two slugs. She reloaded quickly and snapped the barrel shut. Just then the door creaked, wiggled, and tore away from the door frame.

Miriam leaped to her right as the door fell inward toward her with an immense fifteen hundred pound brown bear crashing backward and smashing to the floor along with the door. She took quick aim and shot twice, discharging the two slugs into the massive brown bear at point blank range… one blast to the throat area, one to the head. The bear's eye ripped away from its socket, the right side of its snout was torn off and blood gushed four feet into the air from its neck, squirting wildly up toward the ceiling in continual pulsing bursts. The bear twitched, let out a thunderous agonizing growl and then lay motionless, blood still spewing out from the wounds. Miriam drew in a lung full of air. She realized she had been holding her breath. Suddenly the bear rolled a quarter turn to its right and lunged at her with a shredded bleeding left paw hanging by muscle and tendon tissue, six-inch claws fanned outward. Miriam jumped back farther and thrust her hand into her pocket. Her fingers curled around the last shell.

One shell left.

The bear tried to roll to the side from its back but its midsection was wedged tightly between the two sides of the cabin where the doorframe had been. Its back legs were bloody, not moving. Looped and gruesome red, brown and gray bowel — steaming as it hit the warmer air of the cabin — slipped onto the floor from the bear's abdomen. The bear struggled and twisted, arching its head and its upper torso to free itself. It tried to growl fiercely but it screeched and gurgled pitiably, whipping its head from side to side, blood and saliva spraying out from between broken teeth through the hole where its mouth once was. Miriam loaded the last shell — buckshot — into the breach and snapped shut the gun barrel. Her arms were shaking from the weight of the shotgun, adrenaline and frigid gusts of wind blowing in through the torn siding.

"Kyle! ANSWER ME!" Miriam shouted. But there was no answer and she didn't wait for one. She aimed at the bear's neck and fired the last shell.

❉❉❉❉❉

Chapter 9

❈❈❈❈❈

ROC East HQ, Route 2 Templeton, Massachusetts,
August

Colonel Falcon Colby frowned and then winced. The noise, jouncing, and vibration inside the Hughes AH-64 Apache helicopter magnified the massive throbbing in his head. He felt like a horse had kicked him. The pandemonium that had erupted in the hours following General Tucker's speech at the ROC graduation ceremony had been a frightening blur. Yet Falcon would not voice his fears or anger. He was a military officer trained to endure... to follow orders without question or hesitation. That was the official version. The truth was... he was as mad as a fly stuck to flypaper on a humid summer day. He would have fired out questions to anyone who would listen except for one thing; it was his own commander, a general, who had ordered the attack — an attack on his own officers. Falcon had no idea who to trust.

In seconds Falcon had been transformed from feeling like a hotshot celebrity, his ego puffed to the max after receiving a medal and a double promotion to full colonel, to what... prisoner? The whole thing was ludicrous... surreal. But real or not Falcon had made up his mind as the armed MPs shoved him toward the Olympus Hall exit that he would not open his mouth — to anyone — until he knew who he could trust. The general's vicious threats echoed in Falcon's head as clearly as Salvation

Army bells at Christmas, "... *Every trace of you, your family, your friends, your acquaintances, will be wiped from the face of this earth...*" It seemed apparent the other graduates had not been prepared for the instantaneous assault and seizure either — except perhaps Whitehawk. Yet that notion raised more questions. What was the connection between the mayhem at the ceremony and Whitehawk's warning about the champagne? Clearly, there was some connection. What did Whitehawk know, how long had he known it, and how could he have kept something like this from Falcon? Falcon supposed this was his hurt feelings surfacing. Whitehawk had not confided in him and he felt slighted. Yet what right did he have to complain about Whitehawk's failure to talk about what he knew? Wasn't this exactly what he had done when he had not uttered a single syllable to Whitehawk about his Uncle Caleb's concerns?

Falcon stared out the chopper window into the darkened sky. The night horizon suddenly appeared as dim to Falcon as his future. He had given everything he had to ROC training. Now he didn't even know if he was sure of the project's mission. How could something like General Tucker's actions have been sanctioned by the U.S. Government? It was easier to believe General Tucker was a rogue madman than a bonafide general in the U.S. Army acting under orders. The doubts that had begun to plague Falcon in the last months of ROC training didn't seem so groundless now. His Uncle Caleb had bared his soul to Falcon. Caleb had taken him into his confidence and knowingly left himself open to ridicule. Caleb had trusted him. Unfortunately, Falcon had been hesitant to take his uncle's warnings as anything more than paranoid theories and ludicrous tirades — delusions of an old man that would be deemed outrageous to any rational being. He had convinced himself his great uncle was losing his grip on reality. Now Falcon felt ashamed and guilty that he had so easily dismissed Caleb. *You superior, arrogant bastard,* Falcon told himself. *What do you think now, you sonofabitch, after your ROC graduation ceremony!*

It had happened so fast... before Falcon could process it. The troops appeared from nowhere and ambushed them — as if these soldier hijackers had been spontaneously generated out of thin air. Suddenly they were on him. In a microsecond Falcon had found himself strong-armed and held captive. The *seizure and restraint* had been perfectly executed with meticulous precision. It was over in minutes. The attack had followed the guidelines for a ROC crowd control exercise: *seize, restrain, subdue, dominate, remove.* It was brutally violating... at least to Falcon. His fellow trainees on the other hand were docile during the entire incident — like zombies in a B-rated sci-fi movie. Falcon clearly remembered the chaos had begun with the general's nod following the last syllable of his speech. That was that. Troops were on the graduates in seconds. Two heavily armed soldiers had grabbed Falcon's forearms and pressed into him with their bodies, crushing him and forcibly steering him toward one of the exits. The soldiers had gripped Falcon with focused mania, like mad chefs cramming meat down through a sausage grinder.

At first Falcon thought it was a military exercise. But even if that were true someone would have been notified beforehand. Those surprise exercises were hardly ever a surprise. Falcon had tried to look his captors in the eye, to appeal to their humanity, to find some common ground for empathy. But his abductors ignored him and stared ahead vacantly as if they were drone robots programmed to *target*, *grab* and *remove*. The situation was absurd. Here they were, supposedly the most highly skilled force in the world — that was the general's description — *"Leaders... the world's twenty-first century warfighters."* It hardly seemed to fit now. For two years Falcon had been conditioned to believe no power could overcome his expertise or his exceptional skills. In a split second, nothing made sense. The simple truth was... the last ten minutes of the ceremony had left Falcon feeling disposable — like unwanted garbage.

Falcon's hope to discuss it with Whitehawk after the ceremony vanished quickly. He lost track of his friend the instant the havoc began. Bedlam had deluged Olympus Hall faster than a freak Missouri hailstorm. Should Falcon have known what was coming? Had he been so stunned — so intoxicated with pride — after receiving the strokes to his vanity that his consciousness deserted him and he missed some forewarning of what was about to begin? He had not even had time to open the sealed envelope containing his orders. Where was the envelope now? Would that provide him an explanation? If he and the other officers were such valuable assets to the world, why had this happened? Would any of this ever make sense to him?

Falcon drew his gaze away from the chopper window and surveyed the inside of the Apache. His head pounded more intensely than any hangover he'd ever had. He tried to put his discomfort out of his mind. Where was his duffle bag... his packet of orders? Okay, the bag could be stowed in a side compartment of the chopper. But his orders should be in hand. He scanned his immediate area. He saw a water bottle in a pocket on the chopper door. He suddenly had a strong urge to grab it and drain the contents but he remembered the champagne incident. Right now he was feeling a little too skittish to put untested liquids to his lips. He decided against the water and left the bottle where it was.

He looked to the empty seat next to him. No orders. He saw no envelope anywhere near him. He saw nothing but the empty seat with ear protectors hanging above, draped over rubber-coated metal hooks. He saw the back of the pilot's head, the metal seams and rivets of the aircraft and the chopper side window that provided a view into the darkness beyond. He saw a lieutenant sitting across from him on an odd mini bench that looked as if it had been added as an afterthought; but he saw no envelope. He sensed the lieutenant watching him. Falcon tried to wipe the pained expression from his face before he remembered his helmet obscured the view of onlookers. Still, the hammering in his head seemed so loud he couldn't be sure the young officer didn't hear the pounding. The lieutenant lifted his wrist and checked the time.

"About twenty more minutes Colonel," the lieutenant said into his helmet mic.

Falcon nodded. Just then the helicopter veered wide left and hit moderate turbulence, thrusting Falcon's six-foot frame against his shoulder harness and shaking the aircraft violently. Falcon tried to pull in a deep breath but it felt as though a thousand pound block of cement were crushing his chest. He wedged his thumb between his torso and the strap and it provided just enough relief, physically and psychologically. He gulped air into his lungs. Grinding and grating of metal struts and riveted panels echoed painfully in his head. He fidgeted in his seat but his movement was restricted by the safety belts. He looked toward the lieutenant and pressed the radio button on his helmet mic.

"I thought these things were supposed to be smooth...

or quiet at least," Falcon said.

The lieutenant shifted his weight on the bench. "Well not so smooth sir," the young officer explained. "But quiet yes... from the outside."

"Maybe I should be riding on the roof," Falcon quipped.

The lieutenant shook his head and laughed. "A little breezy up there sir." Falcon smiled, relieved they would soon be landing. The incident at the ceremony was unsettling. Dwelling on it was a waste of time and it surely wouldn't do him any good to start his new assignment with a major chip on his shoulder. He would have to put the episode out of his mind. Something as bizarre as that ceremony couldn't possibly go unaddressed or unquestioned forever. Right? Falcon looked out the window where moonlit silhouettes of the topography appeared sculpted into the gray-black horizon. Fifteen hundred-foot hills and huge pines rose up into the night. Even in darkness, Falcon was certain he knew where they were. He had been raised in New England. He could see the long, wide, winding break in the trees to his right in the glow of the quarter moon and diminishing smattering of ground lights.

The Connecticut River Valley and the Berkshire Hills of Western Massachusetts stretched out below him as silhouettes etched into the night horizon. He could see red taillights from the occasional automobile moving east along a winding section of the two lane divided highway — Route 2 — an infrequently traveled road at this hour. The throbbing in Falcon's head seemed to diminish with the increasing familiarity of his environment. After a short while the Connecticut River gave way to thick woods as the chopper continued eastward. In minutes the Apache's halogen spotlight shined down on a smaller break in the trees and the helicopter began its descent, setting down with only a slight dip and wag to the right. The only question in Falcon's mind now was their exact position along Route 2.

He followed the junior officer's lead and unbuckled his safety belt and harness. He removed his headgear, quietly basking in joy now that his bones were no longer jostled by the chopper's flight. He put on his top cover. The lieutenant slid back the door of the Apache and a cool wave of crisp country air tinged with the slight odor of jet fuel washed over Falcon. He felt a new surge of energy and anticipation. The young lieutenant jumped down from the Apache. He turned to help Falcon down from the helicopter but Falcon was already outside the chopper standing next to the lieutenant. The young officer's eyes widened. For an instant he stared at Falcon with visible bewilderment. Then he cleared his throat. "Uh… don't worry about your gear Colonel," the lieutenant reassured him. "Everything's been taken care of."

What did he mean… everything's been taken care of? Falcon wracked his brain. Where were his bag and, more importantly, his orders? Who took them and when did that happen? The young man's statement puzzled Falcon but he shook off the urge to pepper the lieutenant with questions. He nodded instead. The lieutenant turned toward a small wooden building eerily bathed in a soft blue haze of light from a street lamp wedged between the tall pines. The blunt quiet of the wooded area was a welcome relief. The vicious pounding in Falcon's head was already fading.

"This way sir," the lieutenant said, nodding toward the building. The young officer walked from the landing area with quick steps across a short strip of blacktop toward the wooden clapboard structure. Falcon followed.

He stared upward toward the sky, then left and right into the trees. The building, no bigger than a four-car garage, sat nestled in the pine forest at the end of a small parking area. Falcon had a thousand questions for the junior officer but doubted the young man would be willing — or able — to give him much information. Besides, after the long ride Falcon relished the silent walk in the night's stillness. He couldn't even hear the chopper and that astounded him. The lieutenant had been right. The chopper was nearly soundless from the outside looking in. The pilot had not shut down the engine yet the woods were silent. Only a soft breeze and an indeterminate distant *hoosh* — from the rotor — betrayed the helicopter's presence. If Falcon had not known the Apache were there he wouldn't have had an inkling of its presence. As if he didn't trust his own senses he briefly turned to look back as he walked. Not only was it silent but he couldn't see it either — the midnight-black aircraft was simply absorbed into the night.

Falcon squinted and focused on the path in front of him. He tried to peer ahead beyond the bluish glow of the streetlight but found it nearly impossible to distinguish anything to the left or right of the building. This was a military facility — intellectually he knew it — but its very existence screamed plausible deniability on the grandest of scales. Gauging flight time from the Connecticut River, he would guess this rest stop was located in or near Templeton, Massachusetts — a village of eight thousand. In all his years of travel along Route 2 as a young man growing up here, Falcon had never seen a black military helicopter land at a rest stop. That would have been a major news story in this quiet country setting. It would have been an anomaly the locals would most assuredly have questioned, especially if it had landed at this particular rest area — built yet never opened to the public. It was deemed too conducive to criminal activity because it could not be seen from the highway. So how long, Falcon wondered, had this seemingly innocuous roadside stop been an underground ROC facility? It surely would have taken longer than two years to build. To thoroughly disguise the entire operation during its construction... how could they possibly have pulled that off?

What about the equipment they would have brought in... the trucks, the workers, the TBM — the tunnel boring machine or mole? These TBMs were usually comprised of a rotating cutting wheel — cutter head — with a main bearing, a thrust system and support mechanisms. The type machine selected depended on the geology of the target area and ground water levels. TBMs were huge. How would the army hide something like that? One TBM in use in Washington State was three hundred twenty-six feet long and fifty-seven and one half feet wide with a weight of seven thousand tons. Wouldn't this be an eye-catcher? Wouldn't someone have noticed an eighteen-wheeler TBM transport chugging along the two-lane road on a Sunday afternoon... most especially if it pulled into a tiny closed rest area in a village of less than eight thousand? Where would the Army hide all of this activity? How could they accomplish this entire project without one of the thousands and thousands of travelers using this highway ever raising an alarm? Didn't anyone at any time realize this rest stop wasn't what it appeared? The fact that this particular rest area was built and never opened should certainly have piqued someone's interest. The crime excuse made no sense. Hadn't officials noticed when they were building it that it could not be seen from the road? The secret existence of ROC headquarters in this obscure location for God knows how many years was a difficult reality for Falcon to conceptualize. He was beginning to wonder just how well he could actually determine what reality *was*... and what it *wasn't*.

❄❄❄❄❄

Takotna, Alaska, August

Miriam Goodriver trembled uncontrollably from the cold, from fear, from concern about Kyle. She held the 12-gauge shotgun out away from her and jabbed the barrel at the apparently lifeless brown bear, mangled and bloody, wedged into the broken doorframe of the cabin's back door. Her immediate inclination was to leap over the carcass and get into the shed as fast as possible to find Kyle — or his body. Yet she knew this was no time to be careless. She still had one live child to consider. If Miriam allowed herself to get into trouble, where would that leave her daughter? It didn't matter how many shells she had pumped into the bear, she was well aware of the number of people who had foolishly approached a dead animal too soon only to realize the thing was still alive. It was usually one of their last realizations.

"Mama," her daughter whimpered from behind her. "Where's Kyle? Is... is he... okay?" Miriam was startled by Kenzie's voice. She moved slowly away from the bear, far enough beyond its reach to remain safe should it suddenly stir and lunge at her with its massive front paws. She turned to look at her daughter.

"He's in the shed, Kenzie." Miriam answered, feeling her throat constricting. "I need to make sure the bear is dead. Then I can get your brother."

"But, is Kyle..." Kenzie was clearly working hard to steady her voice. Miriam was deeply burdened by

Kenzie's despair. The final vestiges of innocence dangled from her daughter by a very thin thread. Losing her father when she was six was one thing, losing her brother on top of that was going to be a painful hardship for Kenzie. After Henry Ivan's death, Miriam had tried to insulate her children from tragedy. She was failing and she didn't know quite how to handle it.

"Why don't you put on the tea kettle?" Miriam suggested to Kenzie.

"I'll be in the kitchen in a few minutes. I'm sure we can use some hot chocolate," Miriam said, stalling — delaying the awful truth. She had no idea how to soften the blow for Kenzie.

"But can't I help find Kyle?" Kenzie pleaded softly.

"No but you could light a lantern and put it on the little hall table for me," Miriam replied.

"But..." Kenzie complained, as wounded as Miriam had ever seen her.

"Go on now, light the lamp and put on the kettle. There's nothing else you can do here. If I need you I'll call you," Miriam told her, trying not to seem harsh. No doubt Kyle had been mauled, or worse, and Miriam needed time to prepare herself to deliver the news to Kenzie. Miriam needed time to adjust to it herself. Kenzie nodded gloomily and backed away reluctantly. Miriam tried to smile but she knew her effort fell short. She moved a step closer to the bear and focused on its chest. She saw no evidence of life... no twitch, no sound. She jabbed at it twice more and then waited, listening.

"Kyle," Miriam called softly. "Can you hear me?" She stood the shotgun in the corner and took in another breath, exhaling slowly. She gave the bear a final quick assessment, looking for the best spot to set her foot. The animal was a bloody mess and she didn't want to lose her footing. She decided the best approach would be to hang onto the wall and start climbing over it. If there were even the slightest chance that Kyle had survived, there might not be time to waste. Miriam stabilized her balance with a hand against the cabin wall and tried to find solid footing under the bear's thick neck, setting her left foot there cautiously. The minute she shifted her weight to her left the bear expelled a great volume of air and emitted a guttural noise. She recoiled and instinctively jerked back her leg, cringing and clamping shut her eyes. She braced herself for the impact of a powerful bear claw to her head. Yet the bear remained motionless. Assured now it was dead, she again placed her foot onto the bloody carcass and began climbing over it. She steadied herself, hand on the wall, and inched her way over the bear into the aluminum shed. There was little room to walk. The lean-to was full of bloody, gnarled, gruesome flesh and fur.

"Kyle," Miriam called out, but there was no answer. Miriam's adrenaline steeled her now and diminished her shivering even as the frigid violent wind rushed through the shed. It was dark but a faint light filtered in from the kerosene lantern Kenzie had set out in the hall behind her. Miriam could see the gaping hole in the siding, the two by fours hanging loosely around the edge of the exterior cabin wall where the shed had once been fastened. The snow blowing in through the demolished siding stung her face. "Kyle," she called again, squinting and peering into the semi-darkness. The long shelves where she had so neatly stored her provisions were partially ripped from the shed wall. Some of the paper she had used to wrap caribou and moose meat was shredded. Strips and chunks of meat and whitish tendon like strings dangled all around her. Splattered blood from the bear and probably from... her son... streaked the walls. She was horrified. Terror clawed at her stomach and she thought she might vomit; thoughts that the blood, or tissue, could be Kyle's were nearly overpowering.

"Come on, Kyle," she coaxed. "It's okay. Everything's going to be all right. Answer me so I can get you out of the cold." She hated herself. She suddenly realized a part of her expected no reply. Kyle could never have survived this. She had made a grave error in not repairing the shed immediately. This was her fault. The wind howled viciously, rattling and shaking the shed. The smashed siding creaked, groaned, and slammed against the shed frame. Winds drove through her like sharp knives slicing through butter. There was a battle going on inside her — exhaustion, fear, cold — and she could not tell which was most responsible for her shaking. She desperately wanted to cry yet she refused to allow herself to do so. Maybe there was still a chance... wasn't there?

Yet she had no right to hope. How could anyone survive an attack from a ravenous fifteen hundred pound brown bear in this confined space? The August snow had caught the bears by surprise and confused their environmental and seasonal clocks. They should be in the fields filling their bellies with the last of the berries and down by the creeks gorging themselves on the fat of the spawning salmon. They should be making their own provisions for their long winter's sleep. Instead, these bears were angry and confused — desperate to survive — and so had encroached on her food cache. How could Kyle's small body ever withstand a blow from this bear? But it wasn't her nature, or God's will, that a mother should give up hope so quickly. "Please God," she whispered, "Let this be one of your miracles."

From what little she could distinguish in the lean-to

within the dim arc of faint light slipping in from the cabin, she estimated a full half of the north side of the shed was peeled away from the frame. Miriam felt the full force of the arctic winds blustering in from that wide opening. Her feet grew numb from the cold and she found it difficult to maintain her balance. She teetered as she stepped over the bear's massive legs, over the broken shelving and over the torn packages of meat. She strained to see. Could that be her son? "Kyle!" Miriam tried to yell when she saw what might be Kyle but her teeth were clenched to stop them from chattering. All she had managed to utter was a haunting squeak. She could only discern what must be the outline of Kyle under wooden racks hanging from the wall near the end of the shed. She weaved and tottered on numb feet and made her way to the silhouette. She fell to her knees, stretched her arm under the splintered shelves and frantically felt for her son's body. When her hand came to rest on his icy flesh, she searched for some indication of life. Her hands were too numb; she had little sensation in them. She mouthed Kyle's name but no sound slipped past her gritted teeth. She reached in with her other hand and grasped him by both shoulders. She dragged him out from the debris and cradled him, rocking him gently on her lap, while searing anguish ripped through her chest.

❄❄❄❄❄

ROC Northwest Takotna, Alaska, August

Pyat' — five...

The sensor did not trigger.

"Blyadskiy rod!" — Goddamn it! Malikov muttered under his breath.

"Strike three," the MP said, decisively.

"I tell you, *deece* sensor *eece* defect," Malikov

complained, even though he knew his protests were pointless. He had slipped over the precipice into that cold, dark well — the abyss from his childhood where he was powerless to control the world around him. His third attempt to trip the sensor to open the door had failed.

"Let's go," the MP said. "Don't make this any harder than it has to be." Malikov stared at the MP. The bastard, he thought. He has the gun. Malikov has no gun to defend himself. He stared at the nametag sewed over the MPs pocket. *Lutzcot...* Malikov repeated to himself. *Lutzcot...* he said the name again in his mind so he would not forget it. He did not resist when the MP grabbed his shoulder with vise like power, spun him around and cuffed his hands behind his back. Malikov remained passive, feet spread, while the MP gripped his shirt collar from the back with one hand and rifled through his pockets with the other. The MP pulled everything — every last item down to an old piece of lint — from Malikov's pockets. Malikov said nothing when the MP told the POD driver to shut down the POD. He had listened in silence as the MP directed the driver to radio for backup so another MP could meet them and take his place as POD escort. POD drivers must have MP escorts for delivery of workers to stations. Everyone knew the rules.

Malikov said nothing. He didn't have to, it was no longer a time to speak. It was a time to build the wall — his private fortress — brick by brick. From that place deep in his mind, from the black murky corners of his memory, the same old descant ran through his thoughts. It was the melody he had come to find quite comforting, the one that first came to him as a child of nine. As usual, as with each crisis in his youth, his personal song ran through his head. Each time Aleksi had beaten Malikov — or anytime the world overwhelmed him — he could hide himself away in that same safe place in his head. He could block out the universe with his silent mantra. The words might change but the melody was always the same. It was his private escape route and he was in complete control of it. So as his heart thumped madly in his chest and the thin arteries at his temples pounded, all in perfect synchronized rhythm, Malikov's mind went to work building his applicable opus from the MPs distasteful name: *Lutzcot... Lutzcot... peece of sheet; Lutzcot... Lutzcot... peece of sheet.*

❋❋❋❋❋

Takotna, Alaska, August

Miriam sat, rocking back and forth among the debris in the shed, cradling her nine-year-old son in her arms. She called his name. She touched his cheeks, his forehead, and ran her hand along his iced limbs — checking for breaks and wounds — but it was futile. The flickering light was too weak; it was impossible to assess him from where she was. She couldn't even tell if he were breathing. How could he be? The cold was beginning to weaken her. She was shaking, equally from the temperature and the awful ordeal they had been forced to endure. She would have willingly laid down her life if she could only take Kyle's place. But she could not change these circumstances any more than she could have taken over her Henry Ivan's battle six years earlier. "You must be so cold, Kyle," she mumbled and pulled him closer. She had to get him into the warmth of the cabin. She had little sensation in her feet and hands. She must get out of the shed before she herself freezes to death.

Miriam wriggled herself up onto her knees — her son

cradled in her arms — using her shoulder and back to support her weight by inching her way up against a section of siding that was still intact. Slowly, she got back to her feet, maintaining her grip on Kyle. For an instant, Miriam felt an overwhelming need to scream — to give in to this despair — but...

Had Kyle moaned?

She couldn't be sure. It was impossible to hear clearly over the roaring wind. It could be that her mind was playing tricks on her. She stepped toward the bear, struggling to hang onto her son while she maneuvered over the animal carcass. She was terrified she would drop Kyle and hurt him more than he was already hurt... if he were even alive. She took one last giant step over the bear and staggered, off balance, back into the cabin. Her shoulder took the full impact as her forward momentum jammed her against the opposite cabin wall. She took a deep breath and stumbled forward, wobbling, down the short hall to the living room on feet she could no longer feel. She laid Kyle down on the sofa and knelt beside him.

"Kenzie, light the other lamp quickly," Miriam said.

"Is he all right?" Kenzie asked as she ran to the lamp holding a box of wooden matches.

"I don't know," Miriam answered. "Light the wick, hurry."

Miriam worked swiftly. "Kenzie... put another log on the stove!" Miriam screamed without meaning to. She rested her open palm on Kyle's pajama top. She could see her hand sluggishly rise and fall with the movement of his chest; she could only barely detect it. He was breathing. It was not her imagination. She drew the heavy quilt down from the back of the sofa and draped it over him.

"God," Miriam whispered softly. "Thank you God.

Please let him live." Miriam vigorously rubbed her palms on her flannel pajamas to warm them. It took many minutes to work the sensation back into her hands. The delay in tending to Kyle seemed interminable. Finally, when most of the numbness was gone, she ran her hands along Kyle's chest and down his arms and legs, searching for broken bones, large bulges, open wounds and areas that didn't look or feel right. She inspected his face, his head, and ran her fingers cautiously through his hair. The lamp light flickered. Something large seemed to be at the back of his head. Her hand grew sticky and wet from touching it. She couldn't see clearly at that angle but when she drew out her hand and held it closer to the lamplight, she could see a large area of dark on her skin. She knew it was the stain of blood.

"Bring me the flashlight," Miriam ordered. "The big three million candle lamp." Miriam rubbed more warmth into her hands. Kenzie ran to Miriam's side in an instant, flashlight in hand, its weak beam bouncing off the quilt as she hurried. Recharging the light had been impossible once the electricity had gone out. Little life remained in the battery. The flashlight would die any minute. Kenzie was sniffling, her breath coming in small wispy heaves as Miriam took the light from her. Miriam wanted to comfort her but every second now was crucial.

"Go and get the first aid box from the bathroom," Miriam directed Kenzie. She cautiously rolled Kyle on his side to more readily see the back of his head. "Bring two clean towels, one small, and one medium size." Miriam shined the failing flashlight beam on the back of Kyle's head. His hair was matted and growing stiff with blood oozing from the wound. She couldn't see well enough to determine how deep this was. While she waited for Kenzie to return, she checked Kyle's back for wounds, running her palms on his shoulders and torso. Satisfied he had no other visible injuries... she wrapped the blanket around him. Kenzie returned with the large box and the towels. She set the first aid kit on the floor near her mother and opened it. Then she laid the towels on the arm of the sofa. Miriam took out a large bottle of peroxide and twisted off the cap. The cap fell to the floor. Kenzie bent down and picked it up, clenching it in her closed hand until her knuckles blanched. Miriam took the smaller towel, soaked a palm size area with peroxide and began gently dabbing at Kyle's open wound.

"Kenzie," Miriam said, "Light candles... quickly. I need more light." Kenzie retrieved and set out additional candles... lighting them after multiple tries. Miriam worked frantically... holding first the scissors and then the needle over the open candle flame. After sterilizing her tools Miriam wiped the light carbon stains with a sterile gauze pad. The sense of urgency tied her muscles into knots. She struggled to cut the hair at the back of Kyle's head — hands shaking incessantly... violently; and then she bathed the wound once more with peroxide. Despair burrowed into her heart muscle as surely as a wood tick bores into flesh. She could not stop her fingers from fumbling with the needle; how could she possibly work in this condition? Panic gripped her intestines... it was futile... she couldn't do this...

So she stopped. She closed her eyes and did the first thing that came to mind:

The Lord is my shepherd; I shall not want.
He maketh me to lie down in green pastures: he
leadeth me beside the still waters.
He restoreth my soul: he leadeth me in the paths

of righteousness for his name's sake.
Yea, though I walk through the valley of the
shadow of death, I will fear no evil: for thou art
with me; they rod and thy staff they
comfort me.
Thou preparest a table before me in the presence
of mine enemies: thou anointest my head with oil;
my cup runneth over.
Surely goodness and mercy shall follow me all the
days of my life: and I will dwell in the
house of the Lord for ever.

It was the 23rd Psalm that ran through her mind in her bleakest hours. "Please dear God," Miriam pleaded quietly. "Fill me with the tranquility and the skill to do this." As she grudgingly opened her eyes, she felt strangely... healed — confident and calm — as if something or someone stood beside her, steadying her hand. The serenity flowed wholly through her, down the length of her arms, into her hands and seemed to pool in her fingertips. The panic and angst were gone. Her fingers became nimble tools, her skill as finely honed as was any surgeon's. It was inexplicable. It was incomprehensible... this stirring, ethereal essence of total peace and competence — this invisible force guiding her hand — as she sewed one stitch and then another, to close the gaping wound in her son's head.

❊❊❊❊❊

Route 267 Shepherdstown, West Virginia, August

"It's cold," Stephy said.

"The car is almost warmed up," Nick replied. "Turn up the temperature on your side."

"It's supposed to be summer, for God's sake," Stephy said, as if she hadn't heard him. She was shivering and clearly annoyed. "Why is it so damn cold here? I thought this storm business was confined to Alaska and the Pacific Northwest and up at the North Pole somewhere." Nick shrugged. How could he answer that?

"If I remember correctly, there's a drive-through doughnut shop ahead, we'll get some coffee," he told her.

"I assure you, that will put a smile on my face," Stephy said. "On the other hand, we could stop and go inside the shop for a few minutes. You know, sit and drink coffee, relax and warm up like people on a real vacation. Maybe even chat a bit... I mean if you feel like chatting about anything." Nick briefly glanced at his wife and then looked back toward the highway. She was right. He had promised her a heart-to-heart; *soon* was what he had told her hours ago. He supposed *soon*, was now. It wasn't going to get any easier for him no matter how long he put off the discussion. Not only had he grown angrier over the last few hours — smoldering like a nearly spent bonfire ready to reignite each time his mind replayed the general's attack on the ROC trainees — but he had begun to dwell on his own sense of violation. Those officers were *his* trainees. He had invested countless hours in them, sacrificing time he should have spent with his wife, to attend to their needs. Didn't he have a stake in their futures?

For two years those young officers had been in *Nick's* care as surely as if they had been his younger siblings, or his children. He had expended massive emotional energy to develop a personal relationship on some level with almost all of them. He never intended it, yet he had come to regard some of them as his extended family. Yes, he'd had his favorites — Falcon and Whitehawk especially, both extraordinary officers and good-natured young men. Nick had invested much of his own time and effort — and passion — in the ROC candidates' lives. Yet in a matter of seconds, those four hundred military officers had been rounded up like stray cattle and herded off to... to where?

Every trainee in that great hall had been overpowered and seized... stripped of their liberty, their will and their dignity as brutally as if they had been jumped by a gang of thugs in a dark alley. The plain fact was... Nick had been duped — used — and kept in the dark about the general's sordid plan. He thought it was a damn good thing he had not had the chance to chat with the general at length directly after the ceremony. Otherwise, he might have done something he would have regretted. He supposed he could just as easily have been on his way to Leavenworth right now instead of his parents' farm.

Stephy had been waiting patiently for hours to find out what in hell had turned their lives upside down. No man had a right to expect — or hope — his wife or anyone close to him could be as empathetic, patient or understanding as was she. He had thought she was pretty amazing when they had first met... with her optimistic, perky, bubbly personality and her unquenchable need to nurture. And that red hair... that gorgeous red hair... it still drove him crazy. She was more amazing now than she had been the day he met her. He was kidding himself if he thought keeping his mouth shut would have no effect. This wasn't like a boil he could keep hidden under a couple of layers of clothes. It was time to get this big fat elephant out of the room... or in this case out of the car. Decisions had to be made, decisions Nick wasn't willing to make alone. He glanced at Stephy from the driver's seat.

"That's a good idea," he told her. "We're not in such a rush that we can't sit down and chat over a cup of coffee." Nick set his focus back on the highway but he already felt better. Stephy reached over and laid her open palm on his thigh. He jumped.

"Cripes! You're like an ice cube," he said. She pulled her hand away.

"I told you I was cold," she complained. "You felt the cold through the fabric of those pants?"

Nick cleared his throat. "Yes... but put your hand back," he said. "I'm happy to share whatever warmth I have stored up."

She did.

He smiled.

❈❈❈❈❈

Adit 17 Perseverance Mine Juneau, Alaska, August

Whoosh... Whoosh... Whoosh...

What is that sound?

Whoosh... Whoosh... Whoosh...

I hear this sound but yet... I cannot see.

The fog distorts the world. You must know what is beyond the fog before you can see it.

I hear you. But I cannot tell where you are.

The fog distorts the world. Sound bounces in the fog.

Who are you?

That is not so important.

It is. It is important to me.

Whoosh... Whoosh... Whoosh...

Please... tell me, what is that sound?

You need not worry. It is only the sound of my wings...

Wings?

Yes.

Are you an angel?

No... not an angel. Many creatures have wings.

Creatures... what kind of creatures? Who are you?

That is not so important...

I want to see you. Why can't I see you?

Whoosh... Whoosh... Whoosh. Because of the fog... you do not need to worry. The fog is not such a mystery. Have you not seen the fog before... on the bridge?

Well... yes, I have seen the fog many times... on the bridge.

Then you know the fog will lift... and then you will see. You do not need to worry about the fog. Whoosh... Whoosh... Whoosh...

Oh please... what is that sound?

I have already told you. It is only the sound of my wings.

Yes. I forgot... it's your wings. I'm sorry. I am very tired... and... and I'm worried.

Whoosh... Whoosh... Whoosh... You worry too much. What worries you?

Many things...

You should not worry about things you cannot change.

I can change this. I... I think that's where I'm going — or where I was going — to change something.

Well... yes. Something is broken. Something you think is important is not working. You must not worry about that now.

I... I can't forget about it. It's something critical. I must fix... something. But I'm not sure what.

Things like that are not important right now. It is important you rest. You must rest until the fog rolls back out to sea.

This is very important. There is no time. I must fix it... whatever it is. I must fix it now... time is critical.

You should be patient. You should not worry about this now. There will be time to repair this equipment later.

Is that what it is... equipment? Something I must fix... yes... at the adit... Adit 17.

Yes, it has failed. But you do not need to worry about it now.

How do you know these things? Who are you?

It is not important who I am.

Please tell me...

That is not important.

But I can't see you. Why can't I see you?

Tell me... what do you see?

I see only fog.

That would be expected.

What do you mean?

It would be expected that you see the fog. Whoosh... Whoosh... Whoosh...

Where am I?

You ask many questions. You must be patient. These things must not be rushed. You must wait until the fog rolls back through the Gastineau Channel and flows out to the bay with the tide and the calmer seas.

Please, tell me where I am...

Where do you think you are?

I... I... could be on the bridge...

Why do you think you are on the bridge?

I hear... the horns... from the fishing boats; and... I hear the wings.

Yes. Those are the sounds of my wings... Whoosh... Whoosh... Whoosh...

Am I on the bridge?

Would it comfort you... if you were on the bridge?

I think it would... Is that where I am? Am I on the bridge?

Let me ask you a question.

Okay.

Did you know eagles mate for life?

What?

Did you know that eagles mate for life?

Well... yes. I did know that. But what does that have to do with this?

Have you seen the eagles near the bridge? Whoosh... Whoosh... Whoosh...

Yes! I have seen eagles there. Almost every day eagles are on the bridge.

Which bridge?

There is only one bridge here... the Juneau-Douglas Bridge.

Yes. That is the bridge. Where on the bridge have you seen the eagles?

I have seen them. They always sit on the utility poles in the middle of the bridge. Well, not in the middle of the bridge. The utility poles are in the middle of the Channel, right next to the bridge... midway between Juneau and Douglas. Why do you ask about the bridge? I asked you who you are... Can't you tell me who you are?

Whoosh... Whoosh... Whoosh... You are not patient. You must think. I am trying to answer your question.

Okay. I am thinking.

Are you thinking about the bridge?

Yes.

Whoosh... Whoosh... Whoosh... Do you hear the sound of my wings?

Yes.

Do you know who I am?

I... I don't know.

You do. You know who I am. You see me almost every day...

You are... an eagle?

No. Not simply any eagle.

Are you... the eagle on the bridge?

Yes. I am the eagle that sits on the bridge.

I have seen you! Many times!

Yes.

There are two of you.

I told you. Eagles mate for life.

But why do you sit on the bridge? Day after day... you sit on the bridge. For hours and hours... you both sit on the bridge and you don't move.

Yes.

But why?

Whoosh... Whoosh... Whoosh... It is not a secret.

I don't know why you sit there. Couldn't you tell me?

Yes. I can tell you. We are waiting...

I don't understand. You sit for hours on the T-bar of the utility pole. You hardly move. It drives me crazy.

You are too impatient. That is why you do not understand. Whoosh... Whoosh... Whoosh...

Yes. I guess I am impatient. But you sit... day after day... hour after hour and you hardly move at all. Sometimes you face north... your mate... faces south. Sometimes you sit close together facing the same direction, like you're whispering, and sometimes you sit at opposite ends of the same T-bar on the utility pole. Why?

It is what we do...

But why do you do it?

It is what we do. Maybe sometimes we sit on the utility pole because we want to know why the cars and the people go back and forth on the bridge... every day, back and forth, over and over. But truthfully... there are not so many cars and people. It is only that they go back and forth... over and over.

Is that true? Is that why you sit on the pole day after day?

No. I told you. We are waiting...

Yes, you did. You said you are waiting. You didn't say what you are waiting for and I don't understand.

Whoosh... Whoosh... Whoosh... I do not believe that is true... not exactly true. I think you know. Deep down in your heart, you know why we sit on the utility pole. See... that is the thing. Deep down you know why we are waiting.

I am so tired...

Yes. You should sleep.

I don't want to sleep. I want to know what you are waiting for... It's driving me crazy...

You must learn patience. Whoosh... Whoosh... Whoosh...

Wait! Where are you going? Don't leave...

It is time for me to leave.

But I want to know...

There will be time for that later. You must sleep now. Whoosh... Whoosh... Whoosh.

Please don't go...

You must sleep.

Will you return? After I sleep, will you come back?

Whoosh... Whoosh... Whoosh... I do not know for certain.

Please... please don't leave.

Whoosh... Whoosh... Whoosh...

❀❀❀❀❀

Chapter 10

❊❊❊❊❊

ROC East HQ, Route 2 Templeton, Massachusetts,
August

Falcon inspected the tired but freshly shaven image peering back at him from the full-length mirror in the bathroom of his new quarters. He snipped at the few small wayward threads poking through the seams of his new black dress uniform. He had been a full bird colonel for less than twenty-four hours and this was the first time he had seen this new portrait of himself.

There had been no time to adjust to his new rank. No colonel-select list had been posted announcing his selection and providing a future effective date. His double promotion had been a stunning break with standard army protocol and he was having difficulty digesting the reality of the image of this new Falcon Colby staring back at him. Merely hours ago he had been a major like most other officers at ROC training. Now, everything had changed. He had been dropped into the middle of the real army as a full bird colonel. There would be expectations.

God does not shape full bird colonels from clay one day and plop them down into command situations the next. Colonels are presumed to know what they're doing. Right now, Falcon didn't feel like he knew much of anything. He felt like an imposter passing himself off as an O-6, a full colonel. He had a brief, disturbing, premonition-like fear that at any moment a zealous MP would kick in his door, cuff him and stuff a one-way ticket to the FOLT SHIDS — or worse, to Kansas — into the top pocket of his crisp new uniform. The double promotion had complicated his life.

Falcon wanted time to sort out the confusion of the last few hours. But time was a rare commodity, something he more than likely would not get. This wasn't the way the army operated. Falcon was obligated to set aside his personal concerns and execute his responsibilities to complete the next mission, and the next, and the one after that. He felt like a newborn — not that he could remember his own grand entrance into the world. Nonetheless he felt naked and vulnerable as surely as if he had no pants, no shoes and no shirt. He was tabula rasa — clean slate. One minute you're safe in mom's womb and the next... poof... you're a member of the human race. It's taken for granted you will follow the paths of all other humans before you and conform to expectations. All Falcon needed right now was a *How to Be a Full Bird Colonel* self-help coffee table pamphlet.

This morning when Falcon had awakened his life was nearer to that blank slate than it had been in many years. Today was the first day of his first ROC assignment. It was the day he would establish the new routine of his life as a full bird colonel. It was the first day he would meet his new commander and, as the overworked saying goes, the first day of the rest of his life. Falcon's initial encounter with this ROC general could very well serve as the catalyst for the remainder of his military career path, the decisive factor for determining the course his life would take over the next forty or fifty years. Whatever notes that general recorded in Falcon's personnel folder would be the first draft of the map to the rest of his life. It was a daunting notion.

Falcon couldn't help but think back to his youth. He had played hours on end with toy soldiers, selecting one and then the next from the battlefield and setting them down wherever he chose, dropping them into the middle of his toy war — or not — reordering the toy soldier's environment without giving it a second thought. His actions could have been compared to the mythical god Zeus reaching down to earth in omnipotent indifference... capriciously shaping the lives and destiny of his minions, plucking them from one situation and dropping them into another. By Falcon's own design his toy soldier world was an environment that neither required nor tolerated his pawns' concurrence. But Falcon wasn't the god Zeus and he wasn't in control — as far as he could see — of anything. He was simply another pliable underling. Falcon *was* sure of one thing; these were strange times and he needed clear rational thought to keep him grounded.

It was true he had little say about his own destiny. This was army life. He was programmed to adapt quickly and adjust to change... to unhesitatingly follow orders. His brain had been rewired to mechanically follow his superior's direction without question. Until now he had succeeded in epitomizing the loyal and dutiful officer — the order taker. But he had been told many times he had not yet seen the *real* army. His advanced education and training had swallowed up an exorbitant amount of time... all of his years in the military so far. But now here he was — overnight — plunged into a new reality.

※※❖※※

When Falcon had first arrived at the ROC-HQ East facility he had not had time to explore the layout of his new quarters. The chopper had landed only four hours earlier at what he had believed to be a Massachusetts rest area. After the chopper's lieutenant had led him through the maze of processing and deposited him into the hands of security, he had been too exhausted to do much more than grab some rack time. ROC Headquarters had scheduled Falcon for a meeting with the three star general at 0730 hours sharp. He had been told he needed to allow one hour's travel time. This left Falcon little opportunity for more than a quick nap. When the alarm had rudely screamed at him he had sat up — bloodshot eyes closed — and run his tongue along the inside of his mouth. His teeth were right where he'd left them but they felt coated with a glob of fuzzy, sticky white paste — the type Falcon had occasionally been dared to eat in elementary school. That sensation coupled with his pounding head and sandpaper throat suggested he might have sleep walked down to a local bar and guzzled enough scotch or wine to leave him with a grisly hangover.

Once he had sorted out his initial confusion at awakening in an unfamiliar place he slid out of bed, stumbled into the bathroom and climbed into an elegant jetted shower. While he dried himself he caught the scent of strong coffee brewing. Frowning, he wrapped the towel at his waist and followed his nose into the kitchen. He figured the coffee had been on a timer; but what little elf had turned it on? He had shuffled over to the wood cabinets and found a coffee mug. The kitchen was fully stocked right down to his favorite hazelnut-flavored creamer. That creamer was the only morning indulgence he generally allowed himself — when he was sleeping alone that is. He found the creamer perplexing. Was hazelnut flavor standard army issue? He didn't recall any surveys exploring his culinary preferences. What possible means could the Army have used to determine this insignificant fact about him? Even more disconcerting why would the army care? And what about the damn sheets — silk sheets — that was nuts.

He had stood at the counter a full forty minutes sipping hot coffee and leisurely mulling over the mysteries of the last twenty-four hours. When he happened to glance at the wall clock he was shocked to realize he had wasted so much time. He had sprinted back to the bathroom and finished dressing. When he in-processed hours before, Falcon was told his uniforms and shoes were cleaned, pressed and already in his apartment. They hadn't lied. Everything he needed, including his dress blacks — complete with two silver eagles — underwear and polished shoes were lined up and waiting for him in the walk in closet. It was impressive.

Now dressed, he stood in the middle of his apartment waiting for his escort. He was perplexed by the modern lavish furnishings: recessed lighting, a huge built-in flat screen, desk, laptop computer and music system with wireless speakers. Two steps down into the center of the room looked to be a freestanding gas or electric fireplace, a rich brown leather sectional and a recliner. One entire wall was a floor to ceiling bookcase with leather bound volumes of multiple classics, the sciences, technology, military history and a few historical novels — all his favorites without a doubt. Chalk up another one for the unnerving, Falcon thought.

He didn't remember filling out any *favorite book* lists for the army. This was puzzling and of course, like everything else, he was probably over analyzing. Was it possible many officers his age shared these specific eclectic tastes and the army simply furnished his apartment according to statistical averages? Still... this apartment seemed a little over the top for the military;

but maybe he simply didn't know what to expect from the *real* army. It could be this upscale apartment was a military courtesy extended to all senior officers. His army career up to now had been limited to part time soldiering and training. So what did he know? But the extent of the creature comforts only left him with more questions. He heard soft knocking... picked up his briefcase, top cover, and opened the door to a young blond, green-eyed lieutenant. The officer stood a lean five foot nine or ten inches tall and snapped smartly to attention.

"Good morning Colonel Colby," the lieutenant said.

Falcon smiled. "Good morning lieutenant," he said, stepping through the doorway. The door slammed shut behind him. Falcon was caught by surprise. He instinctively patted his top pocket, looking for his key.

"Don't worry sir," the lieutenant said. "You can't get locked out." The young officer tapped a matchbook size fixture on the outside wall, "Iris recognition. You don't need a key." Falcon nodded, remembering security forces had entered his vitals into the system when he in processed.

"Lieutenant Packlander sir," the officer said, thrusting out his hand. "Most people call me 'Rabbit'. I've been assigned as your aide sir, temporarily anyway."

"Nice to meet you, lieutenant," Falcon said, firmly grasping the young man's hand.

The lieutenant nodded in the direction of a waiting vehicle. "I'm here to see you to headquarters. If you're ready, we should go."

"All set," Falcon said, nodding his head. He tried not to let his expression betray his eagerness as he eyed the waiting sleek, shiny, black and red machine... a hovercraft. Falcon was astonished... a hovercraft perfected to this advanced stage of use? He felt like the old country bumpkin on his first trip to the Big Apple. He had never seen one of these in action. Now he was about to hop into one in his first hours in this new underground world as if this were something he did every day.

Falcon knew the history of this machine, or so he thought. He followed the research closely before he entered ROC training. He had believed he understood the projected phases and time line of development. Yet apparently he hadn't been as knowledgeable as he thought. Supposedly the first hovercraft, or flying car, had been designed by a Massachusetts company only a few years earlier. It had initially run on normal unleaded gasoline and had a cruising speed of about 185 miles per hour. His Army Technology and Weapons class at ROC training had included briefings about the flying car. Falcon knew the army had been working on variations of vehicle payload and fuel systems but he could not have conceived they would have progressed to this level of technological sophistication in a mere two years. When Falcon had first read of the development of this technology four years earlier it confirmed something he had long suspected about UFOs.

Reported UFO sightings had fascinated him as a child. While he had never believed alien spaceships zipped around the universe scooping up humans for experimentation, he did believe people had actually seen unexplained phenomena in the skies. There had been too many verified anomalies reported by reliable sources to dismiss these sightings outright. Falcon was convinced most, if not all, UFOs were classified military and scientific test vehicles not unlike this hovercraft. He had long thought that by the time the public became aware of new technologies the military had already perfected the science and researched its military applications in secrecy. Considering how thoroughly the government scrutinized drugs and medical procedures before allowing them on the market, it only made sense to Falcon that the truly great innovations would be held back from early public scrutiny.

Falcon was certain these high-end technologies remained buried in secrecy until all military applications had been examined and extracted. The military would have a first go at grabbing anything of strategic value. Then, and only then, would the science be released into the public domain. Personal computers and Global Positioning Systems — GPS — were prime examples. What other logic could reasonably explain how this technology would have reached such a sophisticated stage if it had only been designed in the last couple of years? When Falcon reached the parked vehicle he couldn't fight the temptation to run his hand along its shiny exterior.

"A beauty sir isn't she?" the lieutenant said, smiling.

"Impressive," Falcon nodded.

"Department of Defense modification of a hovercraft," the lieutenant said. "These models are enhanced. We have different sizes and variations with room for cargo and greater passenger capacity as well as other... uh... frills... you might say. You'll get to know those up close and personal pretty fast. We call these MODv-PODs, Military Operational Defense Vehicle PODs... PODs for short." Lt. Packlander tapped the top of the back door twice and it opened, upward, functioning much like a door to a Lamborghini. "Climb aboard sir," he smiled. "Please put on your helmet and fasten your shoulder harnesses." Falcon climbed into the back, set his hat and briefcase on the empty seat and put on his helmet. As the lieutenant walked around to the driver's side,

Falcon fastened his shoulder harnesses. The lieutenant got in, buckled up and then both doors closed.

Falcon had arrived at the facility only hours before and had been too emotionally and physically drained to inspect his new environment. His main goal after processing in had been to stretch out and grab a power nap. The one thing he didn't want to do was make a bad first impression on his new commander so sleep was primary on his priorities list. But he now surveyed the tunnel with fresh eyes. He was inclined to compare this area outside his apartment door to the inside of a gigantic MRI machine. The walls were smooth and curved, seamless, bright and clean. The basic design was not much different from the underground ROC training facility he had just left.

"I presume you know about Virtual Retina Display technology sir?" the lieutenant asked, his voice clear inside Falcon's helmet.

"VRD," Falcon nodded. "Yes."

"Well, you will find several options for selection on your helmet visor display. There are several VTNs — Virtual Telecommunications Network Stations — including military history and news, documentaries, and a number of ROC headquarters orientation briefings you might find useful. Also, a full global ROC map display, allows virtual location browsing. You'll find a complete library with eight hundred thousand titles and of course full computer functionality with a document section that allows creating, editing, commentary review, uploading, downloading and access to the shared files on the ROC-GPCS... uh... that's the ROC Global Point Community site. If you want me to stop at any of the locations along the way that you find on the VRD maps, tell me. I'll bookmark the spot and we'll catch it on the way back. We'll have more time to putz around on the return. I don't want to get you to the General's office late on your first day."

Falcon chuckled. "Agreed," he said.

The lieutenant nodded. "If you don't have any questions sir, we should probably get underway."

"Hit the road," Falcon responded. The POD engine was super quiet... more like a muffled distant whir of one of those gag two-inch desk fans. Falcon felt a slight sway in the POD as the lieutenant brought the craft up approximately three feet off the tunnel floor. When the POD entered the flow of traffic the initial jolt pushed him backward into the seat. Falcon's stomach lurched along with the vehicle's movement. He gripped the handles on the back of the front seat until his insides settled down.

Once they were underway the POD moved slowly through the congested zones — fifteen miles per hour in the area of apartments. Falcon could easily see the dashboard digital speedometer readout from his seat. The vehicle continued to move slowly as it approached a four way cross tunnel intersection about one thousand yards straight down from Falcon's quarters. As they sat in the hovering POD at the junction of the corridors Falcon remained quiet, sated with technology overload.

The massive size of the intersection was overwhelming. The ROC training facility had been nowhere near the magnitude of this network. Other PODs of varying sizes and colors whizzed by at what had to be one hundred to one hundred twenty miles per hour, astounding speeds for such a relatively enclosed space. The distance between each of the PODs appeared to be about two or three normal compact car lengths. The PODs traveled at about three to five feet off the tunnel floor. Falcon had seen one or two crafts with security markings pass the intersection at double the height from the tunnel floor. He guessed it was an emergency or express corridor.

Falcon could see Lt. Packlander's fingers drumming on the half-moon steering wheel as they waited to enter the stream of traffic. He found it hard to believe he had been sequestered for only two years. He felt as if he had been plunked down a hundred years into the future. Was everything going to be so overwhelming? Without warning the POD shot out and swerved to the left into the flow of traffic. The lieutenant's fingers had never moved on the steering wheel. Falcon's mouth momentarily dropped open at the sudden lurch into traffic. His stomach had not been prepared.

"Wasn't ready for that," Falcon said into his helmet mic.

"E-GPS" Lt. Packlander explained matter-of-factly.

What a rush, Falcon thought, nodding to the lieutenant. He knew about GPS and in theory, the technologically superior E-GPS — Enhanced Global Positioning System. But obviously scientists had made a technological leap from using hands free GPS smart parking systems — limited to high-end luxury cars — to equipping these PODs with an enhanced version of the system. Commercial GPS hands free systems had been restricted to inching cars into parking spaces. It appeared the E-GPS might control POD acceleration, braking, landing and takeoff — and steering of vehicles as well? But Falcon was only guessing about the scope of E-GPS control systems. Still, he imagined that soon no human drivers would be needed behind the wheel of any land-based transport. UAVs — Unmanned Aerial Vehicles — or drones, were a prime example of such technology... but this level of E-GPS sophistication in two years? That was not likely, Falcon thought. It was more probable the military had developed this technology long before the more primitive mechanisms were approved for installation in commercial products. He was curious about the status of this technology in mainstream America. Were the systems in luxury cars still at the more primitive automatic parking phase?

Surely ROC trainees' top-secret clearances should have authorized them for briefings about such routine use of these advanced technologies across the U.S. military tunnel network. Falcon found it increasingly disconcerting that he and the other officers were provided only enough rudimentary knowledge to make it through ROC training. What other secrets and half-truths were out there? Only an idiot would believe this massive underground smart tunnel network had been technologically refined to this degree in the two years since ROC training began. So who had initially envisioned this secret tunnel world and how long ago had they started building it: the forties... the fifties? How much more did Falcon *not* know? He couldn't dwell on these questions. They would consume him. Yet he was overawed by technology, had no idea who he could trust and, based on the surprise at the ceremony, he couldn't even be sure what would happen in the next five minutes.

For now, he had to force himself to focus on the mission. He had one clear objective... get his head into the army game and impress this new commander. If he fell short he was going to have major problems from the start. Falcon moved his head slightly and glanced at the VRD screen on his helmet display.

"So, why Rabbit?" Falcon asked the lieutenant.

The young officer chuckled. "A little thing that happened when I was about eleven. It was no big deal. It started then and stuck. It's better than 'bunny' I guess." He laughed.

"Definitely better than that," Falcon said, nodding. Falcon focused on the virtual 3D 'Regional Operations Command' welcome screen that popped up on the inner surface of the black fiberglass of his facemask. VRD technology had been around for some years. Yet Falcon now found the sophistication of the system to be far beyond what he might have expected... hardly surprising after what he'd seen so far. Falcon supposed all of these technological advances had been developed under special access programs. They were probably funded by chunks of the defense budget that had been diverted to top-secret programs where the prying eyes of Congress and the voters couldn't reach. There were no audits for these defense dollars. The military stashed these programs under the national security veil. It was exasperating to him. Where was the transparency in government? Who was running this show? And what about the popular army demand for officer team work?

While Falcon had done his best to excel individually he had also enjoyed profound satisfaction as a team member. He supposed this had as much to do with his choice of career paths as had his Great Uncle Caleb's influence. Caleb had retired as an army colonel. Falcon had envisioned the military as a rock solid family... a band of soldiers pledged to one goal. From the start of his military service he had felt a deep sense of commitment and camaraderie. But right now he felt more like an outsider.

After a two-year ROC sequestration — total isolation from the rest of the world — Falcon felt excluded. He wasn't feeling much different today than he had during his bench warming years when he had first started school sports. He had been too awkward to run a straight line down court, too clumsy to dribble and too slight of a build to absorb even the weakest hit on the football field. He had felt left out and was brutally teased as a misfit by the other boys. But that didn't last long. Falcon had quickly grown into his body. He filled out and developed an unbeatable agility. As his confidence had grown, so had his interests until soon he had excelled in most everything he tried — physically and academically. But now he felt as though he had been yanked right back to his awkward stage, snatched from the top of his game and dumped on the bench — right back to the bottom of the pile. He felt six paces behind the human race. If he had to assess his technical knowledge of these systems, he would say he was about as in synch with this technology as would be a cave man with a laptop computer.

When Falcon had entered ROC training two years ago the mechanism of Virtual Retinal Display technology was anchored in the projection of red, green and blue laser lights directly onto the retina. At that point in its development, shining colored lasers onto the retina and using a particularly placed small cylindrical lens made it possible to produce — inside a helmet or special type of glasses — a picture as rich as a giant screen High Definition documentary. The image could be displayed over a one hundred twenty-degree field of vision with a resolution of 1600 by 1200 pixels. The display on the inside of Falcon's helmet that now both awed and intimidated him was unfathomably far beyond those initial capabilities. Yet while these amazing new technologies fired up Falcon's imagination, he couldn't help but admit to himself that these scientific leaps disturbed him. He had given two years to this military ROC project, agreed to drop out of the world for that long period and fully surrender ownership of his life on the promise that he would be a key leader of the most advanced and sophisticated military force on the face of the globe. But his heart lay heavy in his chest. The present state of science and technology was overwhelming. Even this young lieutenant manipulated these futuristic innovations without a second thought. How could he lead ROC forces when his own skills were so deficient?

He felt as if he had been benched for the biggest game of his life. Whatever skills he had honed, whatever knowledge, strategies or tactics he had amassed at ROC training, paled miserably in comparison to the world he was now expected to lead. Plainly put, Falcon felt inept and used. He could never recover those years taken from him.

Falcon's youth grounded him, instilling him with the concept that he had to earn his own way in life. He learned he had to work to achieve his objectives because no one would be providing him handouts. He had worked damn hard in his young life and now he felt cheated. He felt like he had run the longest, most desperate and difficult course in his life — and had come in first — only to find at the end of the race the officials had sent him down the wrong road.

He tried to remind himself he had agreed to the terms of ROC training, but what if the army had misrepresented the program. That would make sense if there had been some underlying objective to rewire the army with a new force of conditioned officers — as his Uncle Caleb had suggested. Maybe the goal had been to strip ROC trainees of their will... give them only the particular skills and strategies with the right army twist... to ensure they blindly followed orders that any other seasoned soldier would challenge. Maybe the objective of sequestration had been to keep new officers off balance. After all, the army spent two years training ROC candidates to be the best of the best and then in a few seconds — after the ceremony — stripped every officer of his will and his capacity to react. By sequestering the pool of potential top leaders and keeping them isolated until the ROC program was implemented, the army could prevent any individual officer's doubts or contradictory viewpoints from poisoning others during the development and planning stages. Wasn't that the theory behind Hitler's SS and his youth movement — *Hitlerjugend* — which robbed German youth of their innocence and instilled in them false teachings and absurd senses of invincibility and power?

He blinked his eyes until he located a military news channel on his helmet display. The newscaster, dressed in the black uniform of the ROC command, sounded like a robot... not a stitch of emotion. Falcon gawked — bewildered — at the image as the video panned to hundreds of police in winter riot gear brandishing weapons — and what looked like Tasers — and pushing into crowds. The announcer droned on in monotone as if he were mulling over the price of a box of prunes. *"More riots began today in Seattle and Oregon. Governors from northwestern states, including California, declared a state of emergency across their regions. National Guard units have been activated and are assisting local police in controlling crowds. The Department of Homeland Security — DHS — is onsite. Hundreds of injuries and deaths have been reported. Extremist groups and suspected terrorists have been arrested. The President has scheduled a State of the Union address for seven o'clock Eastern Standard Time tomorrow night. We will carry the full Presidential address."*

Falcon's mind replayed the video — riots in Seattle... Oregon... states of emergency? Why were they rioting? The newscaster hadn't said. How could L.A. and Seattle have snow... in August? This couldn't be a newscast. These videos must have been taken at some other time, in some other place... or this was an elaborate training exercise — a test on crowd control tactics or emergency response efficiencies? He tried to bring up a weather forecast on the screen but his anxieties interfered. He couldn't make the VRD take him where he wanted to go.

"Lieutenant," Falcon said, fumbling with his helmet mic. "What's with this video? I must have pulled up a training film or something. How do I get a current newscast?"

"Please sir feel free to call me Rabbit, everyone does," the lieutenant said, "At least when the general's not around."

"I'll try to remember," Falcon said, working hard to not sound indifferent to the lieutenant's preoccupation with his nickname. Falcon felt an urgency gripping him. He had to know what was happening across the country.

"That'll be great sir because I can't get used to 'lieutenant.' I'm not the career type, decided that after about six months. I'll be doing my four years and then I'm going to head home. Anyway that's not a training video Colonel, a lot has happened in the last twenty four months. I'm sure you'll be briefed by the general." Falcon tried again to bring up a weather forecast but found he had been so rattled by what he had seen he was making a mess of it. Screens were popping up, flickering and then switching to something else after a few seconds. He grew impatient.

"So what's with the riots?" Falcon asked, trying not to sound as flustered as he was.

"Well it's complicated sir," Rabbit explained. "I guess there are a lot of causes: the economy, the weather, the new legislation. I guess a lot of folks are pretty much fed up with unemployment and such too."

"What new legislation are we talking about?" Falcon prodded.

"Well there are a few biggies," Rabbit told him. "Mostly new gun restrictions, curfews, agriculture regulations... Maybe the biggest complaints are about the new Mandatory Corporate Community Service League Act — MCCSLA — we call it 'MIKSLA'. A lot of people are pretty pissed off... uh... excuse me sir," Rabbit said, clearly embarrassed.

"Don't worry about it Rabbit," Falcon said, chuckling. "I have a thick shell. Go on."

"Well like I said sir it's complicated and I don't think anyone understands all of it. You know, I heard those congressmen don't even read those bills before they vote on them. They have these little flunkies that work for them who are supposed to read this stuff and sum it all up so senators and representatives can waltz into that big chamber and raise their hands for yay or nay. Then they slip out the side door and go back to the bar. To tell the truth sir, I don't think those congressmen's peons read this stuff either," Rabbit sprinted to each new paragraph of his explanation like a runner passing the baton in a relay race... never stopping and barely slowing for a breath.

"I have a friend in D.C. at the Pentagon — D-wing," Rabbit went on, "I went down to see him last year. Man, that place is something else. What a maze. I'll never set foot down there again. Do you know they have all of these new security gizmos that basically tear you apart from the inside out in a few seconds before you ever get a foot into the building?"

Falcon wondered how Rabbit had managed to slip in that last breath without him noticing. "So..." Falcon said, catching Rabbit right at the end of his last syllable. "Tell me more about these new bills."

"Oh… yes sir," Rabbit said. "Absolutely sir… well like I said sir I don't think these congressmen read these things before they vote on them. I think it's a matter of what lobbyist gets to them first. You know, which lobbyist makes the most noise. Then too, I think their vote depends on what they think they can get out of it. You know… what they can grab for their own districts and stuff."

Falcon fidgeted in his seat. He looked at his watch. "Uh… Rabbit, it would be great if you could give me specific details about these bills," Falcon said. "It would be helpful to have a handle on some of these things before I see the general."

"Oh absolutely sir sure… I will do my best to stay on point…"

"That would be great. I'd appreciate it," Falcon said.

"Okay, where was I?" Rabbit said. "Right, I just started in on the bills. Okay, so first off the MIKSLA Community Service Program requires two years community service starting with every person at age twelve. This is the same program that used to be voluntary. The President first changed it by executive order… you know… made it mandatory. But even Congress griped about it so they had to put through a new bill. It passed anyway. Right now the first two years, from twelve to fourteen, require part time commitment. You know… like a couple of hours after school three times a week, or something like that, and mornings on Saturday and Sunday. Then again when kids turn eighteen they have to give another two years but that's full time and that's what most people are so pissed off about I think…"

"That's a big commitment," Falcon said. "I guess that might have pissed me off when I was eighteen."

"Exactly!" Rabbit exclaimed. "It's huge isn't it?"

"So what does this *commitment* entail?" Falcon asked. "I mean, what are they expected to do for those two years?"

"Dunno sir," Rabbit said. "I'm not sure. It's all kind of hush-hush. They don't tell you what you have to do before you go. But I know one thing... no one is paid for it. The Community Service League scoops you up and sticks you somewhere for two years. They provide you food and a bed and that's it. It's basically — and pardon me for disagreeing with the government sir — but it's pretty much like slave labor."

"What about a selective service board?" Falcon asked.

"No. No military draft sir," Rabbit answered. "I've heard people can't sign up even if they want to. I have a friend back home who lost his job and tried to enlist. D'you know what they did... '1-knock' right off the bat. He didn't even get to the physical and he got a '1-knock' rating right off."

"1-knock?" Falcon asked, pleased he was getting the hang of it now... *Rabbit talk*, he mused. That's a great way to describe talking with this lieutenant. Falcon had figured out how to interrupt him without seeming to interrupt at all.

"Not-Qualified sir," Rabbit explained. "You get a 1-NQ — we call it '1-knock' — it means you'll never get into the military no matter if we're at war or what. A '2-knock'... er 2-NQ... means you have some chance of getting in if we're at war and... and '3-knock' means, we're at war and you will be called up to serve at any time."

Falcon was baffled. "When did all of this happen?"

"About eighteen months ago," Rabbit said. "But the thing is sir, it's so nuts... the way they classify you. This friend back home was top of the heap, if you know what I mean. He was class president, most likely to succeed, captain of this and captain of that. He was in all the sports, went to church every Sunday. Crap he went to church during the week. It makes no sense. And he was as physically fit as anyone," Rabbit said, shaking his head.

Falcon focused on his helmet VRD when he realized he had stumbled upon a weather report. He listened intently. *"Another foot of snow fell today in Seattle as temperatures hovered at minus ten degrees. All across the eastern edge of California the weather was similar. Snow fell in Arizona and Texas where blizzard conditions have raged for a week now. Most residents have followed authorities' orders to stay inside their homes but members of some extremist groups have ignored these warnings and taken to looting shops and markets that have been closed due to the freakish weather."* The camera panned to crowds of men, women and children running and screaming. *"Police, DHS and national guardsman are working together to control outbreaks of violence. Residents are again ordered to stay in their homes."* The screen then went black. Falcon's chest felt heavy; he drew in a deep breath.

"We're here sir," Rabbit announced. "Sorry about the streaming video but the VRD automatically shuts down when we are within five hundred yards of our D-Grid — er... programmed destination." The POD swung violently to the right out of the main corridor, decelerated, continued on for a few hundred yards and then eased down three feet until its underbelly rested on the tunnel floor. Falcon released his shoulder harnesses and gathered his things. He tried to ignore the twisting and gnawing in the pit of his stomach. He wasn't sure if the cause was more attributable to his lack of sleep, the manic pace and events of the last twenty-four hours or the horrific video he had witnessed. Whatever the cause, he had to put it out of his mind.

He waited as the POD door opened and then exited the hovercraft. He looked up and surveyed the tunnel, his gaze falling on two impressive thick columns framing a pair of doublewide glass doors. He read the sign above the entrance of G Sector... *Headquarters, Regional Operations Command, Eastern Division, Lt. General H.B. Hazkill: Commander.* Falcon swallowed hard. His mind raced a thousand miles an hour. Images flashed in his head... riots, snow — where it had no business snowing — violence. How could the world be in such a state of chaos after only two years?

He reached into his right pants pocket for a hard candy, unwrapped it and popped it into his mouth. He crunched it into small bits, hoping a sharp piece or two might take his mind off the visions in his head... the police, the guardsman, the cruelty of this world he no longer understood. He may as well have awakened in the grass next to Rip Van Winkle after a hundred year nap. He had seen women and children pursued by SWAT teams in body armor who dished out brutality like it was the main side dish at the local Saturday night prime rib buffet — everybody got some. Mothers, toddlers and babies were beaten... on camera. These people were so-called extremists now? Was that the objective of this new world he didn't recognize... to demonize the innocents, subjugate and bully and brutalize the most vulnerable of society? There had been screams... terrible, agonizing wails in the background of that newscast while weapon-laden police, DHS troops and guardsman tromped around like Hitler's storm troopers. They had used brutal force, and Tasers. On Americans! How can they justify using such lethal force against mothers holding young children? What the hell kind of world was this?

He focused on the sharp edges of candy against his cheek. He popped another piece into his mouth as they walked toward the G Sector entrance. He bit hard into it, his jaws clamping down with the great force of his inner torment. He had so many questions. The lieutenant led the way up a short ramp and peered into an iris sensor. Falcon followed. Rabbit held the door and they both walked into ROC headquarters. He and Rabbit walked down the corridor, passing closed doors on each side of the hallway. Falcon was strong enough to put these terrible issues out of his head for the moment. For the sake of his future he must focus only on his own present mission... meeting and impressing this general. He might look good on paper but he had to show he was as good if not better in person. As the saying goes, you only get one chance to make a first impression.

"This is it sir," Rabbit told him, nodding his head toward the stenciled glass doors. Rabbit leaned in toward the security box and glanced into the sensor, "One more spot check. If you'll just take a peek into that last box sir we can go in."

Falcon nodded once and then peered into the iris scanner. He took in a quick breath, arched his back, flexed the crick out of his neck and stepped past Rabbit as he held the door.

"I will be waiting in the POD for you sir," Rabbit said. "Good luck."

"Thanks Rabbit," Falcon whispered.

As Falcon entered the general's outer suite of offices the lieutenant's nickname flashed across his mind. The irony of the name — Rabbit — wasn't lost on him. How appropriate for someone to have a moniker like that around here in this underground world he didn't understand... in this place where he felt as if he had fallen into Lewis Carroll's rabbit hole right alongside Alice. Carroll's setting in *Alice in Wonderland* was a world where everything was upside down... where yes meant no and nothing — absolutely nothing — was as it seemed.

❀❀❀❀❀

Chapter 11

❄❄❄❄❄

Route 267 Shepherdstown, West Virginia, August

As Nick related his story to Stephy in the coffee shop off Route 267, he paused occasionally to study her. She sat quietly across the small table from him, her eyes fixed on his face, her gaze and breathing steady. He laid everything out in the open. He told her all the things he shouldn't tell her... the things he wasn't authorized to tell anyone. He tried to evaluate his wife's body language, to get a bead on how badly he was uprooting her reality but Stephy gave little away. Normally she was an open book to him. Tonight she would have made the most steadfast poker adversary blush. Nick worked hard not to omit anything important from the summary and he included some of the torment and doubts he had endured over the last few years. Not once had he looked at his watch and neither had his wife.

"So you say this... this Olympus Project has three phases?" Stephy asked.

"Basically yes," Nick whispered, although there were no other patrons in the coffee shop to overhear him.

"Well what are they?" she asked. "What phase... where are we now?"

"Essentially we have been dancing around Phase I since the last American terrorist attack," He said. "Which, I should add, was not what it seemed," he muttered softly.

"What does that mean?" she asked, narrowing her

brow, "Dancing around, I mean."

"Phase I is basically a phase of flux and preparation," he told her. "It starts with a period of heightened security. They implement new vague laws and broad changes and the president issues a multitude of executive orders. For example, maybe the government issues new executive orders to grant rights to women to breastfeed their babies and then in a year or two the next order rescinds that right... making it *illegal* for mothers to breastfeed babies. The government will easily be able to do that because they granted the right to breastfeed in the first place, even though it's none of the government's business. However, because they did step in and grant the protection by force of law, they have created a situation where they can rescind the permission and then make it illegal. One excuse they might use is that all mother's milk is contaminated due to some source of poison the government says exists in U.S. farms. The beauty of this concept," he continued, "Is if the government had not interfered in the first place and taken it upon itself to grant something under man's law — to which nature's law already inherently entitles us — then they would have been in no position to make it illegal. Establishing government control over something is the first step. The first step is usually easy. Who would argue against solidifying by law a mother's right to breastfeed her infant?"

"That's the type of flipping that will occur during this phase," He continued. "The government will exert more and more control over all areas of life, testing different platforms at various sites across the nation to see how intrusive they can successfully be... how far they can push Americans into a corner. All efforts are meant to hack away at our freedoms — one tiny chunk at a time. It's a time for evaluation. You know, to see how people adapt." Nick sipped his coffee.

"You mean to see how much the government can get away with?" she asked him.

"Exactly… we have in fact been living in Phase I for a long time. Some think Phase I will last for years, some think decades. It's going to take the right crisis to push us into Phase II — initiated by the government — or in some weird ironic twist… it might start with a freak natural catastrophe the government will use, opportunistically, as an excuse. When that happens there will be no easy way to turn back the clock," Nick said somberly.

"So… so what is this Phase II?" Stephy questioned timidly.

Nick shook his head slowly. "Phase II is serious business. ROC forces will be deployed. The government will use some excuse to justify broad sweeping changes in a multitude of areas — or maybe it will be one area they select… like banning shortwave radios or something — but it will happen in plain sight of the American public. ROC forces will be necessary to *control* the situation for America's protection. At the start of Phase II, most Americans will do absolutely nothing, even if they think whatever is happening is outrageous."

"Why?" Stephy asked. "If the government stormed into my house and hauled my husband off to jail because he was tinkering with his radio or because he said the Pledge of Allegiance in Times Square or something, I'd go ballistic. I wouldn't sit by and do nothing."

"You might," Nick explained, wrinkling his nose as if a skunk sat down beside him, "If you had been sufficiently conditioned. That's the purpose for these scattered tests… consider the shootings of, and by, schoolchildren. As a society, the sheer volume of such news stories desensitizes us. Second, the goal is to condition people to blame guns for murder, not society's immorality, lack of value base, education, or sociopathy. The objective is to outrage the public against private gun ownership to fire them up to demand the government outlaw guns. A disarmed society is a vulnerable society. The sad thing is... the same people who cry for gun confiscation are the same people who are using such tragedies to push their own agenda. Sure, stiffer gun laws *should* make sense... take the guns away from everyone so bad people can't get their hands on them. Will that stop murders? No, and the people who sincerely believed in disarmament to save lives will wonder... well, gee, how come removing guns didn't stop murders? It will be too late then. Once the guns are confiscated, it doesn't matter if the statistics show violent crime goes up... it wouldn't matter if murders rose fifty percent. The objective was accomplished... the fact that the ends didn't justify the means is insignificant... meaning the disarmament didn't accomplish the publicized goal — the saving of lives of innocent people — but it accomplished the hidden agenda. And believe me, when disarming society is shown to be ineffective Americans certainly won't be getting their weapons back any time soon. The worst users and abusers of the suffering are those who use what appear to be noble or worthy platforms to reach an end where the consequence is not what the public expects. Our society is causing the violence, not our weapons."

"I don't see myself falling for that kind of conditioning," she said, defensively. "I don't believe for a minute that outlawing guns will stop gun violence. We already have laws. People aren't supposed to steal either, but laws don't stop them from doing it. And felons aren't permitted to own guns, but what do they do when they're released? They get a gun because society is too damn violent to survive the inner city without one. People kill with knives and baseball bats and pillows and they use legal drugs — vital for saving lives, like succinylcholine... critical for operating rooms — so do we outlaw those things too?"

"Well, that's another thing," Nick said. He had started this, no sense holding back now. He was beginning to feel he had an obligation to bring these things out in the open... whether people believed him or not. Stephy is strong; she can handle this. "The government might help you out with that, you know. Give you a little boost to make their irrational arguments sound... rational."

"What do you mean?" she asked.

"I mean you have no idea how far the government has taken advanced technology," Nick took a small bite of his doughnut and a gulp of tepid coffee. "There are ways available to make... strong suggestions to people," he told Stephy.

"You're talking about... mind control?" she frowned.

"Not an entirely accurate name for it, but yes," he answered.

"That's pretty far off the deep end Nick," she said.

"It sounds pretty far-fetched," he agreed. "But it's only — as they say — the tip of the iceberg. And let me mention something else. You said you didn't believe you could be conditioned but it seems to me not two hours ago you subjected yourself to a search of your belongings and a full body x-ray at the airport by the TSA — Transportation Security Agency. You gave up your right to privacy because the government has conditioned you. We both stood by and watched while that wheel chair bound thirty-something brain-injured, double amputee on oxygen — the one who said he fought in the Middle East — was frisked by a security agent whose supposed liberty the veteran thought he had fought to protect. Then we witnessed another TSA agent run her hands up and down a blind eighty year-old woman with a white cane and a hip replacement because she set off the metal detector alarm."

"You're right," Stephy agreed dejectedly. "We did. And we didn't say a damn thing about it."

"We're all vile terrorists — guilty *until proven otherwise.*" Nick argued... feeling like his blood pressure was creeping higher. "You, I, and the rest of the country have given up our constitutional right to be considered innocent until proven guilty. And every time we lose another right we all look away and pretend it's not so bad... the government is protecting us."

Stephy nodded. "You're right," she said softly, staring at the table for a long while. Nick didn't intrude on her thoughts. Soon she sighed and shook her head. "So, when you say that in Phase II the government will implement broad sweeping changes what do you mean? Give me an example," Stephy demanded.

Nick was pensive. "Well, it could be pretty much anything. For instance, the government might crash the internet and then outlaw it using the rationale that America is under cyber-attack. That's going to cause a domino effect. Banks will close because all government and most private banking transactions are accomplished through electronic transfer now... exactly the way the government wanted it. You won't be able to pay your bills or buy food or clothing so maybe the government will determine it's time to introduce the infamous 'mark'; you wouldn't be able to buy or sell without it. Or maybe they will stage another terrorist attack and in the aftermath, set up internal domestic checkpoints everywhere. They could make it as difficult traveling from one state or city to another as it is to get on an airplane. It would be common practice to have to produce papers. The universal I.D. card would become mandatory. Those refusing to comply wouldn't be able to obtain food or water... or public services like electricity... because they didn't obtain their I.D. card. But the worst... the absolute worst part of Phase II... is that once these problems are set in motion, the government will announce the need for additional mobilization."

"What... the National Guard?" Stephy probed. "National Guard Units have been called up lots of times."

"ROC forces," Nick said, "And U.N. peacekeeping forces will be mobilized... droves of those troops will be called up under Phase II."

"Peacekeeping forces," Stephy exclaimed in a loud whisper, "U.N. peacekeeping forces on American soil? Nobody would stand for that!"

"Companies and battalions of them will pop up all across America. It will seem like they have materialized out of thin air and honestly... that's kind of what they will be doing," he expounded.

"How is that possible? Wouldn't there be a revolt the minute U.N. foreign troops marched into America?" she asked incredulously.

"No," Nick said. "There won't be a revolt when that happens."

"How can you be so certain? What about the NRA and doomsday survivalists and people who are already picketing about losing their rights?" Stephy argued, leaning across the table. "They'd go ballistic!"

Nick shook his head. "They might go ballistic, but it won't change the outcome. Even if they did try to fight it, that kind of disorganized rebellion would be crushed rapidly. Part of Phase II includes extraction of 'extremists' and 'terrorist groups' from society. People will be hauled off to... to special reeducation centers in the middle of the night like they did in Germany and the Soviet Union and China. People think America is immune to this."

"I don't believe it. I'm sorry Nick," Stephy said. "I can't believe that this country would look the other way — not revolt the minute foreign troops landed on our coastlines. It would take weeks to pull together foreign peacekeeping forces anyway. Then you have to equip them, organize them and transport them. By that time... the shorelines and airports would be blocked by American patriots."

"Well in one respect you're probably right," Nick agreed. "It would take time to ready a force like that, mobilize it and then invade America."

"There, see?" Stephy said. "Maybe you're more worried right now than you need to be. Sending troops across to our coasts or landing at our airports couldn't work."

"It doesn't make a difference Stephy." Nick explained.

"What do you mean?" she asked. "I'm saying we will have time to organize and stand off any invading foreign troops."

"Nope," Nick said.

"Nope... nope?" Stephy repeated. "What do you mean... nope?"

"I mean," Nick clarified, "Even if we had time to organize and equip some kind of revolutionary force — volunteers or whatever — and we run off to wait at the airports or the coasts to block foreign troops from getting in, all that wouldn't matter."

"Why in hell not?" Stephy frowned. "Give me one

good reason why we couldn't join some survivalist group and stage a revolution to keep foreign troops out of our country. Give me one good reason!" Stephy demanded, breathlessly.

"Because they're already here; U.N. peacekeeping forces are already in place... here... in America right now," Nick told her. "They're already inside the country. Check the Internet. The government has not been able to keep this entirely quiet so they explain away the thousands and thousands of U.N. vehicles and foreign troops — that are visible to the average American — as 'visiting' Global Special Forces units. The government's justification for allowing these vehicles and troops in America is that they are simply part of a U.N. training exercise for the MJTF — the Multijurisdictional Task Force. According to the U.S. Government, the task forces training on U.S. soil are simply tools in the global war on drugs and terrorism." Nick watched Stephy's face blanch white. "And of course they're only in America to aide in times of... earthquakes or tsunamis... or pandemics."

"But these vehicles and troops are only the parts of this plan that are visible to Americans," Nick continued. "The government specifically does not try to hide them in order to desensitize us. It is part of a ploy to get our brains used to seeing machines of war and visiting foreign troops on our streets so we are conditioned to shrug off their presence in the U.S. as simply another military exercise. It has become normal — a trivial inconvenience — to be delayed at railroad crossings witnessing hundreds of freight cars loaded down with tanks, military transport vehicles, military ambulances and war weaponry... and the drive to condition us doesn't stop there."

Nick fiddled with his doughnut and ate a few crumbs

before continuing. "Americans are programmed to ignore questionable government activities like the building and manning of strange vaguely-defined facilities across the nation. After all, the media tells us our prisons are overflowing with drug users and dealers that we must root out of our neighborhoods. These little publicized centers could handle the rash of criminals rounded up from the accelerated efforts in the war on drugs and terror. But the intent of these facilities is to house dissenters, extremists and suspected terrorists — anyone who speaks out against the plan. And what's really horrifying is that these secret objectives — and the forces that will carry them out — remain hidden inside America... for now."

"You're frightening me, Nick," she said.

"I don't mean to. I should stop. I shouldn't be unloading all of this on you," Nick apologized.

"Doesn't it scare you?" Stephy asked.

"Truthfully? It terrifies me," Nick told her.

"So are you going to go bury your head in a sand dune somewhere?" she questioned.

"I get it. I know what you're saying. But sometimes ignorance — maybe for a while — isn't so bad," Nick explained. "I mean, I had no choice. I was dumped squarely into the middle of this freaking party. But you, you have a choice to ignore it if it frightens you." Nick reached across and held Stephy's hands. "Maybe you should — ignore it all — at least for now."

"Seems to me, that's why America is in this fix in the first place," she mumbled.

"There's no denying that," he agreed. Nick watched his wife. She was quiet. He couldn't blame her for being stunned. The thing was... she only knew half the story. Still, he didn't have it in him to go on with the rest... not tonight anyway.

"Nick," Stephy said, breaking the brief silence. "One thing you said... I don't get. You were talking about U.N. peacekeeping troops and you said... *It will seem like they have materialized out of thin air...* what did you mean by that?"

Nick shook his head. "That's a long story for another day Stephy," he said. "Let's just say... these U.N. peacekeeping troops will seemingly pop up from right under our feet." Stephy nodded but she seemed to be moving in slow motion, as if her thoughts were stuck in the mud going uphill.

"Are you okay?" Nick asked, smiling when she looked at him.

"Sure I guess so," she nodded. "It'll take me a while to... to adjust to the reality that's all. Those nuts — those rogue internet conspiracy theorists — well, you know... it's hard to get used to it. They were right about so much of this."

"Yes... it's pretty amazing for sure," he said. "And it *does* take time to adjust."

Neither one of them stirred from their seats. They were silent. Now that he had finished his account — for the present — he picked apart the doughnut on his paper plate, breaking off tiny crumbs and spreading them around into an odd circular design with his finger. *Food doodling*, Stephy had christened it. Nick knew she was aware it was a borderline compulsion of his that reared up when he was nervous or preoccupied. Stephy had the exceptional good sense a long time ago to recognize it was a habit from which he would never break free. She always gave his finished edible sketch her own once over version of the inkblot test analysis.

"Are you going to eat those doughnuts? Or are you content to merely torment and dissect them?" Stephy asked, smiling lightly.

Stephy's sharp wit could chase away his anxiety no matter how grave the circumstances. He looked up from his plate, laughed and reached for her hand. "Everything I told you," Nick said, "Well... it really is a lot to process."

Stephy nodded. "That's a bit of an understatement," she said, eyeing him. A pixie smile brushed her lips. She took a sip of coffee and wrinkled her nose, realizing the coffee was long since cold. She set the cup down. "What does this mean for you Nick? Can you honestly head back to Georgia and stroll into the office in two weeks as if nothing has changed? I mean... you said that Phase I could last for decades... but where does that leave you right now? Things have changed for you... right?" Stephy asked, frowning. "I mean this general thing has to be unsettling... to say the least."

"Now *that's* an understatement," he said. "Of course things have changed. General Tucker's actions... well... I don't know what meaning to take from... from what he did. I guess I'm not sure *how* I feel right now... besides angry, that is."

"Well I think it was pretty low of the general to leave you in the dark," Stephy complained.

"Sure," Nick agreed. "It was pretty crappy." They sat silently for a long while.

"Hmm," Stephy mumbled. "Your... anger at him seems a little subdued and understated I think. I get the feeling twenty-two years of army loyalty is kicking in." Nick sighed and nodded in agreement. He picked at the doughnut on his plate.

"Well, the good thing is, you have two weeks leave so you have some time to think about what you want to do next," she said.

Nick looked up from his plate. "No."

"No?" Stephy asked. "No, you don't have time to think

about it?"

Nick shook his head. "Nope..." From his plate he picked up the intact half of the chocolate-covered doughnut he hadn't yet decimated and stuffed it in his mouth. Then he gulped the last few sips of his cold coffee and reached into his top pocket for the key fob. He stood and gathered up the trash from the table. Stephy watched him closely, obviously waiting for an explanation.

"*We...* have time to think about it," he said grinning broadly, "*We...* not *me.*" He reached out his hand to her. "Come on baby... let's blow this joint," he said in his worst ever Bogart imitation. "*We* haven't had a proper vacation in two years."

❅❅❅❅❅

ROC Northwest Takotna, Alaska, August

Malikov, still clad in his parka, brow drenched in sweat, sat on a heavy iron chair jammed up far too close to a metal table. The harshly lit interrogation room at the SHIDS — Short Term In-FOLT Detention Sector — was stifling. His armed MP escorts had manhandled him and physically wedged his body into the seat. The chair was crammed so tight to the table he couldn't get the proper leverage to stand without assistance. Malikov assumed the chair was fixed somehow to the table or the floor. His anger burgeoned as the minutes ticked by. The MPs had left him sitting alone with nothing to occupy his mind in the silent bare room.

They had abandoned him for almost four hours. He was ravaged by thirst; his tongue began sticking to the roof of his mouth. His bladder was full. He could have documented every minute of this evolving nightmare and chronicled his thoughts down to the second, synchronizing them with the droning *tick... tick...* of the wall clock staring down at him. Sweat pooled under his buttocks. When he shifted his weight, he could feel the damp heaviness of his pants. He fidgeted, trying to lift the lower half of his body off the chair by extending his legs and feet forward, his hips up toward the bottom of the table. His anger intensified the pounding and pressure inside his skull. How dare they treat him like this... *Senior Starshiná,* Pavel Aleksandrovich Malikov... how dare they! He was a Chief Master-Sergeant; military protocol demanded they show him respect. He would never forget these MPs... someone would pay.

His parka was unzipped. The MPs had purposely opened his jacket far enough for Malikov to feel his shirt brush the edge of the table with every breath, but not far enough for him to gain any relief from the sweltering temperature. He scowled and gritted his teeth. Discomfort gnawed at him like a Chinese water torture... the glaring light, the oppressive heat. It was all right out of some sleazy American spy movie. It was exactly what he would have expected... from sadistic bullies.

Malikov tried to work out the soreness from his wrists. Why couldn't they have unlocked his handcuffs? He could have at least removed his parka. He rotated his wrist joints and massaged his skin... anything to take his mind off the walls that seemed to be sliding closer and closer toward him. He felt like an animal caught in a trapper's snare. The more he thought about the abhorrent situation, the more he sweated. The more he sweated, the more enraged he became. The pain in his wrists plunged his mind back to the minutes the cuffs were slapped on him... his initial seizure outside his laboratory. The MP had maliciously done this to him... denigrating him from the start, zealously handcuffing Malikov while the POD driver and passenger looked on. The MP had searched through Malikov's pockets, violated his personal space and never bothered to hide his satisfaction at finding additional evidence — the prohibited flask — to further justify detaining Malikov. News of Malikov's arrest would spread through the FOLT facility like a rampant wildfire across a dry field of wheat. Contemptible bastards! Malikov grumbled in his head.

In a moment of utter futility and anger he stomped his shackled feet on the hard cement floor. Then he quickly regretted his display of emotion. It only served to reveal the MPs were getting under his skin. They were probably watching him now — laughing at him. Bastards, he thought.

Malikov's insides were twisted as tight as piano wire and that made him think. If only he had a piano wire in his sweaty hands at this moment. No, not a piano wire... a garrote. If he had a garrote he would not hesitate to use it. Malikov could almost feel the ends of the garrote cutting into the flesh of his own hands as he imagined pulling it tightly around the neck of an MP, any MP. One MP was the same as any other. They were all like Booner... and Aleksi. All of this melodrama... and for what — an empty flask of vodka and a defective sensor — this was not even his fault. Why didn't they lock up the real criminals? Why didn't they throw obnoxious drunks like Booner in jail instead of him? He was minding his own business. *Govno sobach'ye!* — Dog shit! Malikov thought to himself.

Malikov's breaths came faster now. He cursed himself; he should have made a run for it. At least he would have acted instead of simply standing there — submitting. But no, Malikov had done nothing. He should have lashed out. Even if the MP had overpowered him and shot him dead on the spot, at least it would be over. But Malikov had not lashed out. He had stood — frozen to the tunnel floor — and he was furious with himself. Malikov had acted like the *Amerikantsy* he despised — like a mindless, spineless sheep. He had broken no law. Malikov had committed no crime. The fools had created all of this drama over tiny administrative infractions. Now Malikov would be ruined. He was ashamed he had not fought back. He had meekly allowed the MP to handcuff him and for what? He had not assaulted anyone. He hadn't been insubordinate. He hadn't sold classified secrets. Yet he had stood there without protesting, allowing the MP to subjugate him, surrendering to the MP's authority. Aleksi would never have just stood there unless he had been sober, which he rarely was. What *would* Aleksi have done?

Aleksi had allowed himself to be destroyed by inner torment from the fighting at the Battle of Stalingrad. But perhaps Malikov had been too quick to judge. Perhaps Malikov should have overlooked the coward Aleksi had become and focused more on the Aleksi who had fought that battle. Had that been what his *babushka* had done? Was that the reason she had still loved his grandfather?

Malikov let his mind drift back to the Penza *oblast* in his beloved Mother Russia. He pondered his life in the small village of Zolotaryovka and his tumultuous youth. He remembered that first horrific day where he met head on Aleksi's violence. He remembered the day of the dogs and the horror in the neighbors' eyes, the mask of dark foreboding carved into the face of the dazed farmer who was sprawled helplessly on his parlor floor. Malikov recalled the farmer's wife who shook uncontrollably, pleading for Aleksi's mercy. Then Malikov asked himself, who had the power that night?

He tried to consider how Aleksi felt back then as he had terrorized the lot of them. He was the bully, yes. That night, he was also the one in charge. The destinies of the farmer and his wife, *Babushka* — and Malikov himself — had all belonged to Aleksi. Malikov was sure no coward could have instilled such terror as Aleksi had instilled in them. No man could bully Aleksi. Malikov must never again surrender control as he had done today when he had been handcuffed. From here forward, no reproof, no accusation of the least significance against Malikov would go unanswered. Malikov swore... in the future nothing like this would happen; Malikov would never again act so cowardly.

The door to the interrogation room flew open.

Two uniformed MPs barged into the room. One slammed a thick folder onto the metal table. Both then pulled their chairs away from the table and sat down. Malikov immediately struggled to try to slide back his own chair. He planted his feet firmly on the cement floor and strained to push away from the table.

"Don't bother, Chief. Your chair is bolted to the floor... right where it ought to be," the first MP said, with a contemptible tone of indifference exactly like Aleksi's that scraped Malikov's nerves raw.

❊❊❊❊❊

Takotna, Alaska, August

As a buffer against the frigid air Miriam hung a blanket across the back hall of the cabin. It fluttered as arctic gusts funneled in through the ragged siding of the shed and rushed down the hall toward the living room. At first light, she must somehow shore up that torn siding and search the woodshed for planks to fashion a back door for the cabin or they would freeze and her food cache would remain open to predators. Perhaps she could salvage some wood from the old door, now underneath the bear, mangled and splintered. But she must first tend to the dead animal.

She knelt on the floor at the rear of her cabin, her left elbow bent, forearm flat against the chest of the decimated animal. The bear's cinnamon brown fur was torn, bloodied and gruesome. Miriam resented having to dress and quarter it while Kyle lay battered and unconscious on the living room sofa... how battered Miriam was not sure. He could have internal injuries she had not detected. But she could do no more for Kyle right now and she certainly could not ignore the massive carcass on her cabin floor. The bear's perforated intestines had spilled out of its open abdomen. Miriam was well aware that all three of them were in grave danger from exposure to bacteria. She had already caused one disaster by delaying repair of the shed siding and she couldn't stomach the thought of triggering another crisis.

As angry about the circumstances as Miriam was, she found it difficult to feel malice toward the bear. Normally in August, bears would have been congregating at the salmon spawning creeks, their instinct driving them to supplement their diet with as much fat as possible to prepare for their winter's sleep. But none of nature's creatures had been prepared for the August blizzard that encased the creeks in ice and obscured the berry bushes under mounds of snow. The bear's nature was to survive; it would pursue any avenue toward that end. Now, Miriam must consider the practicalities of her actions in killing this bear. She must not anger the bear's spirit. She could not adhere to all of her cultural traditions because of the close quarters and the brutal weather, but she must do what she could under these conditions to show her respect.

If Miriam had been in the field she would have first skinned the bear with an incision down its belly and legs. Then, after separating the hide but before removing it from the site, she would have shaken it three times. Then she would have stripped away the flesh from the bones and saved the entrails. She may have fashioned a pouch from the bear hide to carry the meat more easily. She would have buried the feet and head bones for several days... burying the bear's head pointing toward the sun, fur side out. She most assuredly would have drawn a likeness somewhere nearby in the dirt floor of the forest showing the sun along a half moon to ensure good weather for drying. Some would also argue she should place eagle feathers on the bear's fur as a genuine sign of peace. Yet she had no eagle feathers. Still, she was sure the bear's spirit would forgive her if she showed as much respect as she could, honoring the bear in other ways. Many songs could be sung on such occasions as this to honor the bear and as she began her work she sang in a soft low voice:

> Ee-hee-yei-aahaa-haa,
> Ee-yaa-hei-hei
> ayoo hoo haa
> aaa
>
> Tleix gwaadei hei,
> ax nak xa niyaagoot xwei,
> shei hei ax kaagei
> ayoo hoo aa
>
> Have you gone away
> From me forever,
> My mother's brother?

This was the song of Kaats' bear wife. Kaats was a hunter who one day went bear hunting... a dangerous thing to do. While tracking a particularly fierce bear Kaats found himself trapped in a bear den occupied by a female bear... the ferocious bear's wife. As Kaats' gaze met the female bear's, the bear fell in love with Kaats and she protected him. But it was a dangerous thing... getting too close to bears. In the end the three bear children he had raised with the sow ultimately killed Kaats because he went back to his human wife. This song was the melody Kaats' bear wife sang after he had been slain... after she futilely tried to restore his life. Miriam had heard this tale as a child. It was one of many tales from her Southeast Alaskan Tlingit roots passed down from the elders. So even though Miriam could not perform all of the traditional activities commonly done after killing a bear, she was hopeful this song would be an acceptable sign of respect.

The buckshot had punctured the bear's stomach, heart, liver, pancreas and most of the animal's intestines. Miriam could not delay dressing down this bear and removing it from the cabin. As she stretched out along the bear's prone body — knife in hand — warmth from its internal organs rose and collided with the colder ambient air. Miriam reached down toward the bear's anus and slipped her serrated knife, awkwardly, into the bear's pelt to split its fur. She had little room to work with the bear wedged in the doorframe, and she was exposed to the bitter cold in her present position. Still, she shivered little as she worked because of the warmth rising from the bear's open abdomen. She was quick to tire because of the awkward cutting angle. As important as it was to show her respect for the bear's spirit her thoughts were not wholly on the animal. Her mind drifted back and forth from the bear carcass to Kyle just down the hallway. This would not do so she forced herself to concentrate. She could not afford to lose her focus. A small slip with the knife could be deadly.

"Make sure those blankets don't slip down off of Kyle," Miriam yelled down the hall to Kenzie. "You holler for me if Kyle wakes."

"I will Mama," she said. "I'm reading to him. Do you think he can hear me?"

"Yes Kenzie," Miriam answered, smiling at the tenderness her daughter was displaying. "I think he is listening to every word." But Miriam wasn't at all sure Kyle could hear Kenzie... or that he ever would again.

✻✻✻✻✻

ROC East HQ, Route 2 Templeton, Massachusetts, August

Falcon looked at his watch... one more time. It was 0750 hours. Another five minutes had gone by while he sat outside the office of General H.B. Hazkill, ROC Commander, Eastern Division. Falcon tried to attract the attention of the captain sitting behind the waiting room desk but the officer kept his head down, intently focused on the papers and folders spread out before him. Falcon was used to waiting but he had been told the meeting was at 0730 hours sharp. He had checked in with the captain promptly at 0725 hours. This delay was annoying him as the minutes dragged on. He was about to tactfully clear his throat to remind the captain he was still sitting there waiting patiently, when he heard the tunnel-side door to the general's outer office open. He watched two majors enter. He knew these faces.

The male officer strode up to the captain's desk and gave his name. Falcon recognized the two majors, Frank Benton and Meg Winters, as fellow ROC graduates. As they gave their names to the captain Falcon distinctly heard that Benton had an 0830 hours meeting scheduled with the general. Benton was early. Falcon laughed to himself. Benton wasn't going to appreciate sitting around in the waiting room for an hour or two, not with Benton's self-inflated opinion of himself. Falcon had not known Benton terribly well at training but he had never witnessed Benton showing up early for anything. What did stick in his mind was that Benton consistently seemed to enjoy making grand entrances into their training classes. He appeared to be aiming for any and all disruptions that put him at the center of attention.

"Please have a seat, sir... ma'am," the captain said to the two officers, motioning toward Falcon and the waiting room chairs. "I will let the general know you're here." The captain stood and moved toward the general's office. He knocked twice on the door and then entered when the general acknowledged him. When the majors turned to find a seat, Benton strode up to Falcon, far too close for Falcon's liking.

"Colonel Colby," Benton said, extending his hand. "It's a pleasure to see you again."

Falcon stood and shook Benton's unpleasant hand.

"Colonel Colby... very nice to finally speak with you," Meg said, extending her hand. "I guess we never had an opportunity to chat during ROC training." This was as close to Meg Winters as Falcon had ever been. He had seen her at ROC training many times but had never had the nerve to walk up and initiate a conversation. Besides, Benton was usually monopolizing her attention. Falcon and Whitehawk had surmised that Benton and Meg had something going but it had never been clear exactly what. Falcon was drawn to Meg's beauty and her warm sparkling smile but he had never approached her, the uncertainties were too great.

At training, Benton had never missed a chance to swagger up to Meg's side. As a matter of fact, he never hesitated to slither up to anyone he thought he could get something from... at least that was the impression Falcon had gotten. Benton was clearly an expert at zeroing in on the instructors, especially whichever instructor occupied center stage at the moment. Falcon had never understood how Benton had so quickly ingratiated himself with every instructor and woman officer at ROC training. It infuriated Falcon when Benton's manipulative antics seemed to go unnoticed day after day by everyone at the training facility.

"Congratulations on your promotion and award sir," Meg said, her eyes twinkling with intriguing sincerity. "That was so impressive," she smiled. Falcon felt himself blush. He had certainly noticed Meg's beauty during training... and so had every other officer. She was a total knock out. She had the deepest, bluest eyes he'd ever seen, a rich brown, shiny bob of collar-length hair, a smile that sparkled like jewels and dimples perfectly nestled into her rosy cheeks... for starters. Speaking with Meg in person after admiring her from the sidelines for two years made Falcon want to jump and laugh like a little kid... crap how ridiculous that would look, Falcon thought.

Falcon had no idea what it was about Meg that had thrown his mind into a dither anytime he was within fifty feet of her during training. He had become an instant clumsy oaf — heart racing a mile a minute, the floodgates of perspiration opening up and his tongue tripping around in his mouth. It didn't make sense. He didn't even know her. Whitehawk had quickly pegged Falcon's weak point and had badgered him relentlessly about his affliction... in a brotherly sort of way. His good friend had made some very specific predictions back then, none of which Falcon had ever given a second thought. Except now here she was not two feet in front of him.

"Oh... uh... thank you," Falcon said. "It's nice to see you," he added, stumbling over his thoughts, looking for the right words as they sat down. "You might as well get comfortable," Falcon told them. "I've been waiting over half an hour."

"Well, lucky we're all used to that," Benton said, chuckling. "After all, it is the army. Hurry up and wait as they say."

Falcon smiled, nodding politely. Benton's remark was patronizing. It wasn't what he said so much as the slightly twisted nasal 'twang' in his voice and the odd twitch playing across his lips. Falcon glanced at Meg but she seemed to be oblivious to any sinister undercurrents in Benton's expression or vocal intonation. She sat, hands folded, smiling at Falcon. So he shrugged off the fleeting nudge from his sixth sense. It was probably his lack of sleep. The general's door opened and the captain — followed by the general — stepped into the waiting area. All three officers looked up and jumped to their feet, snapping to attention when they saw the general enter.

"As you were," the general said, a broad smile spreading across his face. Without hesitation, he walked directly over to Major Benton and thrust out his hand, grasping the major's hand in both of his and vigorously shaking it. "Welcome! Major Benton," the general said, nodding eagerly. "Yes welcome to ROC headquarters. It's good to have you aboard."

"Thank you sir," Benton said, zealously. "It's great to be here!"

Falcon was baffled. He realized the silver eagles

sitting on his shoulder boards were as fresh as morning dew, but if he wasn't mistaken army protocol had sorted out this order of precedence long ago. Falcon outranked this major by two full grades and he certainly expected the general to follow military etiquette and pay him due courtesy. Falcon should have been acknowledged first. As if General Hazkill had heard Falcon's thoughts, the general turned and stepped toward Falcon, his hand extended.

"Colonel, welcome to ROC Headquarters." Falcon shook the general's hand for an instant before the general quickly moved on to greet Major Winters. "Major Winters," the general said, "It's nice to have you with us." Hazkill took a step back from the three officers and rested his hands on his hips. "Well, fine officers. We'll certainly expect good things from you." Then, just like that the general laid a hand on Benton's shoulder and led him toward his office. The general turned, as a second thought, toward Falcon and Meg. "I'm sure you two won't mind warming the bench for a few minutes while I speak to the major." Benton squeezed right by the general as he spoke and went into the office. Hazkill looked toward the captain sitting at the desk, "Major Benton was up first on the schedule," he announced. "Correct captain?" Before the captain had a chance to answer, the general added, "We'll only be a few minutes," he announced matter-of-factly over his shoulder. Without another second's delay, the general disappeared into his office and slammed the door.

Falcon saw a fleeting shadow of bewilderment flash across the captain's face. He appeared as confused as Falcon. The captain shrugged and then sat down to refocus his attention on his paperwork as if he had never been interrupted. Falcon followed Meg's lead and sat down. *Warm the bench*, Falcon thought. Seriously...

had the general just told him to warm the bench? Some first impression…

❀❀❀❀❀

Chapter 12

❋❋❋❋❋

Adit 17 Perseverance Mine Juneau, Alaska, August

Whoosh... Whoosh... Whoosh...

You have come back! You have returned eagle. I hear the sound of your wings.

Whoosh... Whoosh... Whoosh...

Eagle... Is that you? Can you hear me?

Yes. I hear you.

Where have you been?

Whoosh... Whoosh... Whoosh... I think you know.

Why do you talk in riddles?

Do I speak in riddles?

Yes. Where have you been?

You already know.

The bridge... you have been at the bridge?

Yes of course.

Eagle... I need to get out of here. I need to go... to... to fix... the equipment. Isn't it broken?

It is.

How could you know that? You're only an eagle.

If you do not want the answer, why do you ask the question?

Well I do want the answer... but how can you know which piece of equipment?

If you did not think I would know the answer, you would not have asked.

Yes I suppose.

You must understand. I know many things. I know

253

*the answer to your question. The equipment that is
broken is the one with the name like another.*

You make no sense!

You said it yourself... I am only an eagle.

But you ARE just... just an eagle...

No. Not just any eagle.

Well... I know... I mean I know you are the eagle
that sits on the bridge. But you are... a bird. How can a
bird know anything about... about human things like
this?

*Tell me... did you not say you knew eagles mated for
life?*

Yes... but...

*So you know about eagles. Yet you are not an eagle.
Some eagles know many things. I know about this.*

Then... then tell me. Which piece of equipment is
broken?

*I have told you. It is the one with the name like
another.*

The... the name like another?

Yes... exactly.

This is frustrating. You speak in riddles.

*I am an eagle. This is how I speak. You must
concentrate.*

Shhh.... quiet.... do you hear that?

Yes. I hear the breathing.

Is that you, eagle? Is that your breathing I hear?

No.

No? If it isn't your breathing I hear... then whose?

Don't you smell that?

Smell that?

Yes. Don't you notice the odor?

Oh... the odor. Yes, there is an odor.

*Whoosh... Whoosh... Whoosh... She is stirring, you
know.*

Who? Who is stirring?

You should know already.

Please don't talk in riddles eagle. It is hard to understand you.

That is to be expected.

But why?

The fog... it is expected because of the fog. But you must concentrate. She is dangerous.

Who? Who is dangerous?

You already know.

Eagle, you speak in riddles I cannot understand...

Then I will help you. I will sing.

How will that help? Please... just tell me!

You must learn patience. Listen to the song...

> Ee-hee-yei-aahaa-haa,
> Ee-yaa-hei-hei
> ayoo hoo haa
> aaa
>
> Tleix gwaadei hei,
> ax nak xa niyaagoot xwei,
> shei hei ax kaagei
> ayoo hoo aa
>
> Have you gone away
> From me forever,
> My mother's brother?

Eagle... I know this song.

Yes. Whoosh... Whoosh... Whoosh...

But what does it have to do with me?

I told you. She is stirring. You could be in danger. Do you not understand the tale?

Yes. But it is only a story.

Concentrate. Do you not understand the danger?

I do. But it is only a story!

Tell me of this danger... the one in the story.

It's the story of Kaats' bear wife. Kaats was a hunter and the bear fell in love with him... and he went missing.

Yes and there was danger. Do you remember the danger?

Yes I remember. My grandmother told me this story often.

Then you know it is dangerous now.

Why? It's only a story... a tale...

Are you certain of that? There is danger.

Why?

Because Kaats is missing.

But he was not in danger because he was missing. It was the children... they were the danger. Kaats and his bear children...

Yes.

But I don't understand...

Shh... do you not hear her stirring? She may awaken.

But she is not the dangerous one...

No, she is not... that is true. But Kaats is missing.

Yes, but after he was found the bear children killed Kaats. They were the danger.

Whoosh... Whoosh... Whoosh...

Eagle, are you leaving? Don't leave me!

I must...

But you haven't explained! You haven't told me the name of the equipment. And you haven't explained the danger of which you speak... in the story.

I have told you of this equipment. I have told you Kaats is missing. Concentrate... I must go.

Where?

You know where. I must go. Whoosh... Whoosh... Whoosh...

Eagle! Don't leave me!

I must.
Will you return?
Whoosh... Whoosh... Whoosh...
Eagle?
Whoosh... Whoosh... Whoosh...
Eagle! This isn't fair...
Life is not fair.
This isn't life...
This is life...
This is not...
Are you so sure? You must concentrate. I must leave.
Eagle! Eagle! Don't leave me!
Whoosh... Whoosh... Whoosh...

❀❀❀❀❀

Route 267 Shepherdstown, West Virginia, August

Nick Fizer eased his foot off the gas of the rented SUV. He squinted hard, peering into the darkness at the flashing red and blue lights in the road a quarter mile in front of them. "What's that up ahead?" he asked.

Stephy turned off the small book light clipped onto her notebook and looked up from her manuscript. "Police... looks like," she said, "... An accident?"

"I don't think so," Nick said, shaking his head. "It looks more like a blockade or... a... a check point or something."

"Here?" Stephy asked. "Well, maybe General Tucker has the cops out looking for you..." she added. "You know... to apologize."

"Right," Nick said. "That was my first thought too." But he was studying the check point or roadblock or whatever the hell it was. It surely didn't belong out here in the middle of nowhere, he thought. Not an hour after he spills all of this crap to Stephy he drives right into something like this.

"Do I detect a bit of sarcasm?" Stephy whispered. Nick didn't answer. In the last fifteen minutes he had noticed a few flakes of snow falling but decided against drawing attention to it. Stephy had been engrossed in whatever writing she was doing and he didn't see any benefit to disturbing her by saying, *hey look, Stephy... what a pleasant snowy August evening.* Besides, it had only been a few flakes. Now Stephy was looking up and she was bound to notice. There were more flakes and they were sticking to the windshield. Then as if she had read his thoughts...

"Is that... snow?" she asked, stretching her neck up higher as if a new viewing angle would prove her wrong.

"I'm sure it's nothing," Nick told her. "It's only a few stray flakes. It started about ten minutes ago." Actually... he was pretty sure it was *something.* He had a few thoughts about where this change in weather — the cold, the snow — had originated and where it could be leading and it scared the hell out of him. But the truth was, he was only guessing.

"It's August Nick," Stephy said. "I don't think that snow in August is... nothing."

"Well right now I'm more interested in what's up ahead," he said. He tried not to let his anxiety show in his voice but the fact was... this was unnerving. As he pulled up to within about fifty yards of the flashing lights he could see it was, in fact, some kind of roadblock. There were three cars ahead of him and the first car looked as if it were being searched. Stephy, normally as laid back and tough as they came, suddenly gripped Nick's leg, clearly anxious about a roadblock in the middle of *Nowhere-ville*, West Virginia... especially after the story he had spilled to her back at the coffee shop. He noticed he was gripping the steering wheel hard with both hands, his white knuckles shining in the red-blue glow of the flashing lights. His chest was pitched forward in the seat like an eighty-nine year old maneuvering through a jammed post office parking lot on a snowy Christmas Eve. He forced his muscles to relax. Inch by inch he slouched back slightly into his seat. He took one hand from the steering wheel and laid it on top of Stephy's hand which by now had tightened into a death grip on his thigh.

"This is so eerie after listening to that awful story about the graduation ceremony and the Olympus Project. This can't be... *it...* Phase II I mean, right?" She was whispering softly but Nick could still hear the tremor in her voice.

"Of course not, I'm sure it's only a prisoner escape or something," he tried to reassure her. "Martinsburg Correctional Center is pretty close... only about twenty minutes or so from the house. One of the minimum security guests probably strolled away from the facility."

"Comforting thought," Stephy said. "But all of this, for a dead beat dad or check kiter?"

Nick shrugged. "Let's wait and see. We'll find out what it is when we get up to the head of the line." He looked at Stephy and leaned over to give her a peck on the cheek. "It'll be fine." Then he turned back and watched the cars ahead of them. He didn't like this. He had better find out an escapee was on the loose because the alternative was too terrifying to contemplate.

He turned the windshield wipers to intermittent and softly tapped his finger on the steering wheel. Maybe he was reading too much into this. There had been checkpoints and roadblocks all over the country for years: Houston, Seattle, Boston... New Orleans. They were established for a short period and then shut down. Why should this be any different? On the surface these things usually turned out to be spot checks for DUIs, registration checks, or road closures for fires or maybe, as in this case, manhunts — if this *were* a manhunt. Was he rationalizing? He was starting to feel paranoid. Yes, what happened at the ceremony had gotten under his skin. He had never let his job get to him like this before. He was supposed to be on R&R. He needed to leave ROC issues back in Marietta and deal with them in two weeks when he returned to work. Why should he rile up his entire family and disrupt their lives with something that would probably turn out to be nothing — nothing involving civilians anyway.

It was true he had clearly been upset by the mayhem at the ceremony. He couldn't deny all kinds of emotions were roiling inside him. He was wired pretty tight. But he was also no doubt jumping the gun thinking the president had called up ROC forces. He only left the ceremony a few hours ago. Nothing would have happened that fast. He needed to pull himself together before he reached his parents' farm or he was going to turn his family into hand wringing paranoiacs. Besides, if ROC had been mobilized he would have been alerted by cell phone... wouldn't he? The car in front of his SUV drove off down the road and Nick was waved forward. He rolled up to the state cop and powered down his window.

"Shut off your engine and exit your vehicle sir," the police officer said.

"What's this about officer?" Nick asked as he stepped from the car and closed his door. Another state cop walked around the SUV shining a flashlight into the interior.

"Nothing to worry about sir... license please," the officer said. Nick reached into his back pocket for his wallet and removed his license.

"Is this your vehicle?" the officer asked.

"Rental," Nick replied.

"Where are you headed Mr.... Fizer?" the cop asked, shining his flashlight on Nick's license.

"Up the road about ten miles," Nick answered, "... My parents' farm in Shepherdstown."

The policeman eyed Nick as if he were a maggot crawling out from a dung heap. "Farm... a working farm?" the cop inquired.

Nick frowned. This cop was damned annoying. "Yeah... it's small... but a working farm. Is there a problem?"

The state cop scowled. "I'll need to see your vehicle paperwork."

Nick turned toward the SUV and leaned in the window. Stephy was already reaching across the seat with the rental papers.

"What's going on Nick?" she whispered. Nick shrugged and took the papers from her. He handed them to the cop.

"What's going...?" Nick started to ask.

"Wait here," the officer ordered. Nick sighed. He leaned his back against the SUV. It was cold. Wet snowflakes landed in his hair and on his eyelashes. He shivered. He leaned on the car door, crossed his legs and slid his hands into his pockets. He watched the officer take the papers to one of the state police cars parked on the left side of the road. There were five uniformed state cops milling around and six cars that Nick could see. Three of the cars were clearly marked state police. Two of them sat perpendicular to the road at ninety-degree angles, one on each side of the yellow line, about a car length or so apart with sufficient space between the front ends to weave a car through. Two other cars — unmarked dark sedans — were parked about twenty yards ahead, one on each side of the road. Nick couldn't tell what agency they were. The last vehicle was a large black windowless van parked in front of one of the dark sedans. Nick thought he could make out figures inside the dark cars but he wasn't sure.

It was snowing in earnest now. He looked straight up into the sky like he used to do as a kid. It made him dizzy and he felt almost as if he were traveling in space, whizzing by a million stars. Nick chuckled. Kid's imaginations, he thought. How easily he had amused himself as a child. It was too dark to play that game and anyway, he was growing impatient. He was trying to decide whether to reach into the back of the SUV and grab his jacket when he saw the officer approaching him. Nick took the papers as the cop held them out. "What's going on officer?" Nick asked.

"Just a spot check sir," the cop replied. He removed a small pad of paper from his top pocket. "I'll need the name and address of the farm you're headed for..."

"What? Why?" Nick frowned.

"Do you have a problem giving me that information?" The cop stared straight into Nick's eyes.

"Well, no, I suppose not..." Nick said. "But I think I have a right to know why you're asking me for that."

"Actually, you don't," the cop replied, readying his pen. "Name and address..." the officer said. Nick was tired. Stephy was anxious about the roadblock and the serious dose of reality he had just delivered. He was cold, and he wanted to be far away from there, sitting at his parents' kitchen table. Still, what in hell was this cop's agenda? Nick could lie and give some phony name and address. Or he could insist this guy tell him why he wanted that information. Maybe if he had been alone he might have taken that route. But it was late. Now he was growing concerned about his parents. Why was this cop so interested in his parents' small farm? How could this state cop possibly find this information interesting? If Nick had learned anything in his twenty-two years of military service he had learned there was a reason for everything. Someone — somewhere — always had an agenda.

"Mr. Fizer," the cop was clearly getting impatient. "Are you going to give me that name and address?"

"Not to be obstinate officer," Nick said. "But if I decline to supply a name and address, what are the consequences?"

The cop dropped his hands to his sides. "You don't have to give me the information I'm requesting," the cop said. "But if you... decline... as you say, I'm afraid I will have to regard your action as uncooperative, obstructive and suspicious... and..."

"... And?" Nick interjected.

"... And we will need to continue this conversation elsewhere," the officer said... "It's your choice." Nick squinted disparagingly at the cop. *My choice...* Nick thought. What a sonofabitch. The cop stared blankly at Nick. Suddenly, Nick felt like he'd been kicked in the gut by a horse. How long had this so-called checkpoint been in place? Had his parents had to deal with this? Were they in some kind of trouble? Nick hadn't spoken with them since last week. Had something happened since then? Nick no longer gave a crap about this checkpoint. He gave a crap about one thing... his parents.

"William and Julia Fizer, Blueberry Hill Way, Route 7, Shepherdstown," Nick said. The state cop repeated the name and address and Nick confirmed. The cop placed his notepad back into his pocket.

"Thank you Mr. Fizer," the cop said. "You may continue on your way."

"It's *Colonel* Fizer," Nick corrected him as he flung

open the door of the SUV. The officer stared at him blankly. Nick wasn't sure why he felt it necessary to add reference to his rank. It could have sparked an entire new round of questions. That was a pretty lame thing to do. Still, the guy was plain rude and Nick didn't like being shoved into a corner by a condescending narcissist with a loaded gun. He climbed back into the SUV, put up the window and started the engine. He looked once more at the state cop, who nodded. Nick put the car in gear and then drove off toward his parents' farm. He drove slowly until he was out of sight of the roadblock. Around the first bend, he brought the SUV up to five miles over the speed limit, then ten... then fifteen. Snow was accumulating on the corners and at the bottom of the windshield where the wipers didn't reach. Nick listened to the *slap... slap...* of the wiper blades as he drove.

"What was that all about?" Stephy asked. "Was it an escapee? Were they looking for someone?"

"I don't know," Nick said. "He wouldn't say. I had to give him my father's name and address. Seems the word 'farm' piqued his interest."

"Huh?" Stephy asked.

Nick shrugged and shook his head. "I don't know. It was strange. All I want to do is get to the house."

"Well..." Stephy said. "Let's get there in one piece."

"Sorry," Nick mumbled, glancing at the speedometer. He quickly let up on the gas. Stephy was right. He had been going far too fast for this winding country lane and the snow was starting to stick to the road surface.

"Take it easy Nick," Stephy said softly. "I'm sure they're fine."

"I know," he agreed. "I'm sure they are." But this business about the farm, Nick thought, couldn't be good.

❈❈❈❈❈

ROC Northwest Takotna, Alaska, August

The tall MP stared at Malikov. Malikov glared back from his bolted iron chair, his cuffed hands folded in front of him on the metal table. The shorter MP rustled through the papers in the folder. The clock ticked away the minutes in monotonously incessant, rhythmic intervals. Twice now, in the last twenty minutes, Malikov's thoughts started to randomly drift in strange cadence with the patterned ticking of the clock. It was tempting to revert back to his chanting to escape his present dire circumstances as he had when he sat in that Russian police station after his mother's death. The allure to shelter himself within the appealing melodic descant felt as strong to Malikov as any narcotic addiction. He bit his lip, hard, until he had pulled himself back to reality. He was here, in this insipid, boiling hot room, sitting across from two MP goons — fools — Malikov thought. He would not succumb to his urge to escape this madness as he normally would. He was not a coward and he would not retreat behind his imaginary opus veil.

Malikov had been arrested — or rather, detained — and there wasn't much he could do about that now. Yet he could play their stupid game.

"Give me your full name," the short MP ordered.

Malikov frowned. "MP know name," Malikov complained.

"I don't give a damn," the MP said. "Answer the question."

"Pavel Aleksandrovich Malikov," Malikov obeyed. He answered robotically. As the MP fired his set of routine questions at Malikov, the answers to which the MP already had in the folder before him, Malikov went along with their mindless interrogation. It *was* a game, he thought. They will torment him, treat him like shit, try to scare him, and then they will send him back to his room with a slap on his hand. That's the way these MPs worked, he thought. Stupid *Amerikantsy,* Malikov told himself. Okay, he will let them have their fun. But he will be back in B Sector by supper. Then he and Sergei will go to Sergei's room and have vodka and a good laugh. But Malikov wasn't going to forget. He would not forget these stupid American bullies. Malikov looked at the nametags on the chest pockets of these vile MPs and he committed their names to memory. He would not forget them.

"Who are you working with?" the short MP questioned.

"*Vhat eece deece?*" Malikov was unprepared for the question. "*Vork...* U.N... *vhy* MP say *deece?*"

"Who put you up to this?" the MP asked. "Answer me dammit!"

"*Vhat...* up to?" Malikov was confused.

"Who put you up to sabotaging FOLT security?" the MP asked. "Who are you working with?"

"*Ny... et, Nyet*" Malikov stammered. "Sensor *eece* defect. *Nyet!* No *vork* someone. Am U.N... Russian Federation Army."

"Says here you got a bad temper Malikov," the MP said, switching topics. "Says you have no friends... can't get along. That right? You got a bad temper?"

"*Vhat eece deece?* Thirty years... soldier," Malikov said indignantly. "Sergei *eece* comrade," he mumbled.

The MP shook his head, "Not what it says here Chief. Says here you got a bad temper and you don't get along." Malikov strained to see the papers across the desk. He couldn't make out a single letter at that angle.

"Says here, you can't control your temper... says you're violent." The MP angled his head to the side and curled his lips into a despicable smile. "Says here you like to play with knives... you like to play with knives Malikov?"

"*Nyet*... knives," Malikov argued, "*Nyet*, no truth."

"Oh?" the short MP inquired. "It says here you and an MP had ago-round in the B Sector mess hall. A witness says you assaulted the MP."

"*Vhat?*" Malikov scowled. "Who say *deece theengs*? *Nyet!*"

"You were seen..." The tall MP said, "... In the mess hall... by a roomful of witnesses."

Malikov remained silent, staring at the MPs.

"We have statements from witnesses," the tall MP added, pointing to the folder. "You threatened the MP... spit food at him... pulled a knife."

"*Nyet*..." Malikov growled, "MP drunk... *Nyet, nyet* truth."

The shorter MP shook his head. "What then... is it the booze Chief?"

"You got a drinking problem..." the tall MP said, shaking his head.

"Too much '*wodka*,' Malikov?" the short MP mocked Malikov's accent. "Isn't that what drunks do... blame everyone else? You were drunk so you claim the other guy is drunk."

"Right," the taller MP said. "You're the one with the flask in his pocket."

Malikov sat staunchly quiet, his face pale. He glared across the table at the MP's crooked sneer.

"You're in deep shit here Chief," The tall MP said indifferently. "Deep shit..."

"He's right you know," the short MP agreed. "You are in some very deep shit."

"*Nyet sheet,*" Malikov said, consciously trying to slow his breathing and heart rate, drawing from deep inside himself to summon a mask of outward indifference... like Aleksi could do. "*Vhat sheet* MP say? *Leetle* vodka... *Deece* defect sensor. *Nyet, nyet...* no *sheet,*" Malikov contended.

"What he means, you little red commie," the tall MP said, standing, again leaning in toward Malikov with his palms flat on the table, "... Is that you best wipe that smirk off your face. Because early this morning we found an MP, one of our own brotherhood, by the name of Sergeant Eric Booner dead with a knife sticking out of his chest..."

"And the word is, you little bastard," the shorter MP boomed, jumping to his feet, lunging across the desk and grabbing a hefty fistful of Malikov's shirt, "... Word is, you sonofabitch, you're the guy that put it there."

❄❄❄❄❄

Chapter 13

Takotna, Alaska, August

The trek to the creek for water seemed longer and more difficult than usual. Despite the brutal winds and freezing cold Miriam was sweating. She drove the head of the shovel deep down into the snow and hoped it was wedged tight enough to withstand the wind gusts. She did not want to be digging for a lost shovel. If it were blown over it could quickly become buried in the drifts. Now that she had cleared the snow she was ready to cut through what she hoped was only a thin layer of ice on the creek. She took aim with the long chisel and rhythmically stabbed six or seven times, then rested and repeated the cycle. The trick was to let the chisel do the work when chopping through ice and use her strength only to lift the tool.

Miriam's ice chisel was a solid iron pole, five-feet long with a leather wrist strap and a sharp flattened tip that her Henry Ivan had used since he was a boy. It was heavy. A newer hand auger might have been less cumbersome but Miriam thought the chisel to be more reliable and easier for her to maneuver... something about the angle of muscle force she needed to apply. But the truth was... Henry's chisel was the tool she had and that's what she used.

While she had readily chopped through ice many times before she was not at peak strength right now. The biting cold, the relentless winds... her lack of sleep and the stress from Kyle's condition all weakened her. But she faced greater dangers than her own weariness. In weather as severe as this storm, frostbite could occur within seconds of exposure of bare flesh to the cold. She did not worry too much about this because only a small area of her face remained uncovered by her hood and homemade balaclava. Her clothing protected the rest of her from the elements. But hypothermia was still a threat, as menacing as a wolf tracking an injured caribou. It was nearly impossible to stay dry while working. The exertion caused her to perspire and left her clothes and her skin damp. Because water conducts heat away from the body twenty-five times faster than air — due to its greater density — heat loss through the pores in her skin was a constant threat. She could not remain outside — exposed to such conditions — and continue to overexert herself for too long. The temperature remained steady at around fifty degrees below zero. Chopping ice in the subzero cold... even though the creek ice was thin... required Miriam to exert double the effort. But when it came to providing for Kenzie and Kyle her will was fierce. She couldn't give up just because she was cold or fatigued or because she wished she still had her Henry Ivan around to do the heavy labor. Miriam faced risks each day in Takotna. Manual labor and danger were simply part of life.

She was weary from working on the bear, making repairs, worrying about Kyle and carving a path in the snow to get down to the creek. Still, she was grateful. Because the creek water was in perpetual motion — flowing downhill toward the Takotna River — and because the cold weather had been of short duration the ice layer was thin. It was probably far less than three inches thick. Had it been January or February, she may not have had the strength to break through a foot of creek ice. After ten to twelve cycles of chipping away at the ice with the chisel, water bubbled to the surface through the small hole. She had continually checked the leather strap as she worked to ensure it was secure around her wrist. While the creek depth varied from a mere four to six feet, if she lost her grip the chisel could slip into the hole, be driven sideways by the current and wrenched from her grasp. She would be unable to retrieve it until spring.

She chipped away at the small hole until it was wide enough to dip in the metal ladle and fill the two buckets. It would take at least two trips to get the full buckets and her tools back to the cabin. She took the buckets first, trying not to lose too much to spillage. She walked a few feet, stopped and set them down and reached out her hand to ensure the safety rope was to her right. Then she picked up the buckets and continued forward a few feet, repeating the same sequence back up the incline to the cabin. It was not a monumental task but it was tedious and slow. Knowing how desperately they needed the water was impetus enough to keep Miriam's feet heading forward.

When it first began to snow Miriam had strung a rope between two tall pines from the cabin down to the creek. She did this every year. It didn't matter how well she knew the woods, it was insanity to venture into a blinding snowstorm without using this lifeline. She could become disoriented and stranded in a blizzard in only a few seconds. In Alaska there were thousands of different ways to die out in the bush. The environment was unforgiving. Miriam tried to foresee and prevent as many hazards as possible. If taking a few extra minutes to string a rope would help decrease risks it was worth the effort. She had already miscalculated twice in the past two weeks. She should not have presumed the storm would die out quickly and she should never have delayed repairing the siding. Her misjudgments could be costly.

After she had transported the water to the cabin, she set the buckets down outside the door and headed back to the creek to retrieve the chisel, metal ladles and the shovel. When she had completed the last trip to the creek and returned to the cabin she set the tools down and opened the front door. She put the buckets inside the door one by one, brought in the shovel, ladles and the chisel and stood them up in the corner. She wanted these tools close. In a dire emergency she could melt snow on the woodstove. But while heating snow would provide them water in a crisis, it took a lot of snowmelt to fill a bucket. The tools were vital to their survival. The importance of safeguarding the few material items she possessed had been ingrained in her since childhood. In a world where self-reliance was the only means to survival, every possession was more valuable than an Alaskan gold nugget.

She was cold and exhausted but satisfied that she had been able to do what she had set out to do. Because she had used additional water to clean up the mess from the bear, she knew she would soon need to trek back to the creek for water. But the next trip would not be so tiring. The hike back would be easier now that she had established a rough trail through the drifts. There would be far less accumulated snow to move out of the way on the path and a thinner layer of ice to break through. As she closed the front door, Kenzie scurried over to help her with her coat and boots.

"Is that hot chocolate I smell?" Miriam asked her. Kenzie nodded.

"And coffee?" Kenzie grinned and nodded briskly.

"What is it Kenzie?" Miriam probed. But Kenzie, continuing to grin, didn't answer. After she draped Miriam's coat over the back of the kitchen chair to dry and Miriam had removed her mittens and boots, Kenzie slipped her hand into Miriam's and brought her into the living room. There, Miriam's weary gaze fell upon Kyle, propped up with pillows on the sofa and smiling weakly. She hurried to him and sunk to her knees. She hugged him and then kissed his forehead. She reached out for Kenzie's hand and gently pulled her down next to the couch. She hugged them both and held on tightly.

"Don't cry mama," Kyle whispered hoarsely. Yet Miriam had no power this time to stop the wet tears from sliding down her cheeks as magnificent waves of relief and joy washed over her. She had prayed for a miracle and it seemed God had answered her prayers.

❊❊❊❊❊

ROC East HQ, Route 2 Templeton, Massachusetts, August

Falcon drummed a silent finger on his knee as he sat in the general's outer office. He stared blankly at page thirty-two of an old Smithsonian magazine that lay open on his lap. It was the same page he had stared at for almost half an hour. In the back of his mind he knew he was wasting a perfectly good opportunity to engage Major Meg Winters, seated barely two feet from him, in some significant small talk. But his initial annoyance with the general's blatant disregard for him had pushed the right buttons. He was consumed by bitterness and his anger was now a colossal distraction for him. An additional twenty-three minutes had passed since Benton had entered the general's office. This was not what Falcon would call an encouraging first encounter with his new commander.

If this were an indication of what was to come Falcon was pretty sure he and General Hazkill were headed for some cataclysmic head butting. The general's treatment of him had not been the auspicious start to his military career he had imagined. Falcon had been waiting twenty-five minutes in addition to the thirty-five he had initially waited. Worse... the general had passed him over dismissively and given his own scheduled appointment to a lower ranking officer. This was unacceptable. Falcon had rarely been inclined to act on impulse but the longer he sat in that waiting room, the more upset he became. The more upset he became, the stronger his urge to tell the general to go to hell. The vision of flipping off the entire ROC program and walking out the door was looking sweeter by the minute.

"Where are you from Colonel?" Meg asked.

"Oh..." Falcon said, startled by the sudden break in silence. "Uh... New England," he answered, turning his full attention to her. "I grew up in a very small town not far from here. What about you?"

"Portland, Oregon," she said, smiling. "Do you still have family here?"

"One aunt," Falcon said. "At least she lived here two years ago."

"Right," Meg laughed. "I guess we all have some catching up to do."

"Two years is a long time," he agreed.

"Colonel..." Meg began.

"Please call me Falcon," he said. "I'm not at all used to these yet," he laughed, tapping his shoulder board.

"Okay..." Meg said. Her eyes sparkled in perfect harmony with her warm smile. But she paused before saying more, looking at Falcon as if she were debating how to tiptoe across a wet floor without getting her feet wet.

"Ah... you're probably wondering about my name," he said, nodding. Her puzzled expression was a typical reaction... one he encountered often when meeting someone for the first time.

"Well kind of..." she blushed. "I'm sorry," she added. "It's..."

"Unusual," he said, completing her sentence. "There's no valid explanation," he told her, shrugging. "My parents liked birds I guess."

Meg laughed. "Well I love it," she said, smiling broadly.

"Thank you," he chuckled, feeling a slight rosy flush warm his face. "So what about you?" he asked, changing the subject. "Do you have family in Oregon?"

"No," she answered. "My parents passed away a few years ago and unfortunately I was the only child of two only children."

"I'm sorry to hear that," he said. "Well... I don't have much family either. My mother was an only child but my father had one sister, my aunt, and a brother who passed away. I do have a great uncle though," he added. He realized his brow had narrowed slightly when his Uncle Caleb popped into his mind. His uncle was never far from his conscience.

"Is he still here?" she asked. "I mean... in New England?"

"No, he bought a farm in the Midwest a number of years ago. He still lives there... er at least he did two years ago. He was pretty old," Falcon added. "He was in his early eighties but still... we were quite close. We kept in touch, albeit by phone, until I started ROC training of course."

"You should look him up," she said. "I bet he would be happy to hear from you. He would certainly be proud... of your accomplishments I mean." Falcon nodded, knowing already that he liked Meg.

"Yes he probably would like to hear from me," he agreed. He found this genuine caring side to Meg attractive. He was suddenly eager to learn more. The general's office door swung open. He, Meg and the captain stood as Benton and the general emerged. Falcon watched the general's left palm resting with odd familiarity on Benton's shoulder. Cozy already, Falcon thought, Benton moves damn fast.

"Now don't be late," the general told Benton, slapping his shoulder twice and then shaking the major's hand. "1900 hours sharp tonight."

"I won't be late general," Benton told him, flashing his serpent grin over slightly protruding, pearly white teeth. "Thank you again sir," Benton added as the two parted. Benton walked over to Falcon with an extended hand. "Again... nice to see you Colonel," Benton said. Then Benton turned toward Meg. "See you at dinner Meg," Benton told her. He clicked his heels together and kissed her hand with pretentiously noble — and overly presumptive — exaggeration very much as a Transylvanian count with a long cape and stiff collar might do. What was that all about? Falcon wondered, quickly becoming more suspicious of Benton's motives. Benton was overly familiar with Meg. It wasn't appropriate and clearly he was out of line. Unless... unless the implications of his comment, "*See you at dinner,*" was an indication that Meg and Benton were involved. Sonofabitch, he thought.

While it was true that Benton may have known Meg at ROC training, he would have had little to no opportunity to ingratiate himself to her there. The ROC training protocol forbid all distractions. Dating fellow officers was a prohibited distraction. Intimate or romantic relationships between officer candidates would have triggered immediate dismissal from ROC and discharge from the military. So if Benton and Meg were involved they were either more successful at secrecy than the National Security Agency and had engaged in something at ROC training or Benton made his move within the last twenty-four hours. Falcon tried to evaluate Meg's body language and facial expression to gauge her reaction to Benton but Falcon's intuition failed him... presuming he had any in the first place.

"Colonel Colby," the general said sternly, indicating with stiff sweeping arm that Falcon should enter his office. Falcon was annoyed. Suddenly he had little interest in meeting with this rude general. He didn't feel comfortable leaving Benton alone with Meg. Benton had bid her goodbye yet he was hanging around. Why hadn't he left? And what was this dinner he flaunted... a cozy dinner for two? Was that it?

Falcon had seen for himself over the last two years what a manipulative narcissist Benton was. In every instance Falcon had observed him... Benton never failed to wriggle his way to the center of the room to try to exert some measure of control over almost every situation and any superior officer he encountered. The worst part was, these supposedly model leaders at ROC training never seemed to notice Benton's manipulation. In Falcon's estimation Benton was clearly an opportunist — the most treacherous sort of predator — a passive aggressive *player*. Benton was a deceptively polite bully. At training, Falcon and Whitehawk had readily agreed that Benton was a guy to avoid. Falcon thought the man was clearly fueled by some deep delusions of grandeur which, Falcon could plainly see, Benton expertly concealed behind a charming outer façade. Benton knew the right angles and the perfect words to use when he wanted to impress senior officers... and beautiful women it seemed. Benton was a slimy serpent. The only person Benton would ever love would be Benton himself. Falcon could feel his muscles tensing by the second. The general expected Falcon to jump... now... which of course he was obligated to do. But Falcon felt an overwhelming need to stay by Meg's side until he could warn her about Benton. He sensed Meg was far too genuine and compassionate to recognize Benton's toxic behavior and far too polite to mention it if she had. Falcon had no basis to make this presumption of course. He barely knew Meg. Maybe his double promotion to full bird had swelled his head some... or maybe, deep down, Falcon fancied himself as a knight in shining armor. His concerns about Benton were palpable.

Regrettably, Falcon had no choice but to allow himself to be ushered into Hazkill's office. When a general said jump, if an officer didn't ask the traditional, *how high*, his career could go south fast. Falcon nodded — dutifully — to Hazkill as he stepped into the general's office. But Falcon turned back toward the waiting room before the general closed the office door. As he glared at Benton for an instant — a split second — he felt an overwhelming urge to beat the crap out of the man.

❀❀❀❀❀

Fizer farm Shepherdstown, West Virginia, August

Nick swung the SUV onto the gravel driveway of his parents' farmhouse and shut down the engine. The silence from the West Virginia countryside engulfed the car. It had stopped snowing but it was still cold for an August night. The porch light from his boyhood home was burning brightly. Strings of blue Christmas lights climbed — in barber pole fashion — up the two large columns framing the front entrance of the house. It was not unusual that Christmas lights adorned the outside of his parents' home in August. Now that his father was older he didn't see much sense in taking down Christmas lights only to have to string them back up in the same place a few months later. The fact that the lights were on at this time of year however *was* unusual. Nick presumed it was likely his mother had lit them to lend a festive atmosphere to their visit.

Nick was a little nervous, or maybe eagerly anxious was a better description of the feeling that was jumping around inside him. He was usually as excited as a schoolboy at the start of summer vacation whenever he managed some R&R with his parents. A boyhood wistfulness would wash over him as soon as he laid out the plans for a visit. Then, when he set foot on the farm the sights, the sounds and dreams of his youth all came rushing back to him in one massive tidal wave... jacking up his heart rate. But this time was different. His enthusiasm was dampened by the events of the last twenty-four hours and the boiling over of doubts he had kept to himself for two years.

The serious questions about the Olympus Project — and ROC itself — rattled around in Nick's head. He knew he would have hours of soul-searching ahead of him. Then too the commotion ten miles up the road with the state police and whatever other agency goons had been sitting in those unmarked vehicles had unraveled him. The fact that such a thing was happening in his parents' back yard was unsettling. He might as well add concern for the well-being of his mother and father to his growing list of things to worry about.

"Nick," Stephy said softly. "Something seems... different here."

"How so?" Nick queried, loosening his grip on the

door handle. He was about to spring open the car door but stopped himself. He didn't want to appear impatient or disinterested in what Stephy had on her mind. He simply felt a growing urgency to get into the house... to see for himself that his parents were okay.

"I'm not sure... exactly," Stephy said. "But something... something seems... different."

"Don't let the Christmas lights throw you," he chuckled. "I know it's confusing but no one truly thinks it's Christmas. Life's just a little slower in Shepherdstown. See... in D.C. people would say it's only four months until Christmas. In Shepherdstown we say... it's only been what eight months since December twenty-fifth? It depends on how you view the world"

Stephy ignored him. "Don't you feel it too?" she asked. She was twisting and turning in her seat, peering out the window into the darkness and fidgeting as if she were sitting on a bad case of poison ivy.

"Feel what?" Nick probed, hesitating. He stared into the night with no idea what he was supposed to be seeing. "Not much beyond the window except darkness," he said. "I can't see anything beyond the arc of light from the porch bulb."

"I don't know. I can't put my finger on it... not really," Stephy whispered. "It's... it's like emptiness... like there's a void... as if... as if something is... is missing." She heaved a sigh. "I don't know. It's silly and I can't explain it."

Nick shrugged. "Well let's go inside," he said, "That chaos back there with the cops probably got under your skin. You'll feel better once you're in the house."

Stephy nodded. "You're probably right," she agreed. "It did unravel me a little."

"Don't worry about the bags," Nick said, "I'll come back for them after we see Mom and Pop." Stephy nodded and they exited the car. They trekked up the wet stone walkway arm in arm.

"They might be asleep you know," Stephy said. "It's late. We should be quiet until we know whether they're awake."

"Of course they're awake," Nick assured her. "We haven't been home in two years. Take my word for it. They're up." Then, as if someone had bellowed, "Action!" the front door swung open. In an instant Stephy, Nick and Nick's parents showered one another in spirited hugs and kisses. Nick and his father embraced and slapped each other fondly on the back.

"Brrr..." Nick's mother said, crossing her arms and seeming to hug herself. "Let's get inside. It's cold out here."

"Where are your bags Nick?" his father asked. "Are they in the car? Let me get them for you."

"No... no Pop," Nick answered quickly. "Leave them. I'll go back out later. Let's visit for a while first. I haven't seen you for two years."

"Sure... sure," Nick's father said, grinning. "Come on in... decaf is already cooking. Let me take your coats."

"How was your trip Stephy?" Nick's mother, Julia, asked. "You must be tired."

"Oh the trip was fine," Stephy answered. "I'm not at all tired. It's exciting to be on vacation," she added playfully, whispering like a teenager at a sleepover. "It's been a while."

"Well it's lovely," Nick's mother said. "Spur of the moment visits are wonderful!"

"Well it was a little tough to get a last minute flight but we were lucky," Stephy said. "A cancellation came in while I was on the phone with the reservation desk and the woman gave me two adjoining seats on the spot."

"I'm glad it worked out," Nick's father said. "There

would have been no living with Julia if you weren't able to catch a flight tonight. As soon as she heard you two were coming she revved herself up into fast forward."

"As usual," Nick added, laughing.

"Yup," Nick's father said. "Baking, cooking, cleaning... you name it. She could make a marine drill sergeant blush with shame the way she pulls everything together at a minute's notice."

"All right you two," Nick's mother chuckled. "That'll be enough of that!"

"The house looks beautiful Julia," Stephy told Nick's mother, winking.

"Thank you Stephy. You're sweet to say so," Nick's mother said. "Why don't you get settled in the kitchen and I'll get the coffee."

"And cinnamon rolls," Nick's father interjected.

"And cinnamon rolls," his mother repeated.

They all strolled into the huge country kitchen. Stephy, Nick and his father took seats around the long thick pine table while Nick's mother busied herself at the counter pouring hot coffee and drizzling icing on the steaming cinnamon rolls.

"Can't I help you Julia?" Stephy asked, starting to rise from her chair.

"No... you sit and relax," Nick's mother said. "I'm almost done."

Nick looked at Stephy and shrugged.

"I'll holler if I need rescuing," his mother added lightheartedly.

"Okay," Stephy said. "As long as you promise to speak up when you're ready for help, I'll wait for smoke signals."

Nick's mother laughed.

"She's more stubborn than a..." Nick's father started to say.

"William Fizer!" Nick's mother scolded in mock anger. "Don't you dare compare me to a mule!"

Nick's father smiled, feigning the sullen expression of a husband who had landed himself in the doghouse. He tapped his daughter-in-law on the arm and whispered to her. "You stay put. I'll give her a hand before she makes me sleep in the garage," he added mischievously.

Nick glanced around the kitchen. Few things had changed in the two years since he and Stephy had last visited. He would have been disappointed if they had. Coming home after a long absence was comfortably predictable. Nick suspected all children forged similar sentimental attachments to their youth... at least the kids whose childhood memories didn't transform into adult nightmares. He studied his parents as they stood at the kitchen counter preparing the coffee and dessert. They were whispering about something but Nick couldn't make out what they were saying. He heard the word farm once or twice and thought... well... he thought he heard something about the USDA but that made no sense. His mother and father were mom and pop farmers. Talking about the USDA would make no sense except maybe in reference to agriculture regulations. It was probably nothing. Nick had no doubt he had heard wrong anyway. He dismissed it and chastised himself for his shoddy attempt at eavesdropping.

This was his parents' home, Nick told himself, his parents' kitchen. They had every right to whisper about anything they damn well pleased without him sticking his nose... or in this case his ears... into their business. He shouldn't be trying to overhear whatever secrets they shared together. He did enough of that as a kid. He should be content to enjoy their company. He should be concentrating on the joy of having them close. As he watched his mother and father working at the counter Nick suddenly realized they both looked much thinner, more frail and vulnerable than he had remembered. Were his eyes playing tricks on him? It hadn't been that long of a trip — fifty minutes or so from the airport. An hour's worth of drive time certainly wouldn't have been sufficient to skew his perceptions. Yet... something was bothering him. When had Mr. and Mrs. William Fizer grown so old?

Well, he thought, it happens. Except... it should be happening to other people's parents. But he felt blessed to still have his mom and pop with him no matter what their condition. But how much longer was he going to have his own parents around? What will happen if he spells out his concerns about the Olympus Project and ROC and the dangers he is sure are imminent? What if he terrifies his parents with this awful knowledge and it turns out they're too weak or too devastated to deal with it? What if he goes through all of the agony of describing the Olympus Project, ROC and the awful events at the ceremony and then his parents simply die in a year or two before anything hits the fan? He will have destroyed the serenity of their final years of life. He will have ruined everything for two of the three people he cares most for in the world and he will have done it — terrified them with these horrors — for nothing. Maybe telling them is exactly the wrong thing to do.

Nick looked toward Stephy and stared into her hazel eyes. He wanted her to tell him what he should do. But Nick found no answers in his wife's eyes. She smiled at him and seemed lost in her own thoughts. She looked relaxed... happy to be exactly where she was. Nick swiveled to the right in his chair so he could better watch the Fizer seniors work. His father rummaged in the cabinet for matching saucers to the coffee cups and transferred the rolls from the baking sheet to dishes. Nick asked himself how in hell he was going to figure this out. If he does decide to reveal everything how in God's name should he begin his story?

He asked himself these things over and over again until his parents were nearly finished at the counter. Nick stood. He took the cups and saucers and dishes of rolls that his mother passed to his father in assembly line fashion and they all settled back in at the table. Four pairs of hands fluttered about; the *chink* of spoons against saucers and cups was the only ripple in silence. They busied themselves adding sugar and milk to their cups, stirring their coffee, buttering their rolls, and arranging napkins on their laps. They all seemed hot on the trail of the same objective — completing these mundane tasks as fast as possible so they could catch up with each other's lives. As Nick added thick layers of butter to his cinnamon roll — a habit his mother hated — he tried to figure a plan in his head. Where should he start? When should he begin? How much should he say? He had a great jump on giving himself a doozy of a headache.

"You must be glad the two years are over son." Nick's father said.

"Definitely," Nick agreed.

"It was rough?" his father asked.

"A bit," Nick replied. "In some ways... there were some challenges."

"Where do you go from here Nick?" his mother queried. "Will you be transferred?"

Nick shrugged. "I think it's up in the air right now."

"Oh?" Nick's father queried.

"Are you thinking about retirement?" Nick's mother asked.

"Mostly I'm thinking I need to do some thinking

before I go back to Georgia," Nick chuckled. "But... but I have two weeks to do it." Nick tore tiny pieces from his cinnamon roll and half-focused on moving them around on his plate. "I'd rather hear about you guys," Nick said, looking up from his artwork. "How have things been going? I started to get a little worried when we ran across a road block a few miles down the road."

Nick's parents' looked at each other, not saying a word, not diverting their eyes even to blink and a heavy pall of uneasiness settled over all of them. Nick stopped *food doodling* all together and wiped his hands on his napkin. He peered at his parents. Nick was familiar with this eye-lock of theirs. He knew all of his parents' silent codes. Clearly they had something on their minds. This look was reserved for dire circumstances like deaths in the family and catastrophic financial crises.

"We thought about waiting Nick," his father began, "But I guess there's no sense to that. We've always tried to say things straight up to you..."

"Always..." his mother added.

"What's up?" Nick asked.

His parents remained quiet for another minute or two until his father spoke. "Well..." his father began. "We need to talk about something with both of you. Your mother and I have been going back and forth about this for a couple of months."

"We didn't plan to dump this on you the minute you walked in the door," his mother said. "But..."

"But it looks like we don't have much choice," his father interjected. "We don't have the option to wait a few days."

"Or a few hours..." his mother added.

"Right," his father agreed. "Or even a few hours."

Nick's brow rose. "What is it Pop? Mom?" Nick asked, racking his brain with a million different possible scenarios that would have brought his parents to this level of worry."

"You're not sick!" Stephy blurted out. "Is that it? Is one of you...?"

"No... no Stephy, it's not that," Nick's mother said. "Tell them William... before they imagine all sorts of things."

"Right..." Nick's father nodded. "I'm not going to drag this out. But it's going to sound crazy to you."

"But you know we're not crazy Nick," his mother said. Nick's father shot his wife the cut-off glance and pinched his lips together. This was his parents' signal for *keep-your-mouth-zipped and let me talk*. It was a nonverbal parental exchange that Nick knew well. When passed between his mother and father it was a given that Nick was to wait patiently until one of them resumed the discussion. Nick had figured out when he was a boy that the silence following the glances between his parents provided them a cool down moment. Most disagreements never even got a foothold. An anxious minute or two slipped by with the four of them chewing and drinking and fidgeting in silence. Finally Nick's father set down his coffee cup and looked up.

"It's about... we're," Nick's father started, paused, and then began over. "We're..."

"We're in trouble Nick," his mother completed Bill's thought.

"We're being watched," his father added.

"Watched?" Nick asked.

"We've been under surveillance," Nick's father explained.

"For months," his mother added.

"YOU?" You're under surveillance?" Nick asked, his voice an octave higher than normal. "Why? What's going on? What do you mean... you're being watched?" Nick's mother reached a shaking hand into her apron pocket and fished out a folded letter. She handed it across the table to Nick. As he opened it Stephy leaned toward him and read over his shoulder. When they had finished scanning the letter Nick and Stephy looked up at his parents.

"Is this some kind of joke?" Stephy asked them. Nick's mother shook her head.

"It's no joke Stephy," Nick's father said.

"Well, maybe it's simply a scare tactic," Nick suggested.

"It is that..." his father agreed, "Plenty scary. There are a couple of small farms around here being watched. The road block has been out there a few times."

"So you fight it," Nick stated flatly, shrugging.

"We have fought it," his mother said.

"For a year..." his father added. "The paperwork's been lost, misfiled, tied up in the courts and then..."

"And then flat out chucked," Nick's mother said.

"Thrown out of court," his father nodded in agreement.

"Dismissed," his mother said.

"How can they do this Nick?" his father asked. "Implement something like this... steal our property and our home?"

"It says here..." Stephy said, reading from the letter. "That your thirty acres has been reclassified as conservation land and you are ordered to vacate the premises. I don't understand this last line..." Stephy frowned. "Land density quota... what is a land density quota?"

"It's something about... well the town says there aren't enough people living here in our house... on our land," Nick's father said.

"Density quota is an urban planning tool under the

Smart Growth concept," Nick explained.

"Under the what growth?" Stephy sneered. "Everything this century is *smart:* Smartphones, smart goals, smart buses, smart cars... "

"Well you won't find *smart* government on that *smart* list," Nick's father complained.

"Smart growth is a way to compact a society into a smaller area to combat urban sprawl," Nick continued. "The government sells it as a method to accomplish a list of objectives: to decrease pollution by increasing use of public transportation, to improve health by encouraging walking and bicycle travel etc. It's part of the U.N. Agenda 21 plan."

"What's that?" Nick's father frowned.

"It's a so-called non-binding, voluntary action plan implemented by the United Nations in 1992," Nick answered. "It's basically the source of sustainable development."

"So why is the U.S. Government kicking me off my farm in America if this sustainable development stuff is a U.N. deal?" Nick's father asked testily.

"That's a pretty long story Pop," Nick told him. "I'll be happy to explain it more fully but right now I'm more concerned about your situation."

"I agree," Stephy said. "I want to know how the town can simply take your home like this." Stephy was incredulous. "Don't they have to pay you for your land?"

"Oh they offered to pay all right," Nick's mother said. "One twentieth of what it's worth."

"And relocation..." Nick's father added, "To some two hundred square foot hellhole of an apartment in the city."

"Micro-Apartment," Nick's mother added. "They call them Micro-Apartments."

"I don't care what the hell they call them," his father

said. "It's a Nazi Ghetto — Warsaw — all over again. They're corralling us like cattle... boxing us up and corralling us."

"I don't understand," Stephy said. "Is this eminent domain or something... Nick...?" Nick didn't answer. His stomach ached as if he had swallowed a bowl full of greasy rotted peppers. It all started to click: the ceremony, the timing... the urgency of the general's actions the minute the officers graduated. The implications were devastating. Then too, the checkpoint with the unmarked vehicles parked along the side of the road and the cop's attitude... the way the officer's interest piqued when he learned about the farm... all of this was more than unsettling.

"We're at the end of our rope Nick," his mother said.

"Well I still think you can fight this if you want to," Stephy said. "This is America... can't you refuse? You pay your taxes... you pay your bills. This is a little mom and pop farm!"

"We did refuse..." Nick's father said.

"Right off," his mother added. "A van full of USDA men in SWAT gear and rifles came around one Sunday last March in a snowstorm. Your father laughed when they told him what they wanted. He thought it was a joke."

"What happened then?" Stephy asked, sitting on the edge of the chair.

"Well we stopped laughing pretty fast... as soon as they showed us the warrant..." Nick's mother grumbled.

"They brought a warrant... to search your house?" Stephy blurted out scornfully. "What the hell were they looking for?"

"It was a pretext," Nick said. "They probably weren't looking for anything."

"What happened after they searched the house?"

Stephy asked.

"They searched the barn, the woodshed, the tool shed and the grounds," Nick's father answered.

"In a blizzard mind you," Nick's mother snarled.

"Then what happened?" Stephy prodded.

"That's when they told us we had to get off the land, relocate to the two hundred square foot box or somewhere else. Anywhere... as long as we left our home," Nick's father complained.

"Micro Apartment," Nick's mother corrected. "It's not a box."

"Micro Apartment," Nick's father grumbled.

"And then... after we refused..." Nick's mother said, her hands visibly shaking.

"What?" Nick said. "What happened after you refused?"

"They took the stock," his father said flatly, "And gave us the eviction notice."

"The cows?" Nick asked. "They took the cows?"

"The cows, the five pigs, the two horses and the goats... everything," his father said.

"Except my hens and..." his mother interjected.

"Right, except five chickens," his father interrupted. "They said our farmland was contaminated. They told us the animals were infected."

"They killed them all," his mother added softly.

"They killed them?" Stephy asked, snapping in disgust.

"Every last one of them," Nick's father protested. "No proof there was ever any contamination either. No evidence the animals were sick. No blood tests... nothing... they simply destroyed them."

"Except for my hens and..." Nick's mother muttered.

"Right," Nick's father agreed, "Except for the five chickens."

"Wait... what's with the five chickens?" Nick asked.

"Well, your mother said she'd be damned if they were going to take her favorite hens," Nick's father explained, "And you know how stubborn she can be once she gets something in her head."

"Four hens and a rooster Bill," Julia corrected. "It was four trio leiper hatch 40 crossed hens and my Golden Sebright rooster, Fuzzy.

"Right dear..." Nick's father nodded, "Like I said... five chickens. Anyway, she hid them."

"Where did she hide them?" Stephy asked. "I thought they had a warrant to search everything."

"Oh they did," answered Nick's father.

"So where did you hide them Mom?" Nick questioned.

"How did you manage to hide them without the SWAT troops seeing you Julia?" Stephy queried, frowning.

"That," Nick's father said, starting to laugh, "Was the funniest damn thing."

"Oh those SWAT baboons were so damn smug," Nick's mother tittered.

"What did you do Julia?" Stephy probed.

"She hid them in..." Nick's father chortled, his eyes watering profusely. "She hid them in the..." but his father couldn't continue.

"I hid them in the SWAT truck," Julia announced proudly.

"In the SWAT truck," Stephy repeated, instantly infected with the irony of it — her laughter rising out of control. "The SWAT truck!" she repeated, tears rolling down her cheeks.

"Well Mom..." Nick said, trying to maintain his composure. "How did they not see that?"

"Your father distracted them," his mother answered. "He set off a..." but Julia, seeing Stephy and Bill's loss of control, could not continue.

"I set off a cherry bomb," Nick's father blurted out. "And all at once the SWAT cops converged — running at me, tripping over their riot gear and each other — to find out what the hell the big bang was. And the animals went ballistic. They were upset at the noise and commotion and made a grand mess of the barn!"

"It *was* a little chaotic," Nick's mother interjected, sniggering.

"It was," his father laughed. "And while five guys on the SWAT team were occupied hollering at me, lecturing me about being a terrorist and threatening to take me to jail, all of the other cops were chasing the pigs and goats in circles inside the barn. While they were busy inside your mother was busy outside. I stood in the doorway watching out of the corner of my eye. I could see your mother running back and forth from the small chicken coop to the SWAT truck... a chicken under each arm, bundled in her parka, leaping through the drifts, her hair disheveled and full of snow. The chickens were struggling to get free and leaving a full trail of crap droppings along the way!" Tears streamed down Bill's face as his body shook with uncontrolled laughter. "Three trips... three trips! Back and forth..."

"But Pop... you're lucky they didn't shoot you when the cherry bomb went off!" Nick scolded him, not knowing whether to laugh or cry.

"Oh I know, I know!" his father agreed, nodding vigorously. "They drew their guns!"

"Oh my God!" Stephy exclaimed, horrified. "And how did you get the chickens out of the truck before they left?"

"I... I'm so embarrassed," his father said.

"What? What happened Pop?" Nick probed.

"Your father... uh... created another diversion," Julia

interjected, eyeing Bill.

"What?" Stephy pleaded. "Tell us."

"Well I only did this for Julia," his father confessed.

"After they finished searching the house," Nick's mother interrupted, "Bill stood in the barn doorway reciting the Constitution of the United States."

"He did? Well why would you be embarrassed about that Pop?" Nick asked, confused.

"Well," his mother jumped in, "He wanted them to think he was... you know... a little slow — so they wouldn't consider him dangerous — and he didn't think they would pay attention to him so..."

"So I stripped down to my underwear," his father said sheepishly.

"Pop!" Nick admonished him. "I thought you said they came during a snowstorm."

"They did," Nick's mother nodded. "It was twenty degrees."

"But you were very quick Julia," Nick's father added. "I got through Section 3 of Article I and it didn't seem all that cold."

"That was your adrenaline Bill," Julia chuckled.

"What did you do then... while Pop was orating in the barn in his jockey shorts?" Nick asked.

"I rounded up the chickens from the SWAT truck, ran them upstairs and locked them in the bathroom."

"It's so funny," Stephy said and they all agreed. "But not at all funny when you think about what was really happening," she added.

"Damn right Stephy," Nick's father said. "But you know, after battling the government for a year it didn't seem like much mattered anymore. We were an annoyance to them... bugs they were going to squash no matter what."

"Exactly," Julia agreed. "They didn't give a damn

that we devoted our lives to this farm. It wasn't a good feeling. We had no control over our own home... our possessions... our animals. They treated us like traitors or something. They were going to do what they were going to do, and that was that."

"Legal or not," Nick's father added. "They didn't even pretend they needed a good reason for any of it."

"They didn't even have the decency to leave the baled hay," Julia said. "All of your father's work for nothing."

"Nope," Bill said, "They destroyed it all. They told us everything was contaminated: feed, animals, everything." Nick's father sighed deeply. "This farm goes back in my family over one hundred twenty-five years," he mumbled. "All I know is farming."

"What kind of eminent domain law is this?" Stephy asked.

"It's not a taking under eminent domain," Nick said. "It's all done in the name of..."

"Sustainable development... safe farming or some damn thing," Nick's father said. "Only big processing plants know how to grow proper food — so I'm told. I think that's what their bottom line is. They want food production under government control or something."

"Yes," Nick agreed.

"But sustainable development is just... just recycling and caring for the trees and animals and... saving the country and energy for future generations," Stephy argued. "I thought sustainable development was a *good* thing. The causes seemed noble... so noble I felt guilty for days once when I threw out a yogurt container without recycling."

"We're supposed to think these things are noble," Nick's father said. "It's what I thought too: picking up trash, recycling cardboard and paper, cleaning up city streets, rotating crops, organic farming. But that's a joke. The politicians don't give a crap about this country. They only care about power.

"Well they certainly don't give a damn about farmers," Julia complained.

"That's exactly what I'm saying," Bill said hotly. "This government doesn't want safe pure food. They want control. The mega corporations *want* their GMO — genetically modified organisms — in our fields and on our tables. They want modified substandard genetic material on the market instead of natural food so they can introduce toxic substances into our diets and at the same time charge us an arm and a leg for our own poisoning." Bill wiped his forehead with his handkerchief. "They don't have any idea what that food will do to animals and plants in the long run..."

"Or to humans," Julia added.

"Damn," he sighed, "We're starting to sound paranoid."

Heavy silence settled over the Fizer kitchen like a dreary mountain fog rolling into the hollow on a gloomy morning. Nick got up and wandered to the window overlooking the side yard. He stared into the night, then up toward the stars, but it was too cloudy to see them. He flipped on the switch for the spotlight at the side of the house. The snow had stopped but Nick barely noticed. He looked down at his shoes lost in thought.

"One thing I'm pleased about," Nick's father said, smiling.

"What's that Bill?" Stephy asked.

"The truck," Nick's father chuckled. "I would like to have seen those goons' faces when they got back inside that shiny SWAT truck."

"What do you mean Bill?" Stephy asked.

Nick's mother laughed. "My hens are sensitive critters. When they're nervous, they are..."

"Prolific crappers!" Nick's father said, grinning.

This was a lot to digest, Nick thought. So many pieces were starting to fit together. He didn't see how he could possibly go back to ROC or any other military organization. Was he making a rash decision? Probably. He shifted his full attention outside the window to the ground bathed in the glow from the spotlight. He saw a large rectangular shaped depression in the grass.

"Pop," Nick said, gawking out the window.

"What is it son?" his father asked.

"Where's the barn Pop?" Nick asked. Stephy pushed her chair back, quickly padded over to the window and stood next to Nick. She peered out through the pane.

"Where's the barn Bill!" Stephy shrieked. "Julia? What happened to the barn?" She grilled Nick's mother. That was it, Nick thought. That's what had bothered Stephy when they drove up. She had said it felt like something was missing. But it was dark and she wouldn't have been able to see the barn from that angle. So how could she possibly have known it was gone? She had *felt it...* the instant Nick had turned into the driveway... she had *felt it.* Nick's eyes darted to his right. He watched Stephy as she stood next to him. She was looking toward his parents now with a searching, empathetic glare. How in hell had she known the barn was gone? Would he ever figure her out? Well... he wasn't about to let this weird episode pass without some discussion. But that would have to come later.

"Pop?" Nick repeated, turning to face his father. "What happened to the barn?"

His father cleared his throat. "Burned to the ground son," his father murmured. "USDA said it was contaminated.

❊❊❊❊❊

Chapter 14

❄❄❄❄❄

Adit 17 Perseverance Mine Juneau, Alaska, August

"Can you hear me?"

Is that you, Eagle? Look ... the fog is lifting. Do you see? The fog is rolling back out the Gastineau Channel just as you said it would.

"Viktor, Can you hear me?"

Wait... that is not your voice eagle. Eagle... where are you?
Whoosh... Whoosh... Whoosh...
Eagle! Yes! You have returned!
I cannot stay. You must no longer call on me.
But why, what have I done?
Whoosh... Whoosh... Whoosh... You must find your own way now. The fog is rolling out to sea. You must concentrate.
But I must know more. I need to talk with you. I must ask you about the equipment and... Kaats' bear wife.
You have the answers.
Okay then... then tell me if I'm right. The equipment — the piece of equipment with the name like another — you are speaking of ELF... right? Because... E... L... F spells ELF... like little elves. Am I right?
If you believe that is so.
Well that doesn't help. Tell me if the ELF Jammer is

the name of the equipment that's broken.

And... the other, what about Kaats' bear wife. Do you know why there is danger if she wakes?

Yes... maybe...

Tell me.

Well, all I can think of is... because when she awakens... soon the children will come. The bear cubs will come when she awakens and Kaats will be forced to fight for his life... am I right?

If you believe that is so.

Your riddles are exasperating!

Whoosh... Whoosh... Whoosh...

Stay... don't go!

I cannot stay.

Then I will go with you. Take me with you.

I cannot take you with me.

Take me! You must! You can't leave me here.

Whoosh... Whoosh... Whoosh...

Eagle!

The fog is rolling out to sea. Soon it will clear.

Stay with me!

I cannot. Yet I will not be far.

Where? Where will you go?

You know where.

On the bridge?

Whoosh... Whoosh... Whoosh...

Eagle! Please stay. Tell me why you sit on the utility pole at the Juneau-Douglas Bridge... I have to know!

"Viktor, come on buddy... Wake up."

Wait, I know that voice. But... that is not you, eagle! It's not your voice.

Whoosh... whoosh... whoosh...

Please! Please eagle... don't go. Take me with you!

"Viktor... wake up."

No, no! I don't want to wake up! Eagle... take me with you! Don't leave me!

I cannot. You must stay. You will see us there... on the bridge. Now, I must go. Whoosh... Whoosh... Whoosh...

Eagle... please don't leave.

Whoosh... Whoosh... Whoosh...

❀❀❀❀❀

Viktor tried to open his eyes, to move his head, but he was trapped. It was dark and he couldn't see. Something must be holding him. He couldn't move his arms or legs.

"Viktor, come on... wake up."

Viktor heard this voice clearly now. Yes... he knew this voice. He tried to ask where he was but he couldn't drive the words passed his lips.

"Viktor, you're going to be all right. Open your eyes. Come on buddy..."

Oh the warmth... the warmth. It is so good to be warm. Eagle... please come back...

❀❀❀❀❀

ROC East HQ, Route 2 Templeton, Massachusetts, August

"Sit down Colonel Colby," General H.B. Hazkill motioned. The general walked around his desk and sat in his soft brown button leather chair. He slipped a pair of gold-rimmed reading glasses over his ears and pushed them up tight to the bridge of his nose. He flipped open the front cover of a thin personnel folder on his desk. He let it remain there... open. He tapped the eraser end of his pencil on the desk, read for a few more seconds and then leaned back, elbows resting on the chair arms, now rotating the pencil between the thumb and forefingers of his hands. "Double promotion," he said, now peering over the top of his glasses that had slipped down his nose, "Major... promoted directly to full bird colonel."

"Yes sir," Falcon mumbled, somewhat embarrassed. He adjusted himself in the leather straight-backed chair at the front of the general's desk.

"Straight to full bird colonel," the general repeated, shaking his head. "Well now, that's quite a feat. What did you do to deserve that, save the president's life?" the general asked, sneering. "Singlehandedly stop World War III from starting?"

"No sir," Falcon laughed nervously, mumbling — trying not to feel the shame it seemed the general wanted him to feel. He swallowed. Was his shirt collar tightening around his neck? It was a creepy sensation and he felt a strong compulsion to slip his finger between his collar and his skin.

"Well," the general said, "Quite impressive."

"Uh... thank you sir," Falcon muttered.

"Yes sir," the general said, with emphasis on the 'sir', "Damned impressive." The general removed his reading glasses and placed them on his desk. He sat forward slowly, resting his arms in front of him on the desk and leaning toward Falcon. "Well Colonel Colby," the general said in a low voice. "Here's a news flash. This here is the *real* army. You may have been promoted to full bird down in Georgia at ROC training... but we don't play games up here. No sir, not on my watch we don't. As far as this double promotion goes, I want you to think about this... just because those birds are sitting on your shoulder right now, that's no guarantee they'll be sitting there in two weeks. I make the rules here at ROC Headquarters-East, and you would do well to remember that."

Falcon remained silent but that did little to diminish his defensiveness. Why was he under attack? What had he done? He felt like he'd been caught smoking in the boys bathroom. He glared directly into Hazkill's eyes. The general glowered right back. Hazkill's forehead was thickly furrowed with clearly etched lines that seemed more like permanent scarred flesh than folds of wrinkled skin. His bushy eyebrows, barely separated at the bridge of his nose, narrowed to a sharp 'V'. Neither man spoke for a full minute. Falcon watched the general's eye start to twitch. It was gratifying. He hoped he was the cause of it.

The general's hostility toward him was inexplicable and unexpected. Was this the way all new officers were treated in the *real* army? After all, he had been warned many times that training was not the *real* army. He had no idea how to deal with this general's aggression — or even if he should. Was it a test of some kind? What was it with these ROC generals and their stare down contests? First it was General Tucker with his half-crazed scowling at the trainees during the ROC graduation ceremony. That general may as well have sprayed them all with bullets... it probably would have been less intimidating than the sour glares he delivered. Then, lest he forget, what about Tucker's threats at the end of the ceremony... what were those intended to do?

General Hazkill picked up his pencil and put on his glasses. He skimmed the rest of Falcon's personnel record in silence. When he finished he closed the file and reached into a stack of manila envelopes piled high in the wire basket at the edge of his desk. He pulled out one folder with a red 'x' in the corner, and handed it to Falcon. "These are your orders," Hazkill said, shoving the envelope toward Falcon as if he had pulled it from a pile of garbage and couldn't wait to get rid of it. "You'll receive some briefings, sit in on some round table discussions and attend additional G-ROC — Global Regional Operations Command — conferences. Then..." the general said with a twisted smile and a sharp contemptuous edge to his voice... "Then you'll be transferred out of here in about two weeks."

"Out of here?" Falcon repeated hesitantly. "I presumed I would be posted here."

"You presumed wrong Colonel," the general said. "You'll go where ROC needs you."

"Oh... of course sir," Falcon reluctantly capitulated. "It's only... well I understood that following ROC graduation we would be sent directly to our duty station — at least that's what we were told at training."

The general smiled crookedly. "Your orders are being revised," he said.

"By whom sir?" Falcon asked.

The general peered over his glasses at Falcon and then stood slowly, ignoring Falcon's question. "Your first mandatory briefing is 1900 hours sharp tonight," the general said. "Don't be late. It's all in your packet."

"Yes sir," Falcon said. Clearly the meeting was over.

"You'll get your revised orders within the next two weeks. Now if there's nothing else..." the general said.

Falcon stuffed the envelope under his arm and rose to attention. "No sir."

"Good," the general said, "Dismissed." Falcon turned and left the general's office confused... embarrassed. He stepped into the waiting area and glanced around quickly. Benton was nowhere to be seen. Falcon walked over to Meg and she rose when she saw him.

"He's all yours Meg," Falcon said.

"That was quick," she commented. "What's he like?"

Falcon smiled and thought for a moment. "Like a general," he said, thrusting out his hand. "It was nice officially meeting you today, Meg"

Meg smiled broadly, and shook Falcon's hand. "Same here," she said warmly.

"I hope to see you again soon," Falcon said. "Maybe we could have coffee... er... or ... dinner some night?"

"I'd like that," she said. "By the way did the general say anything to you about a briefing at 1900 hours tonight?"

"He did," Falcon answered.

"Well then," she said, "I will see you there."

Falcon's brow rose.

"Oh," Meg laughed, "Major Benton told me about it."

"Right," Falcon said, nodding. "Well..." he added, stumbling over his words, "Uh... maybe we could go together..."

"Oh I'm sorry," Meg began, "Colonel..."

"Falcon," he said. "Please call me Falcon."

"Sorry..." she corrected herself, laughing awkwardly. "I mean, Falcon. Major Benton already asked me. He's planning on swinging by my apartment to escort me," Meg said. "We could all go together if you could meet us."

"Well I'd love to," Falcon said. "But I have some things I should take care of anyway." Hearing Benton's name from Meg's lips made Falcon feel as if he had sucked on a moldy grapefruit; it left a rancid taste in his mouth. Worse, it seemed like Falcon's anxiety about Benton muscling his way into Meg's life had not been so off target.

"Oh that's too bad," Meg said. Falcon thought she seemed genuinely disappointed. "But at least I *will* see you at the briefing," she added, smiling and heading toward the general's office.

"Right see you there," Falcon said. He watched as Meg entered the general's office and the door closed behind her. Falcon nodded to the captain and then he left the waiting area. As he stepped out into the tunnel he could see Lieutenant Packlander — Rabbit — inside the POD parked at the front entrance of G Sector: earphones on, head resting against the back of the seat, fingers tapping out some rhythm on the steering wheel. Falcon rapped on the window. Rabbit's eyes popped open and he scrambled out of the vehicle. He opened the back passenger side door and Falcon got in. As soon as they were underway Falcon cycled through available programs on his helmet display.

"So how was your meeting sir?" Rabbit asked into his helmet mic. "He had you in there quite a while. It must have gone well."

"It went fine Rabbit thanks," Falcon lied, nodding. He wasn't eager to disclose to anyone how badly his first meeting had gone. He couldn't help wondering what Benton had done to get so cozy with Hazkill. General H.B. Hazkill, man of the hour, was tripping all over himself... patting Benton on the back like a long lost drinking buddy. Falcon shook his head. You would have thought Benton returned from a lunar mission the way the general pumped his hand. All the while Hazkill had that stupid goofy smile smeared across his face. Falcon didn't get it. And how did his own meeting with the general go? Hazkill had treated him like a thug... like the scum of the earth... as if he had committed some despicable crime. Well, Falcon thought, no sense trying to understand it. But he did want an answer to one question; what in hell was so damn special about Major Frank Benton?

❄❄❄❄❄

ROC Northwest Takotna, Alaska, August

Malikov sat in a wrinkled lime green jump suit on a

thin plastic mattress covering a concrete bunk in a six by seven foot windowless prison cell... his knees drawn up close to his chest, his arms wrapped around his legs, chin resting on the tip of his kneecaps. The faint stench of urine, decaying socks and stale sweat stung his nostrils. The cellblock was one level below the FOLT interrogation room, B Sector, where MPs had questioned him for nearly sixteen hours without a break. Malikov stared at the inlaid rivets of the thick battleship-gray door and the five by twelve inch food slot set into the center of it. Heavy snoring from down the hall melted into a disagreeable cacophony with the faint steady buzz from a fluorescent bulb and the echoes of distant inmate screams. Malikov heard faint voices and footsteps of guards at the far end of the cellblock whom he presumed were changing shifts. But this was only a guess. He had no watch, no clock, no way to mark the passing of minutes. Without a timepiece he had no tangible means against which to measure distances between the small insignificant diversionary objectives that human beings set for themselves throughout the day to break up the monotony of their banal lives. He felt as if he were adrift in a foundering rowboat dwarfed by gargantuan waves in an endless roiling ocean with no compass to direct him and no means to steer the unstable craft.

Malikov had not slept in nearly twenty-four hours but he couldn't prevent his mind from twisting his thoughts into knots. His brain refused to release him from the brutal reality that surrounded him. Vile MPs had seized him, tormented him, threatened his life, questioned and accused him. So here he was... locked up in this tiny, airless crypt like a rabid dog. He couldn't escape the nightmare. His eyes darted around inside his cement vault from the combination aluminum toilet, sink, water fountain, to the narrow concrete desk with adjoining toadstool seat... all seamlessly fastened to the concrete wall. One dingy gray top-sheet and a scratchy brown woolen blanket with frayed edges and holes remained folded at the end of his bunk. Malikov was waiting... for what he didn't know. The MPs had given him no sign of how long he would be in custody, had not allowed him the famous American phone call and had provided him no indication of what was to come. Anger welled up within him.

A long annoying blast from the wake up horn wailed through the speaker system slicing into the lingering night sounds of the prisoners' own muffled discontent. The unexpected *squawk*... jarred him, sounding like a nuclear warning siren. It had wrenched Malikov away from the only semblance of peace he had found in hours. All at once... talking, sneezing, coughing, yelling and rustling of waking prisoners within the cellblock filtered into Malikov's cell. He turned sideways on his bunk, dropping his legs over the edge of the mattress and planting his feet flat on the floor. He fixated on his cell door waiting for the slot to open.

"Inmate Count!" a husky voice announced over a loud speaker. Malikov leaned his elbows on his knees and buried his head in his hands. He listened to the noises of the most wretched ilks of humanity... caged despicable animals... rousing from a night of tortuous isolation suffocated by the depths of their own despair. He didn't belong here. He closed his eyes and tried to envision what was happening outside his door. He dissected his thoughts... mentally trying to ascribe the actions he couldn't see with the clash of echoes, prison banality and disgruntled complaints he could hear. Time was eternity in prison.

The slot in Malikov's cell door finally slid open with a

metallic *clunk*... "On your feet inmate... now!" a guard screamed. Malikov stood.

"Turn toward the door... hands at your sides... palms facing me..." the guard ordered.

Malikov looked at the door, dazed and numb.

"Do it... NOW!" the guard demanded. Malikov complied. "You do this when count is called," the guard commanded, "Just like I said. Face the door... arms down... palms toward me."

Malikov nodded. "See *advokat?*" — attorney — Malikov asked.

"SHUT UP!" the guard yelled. "Not a word during count! Shut your mouth!" Malikov clamped down his mind immediately, diving deep inside himself where no one could control him... where he couldn't hear the screaming guard or see the exposed aluminum toilet or concrete toadstool or the slot in the door that completely shut him away from the rest of the world. Malikov severed his thoughts from his physical body and transcended the stink of this ugly pit into which he had been dumped. He stood, motionless and silent, as he waited. When he heard the *clunk*... of the door slot closing, he sat down on his bunk and dropped his head in his hands once again, eyes closed. So this was the *Amerikanskaya tyur'ma* — American prison. This was Malikov's world now... a six by seven foot concrete tomb. Thirty loyal years in the Russian Federation Army and here he was... brutalized... thrown into an underground grave like garbage in a stinking *Amerikanskaya tyuremnaya kamera* — American prison cell. They had discarded him... humiliated him. They had rounded him up like a rabid dog and thrown him in a cement cage. "Fools," Malikov mumbled aloud to himself. He rose from his bunk and shuffled in his flip-flops over to the aluminum sink. He leaned over the basin, palms on the rim and spat into the bowl. "*Ve* see," he muttered aloud, "*Ve* see who *eece beshenaya sobaka,*" — rabid dog.

❄❄❄❄❄

ROC East HQ, Route 2, Templeton Massachusetts, August

It was nearly nineteen hundred hours when Falcon walked into the ARES-1 briefing hall at ROC Headquarters-East but he wasn't the last to arrive. Officers were still filtering in and no one seemed particularly concerned about scrambling to their seats. There was a long buffet table set up in the back of the room. Pies, cakes, brownies, puddings and fresh fruit as well as multiple large bowls of red, clear and orange punch were neatly showcased on top of a white embroidered tablecloth. Falcon had already had chow earlier in the evening so the desserts didn't tempt him, but he was overcome with thirst from the ham he had eaten for dinner.

He picked his way through the crowded room and headed for the buffet spread. When he reached the table he stood indecisively, staring at the bowls of multicolored punch, wondering if the mixture was spiked. That was a pretty far-fetched notion. The general didn't seem the party type. Besides tonight's event was scheduled as a briefing not a social affair. Then again simply because the punch may not be loaded with alcohol didn't mean it wasn't contaminated with something else. He went down that road before. No... impossible Falcon argued with himself. Why in hell would there be any reason to repeat the chaos of the ROC ceremony? Of course he didn't know why the ROC graduation had ended up in such a melee so he guessed this question was pretty rhetorical... except maybe Whitehawk could answer this.

Falcon needed to find Whitehawk; he made himself a mental note to add that to the top of his priority list. Preoccupied with thoughts of Whitehawk, Falcon reached for a punch glass. As he did, a disturbing vision leapt into his mind. It was a vivid freeze frame clip of Whitehawk's face awash with desperate concern and urgency in the instant prior to the ROC graduation champagne toast. Falcon recoiled, yanking his hand back from the table as if he had dunked his fingers into boiling oil, knocking over several punch glasses as he did so.

"Is something wrong Colonel?" a man standing next to Falcon asked.

"Oh... uh... no," Falcon replied... startled... feeling as if he had been caught with his hand in the man's cookie jar. He briefly studied the gentleman beside him who had seemed to materialize out of nowhere. He was dressed in a white jacket, bow tie, black pants and cordial smile — a caterer Falcon presumed. "I... I wanted something to drink but decided the punch would be... too sweet," Falcon tried to explain.

"No problem sir," the caterer said. "We have bottled water." The caterer pointed to the far end of the table. "Please sir help yourself."

"Great," Falcon said. "That'll hit the spot thank you." At the far end of the buffet he could see dozens of bottles of spring water. The bottles sat chilling in large silver buckets packed with ice. The water would be cold. Even better, Falcon told himself, the bottles would be sealed. You can keep your fancy punch to yourself General H.B. Hazkill, Falcon thought, and whatever toxic surprise you might have slipped into the mix tonight; and what the hell kind of name was H.B. anyway? Falcon moved down the line, grabbed a water bottle and twisted off the cap. He took long swigs, savoring the icy liquid as it washed away the lingering saltiness from his dinner.

"Colonel Colby," Meg said, coming up behind Falcon.

"Colonel," Benton said, nodding. Falcon recapped the bottle and dutifully shook Benton's extended hand.

"Majors," Falcon said, reaching to shake Meg's hand with a great deal more enthusiasm.

"I've got to get to my seat," Benton told them. "I'll find you two after the briefing," he added quickly, hurrying off toward the front of the room and disappearing into the milling crowd.

"We should sit," Falcon told Meg.

"Yes," Meg agreed. "It's nearly time." Falcon and Meg found two seats together in the fourth row and the remaining chairs quickly filled up around them.

"How was your day Colonel?" Meg asked.

"Busy," he said, "Lots of introductions and meetings throughout the day. What about you?"

"Very busy too," she answered, "Settling into my office. I thought I might run into you this afternoon... you know... at the HQ-East Command. I poked my head into the ROC Field Commander's office to see if you had checked in but they told me you hadn't; and they weren't expecting you. I presumed you were going to be the ROC-FC HQ-East," Meg said.

Falcon peered at Meg and smiled. Logical presumption, he thought. He was the ranking officer just below the general in the ROC HQ-East food chain and he had fully expected he would be assigned the ROC-FC billet. He would love to tell Meg where he was being assigned... unfortunately he didn't know. The packet the general had handed him that morning was simply his original orders with his assignment redacted — blackened out — with an attached memorandum signed by General H.B. Hazkill himself noting that amended orders were being drafted. This was embarrassing, not to mention inexplicable. It was another kick in the teeth as far as Falcon was concerned. He was pretty disillusioned with this *real* army.

"I guess they have other plans for me," Falcon shrugged.

"Are you being transfer…" Meg started to ask but her question was cut short. General Hazkill entered the briefing room and the seventy or so officers came to attention.

"As you were," the general said. The attendees took their seats. When the rustling stopped the general spoke. "Before I get down to business tonight I have a couple of preliminary items on the agenda. First, for those of you settling in at ROC HQ-East I want to welcome you to our superior award-winning team. I expect great things from all of you. You wouldn't have been selected for ROC HQ-East — the largest and most critical command — if you weren't considered la crème de la crème. So again… welcome!" Nice jab, Falcon thought. Had the general been staring straight at him when he twisted that knife in Falcon's back or had Falcon imagined it?

"Now," the general said, smiling broadly, "If Major Frank Benton would please come forward." The general stepped to the side of the podium and watched Benton rise from his first row seat.

"Is he getting an award?" Meg muttered softly to Falcon.

"I don't know," Falcon whispered. Falcon was confused. Twenty-four hours total… that's how long Benton has been at ROC-HQ, Falcon thought. What in hell was this? It certainly wasn't a ROC training award that was just now catching up with him. As many times as Benton had tried to manipulate the staff there, in the end he had fallen short — at least as far as Falcon had seen. Benton had never been the best, the second or even the third best, at anything. He was all talk. He had no talent, no leadership qualities and no common sense. Benton was obnoxious, arrogant and an expert at manipulation but no matter how much effort he had devoted to acting out his private delusions or how determined he was to manipulate every superior officer, the ROC Training Commander had never seemed to be fully duped by him. So what in hell could he possibly have done to gain recognition?

A lieutenant handed a brown and gold folder and a small ornate box to the general; then the younger officer stood at attention to the right of Hazkill. A photographer hurried to the front of the room and aimed his large camera lens at the general, adjusting focus and stepping left, right and forward until he found the position he wanted. Benton reached Hazkill's side and stood awkwardly to the general's left.

"Please rise," the general instructed the audience.

Falcon, Meg and the entire room rose to attention. The general opened the folder and began to read.

"*By order of the President of the United States and with the confirmation of the United States Senate,*" the general said solemnly. "*Frank Benton, Major, United States Active Duty Army, Regional Operations Command, is hereby appointed to the rank of Brevet Colonel, Field Commander, Regional Operations Command Headquarters-Eastern Division. Brevet Colonel Benton's promotion — from Major to Brevet Colonel — shall be converted to permanent full colonel status upon completion of sixty days service as Brevet Colonel, Acting Field Commander, Regional Operations Command Headquarters-Eastern Division. Signed... Thurmond S. Drew, President of the United States of*

America." Hazkill looked up from the letter. "Congratulations Colonel!" the general said to Benton, grinning excitedly. Applause erupted in the briefing room as the general pinned the silver eagles with outstretched wings to Benton's shoulder boards. The general's admin officer led, and vigorously encouraged, continued applause while the photographer snapped multiple photos of the two smiling and shaking hands. The room buzzed with murmurs, comments extolling Benton, and gasps of surprise. Falcon clearly heard some not so flattering whispers coming from the rows directly behind him.

Brevet Colonel! Falcon thought. Benton? Hazkill gave Benton the ROC-FC billet? What in hell was going on with Hazkill and Benton? This was ludicrous. Brevet promotions were used in war, at least historically. These were provisional warrants authorizing a commissioned officer to temporarily hold a higher rank without a corresponding raise in salary. Brevetted ranks didn't become permanent and certainly not in sixty days. These promotions were assigned when no other officer of that rank was available. Funny, if Falcon wasn't mistaken, when he had looked in the mirror this morning, there were two silver eagles sitting on his own shoulder boards. What a damn racket. Okay, this made no sense.

As mad as Falcon was that he was losing his job before he even started it his real point of contention was that he was more qualified and certainly more able to take over as ROC-FC. Maybe Falcon *had* been promoted outside the box — outside standard army operating procedures. Yet at least he had worked for his promotion. When it came right down to it, Falcon's achievements could stand on their own. He could point to tangible justification for his double promotion. But

Benton... Benton was a bottom feeder, a bully. He fit the old saying to a tee. *Those that can work do; those that can't, bully.* Benton had no common sense and certainly no army sense. He was inept. He couldn't strategize his way out of a broom closet. He wasn't a leader. He couldn't shoot. He couldn't command and he damn sure couldn't be trusted. He was a manipulative sociopath, a devious lowlife bastard looking for the shortcut to everything. So it seems once again he found his way to another one. How could Benton have pulled this off? More importantly... what was General H.B. Hazkill's game? There was one other small matter. Brevet promotions had been deemed obsolete in 1940. More to the point, it was unlawful to award a brevet promotion. It seemed there were no limits to what Benton could achieve — legal or otherwise.

The last recipient of a brevet promotion had died in 1952. Brevet promotions were a footnote in history. This wasn't possible. Should Falcon be worried; what surprises did Hazkill have up his sleeve for him? He looked to his left out of the corner of his eye. Meg was applauding. Was she *eagerly* applauding... or was she being polite? Falcon couldn't tell which. She was definitely smiling and she seemed overly enthusiastic. Falcon's stomach grew queasy.

The applause faded as Benton retreated to his front row seat. The general returned to the podium and looked out over the room. "Please congratulate my new ROC HQ Field Commander, Brevet Colonel Frank Benton, when next you see him. The ROC-FC Commander position has been vacant for almost two years," the general said. "Colonel Benton is a fine officer with a stellar record. He will be a huge asset to the Olympus Project and ROC-HQ forces."

Falcon thought he would be physically ill. Stellar

record? Sure... Falcon himself had jumped two promotions and by all accounts he had no right to feel envious of Benton. And the truth was... he *didn't* feel envious. It wasn't jealousy eating at him. It was blatant injustice. Falcon had worked damned hard at ROC training. He put one hundred fifty percent into everything he did there. Benton on the other hand was the man looking for the easy road at every turn... the man quickest to find someone else to do his work. It didn't matter whether it was studying, competing or strategizing; at ROC training Benton was the guy whose first impulse — whose only impulse — was to find the fastest way to circumvent the system. He was the guy looking for ways to jump the rules — rules never applied to Benton. He was the one who felt entitled to take whatever he wanted — whether it belonged to someone else or not. And teamwork... watch out if you were on a team with the guy, Falcon ruminated; teamwork was a joke to Benton unless he could find a way to steal credit for something he didn't do. He had a ready excuse for missing deadlines, failing to produce or not showing up at all to do his job. If Benton didn't know an answer it didn't faze him; he simply made something up. Benton *was* skilled at one thing — deniability.

Benton was the first to deny accountability for whatever he did wrong or failed to do. He was an artist at laying the blame on the closest patsy. If his first excuse didn't work he was ready with the next. He was the quintessence of pathological liars. Benton was a wretched example of a human being as far as Falcon was concerned. He didn't understand this. It simply cheapened his own hard work. Falcon involuntarily shook his head — slightly — in disgust. It was a gut reaction but he was pretty certain no one had seen it. He casually lowered his gaze, focusing on his hands resting in his lap. He fixated on his intertwined fingers... his thumbs silently tapping together... and he felt cheated and nauseated.

As despicable as General Tucker's actions were at the end of the ROC graduation ceremony he at least didn't seem blind to Benton's sociopathy. Falcon had never seen Tucker reward Benton for his pathological behavior. In fact, at ROC General Tucker never rewarded Benton for anything. As far as Falcon could figure, considering his initial encounter with his new commander there could be only one reason that General H.B. Hazkill would hold Benton in such high esteem and reward him for being the screw up he was. Hazkill was as much of a sociopath — hell, a psychopath — as was Benton.

Falcon glanced back to the podium in time to catch a glimpse of General H.B. Hazkill as he nodded to the officers sitting to the left of Benton in the front row. The heavily armed — ten or so — MPs stood and hurried to the four exit doors. Falcon slouched in his chair. Now what, he thought. Images of the ROC ceremony rushed through his head. Hazkill had nodded and set off a bunch of armed MPs rushing toward the exits — as if he had lit a fuse under them. Falcon was trapped. All he could do was watch this fuse burn down to the end. What then? Falcon unwittingly cringed. He couldn't stop himself; this was déjà vu. He didn't think he could sit calmly for much longer. He had the urge to bolt for an exit door.

"What are those armed MPs doing?" Meg whispered to Falcon. He thought he could see her hand trembling and for some reason it calmed him. He had a strong compulsion to slip his arm around her shoulders and protect her. After all she had lived through the ROC graduation ceremony too. What was *she* thinking about the ceremony? This couldn't possibly be a repeat of ROC graduation. Yes, General Tucker had nodded at the ceremony and the moment he had the chaos began. What was this *nod of the head* thing with ROC generals? Was this a *real* army code — some secret signal used by active duty general officers to set off cataclysmic reactions in worker-bee MPs?

"I don't like this," Meg whispered. "Why are those MPs so heavily armed?"

"I don't know," Falcon said, his own voice barely above a whisper. What else could he say to her? He was ready to get the hell out of there himself. Falcon watched — inwardly nervous and wary — ready to leap from his chair. It was the general's move. After a short period of tense silence Hazkill resumed his speech. The MPs were merely standing by the door. There was no mayhem, no chaos, no seizure or capture. It was not going to be a repeat of ROC graduation. Why then the show of armed force?

"Those of you without an Olympus Top Secret Security Clearance," Hazkill said, "Please leave the premises. Move in an orderly fashion to the exit doors." Caterers, other civilians scattered among the crowd and some lower ranking officers quickly moved to the exits and left the ARES-1 briefing room. The MPs stationed at the exits closed the heavy doors. Hazkill smiled from his perch at the podium. "Okay," the general said, "Very good. Now, as most of you are aware," General Hazkill continued, "A brevet promotion is normally awarded during heightened periods of National Security Readiness."

Really, Falcon thought. What is that, a rewrite of history… or maybe a new definition of war? These army twists on reality were ridiculous but innovative for sure. So say it general, Falcon mocked in his head; say anything you want. If a general says it... it must be so. What a load of crap, Falcon told himself as he steamed inside.

"What I am about to tell you is classified," General Hazkill continued. "Any breaches in Top Secret Security Protocol will result in instant seizure and detainment of the breaching source and execution as a traitor in strict adherence to the Olympus Top Secret Security Protocol — OTSSP. If any of you believe you may encounter a problem complying with OTSSP, please leave the briefing now." After a short pause and cursory scan of the room the general continued. "Okay," the general said, looking pleased, "Very good." Hazkill took a sip of water and then continued.

"As it turns out," Hazkill said, "Colonel Benton's promotion is a bitter sweet one. This morning, at oh five hundred, the president of the United States upgraded Project Olympus to Active Phase II Readiness — AP2R. As you know," Hazkill said slowly, "This means per order of the president's *National Security Directive 1-0078*, domestic security now falls under the oversight and control of the Olympus Project. In a few days, the following Emergency Action Message will be authorized by President Drew and issued by the White House for distribution to all ROC and U.N. peacekeeping forces and all support personnel:

> EMERGENCY ACTION MESSAGE: This is a Regional Operations Command Recall. ALERT: Phase II Mobilization and Deployment of ROC Forces Is Imminent. All personnel are directed to report to duty stations immediately by order of the President of the United States.

"Ladies and Gentleman I don't need to tell you what

this means. Within ninety days ROC forces... *will be mobilized.*" The general emphasized each word and a palpable deathly stillness seized the briefing room.

"Oh my God," Meg whispered, "Phase II."

"Mobilization," Falcon muttered quietly. "Holy shit," he said softly to Meg.

"*Let me repeat,*" the general said, emphasizing each word. "Deployment of ROC forces... *is... imminent.*" Hazkill sighed, taking another sip of water as calmly as if he were sipping his four o'clock tea at a London gentlemen's club. If it weren't for the wild thumping of Falcon's heart he was sure he could have heard a feather hit the floor of the briefing room.

❀❀❀❀❀

Chapter 15

❅❅❅❅❅

Takotna, Alaska, August

Miriam opened her eyes and tried to wiggle the crick out of her neck. The stiffness had afflicted her constantly since she began camping out on the living room chair through the night. She couldn't bring herself to leave Kyle's side since his encounter with the bear. She stretched... all the while eyeing her son on the sofa. She listened, waiting to hear the tiny squeak he often made in his sleep as he exhaled. She stared at his chest area looking for the rise and fall of the blanket. Satisfied — thankful he didn't seem in worse condition than the night before — she rose quietly and padded over to him. She looked down at the small vulnerable boy and gently laid the back of her hand on his forehead... no fever. She was hopeful. Another day had passed with no sign of infection from the wound on his head. But something seemed different.

The room seemed bright... brighter than it had been in two weeks. She realized she wasn't shivering from bitter cold. Miriam's heart skipped a beat. She raced to the window and peered outside. Diamonds... she thought. The world beyond the windowpane was twinkling like tiny diamonds, sparkling under the Alaskan sun. She glanced at the old wall clock. It was three forty a.m. — sunrise in Takotna in August. She rushed to the front door and flung it open wide. Gleaming rays of sunlight glistened off the virgin white world and danced along the surface of the snow, shimmering up the small incline to her cabin. The warmth slipped in through the open door, fanned out across the wide board floor and cast an intense late summer glimmer across her son's blanket. As Miriam lingered in the doorway she noticed the outdoor dinner-plate size thermometer wheel fastened to the corner of the small woodshed... forty-eight degrees! A broad grin burst across her face. She softly giggled with joy. God had subdued nature's wrath and restored peace and serenity to her world.

The monstrous blizzard was only a pinpoint memory now. She languished in the sun's rays, allowing the warmth to seep into her skin. Off to her right beyond the creek and across an open patch of field near the edge of the tall pine forest she spied an enormous moose. The moose nibbled on a snow coated pine bough and then tiptoed gracefully — as only moose can do — through the deep snow to the next branch. The snow twinkled as brightly as tiny glowing stars across a cloudless night sky. She breathed in deeply as a long absent sense of peace flowed over her.

She envisioned her Henry Ivan emerging from the forest and turning toward the cabin after a winter morning's hunt as he had done so many years before. The sky would have been darker then, she mused, because if the snows had already come it would have been winter. Yet she would not permit this small detail to ruin the image in her mind's eye.

Years ago she would have been peering out the ice glazed window anxiously awaiting Henry's return. As soon as she saw his moonlit silhouette emerge from the edge of the forest she would scurry around the kitchen setting out his breakfast. She would pour his coffee, remove his heated smoked salmon strips from the warming pan on the new gas stove he had purchased and slice her freshly baked sourdough bread. She would lay out everything for him so she would be ready to help with his heavy boots and parka the minute he stepped inside the door. When he sat down to the table and sipped his coffee he would have grinned and his eyes would have sparkled. He would have described to her what tracks he had seen in the snow, told her of the sounds he had heard in the spruce forest, let her know whether the wolves were speaking to the moon and he would have told her of the successes and shortcomings with his hunting or his snares. Could these memories have been so very long ago? Would this ache in her heart ever fade away?

"Mama..." Kenzie said gleefully in a loud whisper, padding up to the doorway. "The sun's out! It stopped snowing!"

Miriam scooped her daughter into her arms and squeezed her with delight. "It has!" she said, smiling. She released Kenzie — now much too big for Miriam to lift — and then crouched a bit, pointing to the edge of the trees. "Look," Miriam whispered.

"Oh she's beautiful!" Kenzie exclaimed. "Does she have a baby with her? Did you see a baby moose?"

"No," Miriam answered. "It may be hiding. If you look hard enough, maybe you'll see one." As they both trained their eyes at the edge of the woods, Miriam heard the distinctive sound of the bald eagles from the tops of the trees nearest the cabin. She smiled as the soft call of the birds skittered across the stillness of the white wonderland. *Giggling eagles* was the way her grandmother had so long ago described the subdued song of the eagle. How quickly time passes, she thought.

"Look Mama!" Kenzie said, excitedly. "See it? Right there!" she said, pointing to the trees. "It's a baby... a baby moose!" Miriam crouched lower, following the angle of her daughter's outstretched arm. She strained to see what her daughter's young eyes had easily fallen on.

"Yes," Miriam started to say. "I see it. I do..."

"I see it too!" Kyle exclaimed.

"Kyle!" Miriam and Kenzie screeched in surprise at the same instant, both whirling around to see Kyle standing behind them.

"You're up!" Kenzie screamed. "You're up," she repeated, jumping up and down frantically like a Jack-in-the-box toy gone berserk.

Miriam threw open her arms and hugged Kyle. She planted a kiss on his forehead and then separated from him, laying her hands squarely on his shoulders, staring him in the eye. "You should be in bed Kyle!" she chastised him. "You need to rest."

"No I'm all right Mama," Kyle protested. "Really.... I just wanna watch the moose!"

"Kenzie, run and get Kyle's jacket please," Miriam said, wrapping her arm around Kyle and pulling him to her side. "You can watch for a minute then," Miriam smiled. "I don't want you to get chilled near this open door."

"I won't get sick... I promise!" Kyle said.

Miriam shook her head in brief surrender. Kenzie rejoined them, draped Kyle's jacket over his shoulders and plunked his slippers down near his small feet. Kyle wiggled his feet into them, not for a second taking his eyes off the huge animal at the edge of the woods. Miriam smiled at her daughter. As the three of them poked their heads out the doorway watching the moose, the children laughed and whispered.

"Don't eat too much little baby!" Kenzie exclaimed, pretending to be the voice of the huge mother moose.

"Aw... but I'm hungry!" Kyle squealed, settling into the role of the baby calf. As the two children bantered back and forth and the sunshine careened off the snow blanketing the Goodriver's universe Miriam rejoiced in the tranquility of her life. Takotna was the absolute spiritual perfection of the world. It came to her then, once again, as it did in simple moments like these — that she could never abandon this remote settlement.

God, and the spirits of her Henry Ivan and Tlingit ancestors, were watching over them as always... keeping them safe. Miriam's heart glowed as she basked in the joy of God's greatest gift to her... the precious two lives in her care. The only thing that could ever have made this world of hers more perfect at that moment... was the sight of her Henry Ivan emerging from the edge of the woods. But Miriam knew this could never be. So she gently pushed away the thought. She set it into a corner of her mind for now. Yet she knew it would never be far... this vision of her Henry Ivan emerging from the spruce forest on a cold winter's morning... because recalling that tradition was one of the few momentary respites she found from a heart that never seemed to stop aching.

❄❄❄❄❄

Fizer farm Shepherdstown, West Virginia, August

A leisurely summer breeze slipped through the worn window screen and drifted into the kitchen, fluttering the curtains and brushing across the Fizer farm breakfast table. It was six a.m. East coast temperatures had risen dramatically in the last twenty-four hours. The temperature in Shepherdstown hovered around seventy-six degrees. As Nick sipped his coffee and *food doodled* his muffin he allowed himself to momentarily bask in the more normal weather. Yet something in his heart prevented him from becoming too optimistic.

"Are you done beating yourself up?" Stephy asked. She concentrated on the whirlpool she created as she stirred her coffee.

Nick chuckled. "Uh huh," he said. "I think so. I'm pretty drained."

"Nice to have you back," Stephy told him.

"I don't know what you mean," he said.

"Right," she muttered with some sarcasm.

"I haven't gone ten feet from the house in two days," he complained.

"Maybe your body was here..." Stephy said, "But your mind was in the next galaxy somewhere."

"I'm sorry," he told her. "My head has been full... thinking about all of this."

"You were walking and talking... and your eyes were open... but I don't think you had a clue where you were the past two days," she said sighing. "It's a good thing you didn't wander too far from the house. I would have worried you would walk right off the edge of a cliff."

"Stephy," Nick commented, laughing. "This is Shepherdstown... there aren't too many cliffs among our rolling hills." But it was true. Nick's mind had been a million miles from the farm. He had grappled with himself tirelessly over the last two days. He had expended every last drop of energy he had wrestling with these issues. He was on overload. He was unshaven, unwashed and he hadn't brushed his teeth. Sleep had come to him only in ten to twenty minute catnaps. If he had been asked to measure his own level of sanity — maybe using one of those pain scales that nurses so annoyingly interrogate every patient about — he would have assigned himself about a twelve. That would be two points over the max of ten and well into the red zone... a top 'ten' rating being certifiably *not* sane.

"It was a hell of a two days for you," Stephy said, pointing to the crumbled cream cheese muffin on his plate. "I can tell by your artwork."

Nick laughed self-consciously. "I know... you're pretty perceptive. What do you think?" he asked, rearranging a few muffin crumbs into a crude smiley face on his plate.

"Well..." Stephy said, frowning as if examining a masterpiece by Wyeth. "I'd normally say, don't quit your day job. But under the circumstances... maybe that wouldn't be the best advice," she smiled.

Nick laughed heartily. "As I said," Nick returned her smile, "You're very perceptive." And she truly was. He had never been one to brood about things, but over the past two days his waking moments were consumed by the tortuous grueling battle in his mind. One minute he would become despondent. He dwelled on an unchangeable future and sunk deep into depression. He told himself the end of American society as he'd known it was already here; it was too late to reverse the inevitable. Despair and impending doom gripped him. His thoughts tormented him now as intensely as they had during ROC training when he had first learned the full horrors of the Olympus Project. His mind bounced back and forth between the same two extremes like a tennis ball at Wimbledon.

First, he told himself it was too late to prevent the chaos his silence had helped to set in motion because clearly the unstable weather across the country indicated that the Olympus Project was accelerating. Then he decided he was overreacting and the abnormality in weather patterns was unconnected. He convinced himself the Olympus Project could never be fully implemented — at least not in his lifetime. Then he vacillated. He retreated into the belief his silence had been a massive failure that had contributed to ensuring the Olympus Project would become the new reality. Guilt haunted him. His actions — or rather inactions — during ROC training were inexcusable. He had plenty of opportunities to draw attention to the horrible downside of the Olympus Project during ROC training. But he had continued to paste on his normal game face every morning and sprint to the office.

The contradictions in his life grated on him. If he had spoken up, somewhere, against some of the questionable policies he helped initiate during his time in the army, then maybe he wouldn't feel like such a poor excuse for a human being. If he would only have said something — anything — maybe he could have at least found some solace in knowing he tried to do the right thing. And maybe — just maybe — he could have found a way to push back. Yet he never once spoke out against the Olympus Project. He kept his mouth shut and devoted his energy to conditioning ROC officers' thinking as General Tucker had ordered him to do. For two years he had skulked around in his own tormented mind and helped to sell the army hype — that the Olympus Project was the only way America could maintain political order and sustain American life. He sunk to the lowest depths of self-loathing. In his tortured mind, over the last forty-eight hours he became certain his silence had elevated him to major player status in ensuring the success of the project.

Then, like a sudden shift in wind direction, he would rebound to the flip side and leap into a manic optimism, convincing himself he had misconstrued all of it. His failure to speak out was inconsequential, he told himself. There couldn't possibly be imminent plans to implement Phase II of the Olympus Project. Besides, he was delusional to believe anything he did or didn't do would play a significant role in the direction or status of the project.

As outdoor temperatures rose toward normal, Nick started to believe his anxieties were groundless... that implementation of Phase II of the Olympus Project was not right over the next hill. He had overreacted, he told himself. The aberrant weather change was merely another routine test of the IRI — Ionospheric Research Instrument — at the Air Force station in Gakona, Alaska. This was a reasonable deduction. It was as plausible, if not more so, than the alternative. Yet one thing Nick couldn't deny was that he was out of the loop. The general had given him no indication the ceremony would end as it did. Nick realized he didn't know half of what he thought he did. Maybe he had no real basis to believe anything his mind suggested to him.

It was true that severe weather manipulation was one available false flag that could be used to kick off Phase II — deployment of ROC forces. Technically a false flag is used to describe some covert military or paramilitary operation designed to deceive so that the operation appears to have been caused by some other entity, group or nation — other than by those who in fact planned and executed it. The government could announce that the weather aberration — actually initiated by the government — was a terrorist attack. Then the government need only select which group it wanted to eradicate and attribute the terrorism to that group to justify retaliation. This was a common mechanism to start wars throughout history. But there were many available false flags. There was no way Nick could determine the actual false flag that would be used to initiate Phase II — except after the fact. Then again, it might be kicked off solely on presidential whim. That was an appalling thought. It seemed the possibilities were endless.

Banks could fail, another conflict in the Middle East could erupt, someone could pull the plug on the global internet, or a new plague might be introduced. Any of these could be used as false flags or flash points — naturally occurring or man-made — to escalate the Olympus Project to Phase II. Whatever false flag was introduced, the objective was the same. In the present case, the American government could now simply connect the abnormal weather to an imaginary enemy of their choice. The government could publically announce that the American people were in grave danger from domestic terrorist factions that had stolen this ultra-technology and turned benign scientific research into a vile weapon of aggression. The ultimate goal was initiation of martial law to make the decisive grab for total control. A new epidemic or natural catastrophe would serve just as well to get things started. It was all there in black and white in the OPSEIM Directive — the Olympus Project bible — officially christened the Olympus Project Strategic Execution and Implementation Manifesto in 1901. While underlying goals of the OPSEIM text were disguised and tossed around in small doses in classified briefings and in confidential exchanges between some officers who might have quietly shared their own division's need-to-know particulars, these OPSEIM objectives were never directly attributed to the actual OPSEIM document itself.

The contents of the OPSEIM Directive, and its very existence, were closely held at the highest top secret security levels. It was only by accident or some cruel quirk of fate that Nick had stumbled upon the Manifesto. Had General Tucker discovered Nick's predilection for nosing around after hours in the general's classified — not so expertly encrypted — OPSEIM files the general would have had sufficient cause to pencil in Nick's name on the monthly update to the executive black list. Nick would have been history. Stephy, his parents, his friends — pretty much anyone who had crossed Nick's path — would be history. Nick had not learned of the executive black list until later... after he had already sat through many clandestine readings of the OPSEIM text. Had he seen it initially he may have abandoned his snooping early on in fair exchange for his life. But that's not the way things turned out.

Nick knew pretty much everything there was to know about the Olympus Project from the OPSEIM text. He knew the ultimate future of American society depended on when Phase II of the Olympus Project was initiated. But he was missing the most important key to all of this. He was not privy to the timetable. He had no clue when Phase II was scheduled for implementation. Furthermore... he didn't know who or how many people had that information. Who would determine the start of this nightmare?

After Nick's initial discovery of the OPSEIM document and his cursory look through the enormous volumes and the two accompanying supplemental addendums he was confused. His first thought was that the OPSEIM document couldn't be real. It was a fantasy — the sick sadistic fictional fruit of some military lunatic like Hitler and his self-absorbed *Mein Kampf*. Yet Nick found it impossible to totally dismiss the OPSEIM Directive. It haunted him. The OPSEIM document was solar systems beyond the tiny rambling diatribe of Hitler's *Mein Kampf*. The complexity and scope of the OPSEIM text was so mind-boggling it was incomprehensible. If the document were the real thing it was horrifying. If it were only a fantasy why had the military gone to such expense and lengths to adopt it, continually study it, validate it, classify and protect it, adjust it for every potential variant and apparently implement it?

The highest-level managers of the Olympus Project had been inconceivably successful in limiting access to the full details of the plan. By restricting, disguising and compartmentalizing these details the number of people potentially disturbed enough by the objectives of the Olympus Project to take action to stop it prior to its implementation had been severely minimized. Nick couldn't get the implications of this out of his mind. The more extensively he read the OPSEIM text the more it horrified him.

Nick manufactured a thousand rationalizations to dispute its validity. He initially told himself that the vast magnitude and intricacy of the OPSEIM document alone was sufficient to assure any reasonable man that it could not possibly work... that it had never been drafted for actual implementation. After intense scrutiny of the plan Nick came to believe that the top-secret guardians of the OPSEIM Directive had no doubt counted on that very disbelief to maintain the illusion that such a plan couldn't possibly be an authentic directive. It was similar to the old saying if it's too good to be true it probably isn't. This was a slight variation of that; if the Olympus Project plan was too comprehensive and too seemingly perfected to be true then how could it be real? No reasonable man could ever accept what the document proposed as a serious tactical strategy. The context and length of the OPSEIM document alone would persuade most it wasn't worth the time or effort to fully read and understand. For those that merely skimmed the text, it would appear to be a compilation of disconnected notions and disjointed platforms founded on misconceptions and illusions.

For example, one long-range objective of the Olympus Project is to obliterate private ownership of land in America. Why? Control... but the government would never achieve this goal by suddenly issuing nationwide laws to accomplish it. Americans would revolt wouldn't they? Instead, the government is building gradually to the point where laws and regulations will be accepted without question. How? Simple... empower an agency like the USDA to manufacture an imaginary problem — a problem that will require the shutdown of farms because of an imaginary threat. A false flag could easily be initiated. Five words would be all it would take. *The war against substandard food...* isn't America already on that road? The false flag here might be the imaginary contamination of animals and fields — exactly what they seem to be using against Nick's own father. It's all done under the pretext of public safety.

Another means to initiate redistribution of land and wealth — prime sub-objectives of the OPSEIM Directive — would be to start randomly requiring certain farms and properties to be rezoned as conservation land that must be preserved in order to *sustain* the environment for future generations. The government uses propaganda to convince Americans of the multitude of benefits of moving to the city into the micro apartments. The platform strives to covertly eradicate private ownership of land while seeming to pursue preservation of the environment. This rationale was cited when the town determined Nick's parents' property was noncompliant with land density quotas. All of these seemingly noble platforms converge toward one goal... total control.

The professed environmental objectives appear to be noble efforts... the greening of America and preservation of natural resources, right? Remove people from land outside the city to preserve that land for all people to enjoy in its natural wonder and protect wild animals — endangered species — at the same time. Eventually, dissenters against the state sanctioned land grab — accomplished under the pretext of sustainability — are successfully demonized as greedy self-serving opportunists. How dare dissenters disagree with saving our land for future generations.

The OPSEIM text lists sub-objectives that are attainable using the USDA agency in this manner. One sub-objective is to remove the capability of Americans to be self-sufficient. It is a sub-objective because the overall goal is control. The ability of Americans to grow their own food to support their families is counter-productive to a government-owned and controlled society. One consequence of eradicating private farming would be a need to open government food distribution centers to augment dwindling resources. Eventually of course this would lead to food rationing. How many Americans would be willing to hand over their property to the state and relocate to a two or three hundred square foot micro unit like the USDA is coercing Nick's father to do? How many Americans would willingly give up the right to choose what kind and how much food they eat? The disturbing answer is... all Americans... as soon as alternative choices are removed from American society, or when all other sources are declared contaminated. This is exactly what will happen as soon as the food distribution centers open. It is one of the Olympus Project's prime sub-objectives.

A controlled society should be allowed access only to what the state determines its population *needs*, not what individuals can afford or want. Once the masses are equalized, choices will be eliminated. The USDA scenario is but one of the potential means for one agency to pursue the sub-objectives of the OPSEIM Directive — all sub-objectives lead to one goal... control. The text suggests hundreds of methods for hundreds of agencies *to do their part*. It was a terrifying document and Nick had never said a word to anyone about it.

If these actual objectives and sub-objectives — like the drive to eliminate personal ownership of property — were disclosed by the government, how many ROC officers would be willing to enforce outright laws prohibiting their parents, or themselves, from owning land? It would mean that Nick himself might be required to stick an XM10 rifle in his own father's face to make him comply. How long would Americans stand for that? This potential complication was a major consideration in the decision to bring foreign peacekeeping forces to America. Foreign troops won't give a *shit* against whose face they lay the barrel of their rifle.

Instead of outright prohibition and legal restrictions, the government will — and already does — use agencies like the USDA or EPA — Environmental Protection Agency — as a pretext to steal land or accomplish other sub-objectives toward the ultimate goal of control. All it takes is the unjustified unsupportable notification by a government agency that a farm such as his father's is contaminated. Then the agency can issue an arbitrary ruling and act in any manner it wishes. For example, they could announce that because the animals and fields are contaminated everything must be destroyed. *But don't worry America... Washington will provide all of your food and protect you...*

One of the most disturbing aspects of the OPSEIM

Directive is that even the government personnel carrying out these despicable deeds would find it difficult to connect the pretexts for the sub-objectives with the covert underlying sole objective. The concept is much like constructing a web of shell corporations to hide money and prevent tracing the criminal acts back to the real criminals. All information is compartmentalized and very few individuals are privy to the actual agenda. There is no need to explain to USDA or federal troops that there is no justifiable evidence requiring enforcement of regulations against a farmer such as his father. If the enforcers have paperwork whatever they have been told to do must be legal. Government personnel have a duty to follow orders not to question or demand additional proof of legality from superiors.

The OPSEIM Directive made it clear in the case of the USDA that these actions should not appear as a purge against all farmers. The assault should begin gradually as random unpublicized decimation of farms in remote areas where media coverage is scant and residents are less empowered to affect changes in laws and policy. The OPSEIM document encourages illegal seizures like this — on a case-by-case basis — until the public becomes wholly desensitized to such deception and chaos. Once the government has accomplished sufficient illegal takings, the OPSEIM Directives suggests an announcement similar to the following: *Due to the epidemic of farm contaminations across the country the government has determined public health warrants prohibition of the operation of private farming ventures in the United States.* Sub-objective one is accomplished. The results are two-fold. Individual land is stolen and the corporate elite's pockets are filled by proceeds from sole ownership of food production and distribution. Furthermore, the government has moved one step closer to the prime objective... total control.

At first glance reading only random sections of the document Nick found the OPSEIM text laughable. He had been certain the meticulous plan was some general's idea of a sick joke — a delusional parody on how to rule the world — that could never succeed. Yet the more he read and understood it the more tightly the pieces fit together. It was devastating to admit but the OPSEIM text proved the Olympus Project was, in fact, a comprehensive concise blueprint for the bid to take over control of America — and eventually the world. Had he not happened upon the full text of the document he would only have seen the palatable portions of the Olympus Project as apportioned out to him based on his need-to-know... only the particulars necessary to perform his own tiny job. In other words... Nick had no doubt he would have been in the same boat as every other unsuspecting American.

The OPSEIM Directive document was laid out in such detail that every contingency had been addressed and all related research and findings meticulously recorded down through the decades. The most disconcerting realization to Nick was that Olympus Project planners had specifically designed the perfect manner to disguise the blackest components of the manifesto. They hid the project's most alarming objectives in plain sight. They accomplished this by first disclosing a shorter abstract limited to an overview of the major Olympus Project plan objectives. This abbreviated summary was the version that ninety-nine percent of authorized military officers would choose to read. These were the sections that touted great humanitarian benefits under fashionable buzzwords like: biodiversity, smart operations, sustainable development, the greening of America and other expertly disguised sub-objectives that appeared innocuous. But the proof was... as the saying goes... all in the details. In this case the details were all encompassing and incomprehensibly horrific.

❈❈❈❈❈

The drafters of the OPSEIM Directive relied on the premise that no sane man would ever think the inconceivable was possible. No officer in his right mind would hang himself out on a limb to expose or even acknowledge such an insane incredulous plot... one whittled down to the tiniest detail. He would be treated just the same as any other raving conspiracy theorist. No... the OPSEIM document would be viewed either as a joke or a delusion conceived by two or three demented individuals. The OPSEIM text was too ridiculous for any person in his right mind to take seriously. Until a few hours ago Nick had based his own denials on that same reasoning. But that all changed.

Over the last two days he'd been released from his normal weighty responsibilities, freed from the RIF cloud hanging over all army officers' heads, out of earshot of executive orders and due dates and whisked away from the environment that continually bombarded him with propaganda. Here he was in West Virginia in the middle of a sea of tranquility floating on the gentle breezes of a soft summer day. He had been able to devote every waking minute to thinking, or not, about anything he chose. His time... hell his life had not so fully belonged to him for twenty-two years. He was certain this release had sparked his brain — and maybe most importantly his heart — back onto the right track. It was in this environment of mind cleansing serenity that one OPSEIM Directive detail had popped back into his mind. The revelation had changed everything.

The OPSEIM text postulated that from Phase II implementation forward — from the point of no return onward — the Olympus Project concept would succeed in absolute mathematical certainty as the sole foundation for societal global governance. The OPSEIM document tracked researchers' efforts down through the years as they calculated the potential success of the plan. The document was a living text in constant flux that incorporated new data from each subsequent generation. When Hawaii and Alaska became states the drafters merged those states into their overall evaluations, statistics, calculations and forecasts. The results of their analyses had been dissected, verified and proved accurate to an inconceivable point zero, zero, zero, zero percentage point of error. Nick had originally found this claim to be so difficult to swallow, he dismissed it. While he would be the first to admit he was no certifiable mathematical genius, he had performed exceptionally well in mathematical theory, advanced economics, logic and theoretical physics in college. He was intimately acquainted with the history of mathematical certainty formulas purportedly predictive of the collapse of multiple civilizations. These formulas utilized various models based on factors such as inequality curves, gaps between societal classes, education levels and other external criteria. Many have been shown to be quite accurate. But Nick saw a fatal flaw in the logic of the reasoning in the most popular mathematical certainty formulas. It astounded him that no one else seemed bothered by this critical deficiency.

As Nick researched these various formulas he found them convincing down to one common thread that Nick saw as a critical failure. The best of the predictive formulas seemed flawless right up to the end. There, at the critical stage of reasoning, the mathematician or economist postulates the accuracy of his certainty formula but then caveats his entire calculation with language similar to the following: *"The instability inherent in this form of government in country 'X' will reach peak failure potential in the year '0000,' and result in total system collapse... unless there is a drastic reversal of the present downward trend of 'YYY' production and export."* As far as Nick's puny brain could comprehend... the inclusion of this caveat introducing a variable contingent on the possibility of a potential occurrence that could ultimately affect the repetitive predictive mathematical conclusion of a formulaic calculation, logically defies the discrete exclusivity of the purported validation of *mathematical certainty.* So who cares? If Nick spewed out a mouthful of mumbo jumbo like that at one of General Tucker's socials, he might as well have shown up to the party in a pink tutu and tights. But this mumbo jumbo did pop into his head and its significance was enormous. It was the one, verifiable factor proving to Nick that the OPSEIM document was authentic, that it was imminent, and that it was mathematically certain to succeed once initiated.

As Nick's mind had revisited his examination of the OPSEIM text, he remembered reading a small obscure paragraph in the first OPSEIM volume over two years ago at ROC training. A Chinese mathematical theorist had been raised and educated from age eleven under the Olympus Project and trained to serve as lead for the Enhanced Theoretical and Applied Mathematics Research Division. Way back in 1957 this theorist had recognized and adjusted the mathematical certainty formula to compensate for the very flaw that Nick himself had observed as the common critical point of failure in today's most popular formulas. How was it adjusted? Simple... all contingencies had been accounted for in the calculation. Nothing had been left to chance. It was brilliant really. From the start... somewhere around 1901 when the OPSEIM Directive was born... the OPSEIM team had simply worked every possible *what if* situation into the equation. That's easy to do if you have generations to do it. That meant one thing to Nick. The mathematical certainty predicting the absolute success of the Olympus Project once it entered Phase II was, in fact, exactly that... a mathematical certainty.

Considering how accurate today's popular flawed calculations were in spite of their shortcomings the veracity of the OPSEIM formula was daunting. The ramifications were almost unfathomable. The only factor that could destroy the validity of the certainty calculation had been one tiny spot on the global atlas. Consequently, that one minuscule spot on the map was essentially written off. In effect the drafters of the Olympus Project determined that the city and land mass at latitude 58° 18′ N, longitude 134° 25′ W should be eliminated from the calculation because it would skew the predicted outcome of one hundred percent success. The OPSEIM Directive permitted the generation executing and implementing the plan wide latitude in determining whether to extend Phase II to the city at those coordinates... the city of Juneau, Alaska.

The Olympus Project mathematicians had calculated the statistical probabilities of program failure... by protest or revolt... and sworn by their figures the plan would succeed. Using the results of their calculations the drafters and contributors to the project built in sophisticated safeguards meant to prevent history from repeating itself... well... part of history. They built in safety measures to ensure the mistakes of previous tyrannies didn't happen again. The goal was to avert the mistakes that resulted in the fall of Rome, the fall of the Third Reich and the crumbling decimation of Soviet communism. This was the reason the plan was so terrifying.

The American public had been manipulated too expertly, too gradually and too scientifically for it to overcome the Olympus Project. For decades a silent few had surreptitiously set the scheme in motion. They were fully committed to steering Americans through life on seemingly innocent roads, diverting American intellect and common sense away from the real issues that threatened their freedom and survival. The clandestine elite — the self-appointed masters of this plan — had expertly developed an enormous reserve of facilitators to help build their envisioned empire. The few — the most devious, most powerful, most unprincipled wealthiest of the wealthy — had pervasively infiltrated and conditioned huge numbers of the media, the military, politicians, scientists, doctors, environmentalists, sports icons and a multitude of other societally-idolized influential pawns. They did it by buying out the souls of the greedy with baubles, trinkets and promises. They conditioned their minions to prod American society toward subjugation until Americans had relinquished their autonomy — like obedient sheep — and followed their shepherds down toward the barn under the pretext of safety and security. All that remained was locking the barn door.

The rogue and cunning group of elite individuals who had designed this vision of the one perfect world had come together over the past decades in secrecy to masterfully conceptualize the new system and seamlessly engineer its implementation. These individuals, fueled by greed and delusional visions of blood line immortality, had passed along this plan covertly to chosen descendants — from generation to generation — and constructed a network of trustworthy successors comprised of men and women who could be coerced to sell their souls. Their future rewards were tickets out of the lowly working class and a position for themselves and their offspring at the ruling top of the pyramid. It was all structured with one goal in mind, total domination by the designated master class. The only problem was Nick had no idea who comprised the master class. That was the most remarkable element of the plan.

The OPSEIM blueprint was complete to the minutest detail. According to OPSEIM researchers, once implementation of Phase II was accomplished bolder new executive orders and unconstitutional restrictions would follow. They would be easily slipped into American daily life without so much as a collective eye blink. The plan wasn't going to fail. There was no doubt in Nick's mind that weather manipulation could be the actual false flag. But the question was, is it *the* false flag... or is the weather aberration only another distraction. Until he was certain, it was hard to see his own way ahead and difficult to rationalize frightening his family with all the details of these possibilities.

It wasn't that Nick purposefully wanted to keep his family in the dark. He had remained silent about the details of such specific military doomsday tools because they were so inconceivable, their systems so complicated and there were such an infinite number of them. As for his despicable silence about this at ROC training... who would believe this horror?

Nick had no idea how much time remained before the

madness hit the fan. Why should he try to explain the abhorrent weapons the military held ready for the complete subversion of every American, when only one weapon might be chosen? For instance, because the weather had been manipulated, he could try to explain to his family how the government accomplished it. He could lay out the concept of ELF — Extreme Low Frequency — electromagnetic radio waves emitted from the H.A.A.R.P. system at Gakona. But it was a massively intricate system. It would take time to explain in the manner a lay person would understand... and believe.

Over the last two days Nick had searched his soul. He looked at what he knew with fresh eyes. It was clear that while it may not be happening yet, Phase II implementation *would* occur. The proof was everywhere. The rumblings of conspiracies and secret plots to exchange American sovereignty for a one-world government weren't fantasy. The *rumor* was no rumor. It was fact. This was the ultimate conspiracy... the mother of all sinister ruses.

Nick looked across the table at his wife who stared lazily, with sleepy eyes, out the window at oak branches swaying peacefully in the summer breeze. Stephy's red hair was in slight disarray just the way Nick loved it... loose, free, uninhibited and natural. It was totally unconstrained like Stephy's own feisty spirit. Her mere presence released him from the limitations of his world. He felt as if he were floating free like a cloud, as unencumbered a spirit as any soaring angel. As Nick took in the warm vision of his wife, Stephy flashed him a soft intimate smile. He felt... ethereally connected to her as if they were in some parallel universe — the two of them. For a moment — a fleeting instant— his mind wandered without a care in a daze of unfettered closeness with her. The peacefulness and purity of this one moment in time only intensified the stark contrast between the potentialities of thousands of joyful moments Nick had yet to experience in his life with the wretched truth that this terror might crash down on them any minute.

These few seconds where he felt a total connection to Stephy only heightened his dread of the coming reality. His biggest fear was the impending collision of universes — the catastrophic impact of the safer world that once was, with the horror of an unknown world to come. He worried about this world on the horizon. Would it be a future where every thought and sensation could be wrenched from them and transformed into an ugly manipulated moment of blackness? What was he supposed to do with his life now? Where could they possibly go to get away from this impending insanity?

Stephy reached across the table and laid her hand on his arm. It was almost as if she had read his thoughts. "So what did you come up with Nick?" Stephy asked. "You did a powerful lot of thinking. You know I'll support whatever you decide, about work I mean."

He gazed into her eyes and smiled broadly at the mischievous twinkle he found there. "I love you more than anything," he whispered. "You're the most important person in my life." He felt a deep flush rise up in him. He moved his hands to her face and lightly touched her soft skin with his fingers. He rested his palms against her cheeks... framing her oval features... and he kissed her. In Nick's heart he knew now that each moment like this was a fragile gift from a higher power far greater than he could comprehend... and more precious than he had ever before imagined.

❄❄❄❄❄

Chapter 16

❄❄❄❄❄

Adit 17 Perseverance Mine Juneau, Alaska, August

"How long have I been here Dan?" Viktor asked hoarsely. He squinted at the blurry image of his friend hovering over him with an eyedropper. Viktor had the urge to rub the sand from his sore eyes but he knew the grittiness was a phantom sensation. The condition was a common symptom of snow blindness.

"You've been down here about twenty hours," Dan said. "But from what Andy told me you've been pretty much out cold — pardon the pun — for about four days."

"Hmm… long time," Viktor whispered.

"Long time to be hanging onto life by a few threads," Dan said. "How are the eyes?"

"Better," Viktor nodded. Dr. Dan Cordwick was the best doctor in Juneau as far as Viktor was concerned. He was also a good friend. "They still ache and every now and then I get some pretty nasty sharp jabs behind my eyeballs."

"That's normal," Dan said. "Photokeratitis — snow blindness — can be painful but it generally clears up in twenty four to seventy-two hours. In your case, because you were exposed to subzero temperatures for such a long period, the restorative process was slow in getting started. Healing may take a bit longer. Photokeratitis is also called ultraviolet keratitis… it's pretty much like a sunburn to the cornea and conjunctiva. As you know, it's caused by unprotected exposure to ultraviolet rays. While you were wandering around in the blizzard the other day those UV rays were reflecting off the snow and bouncing right up into your eyeballs. You know better Viktor," Dan admonished, giving Viktor a disapproving frown. Viktor only nodded.

"It should clear up pretty fast now that you're out of the elements," Dan assured him. "The cool compresses and artificial tears in this dropper should help speed the healing. But if the eyes become unbearably painful I can give you a few anesthetic drops. We can't use those long term. They interfere with healing and can lead to corneal ulceration and, in worst case scenarios, loss of an eye." Dan placed two drops of artificial tears in each of Viktor's eyes and then sat down. "How about the blurriness?"

"Definitely better," Viktor answered. "I can almost count the freckles on your nose."

Dan laughed. "I wouldn't advise it," he said. "I can't sit here for two or three years twiddling my thumbs until you finish."

Viktor smiled.

"Look Viktor..." Dan said, the sincerity of his tone betraying the genuine human compassion behind his bedside manner. "I'm sorry..." he continued, shaking his head and intensely focusing on Viktor's left ring and pinky fingers. "I don't know if we'll be able to save these two. I should know in about twenty four hours."

Viktor shrugged. "Small price to pay," Viktor told him. "Considering..."

Dan finished bandaging Viktor's left hand and then shook his head. "You're one lucky bastard Viktor," he muttered. "The next time you decide to lie down and take a long winter's nap two feet from Andy's doorstep, don't do it in the middle of a blizzard!"

"Is that where I ended up?" Viktor asked, briefly closing his eyes to relieve the grittiness. It was curious, ending up at Andy's house, Viktor mused. He had been headed here — toward Adit 17 — at least as far as he could recall. That had been his sole objective. Yet Andy's house was in the opposite direction. Had he lost his bearings in the storm and turned right instead of left? With so little remaining stamina why would he have intentionally gone the opposite way? Was it simply coincidence that he ended up at Andy's? If he had come toward Adit 17 and collapsed before he made it he would have fallen unconscious somewhere near the Perseverance Trail... a hiking trail in a forested area sure to be deserted during a blizzard. He would have died right there. Was this detour initiated by human error — his own? Or had someone or something been guiding him all along?

"Damn lucky you picked Andy's house," Dan replied, nodding. "His huskies sniffed you out and raised holy hell: barking, yipping, howling and whining. Andy said they scratched the wood stain off his front door. He told me he was so ticked at the dogs he nearly decided not to bother investigating the commotion. He figured they were riled up over a wolf or a deer. But the dogs wouldn't shut up," Dan told Viktor, leaning forward and frowning. "So Viktor," Dan said, "This is where the story gets weird."

"Weird?" Viktor asked.

"Right," Dan answered. "See, two hours before the ruckus with the dogs Andy had decided to take a nap..."

"That doesn't exactly qualify as weird in my mind Dan," Viktor chuckled.

"Pay attention and don't aggravate me or I won't bother to deflate that little balloon when I yank out your

Foley catheter," Dan smiled.

"Sorry," Viktor said, feigning capitulation. "I'll be good."

"Fine," Dan nodded. "Then I will finish the story. So as I said, Andy laid down to take a nap... which is weird because he never takes naps. The commotion with the dogs woke him. He was about to ignore them and roll over to go back to sleep when he suddenly remembered he had a dream while he was napping. He dreamed there was a huge bear sitting on his deck — which was how the barking dogs had figured into his dream. They were barking at the bear. So in his dream he went out onto the deck to confront the bear," Dan stopped for a minute and peered at Viktor. "You look sleepy, are you listening or am I losing you?"

"Listening," Viktor said weakly. "But I would advise giving me the truncated version."

"Okay," Dan nodded. "So Andy asks the bear why he is sitting on his deck and the bear tells him he's not a 'he'... he's a 'she' and she's there because she's looking for someone."

"Interesting," Viktor said.

"Creepy," Dan corrected. "So the bear says she is Kaats' bear wife and she starts singing:

> Have you gone away
> From me forever,
> My mother's brother?

"Hold it," Viktor said, lifting his right arm and motioning. "I know the song and your singing is a little off key," he said. "You're not going to move on to the Tlingit version are you?"

"Go ahead Viktor mock me all you want but let's remember the little balloon I mentioned," Dan grinned. "Now may I continue?"

"Of course," Viktor answered, "As long as you don't do any more singing."

"All right," Dan said, "I won't do any more singing. So anyway... Andy says in his dream he gets mad at the bear and demands to know who she is looking for and guess what the bear said?"

"Dan, bears don't talk," Viktor tried not to laugh too heartily. He wanted Dan to finish.

"In Andy's dreams they do... So the bear says she's looking for Viktor."

"That's not how the story goes," Viktor admonished him. "Kaats' bear wife should be looking for Kaats."

"It's a dream Viktor not a research paper," Dan snapped, clearly trying not to lose patience.

"I'm just saying..." Viktor told him, wrinkling his nose.

"Right," Dan said. "But that doesn't matter. What matters is the only reason that Andy decided to go outside to see why his dogs were going ballistic was because as soon as he remembered his dream, he suddenly had this dark oppressive despair grab hold of him and he knew you were in terrible danger. No one knew where you were because you had not left the facility with the rest of them. When your name popped up in his dream he freaked out. He said he was certain that if he went outside you would be there. He told me he jumped out of bed, threw on his coat and boots and flew out his front door. He said he got about twenty feet from his house and he tripped over you."

Viktor remained silent.

"Andy said he was sure you were dead. You were nearly frozen solid. He told me it took him and his wife ten minutes to haul you inside and Andy's almost as much of a hulk as you are. He said it was like hauling a fifty foot tree trunk through the doorway, branches and all," Dan said, shaking his head. "So, pretty weird huh?"

"Yeah, pretty weird," Viktor agreed. But sometimes what seemed weird to others did not seem so weird to Viktor. He didn't think Dan would understand but maybe in some way this was a manifestation of some spiritual tether to his grandmother through her sewing art — his mukluks. That could explain some spectral connection that allowed his grandmother to know of his peril. It was an odd intervention, passing along information to Andy about Viktor's danger through a dream. It could have been some ethereal bridge to a higher power he might never understand. No question Ilya is astonishing... a woman whose spiritual essence is far beyond anyone's comprehension. As for trying to make sense of Andy's dream... maybe some things were not meant to be understood by everyone.

"Christ Viktor, what the hell were you thinking?" Dan chastised him. "Who in his right mind picks the middle of a record-breaking super storm to go out for a five-mile jog? What made you do such an asinine thing?"

"I'm not sure how I ended up out there. I mean I don't remember making a conscious decision to jump into the blizzard," Viktor said. "But when I was out there in the middle of it, all I remember thinking was I had to get to the adit. I had to check the jammer. I was sure the ELF — Extreme Low Frequency — signal from Gakona was getting through and I had to stop it. That was my focus."

Dan slouched back in his chair, planting his elbows on the armrests, clasping his hands together in his lap and tapping his thumbs together. He peered at Viktor. "Uh huh... and how did you know the jammer was out?"

"I... I just knew," Viktor said.

Dan eyed Viktor suspiciously. "Uh huh..." he said, peering at him. "Are you still hearing the voices?" he asked him. Viktor closed his eyes but didn't answer. "Viktor," Dan repeated, "Do you still hear the voices?"

Viktor shook his head. "No. No voices aside from your lovely tenor," he said, "Except it was a little off key."

"Thank you," Dan said, "Appreciate that... although you did already mention it."

Footsteps echoed in the distance. Dan straightened in the chair, listening. "Wait here," he said, standing. "I'll see who it is."

"Funny guy," Viktor snorted, motioning his head toward the IV bag hanging on the pole over his right shoulder and the wires tethering his chest to the EKG monitor. He watched as Dan walked out through the doorway of the mini hospital ward.

Not bad Viktor thought, squinting and trying to survey the dimly lit room through blurred eyes. The four-bed mini hospital had been a great idea, especially from his present point of view. Dan deserved the credit for it. He had made this part of Viktor's vision a reality. Dan had been in on this venture almost from the beginning nearly three years ago, when the idea of converting a section of the abandoned Perseverance Mine was nothing more than a rough sketch on a paper towel. The ruddy-cheeked red-headed doctor had initially frowned and wrinkled his nose at Viktor's paper towel proposal for the mine conversion. But Dan had come around to the Five Running Rebels way of thinking pretty fast.

Viktor had christened his original five-member team, consisting of himself, Andy Borca, Matt Cordwick, Gil Pope and Grace Stonewoods, as the Five Running Rebels (FRR) shortly after the bonds of friendship grabbed hold. Viktor had registered their small group with the Alaska Department of Commerce as the FRR Research Corporation in order to engage in a contractual relationship with the state and to add legitimacy to their work within the scientific community. The five original members were young scientists Viktor had met during college. They never seemed to stop running here and there in their zealous drive to investigate and examine everything that most people took for granted. They had been drawn together both by their own strong convictions and a growing united belief that the country was headed down a dangerous path. They had pooled their individual areas of expertise and distinct talents and merged into an inseparable group of pragmatic idealists — an ironic twist of terms Viktor thought appropriately exemplified their collective purpose. Both the oxymoron for their moniker and the crazy idea to convert the mine had originated with Viktor.

Dan Cordwick, M.D. was Matt Cordwick's older cousin, ten years older than the others in Viktor's little academic think tank. It had been clear to the group of five that Dan originally believed they were more than a little paranoid when they first broached the topic of the Gakona, Alaska H.A.A.R.P. research program to him. After some cursory searches of the internet, Dan was swayed by the political and media hype that the research being done there was benign. Yet Viktor and the group had started working on him to explain the real focus of H.A.A.R.P and to demonstrate the criticality of their own little research facility. Viktor and Matt gave a series of overview briefings to Dan but he wasn't easily convinced H.A.A.R.P. was the potentially sinister project they portrayed it to be. But Dan's lingering doubts about the realities of the H.A.A.R.P. program eventually evaporated once the epidemic of inexplicable physical symptoms erupted across the Juneau Borough and the state. Conspiracy theories might be explained away as imaginary but actual visible physical ailments couldn't.

In the last couple of years Dan had witnessed first-hand his patients' intermittent symptoms: rashes, loss of hair, odd changes in behavior, seizures, headaches, cognitive disturbances, peculiar sensations of restlessness and despondency. He listened to patients complain about hearing voices — Viktor one of them — and feeling strange compulsions to do things they would normally never consider doing. Dan had confided to Viktor how maddening it was to sit by and repeat over and over again to his family, his patients and his friends that he had no idea what was causing the rampant symptoms and no clue how to eradicate them. The remedies he had tried had yielded no consistently positive results that would indicate treatment, cure or prevention was even possible. Dan told Viktor he had never felt so inept. He had trained for a decade to help people... to *cure* them — or at least treat their discomfort — but all he could do was emotionally console a few patients. He certainly wasn't making them better. Then, suddenly, the symptoms would disappear. A few days, a week, a month later, the symptoms were back and so were his patients. Dan couldn't verify that anything he tried had actually worked. He suspected some of his patients swore they were improving only because they felt sorry for him — the inept doc who could neither cure nor treat them but who tried his best. Nothing Dan had seen was even remotely encouraging. Nothing suggested he had been anywhere near a solution. It was hit or miss.

When all was said and done, even if the briefings combined with Dan's observations of symptoms hadn't completely won him over, Viktor's infectious eagerness for the mine conversion did. Three years earlier Viktor had planted the seeds in Dan's head about including a small medical services unit in the mine transformation plan. Those seeds of enthusiasm grew faster in Dan's mind than the beans in the *Jack and the Beanstalk* fairy tale. The idea to include a secret mini hospital ward in the conversion proposal had sealed Dan's unwavering commitment to the project. Dan eagerly took over the design of the small hospital ward without batting an eye. His personality and skills merged seamlessly into the group's collective character and scientific impetus right from the start. Dan said the way he figured it, even if they were nuts and were way off base about this H.A.A.R.P. thing, they could use the abandoned mine facility as a bomb shelter for the next apocalypse or as a FEMA station in case of a tsunami, earthquake or other natural disaster.

Dan had quickly become so caught up in the vision he had even included in his version a sterile room for minor surgeries. Once Dan had zeroed in on his goal, he concentrated every waking minute on his dream. No piece of equipment was too costly for his vision. But eventually Viktor had to put on the brakes. Their funds were limited. Viktor was pretty sure that if Dan had a bottomless wallet to play with the final underground medical facility would have rivaled the three hundred forty-five bed Walter Reed Medical Center in Bethesda, Maryland. Viktor had to slow Dan's enthusiasm. "This is Juneau, Alaska," Viktor had reminded him. "You've got bear cubs climbing into the vegetable bins at the Food Market in the center of town and tracking mud all over the store." Reminding Dan of the local front-page newspaper article did the trick. It brought him right back down to earth... and to Juneau.

Viktor had gotten the entire brainstorm for converting the mine from a dream he'd had, although he never told anyone how the notion had come to him. Turning a portion of the old Perseverance Mine into a headquarters for independent research — the rationale they used in their proposal to sell the city on the idea — was a pretty ambitious undertaking. Viktor, Andy, Matt, Gil and Grace had kept the real function secret. The city would have locked them away in a rubber room if they caught wind of the actual objectives they had in mind. Viktor took the need for secrecy up one level and figured it was better if he kept the source of the idea for the mine conversion to himself.

The mini medical facility had been a great idea but the Five Running Rebels were initially stumped on how to go about designing and equipping such a place on their own. None of them had medical backgrounds. They were merely a bunch of idealistic college graduates worried about the future and preparing for something they felt was not only inevitable but imminent within their lifetimes. Hell, the Juneau City Planning Commission was happy somebody was reviving the mine, albeit for non-mining and noncommercial endeavors.

The mine had initially been converted to a tourist attraction after mining activities ceased. Eventually the city had to close the doors on that venture as well. After the mine was closed for the final time the city had a choice. The Juneau Planning Commission could either adhere to the Surface Mining Control and Reclamation Act, erasing all traces of the mine by restoring the top soil to its natural state — as if the place never existed — or let the Five Running Rebels have it. At least that's the way Viktor saw it. He worked hard to convince everyone that granting him access to the mine was the only good alternative. Eventually Viktor's ability to be annoying proved to be a huge asset. The city of Juneau relented and devised a split deal.

It would have been insanity to simply abandon open adits — horizontal passages leading into a mine for access or drainage. The passageways were a catastrophe waiting to happen. Children could have come across those old unattended mine openings and been injured or killed. Viktor's group was too small — and too poor — to maintain the entire mine system and ensure the public was safe at the same time. Besides, the venture was a part-time project for the Five Running Rebels. None of the group could afford to quit their day jobs at SUARS. They would have had no source of income if they resigned and there would have been no insiders left to keep an eye on the research being performed. More importantly, there would have been no trustworthy sources left at the SUARS satellite research facilities to monitor, and understand, the *real* actions coming out of the H.A.A.R.P. facility.

The H.A.A.R.P. researchers continually tested the system's capacity to manipulate. This research was publicized as benign investigation. Official sources swore scientists were merely evaluating areas of the Ionosphere that had been excited by high frequency radio waves from an Ionospheric Research Instrument located at Gakona. Supposedly, VHF and UHF radar instruments, a fluxgate magnetometer, a digisonde device — an ionospheric sounding device — and an induction magnetometer were used to study the physical processes occurring in the Ionospheric region that had been excited by high frequency radio waves. But scientists who understood this system were well aware of the dangers. This radio wave manipulation was not limited to *exciting* external space in the Ionosphere. Extreme Low Frequency — ELF — radio wave blasts were turned inward — aimed internally at the unsuspecting population of the United States.

While monitoring the supposed harmless testing coming out of the Gakona facility the truth became clear. Official assurances that this was a so-called benign research facility were outright lies. Viktor couldn't deny these benign tests were in fact being performed, but neither could he ignore his findings when scrutinizing these tests. Each benign test disguised a hidden embedded objective which, when studied and dissected, unveiled the real purpose of the H.A.A.R.P. system. Viktor wanted his covert group of five to eventually acquire the capabilities to monitor H.A.A.R.P. testing and maybe even develop the ability to interfere with it. But these notions were initially only intangible — perhaps unreasonable — expectations for the future. In any case Viktor had to start somewhere and without a facility of his own to try out his theories none of it would have ever been within the realm of possibility. So the split deal on the Perseverance Mine was a dream come true. It was beneficial to both Viktor and the city of Juneau.

Under the agreement the Juneau Planning Committee would ensure the City Borough maintained accountability for all but two adits under the Reclamation Act. Viktor's group would gain accountability for the two adits, the primary mine entrance, a secondary entrance and a designated portion of the underlying mine tunnel system. As far as the city of Juneau and the general public were concerned the mine deal was a minor administrative burden that would result in highlighting city and state support of budding young Alaskan scientists. Juneau, and the state of Alaska itself, had a well-known propensity to support young people in their educational pursuits — even if those pursuits might have appeared a little odd on the surface.

"Hey tough guy," Andy shouted, as he and Dan entered the ward. "You're finally awake. It's about time. How long can one guy sleep?"

"Andy," Viktor said, smiling warmly and reaching out to him weakly. "I understand you rescued me. I owe you... thank you."

Andy gently held Viktor's bandaged hand. "For what dude?" Andy said in mock surprise. "You're lucky I didn't call the cops. You trespassed on my front lawn and got my dogs pissed off," he laughed loudly. "I thought you were another homeless guy looking for a handout!"

"Dogs huh?" Viktor chuckled, thinking back on a vague nagging memory of howling wolves that he couldn't seem to shake. "And homeless guys... do you get many of those... homeless guys knocking on your door in the middle of the night in blinding blizzards?"

"You have no idea," Andy said, laughing. "I don't live far from the Red Dog you know. Where in hell do you think those guys go after the bar closes?"

Viktor laughed. "Well, I guess we all have to do our part for our fellow man," Viktor said.

"That's a fact Viktor. That's a fact," Andy replied, taking the seat next to Viktor's bed. Dan moseyed over to his desk, sat down and started writing in Viktor's medical chart. When Andy was settled in the chair, he grew serious.

"What happened Viktor? Why didn't you leave the facility with the rest of us, when the storm first started?" Andy asked.

"I... I don't know," Viktor said, frowning. "I don't remember much."

Andy shook his head. "I don't get it. You popped up on my porch days after the start of the storm. Were you at the facility that whole time? What in hell were you doing out there alone?"

Viktor shrugged. "I... I can't remember Andy; I really can't."

"Sometimes low grade amnesia occurs after a traumatic experience like this," Dan said, piping in from his desk. "It might clear up; but then again you might not recover certain parts of your memory."

Andy swung his arm over the back of the chair to face Dan. "I thought you had to get conked on the noggin to get amnesia."

"Not always," Dan replied. "Sometimes amnesia is the physical response to something traumatic. Amnesia can occur after severe illnesses or high fevers. The body has its own funny ways of healing."

"I'm not so sure I would call this funny Dan," Viktor chimed in. "It seems like I lost about two weeks of my life. I can't remember anything from the time everyone else left the satellite facility until I found myself on the highway in the middle of the storm."

"I meant funny... as in strange," Dan said. "By all rights Viktor you shouldn't have survived a five mile hike in that storm. You weren't even wearing gloves from what Andy's told me..."

"That's right... no gloves," Andy said, swinging back around to face Viktor. "It was the damnedest thing... first thing I noticed. Weren't you the one always nagging everyone to be prepared for the worst no matter what? What did you do... lose them on the way? At least that would make some sense."

Andy was right, Viktor thought. At least if he lost his mittens there would have been some sense to this. Diving into the storm with bare hands was absolutely contrary to everything Viktor had ever been taught — not to mention it was an insane thing to do. It was so insane Viktor doubted a city slicker from the Big Apple would have done something so stupid. That was the reason it had gnawed at him as he made his way into Juneau. It had always been innate in Viktor's character, to methodically perform a subconscious mental check — like a pilot's pre-flight inspection. But here, when faced with the most deadly challenge of his life, he simply forgot to do this quick assessment. Instead he strolled out into a colossal blizzard with nothing protecting his hands as if it were a summer afternoon stroll in New York's Central Park.

Viktor knew the voices in his head were a direct assault from targeted low frequency H.A.A.R.P. radio wave bombardment. He was pretty certain they had been the motivation for his blizzard adventure. The Running Rebels knew H.A.A.R.P. had the capability of interjecting these subliminal messages. Until now, Viktor had been confident he could nullify these voices. He could refuse to follow directions interjected into his mind because he understood the origin of the commands and had successfully blocked them — as he did during the rash of symptoms that hit Juneau, as he had in the storm by speaking his own thoughts aloud.

The Five Running Rebels had designed their own primitive ELF jammer capable of blocking some H.A.A.R.P. ELF assaults within a small dome of protection... their Perseverance Mine haven. But going out into the blizzard unprepared, and his inability to remember doing so, was a terrifying escalation of H.A.A.R.P. efficiency. Viktor had been successfully 'puppetized' — for lack of a better word to describe it. He had been victimized, not simply assaulted by annoying experimentation. H.A.A.R.P. had successfully manipulated him into doing something absolutely contrary to his nature. H.A.A.R.P. had become parasitic.

It had fed off Viktor and sucked his free will from him. But why him... had he been specifically targeted? Or had he simply wandered haphazardly into a zone of random ELF wave blasting. Even more terrifying to Viktor... was this merely another test of the system? Or was this something more sinister?

Dan nodded. "If you weren't wearing gloves or mittens during that entire five mile jaunt Viktor, there's no way there should be anything left to your hands. If you didn't keep them in your pockets or under your armpits... with those frigid temperatures and the wind..." Dan's brow narrowed. "Well I'm telling you... no way should you have come through this alive, let alone in such good condition."

Viktor nodded and rested his eyes. He needed to heal fast. He needed answers to these questions. If H.A.A.R.P. had truly entered a new phase — a vile, despicable phase — where Americans could be victimized at will by disruption of brain activity — and by voices that actually could control, not simply suggest — then people had to be made aware. Someone had to do something about it. Right now, he had no idea how to accomplish this, or any concept of how much time they had.

"By the way," Andy said. "It was."

"What was what?" Viktor asked, opening his eyes, straining to bring Andy's face into focus.

"The ELF jammer," Andy said. "It did crash. I checked it out as soon as the winds died down. It was probably weather interference with the rectenna seed," Andy said, scratching his head. "Dan said you told him that's what you had on your mind... you know, while you were out in the snow... that you knew the jammer was down."

"Yeah," Viktor said."

"And it happened exactly as you predicted months ago," Andy added. "The rectenna is the weak point."

"Well," Viktor agreed. "The weak point we know about so far."

"Right," Andy said.

Viktor squinted at Andy. "Gil needs to get that plane up in the air as soon as possible."

"He's already working it," Andy nodded. "But digging out the city is a monumental task right now." He rubbed the back of his neck and frowned... thinking. "Hey..." Andy continued. Let me ask you something else before you drift off to see the sandman for another two days."

"Go ahead," Viktor murmured softly, "Shoot."

"There's one thing I wanna know," Andy frowned. "What the hell were you dreaming about the last few days? You kept mumbling stuff like... like you were talking to..."

"Birds," Dan piped in. "Eagles... to be specific."

"Exactly," Andy added, "Like you were sitting around shootin' the shit with a bunch of birds. It was damned spooky," Andy said, "Creepy as hell! I mean... I swear... you sounded like you actually thought they were... talking back to you!" Andy said, contorting his face in confusion. "Like... like they were answering you! Damn... it was too weird."

"Yeah, that sounds pretty weird," Viktor said, smiling. "It must've been some powerful dream. Too bad I can't remember it," he commented, letting his voice trail off and his drooping eyelids close. He hoped the signal was clear. He was tired and this was a good place to sign off on the questioning period.

But did Viktor remember this dream? It was an odd thing, Viktor thought, the strange euphoria that suddenly washed over him, a warm tranquil serenity... from somewhere deep within him... that was utterly, purely and incomprehensibly comforting to him as he drifted off to sleep.

❄❄❄❄❄

ROC Northwest Takotna, Alaska, August

Loud, relentless pounding on Malikov's SHIDS cell door jolted him to consciousness. He heard the rattling of keys and the unmistakable *clunk...* of the slot opening. Malikov was shaky. He must have been dozing. He searched his scrambled thoughts. What time was it? What day?

"On your feet Malikov," the guard demanded. "Get up!" Malikov's heart raced. The guards give him no respect, no peace. Anger gripped his senses like a vice, driving outrage down into him clear through to his bones. His veins and arteries pulsed with uncontrolled bursts of adrenaline. Malikov's body stiffened, his fists curled into tight balls. He had heard no buzzer for inmate count. No! How dare they storm into his pitiable universe yet again! Prison cell or not, this despicable six by seven foot cement box was his own miserable world. It was his private space now. It was *his* to control, not theirs! Why didn't they just leave him alone so he could think?

"Get up I said," the MP ordered, "Hands behind your back... turn and back-step to the slot to be cuffed." Malikov had only drifted off to sleep moments before — at least he thought it was only moments ago. What did they want: to interrogate him... to humiliate him again... to treat him like scum? His face burned hot.

Malikov stood, slid his feet into his flip-flops and shuffled backwards toward the door, hands crossed at his waist behind him. If only the guard would slip up and step into his cell before cuffing him. If only Malikov's hands were free. Without those cuffs, he thought, he could jam his fist into the MP's contemptible face. One massive surprise blow, Malikov told himself, just one... to crush the MP's bones. There were fourteen bones in the human face. Malikov's doctor had once told him about facial bones after Aleksi had slammed his fist into Malikov and cracked his cheekbone. He had fallen; he told the doctor that day so many years ago. He had fallen onto a stone wall.

Malikov had dutifully told the doctor exactly what Aleksi had told him to say. How could he have told the doctor what had really happened? If Aleksi had been thrown in jail how was Malikov to eat? How was his grandmother to survive? Who would have sweated every day and tilled the ground? Who would have planted and harvested Aleksi's strip of land in the Black Earth Belt? Who would have put food on the table if Aleksi had been taken away? Malikov felt the carbon steel tighten around his wrists. Too tight... the MP had cuffed him too tight yet again.

"Must be your lucky day Malikov," the MP told him as he opened the cell door. "You're lucky on two counts. First, you have a visitor. Second, the commander decided to let you see him," the MP laughed.

"*Da*," Malikov said, watching the MP's twisted grin. "Who visits?"

"How would I know? Another Ruskie I guess," the MP said indifferently. He led Malikov out of the cell and moved behind him. Malikov felt the MP's hand on his shoulder. *Dirty bastard*, Malikov thought. The MP shoved the toe of his boot between Malikov's heels. As his ankles were shackled Malikov had a notion. He could slam his heel into the MP's face. It would split his lip. No... it wouldn't work, he thought. His cheap flimsy flip-flops were useless. If the MPs gave him back his boots then he could do this. From the corner of his eye

Malikov saw another MP standing to the right of them. He was watching... glaring at Malikov... and slapping a nightstick against the palm of his hand.

"Let's go," the first MP said, rising to his feet. "I haven't got all day." He gripped Malikov's arm right above his elbow and they started off down toward the visiting room. The other MP brought up the rear, following them menacingly, with his nightstick slapping his palm. Malikov shuffled slowly. The shackles rubbed hard into his ankles.

Slap... slap... slap... of the nightstick.

Flop... flop... flop... went Malikov's flimsy shoes. The echoes in the hall as the three walked, irritated Malikov. Cowards, Malikov thought. It is two against one. This MP walks behind him with a weapon. The odds are never fair. MPs are cowards. MPs deserved to be pummeled. This MP walking behind him was a bully. He slammed that nightstick into his hand to intimidate Malikov. It only angered Malikov more.

Malikov could envision in his mind how the fracturing *crack* of the MP's bones would sound if his fist were to sink deep into the coward's flesh. He knew exactly what he would hear — the *crunch...* of bones and muffled *rip...* of tearing flesh. He recalled the sounds of mangling facial bones and the splitting of skin as clearly as if it had only been yesterday that Aleksi had slammed his rock hard fist into Malikov's own tender flesh and broken his cheekbone. Wasn't Malikov entitled to payback for his suffering as a child? Didn't bullies owe him?

These MPs were vile bullies. They should not have the right to treat him like this. If he could only lash out at the MP then he could free himself from this dark hole. He was trapped in a black pit: bottomless, empty, terrifying. He had no control over anything around him.

It was oppressive, choking, crushing. He couldn't breathe. He was claustrophobic... powerless. He was nothing. If only he could make one of these MPs suffer, as he was suffering — as he had suffered as a boy — then he would feel free. Without the cuffs, without the nightstick, the MPs would be nothing. Malikov's fear would melt away. He could find himself. If he could only control something, anything, even for an instant... he could take back his dignity. He could crawl from the pit. In the one instant after he had bashed his fist into the MP he would be able to feel again. He would be free, however briefly. He would know he was alive.

Maybe Aleksi felt this way as his fists had plunged into Malikov — the trembling boy. Perhaps Aleksi had found the way to free himself from his inner torment. Could it be that Aleksi was strengthened, renewed in confidence, as each blow had landed against Malikov's flesh? Was this what Aleksi took away with him from each of Malikov's beatings? Yes, Malikov could understand this. Perhaps Aleksi's fists had released him from the demons that had taken hold of him so many years before. Yes... yes... yes... this must have been why Aleksi had taken out his rage on Malikov.

"Pick up the pace inmate," the MP behind them demanded.

Idi k chortu — go to hell — Malikov said to himself. But he could not say it aloud. He was too weak. He was too timid to voice his own thoughts. His body ignored his silent curses and instead of lunging at the guard in protest, he meekly, mindlessly, submitted to the MP's demand and shuffled his flip-flops ahead faster. So this was how it was to be until they let him go. Even his own body betrays him. Fine, Malikov told himself, fine. But he would soon be free and he would find his confidence again. Then *he* would have the final laugh. Maybe he would have that laugh now with his good friend. Was this visitor Sergei? He could talk to Sergei. Sergei would listen to him and Malikov would feel more like himself. Or was this visitor someone else? Maybe someone has come to listen to his story... and believe him. *Slap... slap... slap...* The echo of the nightstick dug deep into Malikov's nerves.

"Stop... hold up. In here," the MP said, jerking Malikov's arm to pull him to the right. Then the MP nudged him hard through the doorway. Both MPs laid hands on Malikov's shoulders, shoving him down into a chair. Across the metal table sat a stiff and austere looking Russian Federation Army captain. The captain nodded to the MPs and they left the room. Malikov peered at the officer but said nothing.

"*Senior Starshiná* Malikov... Chief," the Russian captain said, extending his hand. "*Dobroye utra*" — Good Morning — "I am *Kapitan* Boris Natkorksky, *advokat,*" — attorney. "I have come to speak with you about your crime."

"*My* crime... I have done nothing," Malikov told him in Russian.

"You must speak English. It is the rule," the captain admonished him.

"I have done nothing," Malikov repeated in Russian. There... he had told this officer how it was. Maybe now they would come to their senses. This Russian *kapitan*, Malikov was convinced, would listen and get him out of this bleak pit. Then he would be free from this idiocy and madness.

Maybe Malikov *would* retire. If he were going to be treated like a mad dog by these *Glupyy Amerikanets* — foolish Americans — why should he stick around? What was the point? He had achieved *Senior Starshiná*. His retirement would be comfortable. Maybe he would travel in the United States. Maybe he could find some woman like his *babushka* and raise babies. He would be set. He could live off his retirement, drink vodka and play cards at night. He could talk about his days in the army. People... civilians... they would respect him. He would talk over this retirement thing with Sergei. Once this *kapitan* heard Malikov's side of the story, this fellow Russian would see how bad Malikov had been treated. He would see what a horrific mistake this was and he would get Malikov out of this place. Finally, Malikov thought, this nightmare will end. He will be sipping vodka with Sergei by suppertime. He will talk with him about this idea of retiring and they could plan it together. Hell, Malikov thought, maybe Sergei would want to retire too.

"As I said," the Russian officer continued, "I come to speak with you about your crime and tell you what will happen next."

"*Nyet, nyet...*" Malikov said excitedly. "*Eece* no crime, I say... DO nothing."

"That is not my concern," the officer said. "I am here only to tell you what is about to happen to you."

"But I have done nothing," Malikov said in angry flowing Russian.

"I cannot stay if you refuse to speak English," the Russian officer told him. "It is the rule... people are listening."

Malikov sneered. What did it matter, he thought, no one was hearing what he was saying: English... Russian... what did it matter.

"*Slushayte menya,*" — listen to me, the Russian officer demanded.

"You are charged with murder in the first degree. It is punishable by death. Because of this, you will be transferred..."

"Smert'?" — Death? Malikov seethed. *"Smert...* But I do NOTHING!"

"Chief," the officer said. "You must calm down."

"Da," Malikov spat angrily.

"I have seen the evidence against you," *Kapitan* Natkorksky rebuked him. "There are witnesses to your confrontation with this American Military Policeman in the B Sector mess hall. We cannot let this stand. This could result in serious political consequences."

"I say," Malikov said. "I do nothing."

"You threatened this man in front of a hundred witnesses!" the officer said, exasperated.

"I do nothing," Malikov repeated, shaking his head slowly.

The captain peered at Malikov. He impatiently flipped through the pages of the folder on the table in front of him. "Here," the captain angled the file toward Malikov and slid it across to him. He tapped his finger on the open page. "It says right here. Read it! It's a witness' sworn deposition."

Malikov stared at the captain with blank eyes. Witness depositions... what is this? What is this *kapitan* talking about? Malikov felt like his mind was dragging him down into quicksand. It was so confusing. His thoughts seemed slow, thick, like molasses.

"READ IT!" the captain ordered. "Or I will."

Malikov could feel his body begin to tremble. He tried to look at the file to where the captain was pointing but Malikov's vision blurred. He couldn't concentrate. He could see that the page was covered with words but the letters made no sense to him. They didn't fit together. Malikov couldn't put the letters in the right order in his head. Nausea gripped him again. His abdomen cramped with pain and he felt dizzy. The walls seemed to be squeezing closer to him. Why couldn't they just leave him in his cell? If he could only sleep... after he slept he would find out this debacle was merely a horrible nightmare.

"Fine," the Russian captain said. "*I* will read it." The captain grabbed the file and turned it so both he and Malikov could see it. The officer ran his finger across and down the page so Malikov could follow along as he read aloud each sentence of the witness' deposition from the transcript copy.

Attorney: "What do you recall about the B Sector mess hall incident on August 7?"

Witness: "I was in the mess hall. I heard a fight and saw the Chief, Chief Malikov I mean, jump up from the table and stomp down to where the MP was sitting..."

Attorney: "This MP... it was Sergeant Booner, correct?"

Witness: "Yes, Booner... I mean, Sergeant Booner. So, the Chief, Chief Malikov, stomped down to where Sergeant Booner was sitting and started screaming at him. Sergeant Booner was just sitting there until the Chief spit food onto his lap. Then the MP stood up... he was real tall. The Chief's face was purple. He looked like he was going to explode himself [sic]. I looked away for a minute to say something to somebody and when I looked back, the Chief had a knife in his hand and had his arm up over his head... like this (witness demonstrates) and then he slammed the knife down onto the MP's plate and gravy sprayed all over the table."

Attorney: "Then what happened?"

Witness: "Then, out of the blue, the Chief shouted something in Russian. I found out later what he said when one of the Russian Army guys came over to the table and told us."

Attorney: "And what was it that the Chief hollered to Sergeant Booner?"

Witness: "He screamed, 'Next time, your bastard heart, you piece of shit.'"

Attorney: "And it was Sergeant Booner to whom Chief Malikov directed this threat?"

Witness: "Yep, he yelled it at the MP... Booner, I mean."

Attorney: "What do you think Chief Malikov meant by that? When he said, 'Next time your bastard heart, you piece of shit.'"

Witness: (Witness laughs) "Well it was obvious what he meant. He was threatening he was gonna kill him."

Attorney: "What happened next?"

Witness: "The Chief stomped out of the mess hall."

Attorney: "And what did Sergeant Booner do?"

Witness: "Do? He just laughed and then sat down and finished his uh... supper, you know."

Attorney: "And did this exchange frighten you?"

Witness: "Me?" (Witness laughs) "No, it didn't scare me. But Malikov — I mean the Chief — well, he wasn't screaming at me."

Attorney: "Did Sergeant Booner seem afraid?"

Witness: "No way," (Witness laughs) "Booner's a monster... I mean really big, you know? The Chief is just a puny runt."

Attorney: "So in your opinion Sergeant Booner didn't take this seriously?"

Witness: "Not at all. At least it didn't seem like it. But he should have."

Attorney: "Why do you say that?"

Witness: "Because the Chief has a short fuse. No telling what he'll do. He's always swearing to kill somebody, or punch them out."

Attorney: "Have you ever seen the Chief be violent with anyone?"

Witness: "Well, no. But I didn't see him this time

either and Booner... I mean... Sergeant Booner... is dead, isn't he."

Attorney: "But you said Sergeant Booner was a huge man, how would you explain the Chief overcoming his size to get the best of him — to kill him?"

Witness: "Easy... the way you get any big guy. You either gang up on him or you work it from an angle."

Attorney: "How do you mean? Work it from an angle?"

Witness: "Booner — I mean the sergeant — is... er... was a boozer. All the Chief would have to do is sneak up on him when he's sleepin' one off, you know?"

Attorney: "Anything you want to add?"

Witness: "Nope."

Attorney: "Okay, you're dismissed. Send in the next man in line out there."

Malikov sat silently. He was numb and stunned. Had he said that? Who would remember such a thing — word for word — if Malikov himself couldn't even recall having said it? And who was this... this witness?

The Russian officer slammed shut the folder. He reached into his front pants pocket and fished out a handkerchief. He wiped his brow and under his eyes, then his chin. He methodically folded the handkerchief in thirds and returned it to his pocket. "They have your knife. They have your fingerprints. They have witnesses. Now you must allow me to finish. There is little time."

Malikov's face twisted in painful contortion as he tried to swallow. My... knife, what knife? What fingerprints? Pinpoint beads of sweat erupted on Malikov's scalp between his root hairs and caused his skin to prickle on his neck. He shivered. Where was Sergei? Why couldn't his visitor have been Sergei instead of this irritating Russian officer? What did this Russian *kapitan* mean... *there is little time*? Why wasn't anybody taking Malikov's side? Booner was a bully, a drunk, an embarrassment to loyal soldiers. Malikov was drained, as if he had run five miles in hundred-degree weather with a sixty-pound rucksack on his shoulders.

"As I said," the officer continued. "Because you are a member of a U.N. peacekeeping force presently stationed on foreign soil and due to the fact that your crime carries the penalty of death, your case must be tried under the jurisdiction of the International Military Tribunal. There are presently two active international military courts in session in the United States. One on the east coast and one here on the west coast in San Francisco, California. You are to be transferred today to San Francisco."

"I tell you," Malikov mumbled, his system shocked as if one of Aleksi's punches had slammed into his head and knocked him senseless. "I do... nothing."

"And I have told you," the officer replied unmoved, gathering up the file folder and rising to his feet. "That is not my concern."

❀❀❀❀❀

Chapter 17

❊❊✤❊❊

ROC East HQ, Route 2 Templeton, Massachusetts,
August

Falcon hunched over his oak desk in a cramped visitor's office down the hall from the ROC Field Commander's door — Colonel Frank Benton's office door, to be specific — across the hall from Meg. Falcon was in a fourth quarter huddle with heaps of paperwork that by this time seemed to be glaring right back up at him. ROC regional and sector maps with tunnel latitude and longitude coordinates for the entire continental United States lined his desk. Complex spreadsheets with details on surface terrain, tunnel layouts, discrete missions, capacity and capabilities of each tunnel force and FOLT facility helped round out the two-inch deep pile cluttering his desktop. Data on peacekeeping unit locations, troop specialties, deployment routes and quarters' assignments added to the quagmire. It was overwhelming... hard to imagine getting through it all before his transfer came through. Lucky for Falcon he had something of a photographic memory. He found absorbing large amounts of data easier if he broke it down into smaller segments. Still, one wooden match might put the paperwork in better perspective right about now.

Falcon had access to this same information in the computer, but he preferred paper when it came to initially digesting and absorbing massive amounts of facts. Most officers would skip this step entirely, scoffing at memorizing data that was at their fingertips in their hard drives. Falcon disagreed. Technology and computers were great for office reference but he wasn't about to set himself up for failure.

He could see it now... trapped in a mountain pass somewhere on a pitch black ROC night mission, scrambling around on slippery crags to position himself under the right group of stars to latch onto the cleanest satellite signal and boot up his A-TEONIC — Artificial Tunnel-Enhanced Operational Nano Intellect Cell — computer system. Hell, a week ago he'd never even heard of the thing. He was still having problems with the acronym — one among thousands — never mind understanding the system for which the letters stood. He had one question. If this was the Artificial Tunnel-Enhanced Operational Nano Intellect Cell... where was the real one? He chuckled softly... at least he still had his sense of humor. Falcon's desk lamp flickered. He was annoyed. The bulb began acting up yesterday but his head had been so crammed with the reams of data he forgot to do anything about it.

"Hey Rabbit," Falcon called to the young lieutenant — now the right hand man without whom Falcon couldn't function. Rabbit was standing outside Falcon's temporary office, leaning against the doorjamb, talking to Meg's administrative support lieutenant.

"Yes sir?" Rabbit said, reeling around and stepping into Falcon's office.

"This desk lamp is flickering," Falcon complained. "Any spare bulbs around?"

"Lots," Rabbit answered. "I'll be right back." Rabbit disappeared and returned within seconds with a package of light bulbs. In the next instant, Rabbit was replacing the bad bulb.

Falcon shook his head and smiled, "I have to know one thing Rabbit."

"Sure sir," Rabbit said, pausing from his minor maintenance job and looking Falcon in the eye.

"What the hell do you put in your morning coffee," Falcon asked, "JP-4 jet fuel?"

Rabbit laughed. "No sir. But my mom tells me she put that exact thing in my baby bottles for the first six months of my life," Rabbit chuckled. "Guess it was never flushed out of my system."

"I would like to chat with your mom one of these days," Falcon said, grinning.

There was a soft knock on his open door. Falcon peered around Rabbit who was bending over the desk lamp blocking Falcon's view into the hallway. "Meg," Falcon said, surprised. "Is it noon already?"

"It is," Meg said, walking into the office.

"Major Winters," Rabbit said, nodding respectfully to acknowledge her. "I'm just finishing. I'll be out of the way in a jiffy."

"No problem Rabbit," Meg said with a gleaming smile. "By the look of the colonel's desk it's going to take him a few minutes and one or two pieces of heavy equipment to dig himself out of that paperwork."

"Nope," Falcon said, laying down his mechanical pencil with a beaming grin. "Ready to go in a flash... I'm starving," he said, rising up from his chair. He leaned over the desk and hit ctrl-alt-del ROC-LOCK — the discrete A-TEONIC computer keyboard security sequence — to lock his system into the COMSEC protocol. COMSEC, Communications Security System, is used in the DoD to ensure the security of telecommunications confidentiality and integrity... two Information Assurance pillars. The ROC unit emblem popped up on the LCD screen saver. He walked around the desk at the instant Rabbit chucked the used bulb into the trash with a *pop*.

"The lamp is good to go sir," Rabbit said.

"Excellent... thank you," Falcon was pleased.

"Anything you need me to do before lunch sir?" Rabbit asked.

"No I'm all set," Falcon answered.

"Do you mind if I take an extra fifteen minutes?" Rabbit asked. "I have an appointment today."

"Nope... no problem," Falcon answered.

"Great. I appreciate it," Rabbit said. "By the way Colonel have you had any luck locating your friend?"

"Major Whitehawk," Falcon clarified, shaking his head, "Afraid not. It seems he's disappeared off the face of the earth."

"That's too bad sir," Rabbit said. "I'd be happy to help you look... just say the word." With that, Rabbit disappeared.

Meg watched Rabbit speed out of the room and she laughed. "He moves... doesn't he?"

"Like a *rabbit*," Falcon said. "I swear... I thought I was fast." The minute the sentence popped out of his mouth he felt his face blush. With Meg, he had been anything but fast since they had arrived at Eastern HQ. Something told Falcon this hadn't gone unnoticed by her. He couldn't deny she had an effect on him back in ROC training. Somehow nothing in his head seemed to work as it should when he was close to her; he couldn't think, couldn't speak articulately. Even though he had started to feel more comfortable around her it didn't seem right to set his sights on a relationship knowing he was on his way out of there. He knew it was probably old fashioned to consider Meg's feelings ahead of his own basic physical urges — clearly not something a guy like Benton would know anything about. But he couldn't help feeling that if he started something with her now, knowing he'd be gone in less than a week, it would be a lousy way to kick off a lasting bond. Of course this type of thinking would probably nail him as archaic.

Most guys would jump at the chance for a few nights of uncomplicated — friends with benefits type — R & R with a beautiful woman like Meg. But Falcon figured this would be no better than slapping down a *c note* on her dresser after a quick tumble and a fast shower. She deserved better. Then again what were Benton's intentions? He seemed to be circling her like the lead hyena on the trail of a wounded antelope. But was Benton the real issue?

If by some miracle Meg fell for Falcon, right from the start they'd have this huge obstacle in the way. God knows where Hazkill was planning to send him. It could be the other side of the globe. Falcon wouldn't feel right about starting something he couldn't finish. Hazkill made it damn clear Falcon was only passing through Eastern Division HQ. H.B. Hazkill didn't want him there and under those circumstances Falcon certainly didn't want to stay. Anyway now that Hazkill's little shit Benton was assigned as ROC-FC there was no place to billet Falcon.

Still, he supposed that wasn't necessarily an insurmountable obstacle. Under the right circumstances, and with the right amount of luck, Falcon could hypothetically help get Meg transferred to... to where? Not knowing, that *was* a problem. If he did start something with Meg how could he even think about asking her to go with him if he didn't know where in hell he was going in the first place? It seemed pretty complicated... probably moot now anyway. He would be leaving ROC Eastern Division HQ in less than seven days.

❀❀❀❀❀

Takotna, Alaska, August

"Well young man," Elizabeth began, smiling. "Let me see this battle scar you have."

"I sewed it up as best as I could," Miriam cautioned. "I'm sure it's a very bad job."

"Nonsense," Elizabeth said, gently parting Kyle's hair as he sat on the examining table swinging his legs back and forth. "Sewing is sewing."

Miriam relaxed, just a bit. She marveled at the tenderness in the Nurse Practitioner's tone. She had a way with people. It was clear this woman loved her work and Takotna was lucky to have her in their clinic.

"No sign of infection, no indication there will be a huge scar to deal with," Elizabeth said, peering through her glasses as she studied Kyle's scalp. "Your Mama has done a fine job on this Kyle. It looks wonderful."

"I think he was pretending the whole time," Kenzie said giggling.

"I was NOT!" Kyle whined, suddenly jerking his head to the side and wrenching it free from Elizabeth's light grasp.

"Whoa, hold on Kyle," Elizabeth said, gently turning his head back toward her. "I want to make sure you're all right."

"I'm fine," Kyle protested. "Mama made me stay in bed for days. I'm tired of staying in bed. I wanna go outside and play."

"Well, you have to let me examine you first," Elizabeth told him.

"I know," Kyle said gloomily, hanging his head. "But I wasn't faking," he mumbled.

"I should say not," Elizabeth said, laying her palm on his shoulder. She lifted his drooping head gently with a

AMERICAN RAGE: Alaska Phase I

finger under his chin. "Can you tell me young man how you managed to fight off a huge fifteen hundred pound brown bear and only end up with this little scratch?"

"I curled!" Kyle grinned proudly.

"Curled?" Elizabeth frowned.

"You know," Kyle said. "I curled. I wrapped myself up in a tight ball and played dead."

"I don't think that big old bear wanted you anyway, Kyle!" Kenzie argued. "He just smelled that salmon and caribou Mama stored in there."

"Can we leave now?" Kyle pleaded, instantly jumping topics. "We could go to Mr. Olani's."

"Please Mama? Can we?" Kenzie asked.

"Hush now you two," Miriam said sternly. "We wait until Nurse Elizabeth is done."

"Kyle," Elizabeth said. "Have you had any headaches? Or trouble seeing?"

"Nope," Kyle answered.

"Any trouble walking?" Elizabeth asked.

"Nope," he replied.

"Any tingling or funny feelings any place?" She continued.

"Nope," he repeated.

"Tell me," Elizabeth said with a serious edge to her tone. "I want you to think back to when the bear first hit you..."

"He didn't hit me," Kyle interrupted. "He swatted me."

"Kyle!" Miriam exclaimed, gently chastising him. "You should not interrupt or correct your elders."

Elizabeth laughed. "It's okay Miriam. Kyle is a bundle of energy. I would be concerned if he weren't all knots and sparks right about now. I might even detect a little cabin fever mixed in there."

Miriam laughed, a little embarrassed. She didn't

expect perfection from Kyle and Kenzie. But maybe a little restraint in public would be good. Then again, they were only children. Henry Ivan wouldn't have batted an eye at their exuberance. Besides, wasn't Miriam the one continually telling her children to have patience?

"Okay Kyle," Elizabeth continued. "So when the bear '*swatted*' you," and she emphasized '*swatted*', "Do you remember if you went to sleep right after?"

"Oh," Kyle said, momentarily pondering her question. "Do you wanna know if I got knocked out?" Everyone laughed heartily, except Kyle. He looked confused.

"Yup," Elizabeth said, still chuckling. "That's exactly what I want to know."

"Nope," Kyle answered proudly. "I wasn't knocked out."

"How can you be sure of that?" Kenzie demanded to know. "No one knows the exact minute they go to sleep. People just *poof...* go to sleep."

"Well," Elizabeth explained. "Sometimes there are little flashes of light, or you might feel very heavy or dizzy... like the room is spinning around."

"And I didn't see any stars either!" Kyle said. "I was definitely awake after the bear got me." Kyle was adamant.

"How are you so sure Kyle?" Miriam asked softly.

Kyle became very quiet. His legs stopped moving. Miriam thought he might be about to cry and she had the urge to embrace him. But she also knew that Kyle might not want her motherly comfort in front of Elizabeth. If Kyle had taken on any of her Henry Ivan's traits in the short time he knew his father, it was his strength. Henry Ivan was a proud and brave man. Kyle was most definitely Henry Ivan's son. She had seen this part of Kyle's personality peeking through when he had frequently tried to fill his father's shoes. Still, she found herself at the edge of her chair ready to go to him.

"I know I was awake," Kyle began solemnly, "Because I kept thinking how much I would miss Mama... and Kenzie... when I died." No one said a word for a few seconds. But to Miriam the seconds seemed to stretch much longer than normal seconds would. She worked hard not to let any tears slip down her face though she felt that constricted sensation in her throat sneaking up on her.

"And besides," Kyle added, his disposition instantly flipping 360 degrees, "The bear smelled awful! He was stinky!"

"Well," Elizabeth announced. "That's proof enough for me. I don't think you ever lost consciousness Kyle, but from now on I think you better stay away from anything with sharp claws over five hundred pounds!" Both children giggled.

"Miriam, I think it's pretty safe to give Kyle an A plus in healing and send you all on your way," Elizabeth said. Kyle jumped off the examining table and both he and Kenzie waited impatiently at the door.

"I think he's fine Miriam," Elizabeth said, resting her hand on Miriam's forearm as they walked through the doorway and down the hall. "You did a beautiful job tending to his wound. You did everything right. Kyle did everything right. And all is well. I don't think the unresponsiveness you told me about was from the head injury. I think it was from the cold. From what you've described, it sounds as if he had the start of hypothermia. I don't think we need to worry," she added in a low whisper.

Miriam smiled. Relief and happiness washed over her like a fresh summer rain.

❆❆❆❆❆

The going was rough through the deep snow but the

temperature was in the high forties and Miriam didn't mind. Judging by the way Kenzie and Kyle were diving and rolling in the snow and twirling and leapfrogging, it didn't seem to bother them much either. It was invigorating to be outside in the sunshine. Miriam supposed they had each experienced a little dose of cabin fever over the last thirteen days. As much as she loved Kenzie and Kyle, she had been hunkered down with them in the small cabin for almost two full weeks. A little fresh air and exercise was certainly doing wonders for her spirit. She had found it difficult to wipe the smile from her face since Elizabeth had given Kyle a thorough once over and pronounced him fit. Miriam was normally of steady emotion — not given to highs and lows — and she felt rather silly walking around smiling when no one had made a joke. But there she was... still grinning, enjoying the antics of her children in the snow and feeling blessed the three of them were together and healthy as they headed home from Mr. Olani's store.

"Can we go Mama? Please! Please? Can we?" Kenzie teased.

"Please Mama," Kyle yelled loudly. "We can make it a celebration!"

"We have to Mama," Kenzie whined. "We have to or we'll be the only ones not there!"

"Mr. Olani said there would be games and everything!" Kyle exclaimed, jumping up and down and twirling so fast that Miriam almost became dizzy watching him. Miriam didn't let on to her children, but she had no intention of missing Mr. Olani's impromptu *After the Blizzard* party. Mr. Olani, short on conversation and fond of using initials for everything, dubbed the open house, the ATB party. He had gone out of his way to invite everyone in Takotna — well, the residents that lived close enough to the village center.

He had planned to visit Miriam and her children late that same afternoon but instead, there they were marching into his store after Kyle's appointment at the clinic. The three of them had arrived before Mr. Olani had been able to make the trip to their cabin.

"We can go on one condition," Miriam said seriously. Kyle and Kenzie stopped dead in their tracks and waited.

"What condition Mama?" Kenzie asked.

Miriam turned to face her children who now waited breathlessly about two yards behind. "On the condition that you both..." Miriam paused. She peered at Kenzie, sighing and shifting her weight from her left leg to her right, and back again. Miriam glanced at Kyle as he stared down at the ground where his boot ought to be. His foot was buried somewhere under the snow and he watched as if any minute he expected it to pop up on its own from its hiding place.

"On the condition that you both help me bake for the party," Miriam said, grinning. Both Kenzie and Kyle screeched with joy — baking was a delight they relished. On the trip home they jumped and dove into the deep snow while making wild guesses at what games Mr. Olani would have, what kind of food people would bring and exactly what the party would be like. As Miriam walked along with them through the piles of snow, she gave up attempts to stop herself from doing all that smiling.

❄❄❄❄❄

Fizer farm Shepherdstown, West Virginia, August

"Okay," Stephy yelled to Nick, her hand shielding her eyes from the rising sun as she looked up toward the peak of the Fizer farmhouse. "I have to admit," she said. "I didn't expect to find you up there. I leave the breakfast table for twenty minutes to take a shower and it takes me forty minutes to find you when I get back to the spot I thought I left you. Couldn't you have left breadcrumbs for me to follow?"

"Sorry," Nick yelled down to her. "It was kind of a spur of the moment thing."

"Okay understood. But I give up. Wanna tell me why you're taking a nap on the roof of your father's house?"

Nick laughed. "Neighbors wouldn't let me take a nap on theirs?"

"Funny boy," Stephy said.

"Not sleeping," he answered, "Rigging up a little boost for the short wave."

"Why not just use the phone or watch television like everyone else?" she asked.

"Where's the fun in that?" Nick answered, finishing wrapping several loops of 14 gauge copper wire around a segment near the base of the old rusted television antenna his father never bothered to take down when television went digital. "Be down in a minute." Nick hadn't intended to spend his morning hooking up his short wave radio. He hadn't intended on firing up the radio at all. The only reason he brought it with him was that he felt naked if he didn't have it close by — like Linus and his security blanket he figured.

He inched his way to the ladder that was leaning against the house and eased himself into position so he was on all fours facing the roof. Once he had the right angle, he slid his leg down onto the second rung from the top, careful not to make a misstep. It was a long way down from his perspective. The ladder barely reached up to the height of the roof so it was a little tricky to maneuver his body into the right position. Once he was comfortable and confident his hands and feet were in the right spots, he began his descent.

He saw Stephy at the bottom looking up at him, her hands on either side of the rickety apparatus holding it steady. He didn't hurry. When he neared the bottom, he stopped on the fourth rung of the ladder, simulated losing his grip and pretended to fall. Stephy stepped right up and grabbed him around the waist, obviously concerned, and seeming relieved she had helped break his fall — only it wasn't a fall. It was a ploy to steal a kiss and sneak in a little strategic hand placement when she least expected it.

"Jerk," Stephy said, feigning anger. She slapped his shoulder and then laughed. "You never change!"

"And you keep falling for it!" he quipped, joining in her laughter. He wrapped his arm around her shoulders as they walked back into the house.

"You're not going to leave that ladder resting against the house like that are you?" She asked.

"Well of course I am," he replied. "You don't think this antenna thing is going to work on the first try, do you?"

She sighed. He held the door for her and they walked through his parents' living room into the kitchen.

"Hey Pop," Nick said.

"Morning son," his father answered, peering over his glasses and lowering the open newspaper he had been reading. "Did you find what you were looking for up on the roof son?"

Nick laughed.

"See," Stephy said, chuckling. "You're all comedians."

"Leave me out of it," Nick's mother said, padding into the kitchen on noisy slippers. She was swathed in a pale green terrycloth robe. "These two have the stand-up routine. I'm only the booking agent," she added, pouring herself a cup of coffee from the pot.

Nick went to the dining room and retrieved his small

shortwave radio. He brought it back to the kitchen and set it on the corner of the table. He opened the kitchen window farther, leaned out to grab the wire hanging down from the roof and pulled it inside.

"You're not going to electrocute yourself with that are you?" Stephy said, leaning away from him.

"I hadn't planned on it," Nick said.

"What is that?" his mother asked, sipping from the cup she cradled in her hands and peering over his shoulder.

"Shortwave radio," Nick's father answered. "But where do you talk through it?"

"It's only a receiver Pop," Nick said. "You know... for listening."

"Hmm," his father said, crackling the newspaper as he turned the page and went back to reading.

"Why listen to that?" his mother asked.

"I dunno, just thought I could get some news," Nick replied.

"The USDA didn't take the television you know," his mother said. "It's still early. I can get the morning news for you."

Nick looked up at his mother and smiled. She meant well. But how was he supposed to explain to her, to any of them, that commercial news and media are a waste of time? Mainstream broadcasting was a propaganda platform. Why was it so easy for people of their generation to recognize and accept that the Soviet Union and East Germany dished out propaganda like gumdrops but they can't, or won't, accept that the United States is the most sophisticated and proficient propaganda dispenser of them all?

With the flick of a switch, the government can take over every form of communication. The initial installation of those little boxes at television and radio stations was for the public welfare... to warn of tornados or earthquakes or to provide other emergency information. The goal of those boxes permitting the swap over to government-controlled media was never — God forbid — meant to interfere with the free flow of information or First Amendment rights! Nick doubted he could ever persuade his parents to accept reality. But the sad thing was... it was going to become quite clear to them — to everyone — very quickly.

"You know how I like to tinker," Nick said, turning his attention back to the radio.

Nick's mother shrugged and sat down beside her husband. Nick's father fiddled with the newspaper, snapping it and crinkling the pages until he latched onto what he wanted. His father pulled out a section in the middle of the paper and handed it to Nick's mother. She folded it and flattened it out so that only the crossword puzzle was showing. Then she put on her reading glasses, picked up a pen and set to attacking the empty black and white squares peering back at her. It was pretty bold. Nick had never had the confidence to sit down armed with an ink pen, to face off against a daunting crossword puzzle... not unless the pen was the erasable kind.

It was good to see his parents' attention turned away from the sledgehammer dangling over their heads — if only long enough for his mother to do a crossword puzzle. By three this afternoon they could technically be homeless or moving into a place no bigger than a matchbox — comparatively speaking. The USDA thing was inconceivable. How could American society have sunk so low to literally throw two elderly people out into the street to implement some socialist bunk about redistributing wealth and land in America? It was damn theft... nothing less.

The government was stealing their land and lying about why they were doing it to cover their tracks. The more Nick thought about it, the more he was beginning to realize there wasn't going to be any right time to stand up against this. This despicable situation was never going to get better. It was only going to get much, much worse. During his lifetime he had been nothing more than a simple guy who tried to make his way through a very complicated world. But the idea of him continuing to sit back — knowing what he knew — and pretending none of it was really happening, was starting to make him physically ill.

He wasn't a rabble rousing protestor — a sign carrying 'in your face' kind of guy — but he couldn't look away when people were headed for disaster either. He wasn't the type to stand by and watch a mugging, or pretend he didn't see a madman with an AK-47 heading for a group of teenagers. Someone had to scream, "Watch out!" If he didn't do it who would? Yet he had kept his mouth shut all those years. The guilt over his silence tormented him. But was there anything he could possibly do that would make a difference now?

"Why the sudden urge to listen to the short wave?" Stephy probed. "I thought you were here to relax?"

"This is relaxing," Nick protested. "For me," he whispered. Nick took his time turning the dial on the radio. His expectations weren't high.

"Why is there so much static?" Stephy grimaced.

"Reception has been bad for years," Nick answered. "Until digital television came to town, watching a whole program from start to finish without a snowy screen was cause for a block party," Nick answered.

"Why?" Stephy asked.

"Shepherdstown West Virginia is smack dab in the National Radio Quiet Zone," he replied.

Stephy laughed. "You mean quiet like a hospital zone? Should we be whispering?"

Nick chuckled. "No. It's a thirteen thousand square mile area over the eastern half of the state where cell phone service and Wi-Fi had been banned. According to official explanations, Wi-Fi and cell signals would confuse the Robert C. Byrd Green Bank Telescope, the world's largest fully steerable telescope located at the National Radio Astronomy Observatory. Only in the last year has the law been revised to permit limited cell service during daylight hours."

"How can a telescope get confused?" Stephy asked.

"The purpose of this monstrosity — that's my affectionate moniker for it — is to track energy waves and gases coming from stars. They say for the telescope to work properly, it must be placed in a quiet area."

"Hmm, exactly what kind of energy waves are they expecting?" Stephy questioned. "Illegal Internet pornography broadcasts from the Polaris Star?"

"Not sure," Nick said.

"Why is the government spending hundreds of millions of dollars watching for these signals from outer space? I'll bet there are families up the street that barely have enough food to feed their children?" Stephy complained.

"Damn good question," Nick's father chimed in.

"It is," Nick agreed. Knowing what Nick knew about the OPSEIM Directive he guessed the official explanation for this telescope was at the least... questionable. The more Nick thought about it the more sensible it seemed that his parents should consider leaving the farm. He didn't want to see them lose everything they had worked their lives to achieve, but the future was so uncertain — for all of them. Honestly, West Virginia was going to be a pretty dangerous place to be if the Olympus Project escalated and did enter Phase II. They were too damn close to Washington and the East Coast was too crammed with people.

Nick turned the radio dial half-heartedly. He was looking for — for what? He wasn't sure. In any event, so far he wasn't having much luck. He glanced out the window at the sunshine streaming across the lawn and for a second wished he were ten years old again. He didn't have these monkeys on his back when he was a boy. As he languished in his musings, his cell phone rang. Three pairs of eyes shot glares at Nick.

"Some vacation if work is calling you already," his mother said, annoyed.

Nick pulled his phone from his pocket and swiped his thumb across the screen to take the call. He listened quietly. "Understood," he said. He ended the call and set the phone on the table.

"Who was that?" Stephy asked. "You didn't have much to say."

He wasn't sure he could answer right now. Instead, he smiled, scratched under his chin and looked up at the ceiling. "Hey Pop," Nick said. "I never noticed before but this place needs a good painting."

"The place needs a lot of repair," his father said, laying down the newspaper. "The older you get, the harder it is to keep things in working order. It seems I fix one thing, it leads to repairing a dozen other things, and when I'm finally finished with a good once around, it's time to start over from the beginning."

"Must be frustrating," Nick said.

"It would be," his father told him, grinning, "If I actually worried about those kinds of things anymore." Stephy and Nick laughed. Nick's mother merely squinted at her husband, peering over her glasses, examining Nick's father's expression as intently as if she were looking for a splinter buried in his cheek. William Fizer didn't seem fazed by his wife's apparent displeasure at his lack of concern over the condition of the house. "I'm pretty pissed about how the government is squeezing us out of here," Nick's father said. "But the truth is... part of me wouldn't mind a change of scenery. Things around here just aren't the same as they used to be. I kind of lost my heart for the farm because of this government thing."

"Well," Nick said, "What do you think you might do? Are you planning to continue fighting this... keep it moving through the courts?"

"No," Nick's mother said. She removed her glasses and took a sip of coffee before continuing. "I think your father and I have had more aggravation than we can stomach over this. He's tired, I'm tired and we're thinking it's time to stop banging our heads against the wall."

"I sure as hell don't want to pack up and go live in a shoebox," Nick's father said adamantly. "You can bet on that."

Nick sat back in his chair and looked at the three of them. "Well, I haven't had a chance to talk with Stephy about this so right now it's just a thought..."

"What's up?" Stephy asked.

"I'm hesitant to bring it up," Nick said, leaning in toward Stephy and taking hold of both of her hands. "I told you I wasn't going to make any moves without discussing it with you first."

"It's just a thought right now though... right?" she clarified tenuously, "So no harm in sharing a thought." She smiled at him.

"Well," Nick began, "The phone call I just got was a ROC HQ emergency action message alert."

Stephy sat stiffly in her chair. "They haven't recalled

you, have they? You're not being deployed!" she exclaimed. "Every time you get one of those phone messages you disappear for a year — or two!"

"No," he laughed. "I'm not going anywhere. Not unless it's with you three."

"Does this mean you're resigning your commission? You're not going back to Georgia... to the army?" Stephy's brow angled sharply upward.

"I think that's pretty safe to say," Nick said, "If that's okay with you."

"Me?" Stephy asked, stunned, "If it's okay with me? Oh hell yes. It's absolutely okay with me!" She jumped from her chair and wrapped her arms around him, appearing to Nick nearly as excited as she had been when he had proposed over twenty years before. It caught him off guard but he held fast to her. He was torn between the joy of seeing her happiness and the lingering distress over the devastating message he had just received from headquarters.

"Well," his father said. "I think that's a fine idea!" Bill Fizer stood and thrust out his hand. Nick and Stephy parted and Nick gave his father a firm handshake.

"Thanks Pop," Nick said.

"It's perfect timing," his father agreed. "You've been at this plenty long enough. I think you deserve to kick back for a while," his father grinned. "And get out from under the government!" he added.

"Well," his mother said eagerly. "You're certainly not going to hear any complaints from me!"

"What will you do son?" his father asked. Everyone looked at Nick expectantly and all three wore wide grins. "Can you live off your retirement?"

"You will get a retirement, right?" his mother asked.

"Oh sure," Nick answered. "Twenty-two years in," he

added, "And we have savings." His mother and father were clearly pleased for him. Stephy looked ecstatic. He had no trouble reading her expression this time. It wasn't about the retirement money. It wouldn't matter to her whether he cut short his career before retirement kicked in. He knew his wife well enough to know she figured this was about him, his own struggle and his peace of mind. There was only so much torture a man could put himself through without losing his grip. There was no doubt in Nick's mind this was the right thing to do. He didn't have much choice now anyway. But his parents didn't have to know that part right this minute.

"So what's this thought you've got on your mind?" Stephy asked.

"Well," Nick started. "It depends on you guys," he said.

"We're all ears son," his father told him.

Nick hesitated. Maybe this was too crazy to spring on them without some preparation, he thought. He wasn't an impulsive guy by nature and this probably wouldn't sound rational to them. Hell, it was probably going to sound damned insane. What if they think it's a joke and laugh at him. That's the one reaction with which he might have trouble dealing.

"We can't read your mind Nick," Stephy said.

"Okay," he started reluctantly. "But I want you to know I have been seriously thinking about this. What I'm about to say isn't a joke. So before you laugh, just remember that."

"What is it Nick?" his father asked, with visible concern creeping into his fading grin. "Does this have something to do with the phone call?"

Nick sighed. "It does, in part," he said. "But it has to do with you losing the farm too... especially now that I know you don't want to stay here to fight this in court for the next five or six years. I would have gladly stood beside you — and still will if you decide you want to do that. I'll give it everything I've got... to help you fight this."

"We know that son," his mother said warmly.

"Boy this must be a pretty interesting thought you've got Nick," Stephy said, smiling at him. "The suspense is killing me."

Nick looked at Stephy and realized it was ridiculous to think she would laugh at his idea — knowing what she knows now and understanding the seriousness of it.

"Okay," he said, resolved. "The way I see it, Mom, Pop, there's nothing tying you to Shepherdstown now, correct?"

"Can't argue with that," his father said.

"Then I suggest we leave... the four of us, together, as soon as I resign my commission." Nick watched his wife. He didn't expect she would object to including his parents in their future but it never hurt to be sure. He didn't see the slightest hint of reservation on her face.

"It's a great idea," his mother said. "So far I like it."

"And so..." his father said, "Where are we... the four of us... planning to go?"

"Just remember," Nick said. "Before you laugh... try to understand I have thought seriously about this."

"Okay," Stephy said. "Unless you booked us on the first shuttle to Mars, how strange can this be?"

"She's right Nick," his mother said. "We're not going to laugh at you!"

"Come on son," his father said smiling. "I'm getting older by the minute. What's the plan? Where are we going?"

"Uh... well... Alaska," he blurted out, cringing as if waiting for his car to slam into a tree after a three hundred sixty-degree skid on a patch of black ice.

Seconds ticked by. No one spoke. Nick waited for someone to say something. He studied his mother. Her mouth was open. He peered at his father. His blue eyes looked twice the normal size. He looked at Stephy. She was smiling, that mischievous smile with one eyebrow tipped a little to the left.

"Wow," Stephy said, "Didn't see that one coming!"

True to their word none of them laughed.

Chapter 18

❀❀❀❀❀

ROC Northwest Takotna, Alaska, August

"You being shipped out too?" the man asked Malikov.

"*Da*," Malikov answered after a short hesitation. He watched as the man stared at him from his concrete bench on the other side of the ten by ten foot holding cell. This man's ankles were also shackled and hooked to a thick metal ring in the floor.

"What they get you for?"

"I do nothing," Malikov answered.

The man laughed riotously. "You're gonna fit right in!" he said, slapping his hand on his leg and then wiping spittle from the corner of his mouth with his sleeve. "Nobody's guilty around here."

Malikov peered at the man. His jumpsuit was wrinkled, his hair disheveled, his face unshaven and he looked like he hadn't showered in weeks. Malikov thought he probably didn't look much different from this man. He himself hadn't looked in a mirror and had not cared whether he showered or not. What difference would it have made? No one had come to see him... not the Russian officer, not Sergei, not even the MPs to interrogate him. If no one was going to look at him, why should he make the effort to look presentable? Maybe he would feel different in San Francisco. Maybe he would have visitors there who would listen to him and believe him... maybe let him go.

"You getting off at San Francisco?" The man had one

leg crossed over the other. He was picking at the spaces between his teeth with the fingernail of his little finger. The shabby man was clearly not American but Malikov didn't recognize the accent. Canadian maybe, or British, or maybe South African... they all sounded alike to Malikov. Right now he wasn't in the mood to talk. He wished this foreigner would keep his mouth shut, his questions to himself. Hadn't Malikov answered enough questions? Questions from the MPs were enough for two lifetimes.

"Hey," the man repeated, impatiently. "I asked you a question. So, you getting off in San Francisco or goin' on?"

"Go on?" Malikov asked. "*Vhat... deece* go on?"

"You know... goin' on," the man said, "To the pen."

"Pen..." Malikov repeated, "*Nyet...* have no pen."

"Christ, you moron, did you just get off a boat or something?" The man asked, heaving a sigh. "The P...E...N man, the federal penitentiary, are you headed for Leavenworth or somewhere to serve your bit?"

"I do nothing," Malikov said.

"Yeah I get it asshole. But you don't have to play that game now. It's just us here. I can hold my mud. Did you get your bit yet or not?"

"Mud... bit... *vhat deece* mean?" Malikov frowned.

"Mud... you know... I hold my mud. I'm not a snitch. It means I won't repeat what you say even if they torture me," the man explained. "So?"

Malikov shook his head and shrugged his shoulders.

The man glared at Malikov. "So, how much time you got?

"Two hours," Malikov answered. "Two hours... plane go."

"Are you listening to me?" the man asked. "I'm asking you how much time you gotta serve. How many years did you get?"

"No years," Malikov said. "Two hours."

"Right!" the man snarled, exasperated. "What are you, touched in the head or somethin'? Dumb bastard..." he muttered, pulling his legs up onto the bench, leg irons stretched taught. He draped his arm over his eyes and mumbled to himself.

"Stupid man," Malikov sneered. He leaned his head against the wall behind him and closed his eyes. He was grateful the questions stopped. It will be good to be in California, he thought. Maybe they will listen to him there... or maybe not ask so many questions.

❄❄❄❄❄

"Wake up!" the MP demanded, rapping hard on the holding cell door. Malikov opened his eyes. His neck was sore from the hard concrete wall. He must have dozed. Time stood still except for disruptions... when the MPs came around to question him or when it was feeding time — like at the zoo. So far, prison hit him hardest whenever he opened his eyes after dozing. It was this moment when he knew he was not dreaming and he was truly in this place... the dark desolate pit. This was a place of no hope.

"It'll be a few more hours before you guys leave," the MP said, handing a boxed meal to Malikov's roommate. "These are to tide you over."

"Hey, man," Malikov's cellmate said, clumsily swinging his shackled legs over the edge of the bench and setting his feet down on the floor. "What do you mean it's gonna be a few more hours... how many?"

"I don't know how many hours," the MP said, passing a box to Malikov. Malikov set it next to him on the bench. "What's the difference?" The MP asked his roommate, laughing. "You got a date?"

"Well what's the hold up?" the inmate complained, opening his boxed lunch.

"Plane malfunction," the MP said, "Small mechanical problem or something."

"*Amerikantsy* defect," Malikov mumbled.

"Problem, Malikov?" the MP asked.

"*Nyet*," Malikov said, shaking his head vigorously, fearing he might give the guard reason to beat him. Bullies had short fuses. He just wanted to be left alone.

❊❊❊❊❊

ROC East HQ, Route 2 Templeton, Massachusetts, August

"How's your lobster?" Falcon asked Meg.

"It's great," she answered. "It's nice they have a choice of restaurants. I'm quite surprised."

"I have to admit," Falcon said. "It is surprising." Falcon poured another half glass of wine for each of them. "You know Meg," Falcon said, clearing his throat, "I'm glad we got together tonight."

Meg laughed. "I hope I didn't make you nervous... asking you out I mean."

"No, no, of course not," he chuckled. But that wasn't exactly true. He did experience that sudden language challenge — tripping over his own tongue — when he tried to eloquently respond to her invitation. Aside from that he was okay, but he still had the concerns about starting something so close to his transfer. Yet somehow none of that seemed to matter to him right now. He was sitting across from her... seeing the real woman for the first time under the glow of a soft flickering candle flame. This vision of her was absent the glint from the gold oak leaf clusters that normally rested on the epaulets of her uniform. Instead, her shoulders were enticingly half bare and adorned only with the scooped neck of her powder blue gown. He realized now his hesitancy to become involved with her was partially a reluctance to become involved with Meg *the major*... the uniformed ROC officer to whom he had so far been conditioned to avoid in accordance with ROC training policy. But they weren't at ROC training any longer and he was definitely attracted by her other half... Meg *the stunningly beautiful woman* only two feet from him. No he wasn't nervous. In fact, he was a little bewildered. Being with her seems to have touched off some inner passion he hadn't been sure existed in him.

"Well I had two ulterior motives for asking you to dinner tonight," she said.

"Oh?" he prodded, intrigued.

She nodded and sipped her wine. "Primarily," she began, seeming uncertain about how to say what was on her mind. "Well, I have to be honest," she admitted. "I was afraid you would get your transfer orders and up and leave before we had any opportunity to... to get to know each other better."

Falcon wasn't usually one to hold his breath waiting for someone to finish a sentence. He wasn't normally the passionate type — outside of competing on a football field or a baseball diamond that is. But he realized he was sitting on the edge of his seat as if he were in the biggest game of his life. He quickly picked up his wine glass. At least a glass in his hand might be enough to draw her attention away from the boyish exhilaration that was probably skipping around all over his face.

"And secondly, I felt you would be very easy to talk to... and so far you have proven me right," she said, seeming a little nervous herself. "It's just... this has been so overwhelming... finding out Phase II is going to happen."

"I agree," Falcon said, nodding. "It is pretty

daunting."

"To be honest," Meg said. "I don't think I was ready to hear that Phase II will be implemented in less than three months."

"Well you're not alone there," he agreed.

"I mean..." she started to speak but seemed reluctant or as if she were searching for the right words. "I guess..."

"What?" Falcon asked, setting his glass on the table, hoping to put her at ease with a soft smile. He should reach over and lay his hand on hers. The urge was strong. But was the time right or would he just prove how awkward he was if he reached for her?

"I just think this has changed everything," Meg said. I don't think the world will ever be the same anywhere after Phase II begins. I think life as we knew it will be changed forever. I feel like there's urgency in the air, a desperate need for stability, for something good... something that will last. I feel like there's no time to waste, as if there's this big giant thing dangling over our heads. We need to... to rush to get in the last of as many normal things as we can and then cover our heads before everything crashes down on us. Or... or that maybe we should run away and find a place to hide from it. But I don't think there's any place to hide from this. You know what I mean?"

Falcon was stunned. Meg had pretty much reached down inside his soul and pulled out his own hidden feelings and fears, deep concerns he had not been able to put into words. At that moment Falcon wanted only to catch his breath or maybe pinch his thigh... to reassure himself that Meg was right here, right now. He felt a need to prove to himself that this was real... this connection that suddenly seemed to have erupted between them.

"I feel the same Meg," he told her. "How could anyone paying attention to the world not feel the impact of this?"

"But I don't know how to deal with it," she said. "I don't have anyone to talk to about this. Phase II isn't a simple mobilization... a deployment to a foreign war zone where you stay over there with your unit, support the mission for a year and then come home to..."

"...To everything you knew, and everything you used to believe?" Falcon finished the thought, watching Meg nod in agreement.

"And to the people... you love," she added softly. He saw a flicker of anguish across Meg's brow. This was no casual dinner. She was deeply worried and her worry seemed... urgent. Falcon was touched that Meg trusted him. This was dangerous territory — expressing doubts about the Olympus Project or ROC objectives. Questions — sincere reflections — like these could get a person killed. Falcon felt linked to her in a way he had never experienced with a woman. What had she seen in him over this last week and a half that gave her the confidence to even broach this subject with him? It was clear she had peeled back multiple layers of her outer protective shell. She had just opened herself up to him, left herself vulnerable. No other person had ever done that with him — trusted him so implicitly. Not even Whitehawk. His good friend had held back from trusting Falcon. Whitehawk had only warned him at the last second about the champagne.

At this moment Falcon felt as if he could tell Meg anything. He felt he could even ask her about the ROC graduation ceremony. What did she think about the general's threats and warnings? What if he told her about Whitehawk... about not drinking the champagne? Did she drink it? Did she know anything about that night that would help him understand the chaos? Now he was kicking himself. He had but a few days left at ROC Eastern Division and he might have blown his only chance to connect with Meg. Was there still time? The last thing he wanted to do was to pack up and move on... without her. Falcon started to reach for her. At that moment Benton swaggered into the restaurant and, seeing them, he strutted over to their table. In a flash, Benton was standing next to Meg, bending from the waist and slobbering over her hand.

"I didn't expect to see you here Meg," Benton grinned, releasing Meg's hand and immediately sliding over a chair from a nearby table. He sat down and made himself comfortable, nodding to Falcon in the same manner he would nod to any busboy who had just refilled his water glass. "Colonel Colby," Benton grinned.

"You have something on your mind, Brevet Colonel?" Falcon asked him, his muscles stiffening.

Benton shot Falcon a sweaty glare. "Just being sociable Colonel," he said, his outer façade seemingly full of sincerity — Mr. Charming stem to stern.

"Are you dining alone tonight Brevet Colonel?" Meg asked politely.

"No," Benton answered. "I'm meeting some friends. They should be here in a few minutes. Just wanted to stop by and pay my respects. Besides I didn't think Colonel Colby would mind sharing the most beautiful girl in the FOLT for a few seconds. I also wanted to set up a time next week for us to have dinner," Benton said to Meg. "We need to talk about your role here at headquarters. You're a critical member of my staff."

Falcon wondered if Meg was blushing. Benton could lay it on thick. Sure, Falcon thought, dinner next week after Falcon had moved on to his next billet... how convenient. Falcon suddenly felt an overpowering urge to run to the men's room and wash his hands. Instead, he tried to maintain his composure. He raised his glass and sipped his wine, watching Meg's expression as Benton talked. Falcon reconsidered. He was pretty sure Meg wasn't blushing even though he first thought she might be; the wine must have flushed her face. So Falcon decided he shouldn't worry about it. It didn't seem that Meg was falling for this guy's crap. Even if Meg didn't outwardly betray disdain for Benton Falcon sensed now she must be smart enough to figure out what a phony he was.

"So," Benton said to Meg. "I trust you've settled in by now. Do you need anything? Is there anything I can help you with?"

"Everything's going well," Meg replied. "Thank you."

"Great," Benton said to Meg. "Tomorrow we'll firm up a date for dinner to go over a few things." Benton turned to face Falcon. "Oh and Colonel, I understand your orders have come through. You should be receiving them in the morning."

Falcon set his wine glass on the table. "And you know this because..."

"General Hazkill happened to mention it in passing," Benton said, with a toothy grinning snigger. "I thought you'd like to know."

"Big of you," Falcon said, unable to prevent the nasty snarl in his upper lip.

"Any idea where you're off to?" Benton asked.

"None," Falcon replied.

"Well," Benton said. "Be sure and let me know then won't you? We should have a sendoff luncheon or something."

"That won't be necessary," Falcon said.

"Oh no," Benton pressed. "I insist. It's the least we

can do." Benton leaped up from his chair when he saw three older distinguished-looking men enter the restaurant and amble up to the hostess station. Benton waved to them. "Gotta go," he whispered, "Can't keep these gentlemen waiting." He took Meg's hand, kissed it and flashed his protruding teeth at both of them in a Machiavellian grin. He turned and hurried to the waiting men. Falcon and Meg watched Benton rush over to them.

"Isn't that taller man General Hazkill?" Meg asked.

"It looks like him yes," Falcon said. It was indeed General Hazkill, his palm on Benton's shoulder while he chatted with the restaurant hostess and two other men Falcon didn't recognize. What a sniveling bastard Benton is, Falcon thought. He wouldn't admit it because he didn't want to let on that he gave a shit about anything concerning Benton. But the truth was... his curiosity was killing him. How in hell had Benton weaseled his way into Hazkill's inner circle so fast?

"I wonder how he knows him so well," Meg remarked offhandedly, sipping from her wine glass.

"No idea," Falcon answered, pushing his plate toward the center of the table. He had lost interest in his dinner. He drank from his water glass and set it back down. It infuriated him that Benton had strutted over to their table, barged into their conversation and disrupted them just when Falcon thought he was about to glimpse the core of what made Meg tick, just when he was thinking about bringing up the ROC ceremony fiasco... the sonofabitch, he thought. Falcon became distracted. He wrapped his hand around his glass and let the coolness seep into his palm. Benton had snuffed out... extinguished... an incredible spark between him and Meg. The moment had dissipated into thin air like a puff of smoke. He would never get it back now... that inconceivably instantaneous, deep emotional link to Meg. There simply wasn't enough time left before his transfer.

"I would like to continue our conversation," Meg said.

An instant of confusion wafted across Falcon's thoughts before he could grasp what Meg had said. Was she opening the option of... of exploring their earlier train of thought? He looked up, catching her electrifying blue eyes with his deep gaze, his own brown eyes twinkling.

"But I'm thinking this is probably not the best place to do it," she added. Maybe it was something in the way she looked at him. Or maybe he was hoping he would see something in her eyes... wanting so much to see it that he imagined he had. Whatever the case it didn't matter to him right now. Something was stirring deep within him and it wasn't the wine.

"Let's go," he said.

❄❄❄❄❄

Takotna, Alaska, August

"I can carry them," Kyle promised. "I won't drop them on the way to Mr. Olani's blizzard party. I'm sure I will be careful."

"But it's a long way to carry them Kyle," Miriam argued. "Why don't you take the fry bread, it's much lighter and even if you drop the basket nothing will happen to it. Let Kenzie or me take the jam."

"Girls shouldn't carry heavy things," Kyle said.

"I'm stronger than you are!" Kenzie teased.

"All right," Miriam said, we don't need to argue. This is a time to discuss calmly. "Now son, if the jars break I cannot replace them. Do you know what that means?" Miriam looked straight at Kyle.

"I do Mama," Kyle said, nodding. "It means we will

not have *Tléikw,"* — berry — "Jam for a long time and it will be my fault."

Miriam smiled. "That's right son," she said. "Now do you understand why I don't want you to carry the jars?"

"Uh huh," Kyle acknowledged, nodding vigorously. Still he continued, cautiously placing the five canning jars into the cloth sack and reading aloud Miriam's hand written labels as he went along. *"Was'x'aan Tléighu,"* — salmon berry, *"Kanat'á,"*— blueberry, Kyle read proudly.

"Kyle," Miriam said, struggling to be patient.

Kyle looked at Miriam solemnly. "Mama, I know I'm only nine years old but I did fight off a brown bear... and live through it."

Miriam looked at her son and studied his expression. She was quickly reminded her living breathing son was nothing short of a miracle. A few canning jars no longer seemed so important... in the scheme of things.

❄❄❄❄❄

Adit 17 Perseverance Mine Juneau, Alaska, August

"Maybe I should have gone up with you," Viktor told Gil.

"Are you crazy?" Dan interrupted. "You just had surgery this morning."

Viktor brushed off Dan's concerns. "You mean my fingers? I could have snipped those off with a pair of dull scissors... not that you didn't do an awesome job Dan. And I did enjoy the buzz from the anesthesia."

Dan shook his head.

"Look Viktor," Gil said. "I took the plane up this morning, took the photos and then scattered the SEEDS. I did everything we talked about without a hitch. The rectennas took hold in the clouds at the right altitude. All you have to do is test them. If something isn't working right, I'll just go up again."

"How do these damn seed things work anyway? I have a pretty elastic mind but I'm having some difficulty grasping this concept," Dan said.

"I'll let Viktor explain," Gil answered. "This is his brainchild."

"Not really," Viktor argued. "I only took what's already out there and added my own little tweaks to it."

"I don't care how you got the idea," Dan sighed. "Just give me a little background — the short version — so that every time you bring up these seed things I won't be visualizing a field of daisies in my head."

Gil and Viktor laughed.

"Fair enough," Viktor said. "Okay first, this whole jamming idea is based on nanotechnology. You know what that is right?"

"Treat me like a blank slate in this Viktor," Dan smiled. "Don't be shy about presuming I know absolutely nothing here."

"Okay," Viktor agreed, grinning. "I have no problem presuming that."

"Asshole," Dan laughed.

"So here goes," Viktor began, taking a gulp of bottled water. "Nanotechnology is the manipulation of matter on an atomic, molecular and supramolecular scale. In other words, we're talking smaller than small here. The National Nanotechnology Initiative defines nanotechnology as the manipulation of matter with at least one dimension sized from 1 to 100 nanometers. The possibilities are endless. The U.S. has already invested 3.7 billion dollars, the European Union 1.2 billion and Japan 750 million dollars."

"What I'm trying to do," Viktor continued, "Is develop a way to jam electromagnetic radio waves emitted by the H.A.A.R.P. facility at Gakona, Alaska.

Government researchers allude there's no way to do that. I happen to believe there is. We just haven't found it yet. What I'm doing is working with an atom-sized antenna system that, when perfected, will have a heap of capacity all wrapped up in a tiny little package. But as you'll see..."

"Uh... wait a minute," Dan chuckled nervously. "Let's not make any presumptions here. I used to think I was pretty smart until I met you guys. But I'm starting to think my initial assessment of my brain's computing power was a little too rash."

"Okay, no presumptions," Viktor said. "Let me rephrase that. As I *hope* you'll see, what I'm working to accomplish is to use something that's already successful for one purpose and adjust it so it works in reverse for another purpose that is conceptually similar."

"Got it," Dan nodded.

"Okay," Viktor smiled. "Here's where it gets a little dicey. In 1964 a U.S. electrical engineer named William C. Brown invented a new process using a rectenna. He used this rectifying antenna to convert microwave energy into direct electrical current. To demonstrate it, he used a model helicopter powered by microwaves transmitted from the ground and received by an attached rectenna. Since that time, one of the thrusts of rectenna research has been to develop a receiving antenna for proposed solar power satellites to harvest energy from sunlight in space with solar cells and beam it down to earth as microwaves to huge rectenna arrays." Viktor stopped for another few gulps of bottled water. "Are you with me so far?" he asked Dan.

"With you," Dan said. "Kind of..." he grinned, wrinkling his freckled nose.

"Shall I stop?" Viktor asked.

"Hell no," Dan said.

Gil laughed, sat back in Dan's desk chair and rested his feet on the desktop. "Now remember what Viktor initially said," Gil pointed out. "All of the *government* research so far... suggests there is absolutely no way to block H.A.A.R.P. signals."

"Right," Viktor agreed.

"And obviously you guys don't believe that?" Dan asked.

"Oh I believe they may have initially thought that was the case," Viktor said. "But then, I'm not sure I know of any scientists besides us working to disprove that claim."

"So have you accomplished it?" Dan asked... eyes wide. "Can you prevent H.A.A.R.P. signals from getting through?"

"I accomplished my first goal... the inversion of the process," Viktor said.

"How is the process inverted?" Dan asked.

"Well... short version... light is composed of electromagnetic waves like radio waves, but of much smaller wavelength. A nantenna is a miniscule rectenna the size of a light wave, fabricated using nanotechnology, which acts as an antenna for light, and works in converting light into electricity. What I succeeded in doing is creating what I call the inverse anti-rectenna — which isn't exactly the inverse but it's mine and I can call it what I want to call it. So in short, the IAR — Inverse Anti-Rectenna — which we generally just call a rectenna, converts light into larger radio waves that can be conducted from the earth into the Ionosphere, rather than from the Ionosphere to earth. So, that's the kindergarten version. Whether it works consistently and how reliable it is... well that's the part we don't know yet."

"That's the objective of the testing," Gil added.

"So you said something about photos you took while up in the air," Dan said, scratching his head. "Is this something you can actually see?"

"Yes and no," Viktor said. "We can't see rectennas, but their activity leaves a trail in the clouds. Depending on the structure of the trail, we can tell what process is being used, where it was used and where it originated."

Gil swung his legs off Dan's desk, leaped up and brought his camera to him. "See," Gil said, "these are the digital images I took up there." Gil flicked through the images on his digital camera.

"Well shit!" Dan exclaimed. "I've seen weird stuff like that when I've flown. I thought they were storm clouds or something; I couldn't figure out what the hell I was looking at."

Gil nodded and grinned. "Exactly," he said. "It's almost impossible to know what you're looking at when you see these formations and pathways up there in the cloud cover. But the minute you know about the rectennas and electromagnetic microwave technology, it's as clear as the silt free water in the ice-blue pools at the top of the Taku Glacier."

"Okay, one last thing I still don't get," Dan said. "What are these SEEDS you keep talking about?"

"Think of it this way," Viktor explained. "Remember the old analog television antennas that sat on everyone's rooftop?"

"Sure," Dan answered.

"Well," Viktor expounded, "Those antennas inadequate range and direction capabilities because they had what we call a limited capture area. Normally you had only one antenna up there pulling in signals. Sometimes you had to climb up on the roof because the antenna wasn't drawing in strong signals and you had to rotate its direction. Of course later they developed those motorized antennas. But these SEEDS, or rectennas, are something like multiple TV antennas that you can spread over a wide grid to capture a greater area of signal... or in this case a greater area of energy... except of course they are tiny. The concept is not that different from principles used in wireless power transmission. The SEEDS are created using nanotechnology."

"Right," Gil added. "Then I get up there in the plane and eject them... of course that's a pretty simplified version of the actual process. The goal is to ensure they are properly placed and stick to the clouds."

"So these SEEDS, as you call them, are so tiny you can't see them, but you take them up in a plane, throw them out the window and they stick to clouds — or whatever you sprinkle them on — and they're super powerful," Dan said. "Crap, you guys better make sure you never drop one of those things in your dinner by accident!" Dan laughed.

"Uh... Dan," Viktor hesitated, looking at Gil and frowning. "That's not so funny as you think."

"Huh?" Dan's face blanched. "Are you serious?"

"He's as serious as frostbite in Nome," Gil said.

"These little rectennas capture signals — H.A.A.R.P. signals in this case — from wherever they're located. So..." Viktor started to explain...

"So if you sprinkle them on your dinner and wash them down with a glass of beer, you're going to have those SEEDS latching onto red blood cells and riding through your circulatory system like a raft on a perky white water river..." Gil added, completing Viktor's sentence.

"... And pulling in whatever H.A.A.R.P. signals are aimed in your direction," Viktor added.

"And whatever uh... suggestions those H.A.A.R.P.

emissions might be broadcasting at the time," Gil said.

"Sonofabitch," Dan groaned. "So it's something like the nuclear seeds they introduce into the body that are supposed to discourage cancer cell growth?"

"Something like that theory yes," Viktor nodded.

"Well how long would they remain inside the body?" Dan asked. "What kind of signals would they draw in and what effects would the emissions have on the host?"

"I don't think anyone is sure yet. Maybe that's something someone — *someone like an... an M.D.* — needs to explore," Viktor winked. "But we should save that for another lesson."

Dan shook his head and clenched his lips. "You're probably right," Dan agreed. "I'm not sure I could take much more enlightenment today. But I do appreciate the cram session. I'm sure this is a lot more involved than what you've laid out but at least I'll have some vague idea of what you're referring to when you talk about these SEEDS... not exactly a spray of daisies."

"Not even close," Gil laughed.

"Well, when will you know whether your theory works... whether you can block electromagnetic radio wave blasts from the H.A.A.R.P system?" Dan asked.

"It's like any experiment," Viktor said. "Unfortunately it takes time to test and measure success and you just won't know... well... until you know."

"It's like we scientific locals might say around Juneau," Gil said.

"What's that?" Dan asked.

"Oh," Viktor laughed. "He's talking about the standard Five Running Rebels' saying... you know... the proof is in the *Kaneegwál'*."

"The *Ka-nee* – what?" Dan asked.

"The pudding," Viktor said. "The proof is in the

pudding. Or in this case, the salmon egg berry pudding to be exact."

❄❄❄❄❄

ROC East HQ, Route 2 Templeton, Massachusetts, August

If there truly were such a place as Heaven... and Falcon would never imply he had doubts Heaven existed... then he figured he was about as close to Heaven right now as anyone could be on earth. He lay under the silk bed sheets with his arm draped across Meg's naked body and her legs entwined with his. He listened to her breathing and felt the beating of her heart. He was pretty positive it didn't get any better than this. This wasn't what he'd planned... getting involved with Meg... but if he *had* planned it he would have sketched it out in his imagination to happen exactly the way it had. Maybe that's why the fact that Meg was beside him in his bed right now was so incomprehensible and so amazing. Yet he couldn't deny this new situation complicated his life. In a couple of days he would be walking out that door, most likely for a very long time. The question was, where would Hazkill send him and what was Meg going to do? His future... his and Meg's... depended on the answers. But maybe Falcon had this figured wrong. Maybe he wouldn't be sent to some remote outpost at the ends of the earth. Maybe Hazkill would post him up the road only a few hundred miles. That's not so crazy. He had never done anything to deserve Hazkill's wrath so why should he prepare himself for the worst?

"What time is it?" Meg whispered, stirring and pulling her arm tighter around Falcon.

Falcon looked to his left to the blue glow from the clock on his dresser. "Four fifteen," he whispered back.

"Ugh," she whispered more softly. "It's almost time to get up for work."

"Just about," he said, barely audibly. "Meg?" Falcon asked softly.

"Hmm?" she answered.

"Why are we whispering?" he whispered.

Meg laughed, Falcon followed her lead and in seconds they were giggling like schoolchildren. Had he actually fought so hard to avoid getting close to Meg? What the hell was wrong with him? Even if they only had this one night — and never saw each other again — wouldn't the pain of missing her tomorrow be worth these unbelievable feelings that ran through him right now? Why was he so sure that he and Meg would never again be together once he was transferred? Even if Hazkill sent him to China — which of course he wouldn't with Phase II implementation right around the corner — he could be back on Meg's doorstep within hours considering the means of travel available these days. Maybe it wasn't physical distance he feared so much as personal absence. Maybe, deep down, he was afraid Meg would forget him.... pass him over for someone else if he weren't around her every day. What kind of trust was that? It didn't seem a very adult way of looking at a relationship. Besides... his heart and mind were leaping far ahead to the uncertain future. He hardly knew her.

"Where are you going?" Falcon said to Meg. She kissed his shoulder and rolled out of bed.

"Not far. I thought I'd put on the coffee," she told him, slipping her arms into Falcon's shirt he had hung over the chair last night. When she had buttoned it, she sat on the bed, facing him, her legs crossed Indian style. She peered at him quietly and looked deep into his eyes. But suddenly it looked to Falcon as though her eyes were beginning to water. He sat up in bed.

"What's wrong?" he asked, taking her hand.

She shrugged. "I'm not sure," she answered. "I'm worried I guess."

"About what?" Falcon asked.

"Are you serious?" she asked him. "I have a list."

"Well let's start at the top," he smiled at her, his head angled slightly. If he didn't know better, he might think he was in the middle of the most amazing dream of his life."

"How," she paused and then started again. "How bad do you think things will get?" she asked him.

"I don't know exactly," he replied. "I don't see how anyone could know." He took both her hands in his and traced her palm with his finger. "You know, I spent my life wanting to be in the military. It's all I ever wanted to do. Now... if I sit down and think about all of this — and my role in it — I'm totally confused."

"I feel exactly the same," she said. "Some of these objectives and... procedures we learned at ROC training are... are disturbing."

"They are," Falcon agreed, "Without a doubt."

"And we aren't supposed to talk about these kinds of things..." she added, "With anyone."

"So we've been told," Falcon muttered.

"I couldn't imagine Colonel Benton bringing up... doubts," Meg said, seeming to Falcon as if she might be testing his opinion of Benton.

"I'm not impressed by Maj... I mean *Brevet Colonel* Benton," Falcon told her, using cautionary diplomacy. He didn't want Meg to think he was one of those guys who complained about other officers... even though he didn't consider Benton in any way part of a loyal military brotherhood. The only one Benton would be loyal to would be himself.

"He kind of gives me the creeps," she said. "I am

uncomfortable around him and I am not looking forward to being a *critical* member of his 'staff' as he put it last night."

"I don't exactly trust him," Falcon said.

"I don't trust him at all," Meg agreed. "I don't understand how he received that promotion. I mean... what did he do? Who gave it to him and why? It isn't like he accomplished anything. Not like you did. You were tops in everything you did at ROC training. You amazed me. Any time they posted scores for anything I knew you would be at the top of the list... and you were... every time without fail. I used to watch you and wonder how you did it. There were times — many times — when I couldn't think about anything else. For some reason I was driven to know everything about you. Anyone I asked had good things to say about you."

"You asked about me... at ROC training?" Falcon frowned quizzically. "Who did you ask?"

"Oh..." Meg replied, now making small invisible circles on his chest with her finger and smiling. "Pretty much anyone I ever bumped into," she laughed.

"What did they say?" he asked, his brow arching.

"Well," she answered, "What impressed me most was not how successful you were at everything... well that did impress me a little," she giggled, blushing as she continued. "I was impressed that everyone said you were an incredibly nice guy. That was intriguing because most guys who are as successful — as successful as you are — would be full of themselves. Everyone agreed you weren't anything like that."

"Well," Falcon rapidly searched his mind for something to say that wouldn't make him sound egotistical. "It's nice to know what people think about you. I wouldn't want anyone to see me as arrogant. I don't have anything to be arrogant about."

"I think that's a matter of opinion," she said. "I think you have all the reasons in the world to be arrogant... if you wanted to be. Colonel Benton, on the other hand, has nothing to be arrogant about and he's totally egocentric."

Falcon laughed and Meg joined in. Her candor surprised him. "Well I won't disagree with you. Benton does think highly of himself. There's no doubt about that."

"Falcon," Meg said more seriously. "Do you think..." she hesitated.

"What?" he probed. "Do I think what?"

"Do you think there's going to be a civil war? No — never mind," she said quickly. "I shouldn't have brought that up."

"Why not?" he asked her.

"We shouldn't talk about it," she answered.

"Meg," he said softly. "There's nothing to be afraid of. You can talk to me about anything."

"It's... it's not so much that Falcon," Meg explained. "It's just that... I said it aloud. And it... it suddenly felt too real."

"Come here," Falcon whispered, reaching out and wrapping his arms around her. For a few moments neither of them spoke. They held each other so tightly not even words could have slipped between their embrace.

"Look," Falcon said. "First of all you and I can talk about anything..." But the minute he said it he wished he hadn't. He was supposed to get his orders tomorrow according to the weasel Benton... what then?

"You're leaving, Falcon," Meg said.

"That doesn't mean we have to stop talking," he assured her. "It doesn't mean I'm going to disappear off the face of the earth." He angled his head to the side and peered at her with a soft reassuring smile. "It doesn't mean we'll never see each other again. I... I don't want you to think this was... I mean... I don't consider last night a... a... brief... you know..."

"Good," she said, "Because I don't consider it a brief one *nighter* either. I would be very upset if you dropped off the face of the earth," she told him, squeezing his hands. "You probably already know that... well... you probably know *now* that I had a pretty bad crush on you at ROC training."

"You did?" Falcon had not known. Their interaction at ROC training had been limited to a nod and a quick hello and he had barely managed that without his tongue twisting in knots. He had no idea she had asked people about him at training or that he had even crossed her mind outside of their occasional cursory greeting.

"I did," Meg nodded. "So clearly I would not like it if you disappeared from the world. As a matter of fact, I would be pretty distressed."

"You would?" he asked.

"Of course I would," she told him. "I thought you understood."

"Understood what?" he asked, surprised.

"I wouldn't bring this up so fast if circumstances were different; but you and I both know in the next three months the entire world is going to change. Nothing will ever be the same. I don't think there's time to play the normal games people play. I would love to be courted and wined and dined and have all the time in the world to banter back and forth pretending I wasn't interested... just enough to drive you crazy."

Falcon gazed at her as she spoke. She was so beautiful. He never thought things could be so good, and so bad, all at the same time. Why did he have to find her... only to then be ripped right out of her life?

Meg suddenly laughed. "I did think you knew... you're a pretty smart guy. I tried to send the right chemistry your way these last two weeks."

"Knew what?" he questioned. Then he grew worried. Was she not interested in him after all?

"I thought you knew," she said, wrinkling her brow. "Damn... I... I'm in love with you Falcon."

❀❀❀❀❀

Chapter 19

✳✳❄✳✳

ROC Northwest Takotna Alaska, August

"Let's go Malikov," the MP said, unlocking the SHIDS holding cell door.

"Hey," Malikov's cellmate said, rising from the concrete bench. He peered at the guard. "It's about time. How long does it take to fix a plane?" he asked the MP.

"Sit down," the guard demanded. "Plane's not ready yet." The MP walked over to Malikov and unlocked his ankle shackles from the iron floor ring. He then handcuffed him. "Let's go,"

"Go?" Malikov asked. "Plane *eece* broke."

"Move it," The guard said. Malikov shuffled out of the cell and down the long hallway in silence. The MP took him to a narrow room with five small cubicles along the wall. The MP nudged him impatiently to the last cubicle. "Sit," the MP said. Malikov did as directed. The guard then stood along the wall behind Malikov with his hands clasped in front of him.

"*Vhat deece?*" Malikov asked.

"The CO was feeling magnanimous today," the MP told him. "You've got five minutes with your visitor before they haul you outta here for California."

Malikov looked at the thick sheet of Plexiglas straight in front of him. A small round metal speaker was embedded in the divider. He didn't have time to speculate on whether he was going to have to listen to more lies about his crime from the Russian officer again.

As soon as he sat down Sergei was escorted into the room on the other side of the partition and shown to a chair opposite Malikov.

Malikov immediately straightened and leaned in toward the divider. "Sergei!" he beamed.

"Malikov," Sergei said softly, leaning toward the glass on his side of the divider. "Comrade... you well?"

Malikov nodded. "*Da... Da...* well. *Vhy* Sergei *nyet* visit?"

"MPs take to *Amerikanskaya tyur'ma!*"— American prison. Sergei shook his head.

"*Amerikanskaya tyur'ma!*" Malikov exclaimed, leaping to his feet. "SHIDS?"

"SIT DOWN! Now!" the MP demanded. "Or I'll drag your ass right back to the holding cell!"

Malikov ducked down and dropped back into his seat, "*Da, da,* sit, sit." Malikov leaned toward Sergei. "*Amerikanskiy duraki*" — American Fools! He whispered energetically, "SHIDS?"

"MPs say I help *keell* MP," Sergei said, shaking his head. "Questions... questions..."

"But Sergei free... *Deece eece* good!" Malikov exclaimed. "*Da,* I be free, too."

"*Nyet,* comrade," Sergei said with sadness. "*Vitness* say Malikov *keell* MP."

"I do nothing!" Malikov argued. "Sergei tell... I do nothing."

"I tell," Sergei said, shaking his head, so frustrated speaking English he blurted out in Russian. "*Nyet*, they don't listen. They say they will send me back to the SHIDS if I don't say you murdered the MP. They said I lied to protect you."

"Speak English!" the MP ordered. Or I'll throw you in the cell with your comrade!"

Malikov ran his hand through his short hair and

leaned in closer to the partition. "MPs free Sergei? Sergei lie?"

"*Nyet... Nyet* lie. MP's free Sergei... but," Sergei said, "Sergei *nyet* lie. MP's have *vitness... nyet* need Sergei."

"*Vitness*," Malikov clenched his fist. "*Vitness*? *Nyet...* I do nothing."

"Bugak," Sergei said, hesitantly. "Bugak *eece vitness*."

"Bugak," Malikov complained, "*Nyet,* Bugak lie! Sergei tell MPs. Tell I do nothing. *Da*, Sergei tell at court! I do nothing. Bugak lie."

Sergei shook his head slowly.

"Let's go, Malikov," the MP demanded, moving toward him. "Your time is up."

"Sergei," Malikov said, rising from his chair, trying to affirm this was an urgent plan and this was how it must go. "*Tovarishch,*"— comrade — "Sergei tell court ... Malikov *nyet keell* MP."

"I said, let's go," the MP repeated, grasping Malikov's arm.

"Malikov, *tovarishch*," Sergei said, his tone subdued. "MPs *nyet* let Sergei go *deece* court." The MP gave Malikov a hard shove toward the door. Malikov stumbled and looked back into the visitor's room for a last glimpse of his friend.

"Malikov," Sergei yelled after him, his voice cracking. "*Nyet, nyet*! Sergei no go *deece* court. Sergei go *vit* ROC force... MPs no let Sergei go *deece* court. Bugak go *deece* court.." Sergei's voice was fading. As the MP pushed Malikov back down the hall to the holding cell, Sergei's words settled deep into Malikov's brain and hung over him like a guillotine blade.

"*Bugak go deece court.*"

❄❄❄❄❄

Fizer farm Shepherdstown, West Virginia, August

Nick and Stephy sat in the grass a little beyond the edge of the Fizer property on the bank of a small trout pond listening to the raspy croaking of the bullfrogs. They watched the late afternoon mid-August sun dip behind the tall pines and the lazy hollow.

"You know," Stephy said. "I thought it was amazing your parents could laugh about their farm being raided and searched."

"What else are they going to do?" Nick shrugged.

"Well I still think they are amazing," Stephy said.

"I can't disagree," Nick said. "A lot of people would have folded under the pressure... gone off the deep end or something."

"You mean like... running around in a barn in jockey shorts reciting the U.S. Constitution?" Stephy teased.

"He's a character," Nick laughed, "That's for sure."

"They're both pretty strong people," Stephy said. "I think their son is pretty amazing too."

Nick smiled and kissed Stephy's cheek.

"Not having second thoughts, are you?" Stephy asked.

"About what?" Nick replied.

"Resigning your commission," she clarified.

"No," he shook his head.

"Won't you miss the army?" Stephy asked. "Twenty-two years is a long time."

"Oh I might get a twinge every now and then I suppose," Nick said. "But I'm going to miss the army the way it used to be, not the way it is now. It feels good not to wake up and start arguing with myself the minute I open my eyes in the morning."

"I've already seen a change in you," Stephy told him.

"Not for the bad I hope," he said, peering into her shinning eyes as if he had a line in the water and wasn't sure what he was about to reel in.

"Hardly," she replied, chuckling. "You're so much like you were those first seven years of our marriage. You were so less stressed then, so hopeful about the future. Your eyes seem to be smiling again."

"Smiling eyes huh?" he said. "Interesting description... must be the writer in you."

"I'm better with a thesaurus on my lap," she said.

"Who isn't," Nick quipped. They both laughed. Nick leaned over, plucked a dandelion from the grass and gave it to her.

"See," she said. "You *are* back to your old self... bringing me flowers and all." She looked thoughtful at the weed. "I wonder if there are dandelions in Alaska."

"I don't know," he answered. "But if you think you're going to be pining away for some, I'll yank up an armful from the lawn before we leave and stick them in the cooler."

"No thanks," she said. "I can probably adjust." A black-capped chickadee landed in the branch above their heads. Stephy looked up, watching it. Nick listened to the tiny bird singing and chirping excitedly.

"You're not nervous about going are you?" Nick asked her.

"God no," she said. "After what you told me about the phone call and imminent mobilization of ROC forces in ninety days, I'd be terrified to stay here. What's the sense in sitting around doing nothing but waiting to see how bad things get?"

"You do understand why it has to be Alaska, right?" Nick asked. "I mean, I wasn't sure I got the reasoning across as clearly as I should have. If you didn't understand it, Mom and Pop certainly wouldn't have."

"No you explained it perfectly," Stephy assured him. "I know for a fact your mother does understand. We agreed it is an absolutely reasonable plan. Your mother told me last night that she believes everything happens for a reason. She said it seemed all the pieces fit together... the loss of the farm... your retirement. You shouldn't be concerned. Your mom is excited about going and about the four of us pulling together like this. I think it makes them feel useful."

"I think you're right," he agreed. "Do you think they understand why we need to specifically go to Juneau... where the weather is maybe not the greatest?"

"Absolutely," Stephy nodded. "I don't think they doubt your judgment one bit. They both get it. I get it. We're all fine with it, honestly. It makes so much sense I only hope we don't hit a huge traffic jam on the way up there. I mean, what if everyone realizes it might possibly be the only safe place left?"

"We won't have to worry about that," Nick laughed. "I'm probably only one of a handful of people in the entire world since 1901 that have read the OPSEIM Directive straight through. The drafters counted on that. It's right there in black and white but it's obscure so if you don't read every page of the text you'd more than likely miss it."

"Juneau is only accessible by water or air," Nick continued. "And because it is a temperate rainforest it is rainy or snowy or foggy much of the time. That makes it difficult to access and easier for private citizens and militia to defend... if it comes down to a face off. The terrain in and around Juneau is inhospitable. It's a small city nestled in the mountains in the Inside Passage — with the glacial ice field to the rear — and a group of mountainous islands in front of it that are just as difficult to access. So all of these things would make it incredibly challenging to amass, maintain and supply a sufficient ROC and U.N. peacekeeping force to crush a rebellion or dominate the small population. That was a huge worry for the drafters of the OPSEIM Directive and they deemed it likely not worth the risk of failure. When they pulled Alaska into the overall blueprint, they pretty much included all of the populated and more open areas of the state in their insane plan... pretty much except for Juneau. The risks of attempting to subjugate that city far outweighed any potential benefits. They discounted a tunnel system from the start — when the tunnel network was dreamed up; the expense alone of shipping the TBM — the tunnel boring machine — up there, operating it in that environment and keeping it functioning was a huge deterrent. It seemed pretty plain... to me anyway... that the architects of this insanity essentially wrote Juneau off like a business loss."

"Plus," Stephy added, seeming to want to show her support for Nick's rationale by demonstrating she had listened intently the last couple of days when he had finally answered the questions he had initially put off — when he first revealed the OPSEIM Directive contents in more detail. "The only underground facilities that *are* present are old deteriorating mines the government never sunk any money into maintaining. So the strategy they devised to subjugate the country wouldn't work up there."

Nick grinned broadly. He was relieved. He had no doubts going to Juneau was the sensible thing to do but he wanted to make damn sure all of them understood why it would provide them the greatest chance to survive... maybe give them an opportunity to retain some freedom. He felt more confident now that he knew Stephy understood his reasoning. Yet some part of him still worried about his parents. Did his mom and pop understand? Did they know he would never drag them four thousand miles into the unknown if he didn't feel it was critical they go? Stephy and his parents kept assuring him they understood and were one hundred percent behind the decision, but still... it wasn't going to be easy uprooting them and starting life from scratch. They were the three people he loved most in the world. Merely protecting them wasn't sufficient. He had to make them understand that this was the best... the only... chance they had to live out the rest of their lives with some kind of independence. It was important to him that they know this... because if the plan failed he needed them to understand it wasn't because he had made an uninformed rash decision.

"It's getting late," Stephy said. "I think break time is over. We should get back up there and help your parents pack."

"You're right," Nick beamed. "One thing though... are you sure your friend Macey doesn't mind taking care of all of our household goods back in Georgia? I mean, that's a hell of a lot of responsibility for her to take on."

"I have no doubt Nick," Stephy said, getting back to her feet, brushing the leaves and dampness from the seat of her jeans as she rose. "I've known Macey since I was eleven years old. I know that anything I would do for her, without question, she would be as happy to do for me. I would do this for her in a heartbeat."

"Well," Nick said, hopping to his feet. "That's good enough for me. I don't want to delay getting started. I don't know what we might run into on the way. Things are going to start heating up on the political front damn quickly... and of course the weather is a question. I have no idea what kind of problems General Tucker's Uncle Sam is planning next."

"*General Tucker's Uncle Sam?*" Stephy frowned.

"Hell yeah," Nick chortled, "He's not *my* Uncle Sam... I'm a civilian."

❀❀✖❀❀

ROC East HQ, Route 2 Templeton, Massachusetts, August

Falcon couldn't stand the waiting much longer. Meg had poked her head into his office at least four times and he had mimicked her actions by doing the same thing every time he passed her door. Each time they gave each other the thumbs up to express solidarity. They had made their pact. It didn't matter where Falcon was assigned. Their prime concern was finding a way to overcome whatever obstacles stood in the way of their being together. Nonetheless, it was stressful waiting to find out where he was headed. Falcon felt like he was sitting on a ticking bomb waiting for the explosion. He tried to concentrate on the papers spread across his desk but he found himself reading the same lines over and over.

"Hey Rabbit," Falcon hollered, louder than he intended.

"Yes sir?" Rabbit popped into his doorway from somewhere in the hall.

"Anything come down yet?" Falcon asked.

"No sir," Rabbit said, shaking his head.

Falcon laughed. "I'm sorry," he said. "I know I asked you a half hour ago."

"No problem," Rabbit told him. "I understand."

"Well," Falcon admitted, laying down his pencil and standing. "I might as well take an early lunch. I'm not accomplishing anything here."

"Oh," Rabbit said, holding up his hand toward Falcon, looking to his left. "Hold on a second sir..." Rabbit slipped away from Falcon's office and disappeared. Falcon moved out in front of his desk and stepped into the hall. As he did, Meg came out of her office and walked over to him.

"What's all the commotion?" she asked him in a soft whisper. Falcon motioned to the left with his head. Rabbit was in the hallway talking with a courier. He had a large envelope under his arm.

"Are you ready for this?" Meg asked Falcon.

Falcon grasped Meg's hand. "We'll be okay," he reassured her. "Knowing is better than not knowing." Falcon noticed Meg's skin was damp. "Don't worry," he whispered, squeezing her hand. Meg nodded. Falcon watched as Rabbit signed for the envelope.

"Why so much intrigue?" Meg asked.

"Not sure," Falcon answered, "Maybe because we're on alert." The courier left and Rabbit trotted down the hall toward them. He quickly handed the package to Falcon. Falcon took it and turned it over. It was marked in red: *Classified, For the Eyes of Colonel Falcon Colby.* Rabbit smiled sheepishly, turned and sat down at his desk outside Falcon's office.

Falcon looked at Meg, frowned and shrugged.

"I'll be in my office," she said.

"I'll give it a quick look and then we'll go to lunch," he told her. He turned and went into his office, closing the door behind him. For a minute he leaned his back against the door. The envelope could be marked classified simply because ROC forces were on alert for the upcoming Phase II mobilization. It didn't necessarily mean he was being sent on some top-secret mission where Meg couldn't join him. Still, a classified mission was not something he had even considered. That would complicate everything. He moved as if in a trance, robotically walking over to his desk. He sat down stiffly. He examined the envelope in his hand, turning it from side to side, wanting... but not wanting... to open it. It was better to know than not know. Hadn't he said that to Meg? He picked up his letter opener, slipped it into a corner and then slit it open. He pulled out his orders and skimmed through them. In frustration, he slouched back into his chair. He didn't know how to process what he had read, in either his head... or his heart.

❄❄❄❄❄

Takotna Airstrip Takotna, Alaska, August

"Plane?" Malikov inquired, "*Nyet*, FOLT POD?"

The MP shook his head and laughed. "Are you that damn stupid? What the hell? We told you the plane was being fixed. You think we have tunnels under the whole goddamn country? I suppose you think we've got a tunnel heading straight up to Mars too! What a dumb shit!" Malikov felt his face redden. Unsure whether he was angry — or just embarrassed — he tried to ignore the tension building inside him. He focused instead on the sharp breezes against his face. Three MPs, Malikov's cellmate and a uniformed Alaska State Trooper — Malikov thought might be a pilot — continued to laugh at Malikov as the group walked slowly across the tarmac, their boots crunching in the snow.

Malikov's shackles had been removed as soon as they emerged from the underground FOLT. A man could not easily maneuver in this snow with bound ankles. Malikov had spent many brutal winters in his village of Zolotaryovka but he could not recall ever seeing snow piled so high. An entire armored division could easily disappear behind some of these snowbanks. Malikov might have considered making a break for it if he weren't handcuffed. He likely would not get very far but a quick bullet in his back from the Alaska trooper's .40 Glock was looking more attractive than the alternative. Without Sergei testifying for him and swearing they were together, Malikov figured this international court was destined to condemn him. The MPs already had their minds made up; Malikov was guilty. He was probably going to spend the rest of his life locked up in an American prison or worse... he would be sentenced to die. If he tried to run he wouldn't get far but for seconds he would taste freedom and then maybe the madness would be over.

In the arc of illumination cast by the huge floodlights Malikov could see the edge of a thick forest right beyond the runway. It would be difficult to reach the tree line in the deep snow. Perhaps they wouldn't shoot him. Perhaps they would chase him and catch him instead. Then they would probably beat him. Malikov sighed. If he could be assured they would shoot and kill him he might have run but what ends would a beating serve?

It was beginning to sprinkle. Malikov wasn't an expert on the weather but he knew it should be forty degrees or so at this time of night in late summer in Takotna. He guessed it was nearer to freezing. He shivered but he didn't mind. The crisp temperature was a great relief from the persistent heat of the FOLT. At least here, outside, the air was not so suffocating. He had not thought much about life outside of the FOLT since he began this duty. Now he realized how much he had missed the open air. Despite the handcuffs and the guards the outdoors made him feel more a part of humanity.

"All right hold up here," ordered the MP standing closest to Malikov. "Don't make any sudden moves or this jittery young private might get a sudden twitch in his trigger finger." They stood at the foot of the metal stairs leading up into an older Alaska State Trooper Hellcat 650C single turboprop engine, fixed gear, upper winged, short hop Cavalcade Reptile with Sleakaire

9000 floats capable of touching down on land or water. It was a roomy nine seat aircraft with single pilot. Malikov thought the plane might have been equipped with snow skis but the runway looked clear compared to the surrounding area and what did he know about planes? He guessed the troopers knew what they were doing.

"Hey," Malikov's cellmate complained, "This plane's not military. It's hardly bigger than a damn POD. We goin' all the way to California in this thing?"

"Crap," the lead MP said. "You're both dumber than shit. You have to get to Anchorage first... for the JPATS hop, asshole."

"I don't mean to sound stupid sarge, but what's a JPATS hop?" the young private whispered to the MP.

"No sweat kid," the MP responded. "We call it 'Jay-pats.' You can't be expected to pick up every detail in two weeks... it is two weeks right?"

"And a day," the private answered, "Two weeks and a day. "I was posted here fifteen days ago."

"Great... okay. So JPATS — Justice Prisoner and Alien Transport, nicknamed Con Air — is an agency of the federal government. Among other things, the agency transports prisoners between prisons, detention centers, courthouses and other places. The JPATS agency usually shuttles inmates of the Federal Bureau of Prisons or U.S. Immigration and Customs, but JPATS also helps out the military... especially in states like Alaska where getting the cons or detainees to the pickup point is a problem." The private listened intently and nodded.

"They aren't gonna bring a big JPATS shuttle into a half-assed village like this for two guys. So to get these scum bags to a central point in Alaska — namely Anchorage — the state cops help out the military and fly these small hops from anywhere in the state over to Anchorage." The MP's voice trailed off as if he suddenly lost interest in the young soldier's tutoring session. He shifted his weight impatiently from left foot to right and peered up into the plane looking for a state trooper to give him the okay to get the prisoners onboard. It was beginning to rain harder. "So now you understand the JPATS setup?" the MP asked, clearly focused on the aircraft doorway where the trooper would be issuing the signal to board the aircraft.

Just then an Alaska State Trooper poked his head out the door at the top of the stairs. "Load 'em up," the slim trooper bellowed. The MP pushed Malikov who grabbed the railing with his cuffed hands to stop himself from losing his balance.

"Move it!" the MP ordered. "I didn't bring my rain bonnet."

The group trudged up the stairs. Malikov lost his footing and slipped on an icy step but the MP had hold of Malikov's parka. The two prisoners were hustled into the plane and buckled into adjacent seats at the very rear of the aircraft. Malikov's and his cellmate's seats faced the rear of the plane. The MP shackled their ankles and locked the chains to two thick metal brackets bolted to the floor. Malikov's cellmate thrust out both cuffed hands at the MP.

"C'mon dammit," the prisoner argued. "You're not gonna leave us pinned in these seats! What if the damn plane crashes... or burns? We'll never make it out alive!"

The MP grinned. "Tough luck I'd say," the MP said. "Maybe you should have thought about the drawbacks of criminal activity a few months ago before deciding on your new career paths," the MP sneered. He sat in the seat across from them in one of two seats facing the front of the plane. The MP briefly fiddled in his seat, then drew the seatbelt across his lap and fastened it. He looked at the two prisoners. "You guys screwed up. Too bad you're gonna miss all the fun. I heard ROC forces are being mobilized in a couple of months. You guys are gonna be on the wrong side of the checkerboard when all hell breaks loose," the MP taunted, leaning his head against the back of his seat and laughing.

Bastard, Malikov thought. Mobilization was an English word he understood well. He should be part of that mobilization. He was going to miss the deployment of the peacekeeping forces to the American cities. He will miss the chance to have his *Stalingrad*; he will not have his battle. Bastards! It wasn't fair. Thirty years a loyal soldier and now he would never get his one glorious battle. ROC forces will be deployed without him. The action will start and he will be sitting in a prison locked away somewhere probably waiting for his death sentence to be carried out. Instead of loading him up with riot gear and ammo, they will chain and shackle him and throw him in another dark six by seven foot cell and forget about him. Even here, in an airplane thousands of feet in the air, these Americans shackle him! What could he do in the air? Nothing... but they chain him anyway like a rabid dog. It was another meaningless rule.

"Do you believe this?" Malikov's cellmate whispered. "They treat us like cattle... like we don't have any brains or feelings. Too bad I got these cuffs on. I would have slipped my hands around that guard's neck and squeezed until I snuffed out that sonofabitch's lights."

Malikov didn't know if his cellmate was capable of such a thing but if the man *had* lunged at the MP Malikov was pretty sure he wouldn't be the one to make a move to stop him. Malikov turned and looked down the aisle and watched as one Alaska State Trooper armed with a sidearm and what Malikov thought was a Bushmaster XM15 E25 automatic rifle strapped himself into his seat. He faced the rear of the aircraft... his seat overlooking the backs of Malikov and his cellmate. Even though Malikov's daily arsenal in the FOLT was limited to a computer keyboard and a mechanical pencil he was required to qualify on all weapons. This trooper's weaponry was overkill... more appropriate for a beach assault on an enemy battalion or crowd control in Moscow's Red Square.

Malikov stared out the window and watched as a man in a blue jumpsuit argued with the trooper who he suspected was the pilot. It looked to be a heated discussion but the two opponents quickly broke away from each other. The pilot climbed into the plane and strapped himself into his seat. In a few minutes Malikov heard the Hellcat engine revving. Within seconds the radio crackled with tower clearance and the aircraft began taxying.

Malikov's cellmate gripped Malikov's arm tight and started moaning and mumbling. "Sonofabitch, dammit, sonofabitch," he repeated, each time louder than the last. Malikov wrenched his arm free from his cellmate's grip and glared at him. The man's face was ghostly white. Malikov's seat vibrated from the inmate's violent movements to break free of his restraints.

"What the crap is wrong with you?" the MP directly across from them demanded to know, as the prisoner's violent shaking intensified. "Shit! You're as bad as a little girl locked in the kitchen with a mouse!" the MP taunted.

"Pa... pa... panic attacks!" the inmate blurted out.

"Sonofabitch!" the MP grumbled, throwing his hands in the air. "That's just perfect!"

The Hellcat lifted off and began a steep climb.

Malikov closed his eyes, trying to imagine himself as a boy in Zolotaryovka at the cool Kuvaka Springs. He leaned his head back against the headrest but the constant jarring of his seat from his cellmate's wild thrashing decimated Malikov's conjured vision.

"UNLOCK ME!" the inmate shrieked, yanking wildly at his shackled feet and slamming his cuffed hands against his head, then his lap. "Get these goddamn things OFF OF ME!" he hollered.

"What the hell's wrong with him?" the trooper yelled from the front of the aircraft.

"Shut that guy up!" the pilot shrieked.

"Let me LOOSE!" Malikov's cellmate screamed.

"Shut him UP! Shut the bastard up!" the pilot hollered again. The radio crackled and Malikov listened as the pilot shouted to the tower. "Hellcat 177 to Takotna tower... we've got icing. I repeat... we have icing! Mayday, mayday, emergency... one thousand five hundred, 1, 5, 0, 0... descending... heading one, eight zero... seven thousand, 1, 8, 0... 7,000. I repeat... we've got icing! Mayday, mayday..." The Hellcat began to shake and rattle, tipping to the left, then right. Alarms buzzed from the front of the plane.

"WE'RE GONNA DIE!" the prisoner squealed. "GET THESE OFF! LET ME LOOSE!"

"Do something with him. SHUT HIM UP!" the trooper in the front of the plane screamed. Without hesitation the MP flipped the release on his seatbelt and lunged forward, winding up and sinking a closed fist into the prisoner's face all in one motion. The MP gripped the armrests on each side of the prisoner and watched as the inmate's head lolled to the side. There was immediate silence. No prisoner screaming. No pilot cursing. No troopers hollering.

No engine sound.

The MP glared at Malikov... they stared at each other as if suspended... frozen in time and space. In desperation Malikov thrust his cuffed hands toward the man. Without a word the MP grabbed a single key from his top pocket and unlocked Malikov's cuffs. Malikov was confused; he had no chance to understand why the MP had freed him. At that second gravity hurled the MP up into the air, slammed his back into the ceiling, and smashed him back down to the floor as the Hellcat plunged... nose down... toward the earth. While the MP lay on the floor, bleeding from his nose and his mouth, he reached his arm over to Malikov's ankle shackles stuck the key in the lock and turned it. He stretched out his arm and tried to do the same for Malikov's cellmate but the plane suddenly lurched to the left, pitched up to 40 degrees, hung for an instant, banked 90 degrees and spiraled nose first toward the ground. At the same instant Malikov heard the *ping*... of the key hit the ceiling, he watched the MP lifted into the air and shot like a cannon ball to the front of the plane. The pilot squawked into the radio, "Mayday, mayday," 90-degree bank... 90-degree bank! Mayday, emergency, six thousand five hundred, 6, 5, 0, 0... I cannot control the aircraft... descending... one thousand, 1, 0, 0, 0, feet per second..."

Gravity pulled Malikov's legs off the floor. He bent his knees and drove his legs under his seat, straining to hold them there. He leaned his torso forward and covered his head with his arms. The Hellcat spun... and spiraled... down toward the ground while the alarms on the cockpit instrument panel buzzed like a terrifying cloud of ravenous mosquitos on a sweltering Zolotaryovka summer night in the *Chernozemnaya polosa*.

"Takotna tower," the pilot shouted, "Hellcat 177...

mayday, six thousand five hundred, 6, 5, 0, 0... eighty knots, eight-zero knots... 8, 0 knots. I cannot control airspeed. Mayday... mayday, six thousand five hundred, 6, 5, 0, 0, heading one, one zero... six thousand five hundred, 1, 1, 0... 6,500. I'm trying to... I cannot maintain airspeed..."

"Jesus... Oh Jesus... Oh Jesus," the Alaska trooper in the front of the plane repeatedly chanted.

"WE'RE GONNA DIE," Malikov's cellmate screamed, regaining consciousness. "LET ME OUTTA HERE!" he demanded. He thrashed and squirmed, yanking at his shackles and handcuffs.

"I told that damn aircraft chief! I told that sonofabitch to deice this plane again! GODDAMMIT!" the pilot hollered. "Mayday, mayday, mayday... This is Hellcat 177... boot on, boot is not working... I repeat... boot is inoperative. Mayday, mayday... Takotna tower Hellcat 177..." The systems alarm buzzers wailed from the instrument panel.

"Jesus Mary and Joseph," the trooper shouted, "Jesus... oh Jesus!"

"Takotna tower, this is Hellcat 177... diving, diving! Cannot control aircraft, two thousand, 2, 0, 0, 0... feet per second. Heading one, one zero, four thousand five hundred, 1, 1, 0... 4,500. Mayday, we've got icing! Descending at 2,000 ft. per second... May..." Malikov clamped his eyes shut, his arms wrapped around his head, his heart hammering violently in his chest. The sound of his own blood pounded in his ears, deafening him as it raced through his arteries fueled by massive uncontrolled bursts of adrenaline pumping through his body.

"Mayday, mayday, Hellcat 177," the pilot bellowed, "Heading one, one zero, two thousand... 1, 1, 0... 2,000... feet per second. I repeat... I cannot control the aircraft! Descending 2, 0, 0, 0 ft. per..."

❄❄❄❄❄

Takotna, Alaska, August

What a perfect day — almost — Miriam thought as she sat at the kitchen table drinking her tea. Kenzie and Kyle were getting ready for bed. It had been a fine evening. Almost the entire village had gone to Mr. Olani's ATB — *After the Blizzard* — party. Her children had worn themselves out. All of the exuberance they had bottled up inside their young bodies in the small cabin for two weeks spilled out of them. It seemed the village had joined in a collective sigh of relief after surviving such a horrendous blizzard. The massive storm had ended and Takotna could go back to normal. Yes it had been a fine — nearly perfect — day. But watching the husbands and wives and their families at the party made Miriam's heart ache all the more for her Henry Ivan. The void his death had left in their lives told her the family would never again be whole. She could not provide her children with that special father's love. Kyle and Kenzie had lost the anchor to their lives and Miriam had lost part of her soul.

Miriam had grown so tired of longing for the closeness of her Henry beside her in bed at night, loving her and holding her and whispering to her in his low deep voice about dreams he had for them or for the children. Maybe what bothered Miriam most was knowing she would never have a chance to experience that kind of companionship again. Her village was so small... there could never again be someone like her Henry Ivan to make their lives complete. This was how it would be... if she continued on in Takotna.

The children ran into the kitchen to kiss Miriam goodnight. She smiled as she always did as if nothing could ever make her happier than she was at that moment. While that was partially true she knew there could have been a greater happiness in her home. But her children must never know the pain inside Miriam's heart.

"All ready for bed?" Miriam asked. "Did you have fun at the party?"

"Yes! Fun! So much fun!" both children said over and over, their eyelids drooping from the two round trips they had made to town and back, the baking they had done for the party and the massive amount of energy they had released after their many days in the cabin. Miriam hugged Kenzie and Kyle and kissed them on the foreheads. She knew they were exhausted when they did not ask her to tuck them into bed and she did not object to deviating from the nightly routine. Miriam was emotionally spent. Her heart seemed to weigh her down so completely she could not lift herself from the chair.

"Good night children," she said.

"Can we look for berries tomorrow Mama?" Kyle asked.

"Maybe in a freezer," Kenzie chortled. "In Mr. Olani's ice cream section," she teased. Kyle frowned.

"I'm sorry honey. I don't think berries would have survived the storm," Miriam explained.

"Well I think they could have," Kyle whined, looking down at his feet, watching his toes wiggle as if the action were independent of his will. "It's August and that's when we pick berries."

"I'm afraid not this year son," Miriam said softly, taking Kyle's hands in hers. "They might have survived a few hours in such cold but the storm lasted too long. I think all the berries will be ruined."

"I hope the salmon are still spawning," Kenzie said. "The bears will be really mad if the salmon are gone."

"Well hunting then?" Kyle pleaded. "Can we go hunting?"

"No, no," Kenzie disagreed. "We should set snares tomorrow! I bet the rabbits will be mixed up too... like the bears."

"Yes! Yes, that's what we should do," Kyle nodded.

Miriam thought for a moment. It might be a very good time to scout the forest's edge. "Maybe we should," she said. "I'm not sure how well we will do with the depth of the snow. But yes, we could look to see if there are tracks. It wouldn't hurt to set snares tomorrow." Kyle bounced up and down, flung his arms around Miriam's neck, and hugged her tightly.

"I love you mama," he shrieked, bounding off down the hall before Miriam could even draw a breath and respond. Kenzie grinned and skipped off to the bedroom behind Kyle. In seconds the house was still. Miriam picked up the book she had been reading — from Henry's collection. She read and sipped her tea as she sat alone at the thick pine table bathed in the amber glow of the vacillating flame from the kerosene lamp. As she read, she tried not to think too much about the searing pain in her heart... the ache in the corner where her Henry Ivan should be nestled.

❊❊❊❊❊

Takotna River Takotna, Alaska, August

The level was rising, slapping at his chin, splashing into his nostrils and eyes. He tried to turn, to move... to kick himself free... to force his head farther above the water. But Malikov couldn't break free from whatever entrapped him. Was this the ocean? Why was he in the sea? His face was splashed again. He licked his lips and then quickly spat it out. Oil and gasoline and water... what kind of ocean was this? The water held no salt.

This was fresh water.

He was in an airplane.

He was in an airplane, Malikov suddenly realized, *and the airplane had crashed...* Crashed! How could the airplane have crashed? *"Amerikanskiy duraki!"* he muttered. Fools! Sensors... planes... all things in America were defective. Malikov was tilted backwards and the wreckage seemed to be listing to the left making his side of the plane higher than the other. He struggled to pitch his chest forward but something bound him at his waist, holding him firmly. *Seatbelt...* he must release the belt across his lap. He fumbled in the water for the seatbelt and worked it until the latch opened and the belt broke away from his waist. He felt the floor under his feet and tried to stand but sheets of metal and wires and luggage rack pieces hung down from the ceiling. He turned his body to a dog paddle position and half floated, his knees about four inches off the floor, far enough to keep his head out of the water. He heard moaning.

In the dim flickering cabin light Malikov could vaguely see the outline of something in front of him. As he reached for it, hands splashed up out of the water — handcuffed hands — and gripped Malikov's forearms. "Unlock the shackles," his cellmate groaned, his words bubbling on the surface of the water. "Help me."

Malikov moved closer, pried loose his cellmate's grip and grabbed hold of both of the man's shoulders. Malikov shivered in the cold. In the fading light it looked like the left side of the inmate's face was in the water.

"Unlock me," the prisoner pleaded, spitting out water with his syllables.

"Nyet! No key!" Malikov told him. *"Nyet,* see? *Nyet* key." Malikov firmed his grip on his cellmate's shoulders

and shook him. "*Nyet* key. *NYET* KEY!" he hollered at his cellmate, trying to make him focus and understand.

"Don't let me die," the prisoner begged weakly.

Malikov drew in a lungful of air and thrust his head under the water. He stretched his right arm down toward the floor of the plane, feeling around until he found the thick iron rectangle bolted to the fuselage. He wrapped his fingers around it and held on. With his left hand he gripped the chain that tethered the man's shackles to the iron bar and yanked at it viciously. Frustrated, he released the chain and the iron bar and reached up to his cellmate's waist. He tried to unbuckle his lap belt but the latch would not open. Malikov popped back up out of the water, took in more air and returned under the surface to try again to release the man's seatbelt. He could not make the latch work. It was jammed. Malikov brought his head back out of the water.

"I don't want to die," the man pleaded. "Don't leave me here," he cried, weakly struggling against his shackles and the belt across his lap. The wreckage groaned, creaked and swayed.

"Find key," Malikov said softly. But the chain held the man's shackled ankles tightly to the iron bar and Malikov knew there was no key. The MP had lost it; Malikov had heard the ping as the key hit the ceiling before the crash. Even if he could have unlocked his cellmate's shackles, he could not undo his seatbelt. He would need tools for that.

"Close eyes," he told his cellmate softly. "I get key... come back." Malikov smoothed the man's hair on the right side of his face and whispered to him. "*Nyet*, no fear... close eyes. *Tikho vso budet Khorosho,*" – Quiet, everything will be ok. The inmate seemed to understand Malikov was trying to comfort him.

"I don't want to die," Malikov's cellmate muttered, choking on his words as the fuselage listed farther to the left and more of his face became immersed. "Cut them off," he mumbled through the bubbles in the water around his lips. "My legs... cut off my legs." But Malikov had no knife and even if he found one and cut off the man's legs, he would not be freed; he would need to cut the seatbelt. There was no time. "I come back," Malikov reassured him. "I come back... free you." His cellmate was weeping. The man's tight shackles and seatbelt imprisoned him. He could lift his face out of the water no farther.

The plane lurched backwards. A sense of urgency washed over Malikov. He must leave the wreckage or he could be dragged down with it. The plane began rocking as if it were perched on a cliff ledge, battered by powerful winds. Malikov knew the fuselage was sinking. He could feel the plane's instability all around him. He tried to look forward toward the front of the plane but it was too dark to see. He grabbed hold of the backs of seats and hanging pieces of metal and pulled himself toward the nose of the aircraft. One of the guards' pockets... maybe they carried knives, or extra keys. But it was futile. He could never do all that would be necessary to free his cellmate before the plane sunk.

He continued forward to find a way out. When he reached where he thought the front of the plane should be there was nothing there... nothing but water and darkness. The fuselage was definitely sinking, moving and dipping. The cabin light was out now. He could see nothing when he looked back toward the tail of the plane. He heard only the soft muffled sobs of his cellmate... and the bubbles. The water level was rising which of course meant the plane was sinking, fast. He wanted to remove his boots but there was no time. He placed his foot on the edge of the fuselage and pushed himself free of the plane.

He lunged forward kicking his feet madly in the water. He tried to swim but he bumped into fractured ice and debris. His feet were heavy and awkward, his boots felt like stones dragging him down. He tried to grab hold of ice chunks and floating fragments of wreckage to pull himself above the surface but he slid off and the flotsam drifted away, disappearing into the darkness. It was pitch black outside. Not a star in the sky, no lights from the plane... nothing.

He thrashed in the water. If he kept kicking with his feet maybe he could keep his head above the surface. Every time he bumped another piece of ice he tried to grab hold and it slipped away. Each kick with his legs was a monumental effort, as if his feet were encased in concrete, and he was quickly tiring. He swung his arms over his head and splashed them down into the water. He felt his thigh muscles tightening. A cramp now would send him to the bottom. He was growing weaker. If he could only make it to shore... but he had no idea how wide this lake or river was.

He couldn't stop himself from thinking about his cellmate, the terror that must be gripping him. He wondered how long drowning takes. He could not imagine the horror of it — bound into his seat like that. Maybe he could find a knife... then he could cut the seatbelt and then his cellmate's legs. If only the MP had not lost the key. Why had the MP unlocked Malikov's shackles in the first place? He should have buckled himself back into his own seat after he punched his cellmate. He should have saved himself... but he had not. Malikov was haunted by the visceral expression on the MP's face as their gazes locked in that instant when the plane had first stalled. In that second the MP knew he would die... Malikov saw it in his eyes. Malikov thought about the blood that trickled from the MP's nose and mouth. If the MP had not risked his life... using extra seconds to free him, Malikov would be sinking to the bottom right now, strapped into the seat next to his cellmate and shackled to the floor.

Suddenly, his boot hit something under the water... more ice? He kicked and it hit again. It was a rock... and mud... the bottom? He pushed with the toes of his boots... dug them into the mud and pushed himself forward. Soon his chest scraped bottom. He dug his hands into the freezing mud and his fingers curled around small stones. He tried to pull himself forward while pushing with his boots on the bigger rocks. The water was only inches deep.

He struggled against the weight of his soaked clothing and was able to get to his hands and knees. He crawled forward until he was almost totally out of the water. As he set down his right hand he felt something soft. The water was barely a quarter of an inch deep now. He set his hand down again, beyond the edge of the water, and felt something softer than the ground should be. He pulled his hand back. He turned around and sat, feeling the ground around him cautiously. He felt fabric... clothing probably? It was difficult to determine because his hands were cold but yes it was a coat. He could feel the zipper. There was a body in the coat.

He leaned over it and drew his hands slowly down along both sides of the torso. His right hand hit something hard. It was a holstered handgun. He released the snap and slid out the gun. He stashed it in his parka. The corpse must belong to one of the troopers. Only they had been armed with rifles and side arms. The MPs were unarmed. Malikov continued to search the trooper's jacket. If only the moon would rise he would be able to see. Yet this did not concern him so much. It was August. The brief darkness would soon give way to the twenty or so hours of daylight. But he *was* concerned about his wet clothing.

He looked out in the direction from where he had come — across the water toward the plane — but he saw only the blackness of night. When he listened he heard nothing. He could no longer feel the presence of the plane; the feeling was a sensation he sometimes experienced when his eyes were closed. It was a deep visceral awareness that told him someone or something was nearby. He felt only the cold and the presence of the corpse next to him on the ground.

He reached his hand over and felt the trooper's clothing. His fingers touched something rigid in the trooper's top pocket... three rectangular items. He pulled them out. His fingers curled around three Glock magazines each with 15 rounds. He stuffed them in his parka. He continued rummaging in the trooper's coat. He found a four inch sheathed knife and matches. The knife... he had found a knife. He gripped the sheath tightly in his hand and for an instant envisioned himself returning to the wreckage, cutting his cellmate's seatbelt and then amputating his legs. But Malikov realized the knife was too small. He could never disarticulate his cellmate's legs with so small a blade. Would he even have been able to swim back out to the aircraft? He did not think so. And what if he were to try? He would die alongside his cellmate as the plane plunged to the bottom of the river or lake... if it had not already sunk. Yet he had promised to go back for him and his inability to do so weighed heavily on his soul. He shook his head. It was hopeless. He could not save his fellow prisoner. He placed the knife in his pocket reluctantly. The pit of his stomach ached when he thought of how the man must have suffered... drowning, choking... conscious of his lungs filling... slowly.

Malikov tried to light one of the matches he had found but it would not spark. He kept them anyway. He reached down into the dark to rifle through the trooper's pants pockets but he felt only mud and ice mixed with wet snow... and the thicker area of liquid that felt warmer to the touch. He was searching the area with his hand but Malikov must be at the wrong angle. He shifted his weight to the left and reached into the darkness again. But he could not find the trooper's pants. There were no pants. There were no pockets...

There were no legs.

There was nothing below the trooper's waist except the holster that laid there in the inch of water where the trooper's waist should have been. Malikov recoiled from the officer's body... scrambling up the bank of the river backwards, pushing himself away from the trooper, his hands beside him working in tandem with his feet. His arms and legs moved like a frenzied crab's escaping a ravenous predator, driving him up the bank away from the carnage. When he was halfway up the bank the incline steepened. He rose to his feet, turned to face the ground — head on — and pitched and stumbled the rest of the way in the dark until he reached the top. Only there would he feel he was far enough away from the water... and the body. Then he sat down in the cold snow, drew up his legs and hugged them trying to stave off his shivering. But he knew he could not sit for long. His clothes were drenched and becoming stiff. He must keep moving to prevent hypothermia. Malikov estimated the temperature was only slightly above freezing, maybe thirty eight to forty degrees.

He stood and used his feet to carefully tamp down an

area in the snow that would be level enough to provide him a place to walk back and forth, a path safe enough to maintain his footing in the dark. He could not stumble. If he fell and injured himself he could die before dawn. He dared not do more until the sun began to rise. As he paced, his thoughts returned to the MP who had taken the time to release Malikov from his shackles. He searched his mind for some explanation, some motivation that would have led the MP to sacrifice his own life for Malikov's, because it was clear the MP knew he was about to die. But Malikov could find no good reason the MP would have done such a thing.

So Malikov carefully walked back and forth in the same tamped down area at the top of the bank... intermittently flapping his arms and shaking his legs. He tried to formulate a plan in his head so he would know what he must do the minute first light came. When thoughts of the MP and his cellmate crept into his mind, he tried to think of something else. From time to time he thought about his small village of Zolotaryovka in the Penza *oblast,* and the Kuvaka Springs... and his *babushka*... and he wondered how he had come to be here in this unforgiving land. How had he ended up so many thousands of miles from his beloved *rodina,* pacing back and forth in the snow on a pitch-black Alaskan night... alone?

❀❀❀❀❀

Chapter 20

❄❄❄❄❄

ROC East HQ, Route 2 Templeton, Massachusetts, August

Falcon stood in Meg's office doorway and knocked. She rose from her chair as soon as she saw him. "Lunch bell," Falcon said, forcing a smile. They walked down the hallway. Neither of them said a word. They stepped into the elevator as the doors opened and Falcon pushed the button. Meg frowned and studied Falcon's face.

"You pushed the button for the residence floor," she said.

"I did?" Falcon asked.

"Are we calling up for room service today?" Meg quipped, "Pizza delivery maybe?"

Falcon chuckled. "Something like that," he said. "I thought we'd have a light lunch."

Meg smiled, clasped her hands in front of her and stretched.

It was a short walk from the elevator to Falcon's apartment door. They didn't speak. Falcon peered into the sensor box and his apartment door opened. He waited for Meg to pass by him through the open door and he followed her inside. For a split second, a twinge of guilt hit Falcon. He hadn't told Rabbit he was taking a long lunch. But the guilt passed over him as quickly as a stiff breeze.

As soon as the door closed they embraced, their bodies drawn together hungrily. Falcon's lips brushed

Meg's lightly... and then more passionately. They side stepped toward the bedroom, entangled tightly in each other's arms, each of them holding on as firmly as a magnet to a refrigerator door. As they fell into bed Falcon didn't once give a thought to the absurdity of the army's silk sheets.

❄❄❄❄❄

Meg and Falcon huddled together on the leather couch, both staring at the burning logs in the gas fireplace. "Well," Meg said. "I'm guessing your orders didn't bring good news."

"It's not China," he said flatly.

"It's probably not New Hampshire either," she said, "But I'm only postulating." She lightly tapped her fingernail on the sleeve button of one of Falcon's shirts she had thrown on before coming out of the bedroom.

Falcon sighed and turned toward her. "No, not New Hampshire... not anywhere on the east coast."

"Okay, just tell me," she pleaded.

"Alaska," he said, staring into her blue eyes... eyes he thought shined like sapphires today. It didn't seem quite so bad now that he had said it aloud... relatively speaking. It was still the United States. But he tried to remember he'd already had some time to adjust to it."

"Oh," was all she said.

"The good thing is..." he began.

"There's a good thing?" she interrupted. "It's four thousand miles away. There are a lot of rest areas between here and there."

He sighed. "Well the good thing is," he repeated, touching his index finger to her lips. "It may be easier to transfer up there. Very few officers request Alaska these days. That is," he added, "if you would consider joining me."

She looked at him and wrinkled her nose. "You have

to ask?"

"No," he laughed, "Just making sure."

"Of course I will go," she said. "But you know how staffing is right now. ROC's primary mission is to prepare for mobilization... Phase II. They're not going to give a crap about pacifying the troops or beefing up morale. Their objective is... well who knows what their overall objective is. I do know that ROC officers' preferences aren't their prime concern." She was quiet for a full minute before she continued. "I just found you Falcon," she complained softly, running her finger along his jaw line. "You make me feel life *will* go on. Whatever happens to the country I know I won't be facing it alone. Being together makes me hopeful... that at least something will be normal no matter what else goes wrong. And when this *is* all over — however the country ends up — we'll be together... at least that's my hope."

"And mine," he said.

"I don't know how my feelings went into overdrive with you," she mused. "I mean technically I hardly know you; but it feels like I've known you forever. When I saw you had been assigned to ROC HQ I knew this was meant to be. Then... all of a sudden you're being reassigned. I don't understand it. It's driving me crazy knowing I have to wait before we can be together."

Falcon tightened his arm around her. "Look, I don't know why I'm being transferred either. I don't know what the deal is with General H.B. Hazkill or Brevet Colonel Frankie Benton..."

"Frankie?" Meg laughed. "Where did that come from?"

Falcon chuckled. "It's an endearing term I picked up at ROC training... scratched into one of the bathroom walls."

Meg sniggered, "No... seriously?"

"Seriously," Falcon repeated.

"Oh my God… I thought I was the only one who thought he was a jerk!"

"No," Falcon laughed, "Apparently he has a following. He has left a few disgruntled officers in his wake." Funny, Falcon mused, he had been concerned Meg would be duped by Benton's manipulation but she had him pegged all along. Some instinct he has. But he did know one thing. Meg was upset about Alaska… as was he… but what irked him most was Hazkill's treatment of him. How in hell could Benton have sucked in this general so fast and turned him against Falcon?

"Meg," Falcon said softly, "We'll get through this," he assured her. "I swear we will. Finding a way to be together is the only thing that matters."

❄❄❄❄❄

Takotna River Takotna, Alaska, August

At the first glimmer of light Malikov tried to evaluate his physical condition. While he shivered uncontrollably it seemed the bleeding from his head he had noticed earlier had stopped. He had no idea he had been injured until he felt the oozing and his head had begun to throb an hour before. When the first pinch of dawn peeked through the trees he could see it was blood on his hands. He didn't think his injury was serious, at least as far as he could tell, but he had no time to worry about it.

He had heard the pilot's mayday so helicopters and search parties would soon be looking for the downed plane. Quickly he surveyed the surface of the water for fragments of the wreckage but he saw nothing. He could not dwell on the crash or his cellmate if he were going to remain free. He examined his environment. He kept his hand in the pocket of his parka, his fingers wrapped securely around the trooper's Gen4 .40 caliber Glock 22.

He had no idea if the gun had been damaged but it didn't matter. It was there in his pocket and he would use it if he had to. If it blew up in his face… so what. He had already decided he would not return to prison.

As the sun inched higher he could see now that the plane's final resting place was a river at least deep enough to swallow the plane. He looked down the riverbank toward the half-clothed torso of the Alaska State Trooper. His legs were nowhere in sight. Malikov thought he should take the trooper's jacket but it was probably as wet as his own parka. That would do him little good. Maybe he could find the pilot and take *his* clothing if by some good luck he had not been thrown into the river.

Malikov trudged through the deep snow up a small incline to better view his surroundings. Near the top and down about one hundred yards to his left he saw a glint of brightness like the flash of sunshine bouncing off a mirror. He headed quickly in that direction, through the trees and brush. As he neared the spot where he had glimpsed the small flash of light he could see the front windshield of the plane, a thick shred of metal below and above it. But broken trees covered the remainder of the wreckage. He made his way to the aircraft and peered into the cockpit.

The pilot was still strapped into his seat, his face torn and bloody, his left arm missing. He was clearly dead; his trooper jacket lay — still folded — on the floor. He had to get that jacket. But first Malikov broke off pine branches, gathered all of the broken limbs and smaller trees he could find and covered the portion of the wreckage that was visible. Then he took a heavy branch and hit the windshield multiple times with all the force he could muster until he succeeded in smashing it. His goal was to prevent any reflecting sunlight from drawing attention to the downed plane. He realized his efforts might be futile if it turned out the aircraft's black box was somewhere close by pinging distress signals across the silent Alaskan tundra but he decided it was worth the risk. It was America, he thought, there was a good chance the box was defective. This possibility amused him.

He walked around to the rear of the front section and made his way through the fuselage toward the cockpit; but he stopped and stood motionless... staring. In front of him lay the body of the MP who had unlocked his shackles. His corpse was twisted and wedged tightly into the wreckage, his torso mangled against a metal partition directly behind the pilot's seat, his chest impaled by a strip of gnarled steel as big around as a baseball bat. The MP was headless. For an instant Malikov found it impossible to stir; but he had no time to ponder the cruel ironies of life or contemplate the grave carnage he now saw before him. He must keep moving. He was freezing from his wet clothing.

The MP's pants looked usable and were easy to access. Robbing a corpse was a despicable act but Malikov had no choice. He would not think of the MP as he appeared at this moment. He would think only of the MP's face in that second before he had unlocked Malikov's shackles... when Malikov had experienced an inexplicably visceral human kinship to the man. That would be the image he must summon whenever he thought of this MP.

Malikov crawled over the twisted metal and leaned into the pilot's area, looking around the cockpit seat. He reached in and was able to stretch far enough to grab hold of the trooper's jacket. When he picked it up, he found a T-shirt underneath it. For Malikov, nothing would have been a greater miracle at that moment.

Without delay, he removed his parka and jumpsuit, and changed into the T-shirt and lined leather trooper jacket. He spotted a brown accordion file near the pilot's mangled foot and stretched out to grab it. He opened the folder and glanced inside. He pulled out what he was looking for and then backed out of the cockpit.

When he reached the headless corpse, he stopped and removed the MP's pants. He thought about his own wet boots but could see the MP's shoes were smaller. He would gain no advantage with them. He struggled to get his wet legs into the pants. They fit well enough. Except for damp blood stains his clothes were dry now and this would increase his chances of survival. At least that was his hope. He thought about redressing the body in his own wet jump suit but perhaps it would be better if he left no trace at all of himself. Maybe the MPs would not look for him if they thought he had drowned in the river. So he rolled up his old clothing and stuffed it under his arm. He would dispose of it somewhere in the forest where no one would find it. Malikov grabbed his own wet parka... expecting to dry it out later.

One trooper seemed to be missing. The seat behind the pilot where Malikov had last seen the armed trooper... was gone. He wasn't sure if that was the trooper at the riverbank or not. Malikov shook his head and grimaced. He seemed to be confused. His thinking was slowed and it was difficult to focus without becoming distracted. It could be his head injury was more serious than he had thought, or maybe it was the cold, but whatever the cause... he could not recall how many people had been in the aircraft. Yet... what did this matter? He had seen no evidence that anyone else had survived the crash. Malikov checked the interior of the plane one last time, but saw no rifles or other weapons. He backed out of the fuselage, gathered more branches and limbs and covered the remainder of the wreckage as best he could. He returned to the riverbank.

He dragged the trooper's torso from the bank and laid it in the woods. Before he left the area, he threw another pine bough over the corpse and dragged two large rotted trunks closer, draping them across the body. He broke off one additional large spruce branch and dragged it behind him to try to sweep away his footprints all the way back to the front part of the fuselage and then back down to the river. He did not do a very good job. With the temperature above freezing some melting had occurred. The snow was wet, heavy, and hard to move. Still, his attempts might delay a rescue crew and give Malikov additional seconds to get farther away from the area.

He dropped the branch at the river's edge and hobbled along the bank, staying in water up to his ankles for as long as he could, hoping this would confuse search dogs. He tried to tie his wet parka around his waist by the sleeves but he could not manipulate the heavy wet fabric. He settled on carrying it. His body was bruised and aching. His feet were numb from the wet and the cold. He limped for ten minutes and then stopped and rested one minute. He continued in this fashion in the shallow waters along the shore until he came to a narrowing in the river.

A log stretched three quarters of the way to the opposite bank. He rolled up his pant legs and used the downed tree as a bridge to cross to the other side. There, sheltered by trees, he took out the map he had grabbed from the accordion file in the cockpit. He looked at it briefly, refolded it and stuffed it into the pocket of the trooper's dry leather jacket. He paused for a moment, scanning the sky for search planes. Satisfied the sky remained quiet and pleased no one yet seemed to be searching for the wreckage he made his way to the top of the bank and disappeared into the thick spruce forest.

❋❋❋❋❋

ROC East HQ, Route 2 Templeton, Massachusetts, August

Falcon and Meg returned from lunch at 1330 hours. As they approached the suite of offices they could see Benton was leaning against the open door to Falcon's office flipping through a binder of spreadsheets.

"So I guess a party is in order," Benton said, looking up from his document as Meg and Falcon approached. "I heard your orders came down this morning."

"No party Colonel," Falcon said curtly. "I meant what I said."

"Well that's not very sporting of you," Benton complained. "I would have thought you would like a big sendoff to start your new assignment... you know... let these folks wish you success. And I'm sure you would like a chance to say good bye to Major Winters here, at the least."

"Under the circumstances, I don't think people are in the mood for celebrating. In less than ninety days these ROC forces are being mobilized," Falcon said. "Or have you forgotten?"

"Well that's my point," Benton said, chuckling. "It's the perfect time to boost morale with a little gathering. Besides, I thought it appropriate to let the troops acknowledge my promotion... you know... a meet and greet with the new Field Commander. We could combine the two events."

"Sounds like a great idea," Falcon sneered. "You arrange your meet and greet just make sure you leave me off the agenda." Falcon wanted to get into his office and close the door but Benton blocked his way. He had the urge to sink a shoulder into Benton and push him out of his path but it would be a costly mistake. As cozy as Benton was with Hazkill a minor incident like a friendly little shove of Brevet Colonel Benton would no doubt end up in Hazkill's lap as a disciplinary action. By the time Hazkill was done shredding Falcon over it there would be little left to his career. Benton wasn't worth it. So Falcon leaned against the wall and waited. Meg crossed her arms and stood outside her own office watching.

"So," Benton said, staring at his hand nonchalantly, examining his manicure, "Where're you headed? I was expecting you to let me know as soon as your orders were in hand." Falcon shot a glance at Rabbit, sitting quietly at his desk. Rabbit shrugged, sporting a pained look on his face as if he had a particularly bad case of heartburn.

"Yeah," Falcon answered. "They came down but I wasn't aware I needed to report to you."

"Well," Benton said. "I *am* the headquarters FC... I think it only courtesy. No harm done... so what's the good word?"

One positive thing about the transfer out of ROC HQ East... at least Falcon would be rid of Benton. If he had to spend two years working beside Benton he knew it would come to blows. Benton's demeanor was infuriating. No one person could be that slimy and devious going through life as condescendingly as he was without some kind of payback in the end. Life wouldn't make sense if the Bentons of the world came out on top every time. That wasn't the kind of universe in which Falcon thought he could live for long.

It made his blood boil when the military failed to recognize manipulative passive aggressors like Benton.

How could Benton have been promoted to Brevet Colonel? Did the damn president revive this Brevet system simply to get Benton on an inconceivably fast track to colonel — or worse — to general? Where did this guy's connections end? This was the damn president of the United States that authorized this travesty. How could Benton possibly have weaseled his way into Hazkill's confidence to get this kind of backing? To be honest Falcon could care less what connections Benton had or who he manipulated during his career. But the fact was... the guy was manipulating Falcon's life. That pissed off Falcon in a big way.

If Benton had never been in the picture none of this would have happened. Falcon would have met Hazkill and he would have been treated relatively fairly... at least like any other officer. This back room scheming — or whatever in hell it was — wouldn't be happening. How did Benton swing it? How did Benton turn Hazkill against Falcon in less than twenty-four hours and come away smelling like the proverbial rose? One of these days Falcon was going to find out what the sonofabitch held over Hazkill's head because Falcon had no doubt Benton had something — if not everything — to do with his transfer.

"Come on," Benton said, feigning genuine interest, "Don't be shy. Where are you headed?"

Falcon moved away from the wall and stepped up to the shorter Benton. "Alaska," he said. "Now do you think you might move so I can enter my office and get some work done?"

Benton grinned. "Alaska!" he bellowed, stepping aside to permit Falcon to pass. "Intriguing... that's what like four thousand miles from here? That will certainly be an adventure," Benton said, his syllables dripping with sarcasm. He took a few steps toward his own office, changed his mind and turned back. "Well," he said loud enough for everyone to hear. "I know Meg and I will miss you." Benton's face twisted into a despicable sneer as he turned to leave. Falcon watched him swagger down the hallway toward his office. What a specimen, he thought in disgust.

❋❋❋❋❋

Takotna, Alaska, August

Kenzie and Kyle were sheltered under the tall pines at the edge of the forest in the field in back of the cabin. Miriam could see them only as shadowy figures in the glare of the bright sunshine. As usual they had run ahead — this time far ahead — of Miriam. They had moved faster than Miriam realized in their eagerness to execute Kyle's *mission*. The two of them were pulling the sled trying to pack down the snow to facilitate Miriam's walking. Yet the sled was light — much lighter than when weighted down with the chisel, buckets and ice fishing traps. The resulting path was not much of an improvement but Miriam saw the effort for its sentiment and intent. Still, the distance between her and her children was dangerous.

No one could keep pace with children especially not Miriam and especially not today. And now she was nervous at the widened gap between them. So she quickened her pace, her hand gripping the shoulder strap of Henry Ivan's favorite rifle... a Model 444SS, 444 Marlin lever-action 5 shot. The tighter her fingers wound around the strip of canvas, the safer she imagined her children would be... as if the mere gripping of the heavy material would protect them. Henry Ivan had been surprised she had been able to handle it so well at 40.5 inches long and over 7 pounds it was not exactly a feminine rifle... if there were such a thing... but it wasn't for show. It was for survival.

Miriam was a dead on shot with it. The checkered American black walnut pistol grip stock with rubber rifle buttpad fit her hand better than her own skin. Unless she were hunting caribou or moose — and she would use the bolt-action .338 Winchester Magnum if she were — she carried the Marlin without scope. Encounters in the thick Takotna forest rarely offered a clear shot at greater than fifty to ninety yards. A mounted scope at such close range was a dangerous hindrance to her when circumstances demanded quick reflexes. Miriam was perfectly satisfied with the ramp front site, brass bead and Wide-Scan hood, and the adjustable semibuckhorn folding rear site. Best of all Miriam had found recoil from the Marlin to be less a shock to her system than the kickback from the shotgun.

"Kenzie," Miriam hollered. "You're too far ahead. You two stay where I can see you and don't go any farther until I reach you!" But neither child seemed to hear her. Or rather neither child *decided* to hear her just then. This annoyed Miriam. "Kenzie," Miriam yelled again. But the children did not answer. Miriam knew her short temper was partly due to frustration of another kind. It was difficult to keep her spirits lifted after Mr. Olani's party. She truly loved mingling with her friends and neighbors but never did the void in her heart — where her Henry Ivan belonged — seem so hollow and dark as when she saw the happiness on the faces of families that were complete. Her notions about leaving Takotna were serious ones that weighed heavily on her shoulders. But she was torn.

How selfish she was... thinking about needing more in her life than her two children. The idea hovered in the back of her mind that if she moved to a bigger village she might find someone to love her — to make their family whole. This was in part selfish and Miriam was disquieted that this vision of finding love again kept creeping into her thoughts. She was not a selfish person by nature. She loved her children. That should be enough. Guilt over this notion of finding love again plagued her. She had her two precious offspring who loved her unconditionally — and she them — yet she continually silently hungered for more. It wasn't right and she did not fully understand her feelings.

Miriam picked up her pace yet further, wrestling with the deep snow, moving as fast as she could to reach her children, wondering how they had managed to get so far ahead of her. She should have taken more care, insisted they stay by her side. What had she been thinking? There were too many unknown dangers at the edge of the spruce woods because of the freakish weather. There was no way to anticipate wild animals' reaction to the August snowfall. The animals were confused. Even Kenzie and Kyle recognized this. But Miriam had found it difficult to stay focused today. Perhaps she was confused by the weather too.

Her mind had thrown her off balance from the time she awoke early this morning. She could hardly concentrate on anything for more than a minute or two. She knew she must straighten herself out; if only she knew how to quiet the longings inside her. What kind of mother was she... dwelling on things that would make *her* feel better? She should concentrate on her children and be concerned only with their health and their happiness.

Suddenly a frenzied terrifying nightmare engulfed her. For an instant she thought she had just awakened but she knew she had not. This was not a dream. There... in front of her yards ahead was Kenzie — with

Kyle struggling to keep up in the deep snow. They were off to Miriam's right, traveling in a westerly direction along the back edge of the small field away from the forest. But they were not alone. Something was chasing them, gaining on them rapidly, loping through the snow behind them.

Miriam dropped the snares from her hand and her feet instinctively sparked her into overdrive. She slid the 444 Marlin strap off her shoulder as she lumbered through the snow. She could not fire it at this range. She could not clearly distinguish the shadowy figures but she would be ready at the first opportunity. This was a terrible movie playing before her eyes; how could this be real? She could see what looked to be a bear closing in on her children but Kenzie and Kyle knew not to run from a bear. And how could yet another bear be jeopardizing her children? Was this a cub of the sow bear she had killed? Her heart thumped faster; something else was there running behind her children. Two bears? No... something smaller was running out from the edge of the spruce forest toward her children.

Before Miriam could understand what was happening all of the figures merged together into one spot under the blinding sun. Kenzie's and Kyle's screams sliced through the air. Miriam tried to run faster but in her anguish her feet became tangled and bogged down in the snow. She tumbled forward headfirst losing her grip on the Marlin as she fell. It sailed out of her hand and sunk into the snow ahead of her. She scrambled to her feet, plowed forward and retrieved the rifle without slowing as she slogged through the wet snow as fast as she could. This could not be real. It could not be happening again. She struggled to move her legs. Then she heard it...

Boom ... boom... boom boom... Like a muffled canon

it echoed *boom ... boom... boom, boom.* The figures in front of her were no longer running. She strained to see as she lumbered forward. Miriam could not distinguish anything but a dark clump of silhouettes against the white blanket of snow and the blinding sun glaring down on them all.

"Kenzie!" Miriam hollered as loud as she could. "Kyle!" she shouted. But her voice sounded so muffled and weak. Her energy was sapped. It was so hard to move in the deep snow and the world around her seemed to be spinning in slow motion. She felt as though she were treading water... marking time... getting nowhere. As she finally closed the distance she was able to see Kyle running toward her.

"Hurry Mama!" Kyle screamed, pointing to the dark mass against the white snow. "C'mon... quick, quick!" He pulled at her hand and urged her to hurry faster with each tug. They rushed toward the depression in the snow: twenty-five feet ahead... fifteen feet... ten. As they came upon the scene the darkened shapes slowly sharpened into distinguishable figures. She squinted in the glare of sunshine while she struggled to discern the mass of flesh sprawled before her. A thousand daggers pierced Miriam's heart as she stared at the pools and splatter of deep red blood fanning out across the glistening snow. She dared not breathe; she waited for the earth to drop out from under her feet.

❈❈❈❈❈

Fizer farm Shepherdstown, West Virginia, August

Nick stood on the running board of their new SUV and pulled on the metal clips of the tie down straps to secure the car top carrier. Stephy leaned against the passenger side door, sipping from a travel mug and talking to Nick's parents. Nick gave the straps a last tug and jumped down. All four of them now stood together in a group between the two vehicles.

"That's it," he said.

"I'm so excited I can hardly stand it," Nick's mother said. "I can't believe we dropped everything and we're moving to Alaska!"

"It *is* exciting, isn't it?" Stephy agreed. "But won't you miss the farm Julia?"

"No," Nick's mother said emphatically. "All of the good memories are filed away. There's nothing left to miss; it's time to create new memories."

"Well," Nick's father said, "We can stand here talking about it or we can start the damn cars and get this show on the road."

"Maybe we should go through the list once more Bill," Nick's mother suggested.

"We've gone through it three times already Mom," Nick reminded her.

"Even if we forgot something," Nick's father said, "There's no more room to fit anything."

"Let's do it," Stephy said, grinning and squeezing Julia's hand.

"It's already ten o'clock Mom," Nick said. "Three hours later than we planned on leaving. But if you want to go through the list again…"

"No," his mother replied. "No need. I'm sure we didn't forget anything important." The four of them stared at each other. No one said anything. Nick smiled. Stephy grinned and Nick's mother giggled. As if they heard a gunshot to start a 5k race… they instantly dispersed from the group and hurried around to the car doors. Without further delay they climbed into their vehicles. Nick started the SUV and began to pull out of the driveway. He stopped at the end and let down his window. For a long instant he peered at the farm where he grew up. He figured his parents might be doing the same. Then he leaned over and kissed his wife.

"Thank you," he said softly.

"For what?" Stephy queried.

"For believing in me enough to go along with this," he said.

"We've always stood together Nick," she told him. "This is simply one more challenge."

"This isn't an ordinary challenge," he said. "It isn't like anything we've faced before."

"In three months nothing will be like it was before," she said.

She was probably right about that. Nick smiled at her and gave her hand a squeeze. He turned the SUV onto the road, the tires crunching on the gravel, and headed north... his parents right behind him in their own SUV.

❋❋❋❋❋

Takotna, Alaska, August

Miriam, Kyle and Kenzie pulled hard on the rope but the sled was weighted down with the body... legs and boots hanging off the end and dragging behind... as they hauled the sled forward. Progress was slow. At least the sled was not the one with the runners. The children had chosen the newer plastic sled to drag behind them in their mission to create a path in the snow for Miriam. The trick in keeping the sled moving forward was to maintain a steady pace and allow momentum to work for them. That was the theory, but the truth was they did stop to rest every now and then. The past few days of higher more seasonal temperatures had caused melting. The snow was laden with moisture. It took a long while to cover a few yards.

"I don't know whether this is a good idea," Miriam

mumbled warily, concerned about her decision to take the stranger to her home. She had never seen him before and visitors to Takotna were rare. If he weren't semi-conscious and if he had not gotten such a bad wound to his eye she may have decided that taking him to the cabin wasn't worth the risk to her family. But he did save Kenzie and Kyle. Maybe he at least deserved a thank you. She could feed him, tend to his wound and after he rested he could be on his way. "Where did this man come from?" Miriam asked.

"I don't know," Kenzie answered.

"He was just there," Kyle added. "First we saw the bear. Then we saw the man."

"I don't understand why you ran from the bear," Miriam admonished them. "You know better than that."

"The bear was already charging us Mama," Kyle explained excitedly. "We didn't have any choice."

"And the man came running out right behind the bear," Kenzie agreed, "Just like Kyle said. And he started shouting at the bear but the bear kept chasing us."

"I think the bears are confused!" Kyle screeched.

"Yes and when the man couldn't get the bear's attention he hollered something funny and motioned for us to duck down in the snow..." Kenzie said.

"Like this," Kyle demonstrated, motioning with his arms and ducking down low. "And we did exactly like he said."

"And then the man shot the bear!" Kenzie said.

"Yup," Kyle added. "*Pow, pow, pow*," he mimicked the man shooting. "He shot the bear with his pistol."

"Four times," Kenzie said.

"Then the man jumped right on top of the bear!" Kyle said while leaping into the air to demonstrate.

"Yes!" Kenzie agreed. "So the bear wouldn't eat us!"

"And he wrestled the bear and shot him more times!" Kyle shouted excitedly.

"You don't think the man will die Mama do you?" Kenzie said with worry crackling her voice.

"He can't die," Kyle said. "He saved us. He's the bravest man in the world! Well," Kyle added thoughtfully, "Except his bear wasn't near as big as mine!"

"You didn't *kill* a bear Kyle!" Kenzie chastised him.

"I KNOW that," Kyle said sheepishly.

"That bear looked to be about two years old from what I could tell," Miriam said. "It could be a cub of the sow bear that came into the cabin through the siding."

"Yes," Kenzie agreed, "I think so too mama."

"It is good it was not a full grown brown bear. We'll see what we can do for the man," Miriam said. "If his wound is very bad we can take him to Elizabeth at the clinic." They continued to plod on through the snow toward the cabin, stopping every now and then to rest for a second when the children grew weary from pulling. Each time they stopped the man groaned and Miriam slipped her hand underneath the strap of the 444 Marlin that was slung across her shoulder. She let her hand rest there, not sure the man in the sled was one hundred percent trustworthy.

Finally they reached the back of the house and they let the sled rope drop in the snow. The man began to stir again as soon as the sled came to a stop. He moaned — a half-conscious groan — and moved his head to the side. Miriam went over to him and helped him sit up.

"Come now Kyle, Kenzie," Miriam said. "Let's see if we can get him to stand so we can take him inside." Kenzie helped Miriam lift the man under the arms while Kyle tugged at the man's jacket until he was in a standing position. He leaned most of his weight on

Miriam.

"Can you walk into the cabin if we help you?" Miriam asked.

"*Valk*," the man muttered and nodded, taking an unsteady step forward.

"Lean on me," Miriam instructed him. The man did as he was told. Kyle took the man's hand and laid it on his shoulder. The man leaned on them and the three of them staggered through the door while Kenzie held it open. They helped the man onto the sofa. Kenzie took off the man's wet boots. He was bleeding from his face and eye. Miriam propped the man up with pillows.

"He should not sleep with a head wound," Miriam said. "You must help me keep him awake. Kyle," Miriam added, "Run and get me the first aid box."

"Name?" the man asked in a hoarse whisper, his uninjured eye half open.

"Miriam," she answered.

"What is your name?" she asked him, taking the first aid box from Kyle.

"Pavel Aleksandrovich Malikov," he said softly, trying to smile, "Malikov..."

❄❄❄❄❄

Takotna, Alaska, August

Malikov completed repairs on the cabin doorjamb and fastened a large plank into a primitive door with a rope handle. The door now worked and kept the cold from seeping into the cabin. It wasn't airtight but it was functional and much better than a blanket hanging in the hallway and the leaning plank Miriam had temporarily used for a quick fix. What destruction caused by the first bear attack, Malikov thought. The boy was lucky to have survived. Malikov did not feel quite so well. His body was bruised and battered from the plane crash as well as from his own fight with the smaller — but no less lethal — bear. But he was determined to do this repair for Miriam and he was satisfied after his labor. He packed up the tools and went back into the kitchen, still unsteady on his feet. Miriam was at the kitchen woodstove making dinner. She could provide everything for her family even without electricity; this astounded Malikov. He sat at the kitchen table and watched her cook.

"Why do we call you Malikov?" Kyle asked, walking into the kitchen.

"Malikov *eece* name," he said laughing. "*Vhy* say *deece* Kyle?"

"My name is Kyle!" Kyle said. "But my name sounds like a name."

"Malikov too," Malikov told him chuckling.

"Will you play Melli Moose with us after we eat?" Kyle teased.

"Now Kyle," Miriam told him. "Malikov must rest. I told you that."

"Kyle," Malikov said. "*Ve* play *deece* Moosi Moose... after sleep, *da*?"

"*Da*!" Kyle said excitedly.

"Go wash your hands Kyle" Miriam instructed. "And tell Kenzie to do the same."

"*Da*!" Kyle exclaimed, laughing and skipping back down the hallway.

"Kyle Russian *eece* good, *nyet*?" Malikov teased.

Miriam giggled.

Malikov watched Miriam... this family... throughout dinner. She was graceful and nurturing and for the first time since his *babushka* he felt a warmth and comfort from a woman and it filled the entire room. He could not explain this feeling. Throughout dinner he was careful not to shovel food into his mouth or chew like a cow chews its cud. These things were suddenly important to him. Even as he worked hard to be careful not to make mistakes and to make sure he used the right manners, he felt free and happy. He felt free with every minute that ticked by... free from the moment Miriam had taken him in. He felt free... not simply unshackled... but truly free from all of his burdens.

Malikov helped Miriam in the kitchen when dinner had ended even though his body ached and the pain in his eye was great. As they now sat drinking tea with the children playing in the other room he looked around this *dacha* of Miriam's. He saw she had few possessions cluttering her home and this impressed Malikov. She was not like the greedy American women he had met, concerned about fancy clothes and jewelry and all the things that meant nothing to him. Miriam had been kind to him and she had asked nothing in return. Why was this? He wondered.

But she had asked few questions of how he came to be at the edge of the forest and this seemed inexplicable to him. Did she care so little about an unknown man in the woods right beyond her home? Or was she simply being polite until she could kick him out the door, send him on his way and out of her life? Or maybe she was waiting and would go to the police? But she did not seem to be in such a hurry to do this. She seemed more concerned that his eye was healed. Would she hurry him then?

She had done a fine job sewing his face and his eyelid. But in a day or two when the swelling went down and his face looked more normal would she tell him to leave? Leaving Miriam's cabin was something Malikov did not want to contemplate. Where would he go? He could think of no better place in the world than right here... in this cabin... with Miriam and Kyle and

Kenzie. Were the MPs searching for him? Why was he not more concerned about this? In two days he had thought of the MPs only a handful of times. What if they were right now tracking his footprints to this door? Why did this all seem so much like a dream to him? Why did he not care so much about MPs now?

Miriam had a book open on the table in front of her. As she sipped her tea she read from it. Malikov felt an urge to ask her about it. But what did he know about books and stories? He was a soldier. He had no time for such things. It had been a very long time since he had even given a thought to books — not since he was very young. But as he looked around the tidy cabin and spied a small bookcase in the corner he felt driven to touch the books. He stood stiffly — as would anyone who had been thumped to the ground by a wounded thousand pound bear mere hours after a plane crash — and made his way slowly to the corner.

Miriam watched the man, this Malikov, with cautious eyes as he approached her Henry Ivan's collection of books. She wasn't as frightened by him now as she had been at first. But she still felt the pull of her instinct and heard the whispers of her conscience telling her to be wary. She had young children and she did not know this Malikov.

Malikov reached for a book and held his hand short of touching its spine. "See book, *da*?" he asked Miriam, nodding, knowing his *babushka* would be proud of his manners.

"Of course," Miriam smiled. "Do you like to read?"

"*Da*," Malikov told her, returning her smile. It wasn't exactly a lie. He did not think he would lie to Miriam. While he had not read for many years, he had read as a boy... before his mother had died. She had encouraged him to read books and to use his mind. But Aleksi was not so concerned with such things. Malikov had no opportunity to read — except at school — when he had gone to live with Aleksi. Malikov selected the book to which he had first been drawn and opened it as carefully as if he were unwrapping a fine piece of china.

"Did you find something you like?" Miriam asked.

"*Da!*" Malikov beamed excitedly, angling the book and showing her the *Call of the Wild*, by Jack London. "Read... *ven* boy." He hobbled back to the table with the book and sat down, his feet still painful from the wet and cold he had endured. He supposed he was lucky his feet still worked at all after wading in forty degree river water.

"It was one of our... I mean... one of my... favorites," Miriam said, blushing. She stood and went to the sink. She filled the teapot with water from the bucket and set it to boil on the small kitchen woodstove. She returned to the sink and leaned against the counter watching this Malikov. Why was he in the forest, she wondered? There is nothing beyond the forest... except more forest. Where did he come from and where was he going? She wanted to ask these questions but yet did not want to ask questions to which she did not know the answers. But no one comes to Takotna unless he comes to visit someone who lives in Takotna. Why did this man seem in no hurry to leave? Wasn't someone worried about where he was? Why was it that she no longer felt so rushed to make him leave her home? She had no reason to trust this man. Yet, it was peculiar... she seemed to trust him. She watched him slowly turn the pages of the book but he was not reading. Could he not read?

"How is your eye today?" Miriam asked.

"*Neplokho,*" — not bad — Malikov said. "*Da, Neplokho,*" Malikov repeated, but motioned to the book and grimaced slightly. "No see good."

"Oh, your eyes must be blurry..." Miriam said, his meaning now dawning on her. She moved over and rested her hand on his arm. She didn't know why she was compelled to do this. Immediately she withdrew it, trying not to be obvious. He looked up at her and smiled. Her face was red. She could feel it. Of course now knowing it was red, it only became redder. "I will be happy to read the story to you," Miriam said, gesturing with her hands to ensure he would understand. Instantly she wanted to take back her words. He will laugh at me, she thought. How ridiculous she must sound. This was not her Henry Ivan. This Malikov would not understand.

"*Da*, read!" Malikov said nodding eagerly, glowing... passing the book to Miriam with both hands. "*Da!* Read!" he repeated, and then he remembered. "Read... *Pozhaluysta, Bud'te dobry!*" — Please! Be so good — he said proudly.

Miriam laughed, nodding. "I will make more tea for us and then I will read."

"*Da*, read," Malikov said, smiling broadly. He watched her in silence.... working her cooking miracles at the small kitchen woodstove. He let the quiet and the warmth of the kitchen settle into his bones... and then couldn't help himself. "Where Miriam's *muzh*... uh... man?" — husband. He had suddenly blurted it out. "*Nyet*," he said, frowning. "*Nyet*, no ask." Bad manners, he thought to himself. He should not pry.

"He is dead," Miriam said.

"Sad," Malikov said. "*Da*... sad."

Miriam smiled and brought the kettle to the table and poured the boiling water into the cups. "It's okay," she said. "He has been gone many years. Do you have a family?"

"*Nyet*," he answered quickly "*Umer*,"— dead.

Miriam wasn't sure if she could comprehend this. How could a man have no family? Even though Miriam's Henry Ivan was dead these many years, Miriam had her children, her brothers, her cousins, her nephews and nieces and her grandmother. How could a man have no one? Surely, he had someone. She had other questions; questions she did not want to ask this Malikov. What about his clothes? He had the uniform of an Alaska State Trooper. Kyle had been the first to point out his trooper jacket and Miriam had shushed him when Malikov did not seem to want to explain. She had not pushed this because he was in pain. But he has not explained this yet. Should she be frightened of this man?

She had been patient for two days and she had not asked him these questions because she planned that he would leave her house anyway. But now perhaps she was not in such a hurry for him to go. What would be the harm if he stayed a week... or two? He has said he has no family. Who would be missing him? Why would he need to hurry away? But she could not let him stay. Not unless he answered her questions. She must know something of this man. If he will not tell her then she will know she should be frightened. She will take Henry Ivan's gun and she will tell him he must leave. Miriam fixed their tea and then sat down, tapping her finger softly on her spoon, lost in her thoughts. *The Call of the Wild* was open on the table in front of her but she did not read from it.

"*Nyet?*" Malikov asked, pointing to the book. She did not answer him. He became pensive and then tried to explain the history of the book in the Soviet Union. "*Nyet* read in Russia. *Nyet*, read," he said feigning cutting his throat with his forefinger. He felt inadequate and wished his English were better so he could explain the book had been banned in Russia prior to 1962 — at least he thought that was the correct year it was published there. Miriam looked up but it was clear her mind was elsewhere. Malikov studied Miriam's expression but he did not understand her sudden reluctance to read the book to him. He wasn't sure she had heard what he tried to tell her. Had he made a mistake? Were his manners bad? What could he have done to make her not want to listen to him or to read the book?

He had thought things were good... that he and this woman could understand each other. But he could not tell what she was thinking. She wasn't a man so he could not come right out and ask her. Wouldn't that be bad manners? It was clear she wasn't picking up *The Call of the Wild.* She would not read to him now? What could he do to fix this? What would his *babushka* want if she were sad... or if he had done something wrong and she became angry with him? Malikov felt a pain in his chest. This hurt him to see Miriam unhappy. He must make this right.

"Miriam sad," Malikov said softly. "*Nyet, eece* bad. Miriam sad," he said, shaking his head.

"It isn't that," Miriam said.

"I do bad?" Malikov asked.

Miriam looked at Malikov's face, the bandage had slipped and she must clean his wound and change the bandage soon. Yet she was driven to know who this man in her kitchen was. She had to know... in her heart she must find out.

"You have not told me anything about yourself," Miriam said, watching Malikov.

"Russian," Malikov said tapping his palm on his chest. But he knew what she meant. Miriam did not respond and now he knew. He could not expect this woman with two vulnerable children to keep a man under her roof without knowing who he was. Malikov had two choices. It was simple. He could lie or tell the truth. If he lied and made a good story Miriam might be happy for a while. But Malikov would worry. He was a very bad liar. He would never remember what lies he had told or when he had told them. Besides... it was a coward's way. It was what Aleksi would do and in Malikov's mind those echoes of Aleksi's lies came very quickly flooding back to him.

"You must tell the doctor you fell on the stone wall," Aleksi had demanded after beating Malikov. *"You must not tell how you were hurt."* Was this how he would want Miriam to think about him some day? Did he want Miriam to think about the man who lied to her... the coward who couldn't tell the truth? Yet telling her the truth was a very big risk. It might mean the difference between being sent to jail and remaining a free man. It could mean Malikov's own *smert',"*— death.

Malikov smiled at Miriam. "To Miriam I say *deece* truth... then Malikov go... if Miriam say go."

Miriam sat up in her chair. She focused intently on this man before her... this Malikov. *Dear God,* Miriam thought. *Please don't let Malikov's truth be something I cannot understand... or forgive.*

❀❀❀❀❀

Chapter 21

✤✤✤✤✤

Tides Motel Toledo, Ohio, August

"Tired from driving?" Stephy asked, standing behind Nick, massaging his shoulders.

"A little," Nick said, sitting at the motel room desk, his laptop open in front of him.

"What're you looking up?" Stephy queried.

"I thought a little Alaska news would be interesting," Nick answered.

"Did you find anything?" Stephy asked.

"Listen to this," Nick said, as he read aloud from the article he had pulled up from the Internet.

> Chicken, Alaska: Miners said that during the week of August 10, seven armed agents of the Environmental Protection Agency — EPA — descended on area mines, sped past miners on all-terrain vehicles or on foot without identifying themselves, and began checking equipment. The agents were all wearing body armor and jackets with the word "POLICE" emblazoned on them. Miners were used to water-quality compliance checks that usually entail an officer showing up with a clipboard and a smile...

"Did you say Chicken Alaska?" Stephy's eyes widened. "Body armor... what were they looking for, weapons of mass destruction? Is there even such a place as Chicken Alaska?"

"Yes it's a real place. The EPA storm troopers were there looking for violations of the Clean Water Act," Nick said, twisting his face as if he had gotten a whiff of a compost heap.

"My God," Stephy exclaimed. "It sounds like a trailer for a B-rated Keystone Cops' short film." She shook her head. "What's the population of Chicken Alaska? I mean... are there hordes of residents there polluting the water?"

"Well I don't know if they're polluting the water," Nick answered. "But the *hordes of residents* in Chicken Alaska... total the tidy sum of seventeen."

"Seventeen people," Stephy repeated. "The EPA raided a village of seventeen... with a SWAT team? It would be laughable if it weren't so... so damn terrifying. It doesn't do much to support the case for finding sanctuary in Alaska."

"Actually," Nick said. "It proves my point exactly."

"How?" Stephy asked.

"Proves it on two counts... first, you have these EPA enforcers going out to the middle of nowhere brandishing SWAT gear and weapons to lay siege to a town with seventeen people — because they might be polluting the water? Is pollution now a violent offense that authorizes the EPA to use deadly force? Where's the common sense in this? Think about it. What possessed these guys to go along with something like this? Has some notion of power gone to their heads? Or do they still have that common boyhood affinity for playing war? Or was it because their *supervisor* told them to do it? Did these EPA agents go to work and sign a waiver allowing the EPA to remove their brains for a day? What the hell?" Nick said in exasperation.

"Christ," Nick continued, "if you can get men to suit up in body armor and storm a town of seventeen in the middle of the Alaskan bush, and get them to threaten innocent people by waving guns in their faces... because the water quality might be a little off... then you can get people to do just about anything."

Stephy's hands froze on Nick's shoulders.

"What kind of example does this set for school children? And the public wonders why teenagers bring guns to school and commit mass murder. If you ask me... guns should be confiscated from these agencies... not from the law abiding public," Nick complained.

Nick went on, "We're talking interior Alaska here... the middle of nowhere. What place is safe from this kind of mindless brutality? I'll tell you what place is safe. No place is safe. This OPSEIM Directive is so complex, convoluted and far reaching, that there may not be any safe place to go."

Stephy leaned her head against his. "What do we do Nick?"

"We do exactly what we're doing," Nick responded. "We work from inside the document. We go to the one place the OPSEIM researchers found the mathematical certainty calculation isn't valid... the one place they couldn't verify project success. We go to the location they might be willing to write off as a loss. We go to Juneau Alaska, the one place we might be able to hold onto our autonomy... some of our rights. Maybe it's the one place we will find a way to... to get our nation — and our lives — back.

❄❄❄❄❄

Adit 17 Perseverance Mine Juneau, Alaska, August

"So what's up?" Dan asked Gil as they stood just outside Viktor's mini hospital room. "Impromptu visit to the patient today... he won't be happy. You seem to be missing something."

"Shit!" Gil complained. "I forgot the damn pizza!"

"You guys might as well come in; it's not like I can't hear you out there," Viktor told them.

"Here," Gil said, handing a news article to Dan as they entered Viktor's room. "Have a look... I clipped this out of the newspaper for Viktor."

"So," Gil chastised Viktor, "Eavesdropping are we?"

"Guilty conscience?" Viktor fired back.

"Is this for real?" Dan asked, frowning as he scanned the news clipping. "The EPA... Guns?"

"Yuh it's for real. Sick isn't it?" Gil asked. "I brought it over because I thought Viktor said his sister lived somewhere up around there and I wasn't sure where."

"So how *is* the patient today?" Gil asked, turning his attention to Viktor.

"Itching..." Viktor complained stretching and scooting himself up in the bed, careful to keep his hand elevated on the pillow.

"Itching?" Gil repeated, surprised. "Is this a new symptom Doc?" Gil looked toward Dan.

"News to me," Dan answered. "You have something new going on Viktor?"

"Not new," Viktor protested, "Itching to get the hell out of here."

"Uh huh," Dan nodded, disapprovingly.

"Say, I have been meaning to ask you," Gil questioned Dan. "Why didn't you bring Viktor over to the hospital after the snow stopped? You know... for his hand surgery."

"What? You mean the *real* hospital?" Dan asked. "I planned to but he refused to go. He said I needed the practice and he wanted to make sure our little Perseverance Clinic could handle the... as he put it... tough VIP cases."

"Well Viktor you're still modest I see," Gil laughed.

"Not just modest but right too," Viktor chuckled. "A real doctor would have had me back on my feet two days ago."

"Ha ha," Dan mocked.

"Geez Dan," Gil laughed. "I think the man diss'd you right there!"

"Okay quit stalling. Let me see the article," Viktor demanded. "But don't think I'll forget about the pizza... and the beer."

"I don't think there was any beer in our previous agreement," Gil argued.

"Well there is now; we've entered the penalty phase," Viktor explained, motioning for the article.

"You know doc, I think Viktor's forgotten who holds the inventory of paralyzing surgical drugs around here."

"I think you're right," Dan agreed, passing the article to Viktor.

"So what is this?" Viktor asked, squinting at the news clipping.

"Have a look," Gil replied, waiting while Viktor scanned the article.

Viktor looked up with a pained expression. "Chicken?"

"Yeah Chicken Alaska," Gil sighed, betraying his exasperation. "Population a whopping seventeen... no, wait... maybe sixteen now. I heard after the EPA showed their weapons one guy was so pissed he packed up and moved to L.A. where it's safe!"

"I have no clue what to say to this," Viktor frowned, shaking his head in disbelief.

"Well, I brought it over because I thought you mentioned your sister lived up near Chicken," Gil explained.

"Nah she lives in the big city compared to Chicken," Viktor told him. "She lives about four hundred miles east of there in a village of about forty or fifty. That reminds me... I haven't been to see her in years."

"Man I wasn't even close!" Gil laughed.

"Well... comparatively speaking you were," Viktor corrected him. "Four hundred miles is a drop in the bucket for a state the size of Alaska. Chicken is not exactly antipodal to my sister's village."

"True," Gil nodded.

Viktor pulled back his blankets and gingerly dropped his feet over the side of the bed. He reached for his shirt on the back of the chair. Gil and Dan looked at each other.

"Going somewhere?" Dan asked.

"Getting dressed," Viktor answered.

"I told you I would bring the damn pizza," Gil narrowed his brow. "You don't have to go to the restaurant to get it."

"And beer," Viktor pointed out. "Don't forget the beer. Wait a minute! Wait... what am I saying? Now you will have two things to remember."

"Yes Pizza *and* beer," Gil promised. "I won't forget so you can just get back into bed."

"Come on Viktor," Dan admonished him. "You promised you would stay in bed for three more days."

"The way I remember it," Viktor disagreed, "I said I would take it *easy* for three more days. And I will."

"Then what are you getting up for?" Gil snapped.

Viktor had his right arm up in the air, wiggling it into the sleeve of his flannel shirt. "Either of you two want to give me a hand?"

Gil shrugged and walked over to help.

"This isn't taking it easy," Dan criticized.

Viktor stopped fidgeting with his shirt and rested his arm in his lap. He sat quietly for a minute... looking first at the floor then at Gil and Dan. He was still dizzy.

Clearly he wouldn't be going jogging any time soon. Viktor tried to pick up the news clipping but his bandage was in the way and he fumbled with it. He gave up and left it on the bed, motioning to it with his head. "Look," he argued, "You see this article? This is pretty bad fellas." Gil and Dan both lowered their heads, appearing to reflect on what Viktor was saying as if someone had called for a moment of silence. "I know it's not exactly pleasant to think about this stuff..." Viktor pointed out, "But all this talk we've been doing for three years... and the planning... and testing. This whole place..." he said, sweeping the air with his arm. "All the work we put into this mine not to mention this crappy blizzard we all lived through... well it comes down to one thing. We can't ignore events like these; they have to be checked out. I'm just not sure how much time we have."

"But what does this thing in Chicken Alaska have to do with H.A.A.R.P.?" Dan probed.

Viktor sighed. "Does this make any damn sense to you? EPA storm troopers in body armor brandishing weapons to raid a village of seventeen people for an administrative infraction generally penalized by a fine? Is this rational? What kind of people would agree to do such a thing? Don't these people... these agencies... have any boundaries? Who the hell is pulling the strings here... ordering these storm troopers to terrorize this tiny village?" Viktor questioned angrily. They remained silent for a long few minutes. "Look," Viktor told them more calmly. "I don't know what... if anything... this travesty has to do with the Gakona facility but we sure as hell need to find out. Until we rule it out I'm working from the assumption that H.A.A.R.P. *did* have something to do with this raid in Chicken." Dan, Gil and Viktor looked at each other.

"What do you need me to do?" Dan asked.

"Help me get this damn shirt on and pass me my pants, and get me down the hall into the lab," Viktor answered.

"What can I do?" Gil asked.

"You got the plane ready to go?" Viktor questioned.

"It's ready to go," Gil nodded, throwing back his shoulders and standing taller.

"Good," Viktor smiled. "Go get me that pepperoni pizza you owe me... with extra cheese and a six pack." Viktor smiled.

"With my plane... that's what you want me to do?" Gil grumbled. "You want me to fly you in a pizza... from where, Anchorage?"

"Nah," Viktor and Dan both laughed. "*After* you get the pizza... and *after* we eat... you need to take me up. I want to look at those cloud tracks. The beer is for my nightcap... to recover from all this extra work."

Gil smiled and turned to leave the ward. Dan grabbed Viktor's pants and brought them over to him. As Gil left through the doorway and started down the hall, Viktor hollered. "Don't forget the extra cheese!"

"And the damn beer," Dan bellowed.

※※※※※

Takotna, Alaska, August

It was two in the morning before Malikov finished telling Miriam his truth. It was a struggle for Malikov... searching for ways to transpose his Russian thoughts into English words and gestures that Miriam could understand. He used his less than stellar working knowledge of English, his hands, his expressions... anything to get across his points. They had been interrupted several times by the children and had taken short breaks while Miriam replenished their teacups.

Malikov left nothing intentionally out of the story he told but he was not sure she understood all of what he tried to communicate.

Malikov was not proud of what had happened at the crash site but he told her anyway. He wasn't proud of his grandfather either or how he felt about the man but he worked hard to tell her all of that too. He told her about the MP Booner and swore to her he had done nothing. But he could not know if she believed him. Now Malikov was sweating as he sat in Miriam Goodriver's kitchen, *The Call of the Wild* still open to the first page on the table in front of Miriam. She had not spoken a word in at least thirty minutes. The only sound in the room was the occasional *clink* of her spoon against the inside of her teacup.

Malikov wasn't sure whether he would be leaving in the morning or maybe tonight if she asked him to go; but the one thing he did know was that he was relieved he had told her the truth. If the MPs knocked at her door in the morning and handcuffed him while Miriam and the children looked on he could hold his head high. It wouldn't be like leaving Afghanistan... head down, cheated and defeated. It wouldn't feel as it felt the day he stomped out the door of the B Sector mess hall after his fight with the MP Booner. It wouldn't be like any of those things if the MPs came and took him away tomorrow. The only thing he cared about was that he could hold his head up and look this woman straight in the eye. He was pleased about that and he knew his *babushka* would approve. But there was more.

Anyone who ever knew Aleksi... truly knew him... would know that Malikov had kept his word. He had gone off to become a good soldier and he had done better than Aleksi had done. Malikov did not return to spread misery or try to hide from his demons inside a bottle...

not anymore anyway. If Malikov were sent back to Russia tomorrow he would go back to his beloved *rodina* knowing in his heart he was nothing like Aleksi.

Miriam looked up from her teacup and angled her head a slight bit to the right as she looked at him. Malikov thought she might have smiled but he was not sure. The flickering amber light and his blurry vision — increased now due to fatigue — did not allow him the clarity to know for certain. So he waited, now looking down at his own cup and worrying that Miriam was angry or disappointed that he had such difficult truth to tell. He was concerned that his truth would be too heavy a burden for her and she would ask him to leave. What right would he have to expect anything different from her? He had only known her for days.

While he stared at his hands and the rim of his teacup he still found himself hoping for things that could probably never be. He had finished telling Miriam his truth and she had not spoken a word to let him know how she felt. He wondered if he should stand and get his clean dry parka and leave her warm *dacha*. Perhaps it would be better if he did this. Maybe he should not wait for her to tell him to leave. He did not want to give Miriam pain. Perhaps asking someone to leave your home was a hard thing to do in America.

Malikov wasn't sure of proper manners in a case like this. He was confused; that was true. But one thing he decided. No matter how it turned out he would be forever grateful for the day he saw the bear down in back of Miriam's field at the edge of the spruce forest. It seemed to him that he felt about as good as he would have felt after the greatest battle of any war. Perhaps this fight with the bear had been Malikov's *Battle of Stalingrad*. Yes... he should go. It was the right thing to do. Malikov took the last sip of his tea and used his napkin to dab at the corner of his mouth. He hoped it was good manners to do so.

He was ready to make his exit. He was sure this was best. So he began to rise but Miriam seemed to know what was on his mind. She gently laid her hand on his forearm and motioned for him to sit. This time she did not immediately pull away her hand. So Malikov sat back down prepared to listen to what Miriam had to say before he left her cabin. But what Miriam had to say so stunned Malikov that he could not speak. He sat quietly long into the early morning hours watching and listening to this extraordinary Miriam as she smiled warmly at him from time to time all through the night; and he grinned broadly as she read aloud to him from Jack London's, *The Call of the Wild.*

> Buck did not read the newspapers, or he would have known that trouble was brewing, not alone for himself, but for every tide-water dog, strong of muscle and with warm, long hair, from Puget Sound to San Diego. Because men, groping in the Arctic darkness, had found a yellow metal, and because steamship and transportation companies were booming the find, thousands of men were rushing into the Northland...

❀❀❀❀❀

ROC East HQ, Route 2, Templeton Massachusetts, August

Falcon and Meg held hands... not exactly authorized behavior when in a ROC forces uniform... but at this point Falcon didn't care and no one was paying attention to them anyway. Soldiers, ROC troops and U.N. peacekeeping forces dashed back and forth in front of them, beside them and behind them; they rushed in double time... verifying their orders, looking for the right transports, checking their bags, cursing the PODs that were behind schedule — and the ones that were ahead of schedule. Frankly he was surprised to see the huge number of forces crammed into this one ROC HQ East Central Deployment Center. No wonder they carved out these FOLT tunnels a mile underground. The noise and thundering vibrations from the sheer numbers of troops and vehicles would have shaken the ground above and instantly negated project security protocols. The secret Olympus Project wouldn't have been secret for long. But all of this movement left him with questions. Was all of this activity in response to the general's announcement about Phase II? How could all of these orders have been drafted so fast?

As he and Meg sat on the metal bench, Falcon moved his boot every now and then, wiggling his way over to Meg's shoe, giving her foot a few taps in secret code and then sliding his foot back toward his duffle bag. He was trying to lighten the mood with a little army footsie he and Meg had choreographed under the table one night at dinner but it wasn't working. For the last ten minutes Meg seemed to be in a fog, staring straight ahead, occasionally glancing at the droves of troops hustling by them. If Falcon didn't feel her crushing grip squeezing his fingers white he might think she had lost interest in him already. But one thing he learned about Meg... he should never presume anything because he was usually wrong.

To be honest he didn't like the way this felt. It was all new to him... this sensitive love stuff. He couldn't figure it out. His emotions were all over the map. One minute he felt like he had returned a kickoff for a ninety yard winning touchdown in the Rose Bowl game... the next he was more pissed off than he had ever been in his life — angrier even than when he was eleven, struck out on a 3-2 pitch with two outs and clinched the divisional championship... for the *opposing* team. He was so emotionally devastated at coming up short in that game he collapsed to the ground in despair. But he was an adult now. He couldn't very well get away with *dropping out* if things got too tough. Yet how was he supposed to function when his feelings were bouncing all over the place? How was he going to function at all with Meg four thousand miles away? The damn army sucked. His life had become massively complicated. More than anything he wanted to play his role in this new relationship correctly. He wanted to be steady and strong and assure Meg things were not as bad as they seemed... that everything was going to be fine. But it was a damn hard façade to maintain. He couldn't bear the thought of leaving her and it pissed him off that he had to do it. It was an oppressive helplessness with which he was unfamiliar.

He couldn't count the number of times in the last two days that he found himself cursing under his breath. He cursed the whole damn military, the government, ROC, the psychopathic General H.B. Hazkill and his twisted boy Benton, his own assignment — the Arctic for crap sakes — and to round out the cursing he added to his list every teacher and coach he ever had starting with kindergarten. He cursed everything that popped into his head and anything that wasn't nailed to the floor. Through it all he heard the same question over and over in his head... the question his Uncle Caleb had posed right before Falcon had left for ROC training and he still didn't know how to answer it.

"Falcon," Meg said, appearing to force a smile as she rubbed his forearm with her hand. Her eyes still looked bloodshot from their morning's final breakdown prior to leaving for the deployment center. They both had a good therapeutic cry. "I don't know if I can do this."

"Look," he told her, "We promised each other we would be strong and we have to do that. We *will* get through this I promise. I'm going to start working on getting you to Alaska the minute I process in," he said. "You have to remember... it's not as impossible as it might seem."

"It seems pretty impossible," she said. "Haven't you seen what's going on out there? The weather across the country is insane; it's unpredictable at best. There are riots, protests, insane new legislation, looting, arrests and... and deaths... and now Phase II Mobilization."

"You have to have faith," he told her, "After all I'm the archetypal example of impossibility... two promotions in one swipe remember?" He smiled, but Meg remained solemn.

"We only have three months," Meg said, "Before Phase II is officially implemented. We have no idea what's going to happen after that," her head fell against Falcon's shoulder. "I'm scared Falcon. I'm terrified for you and for me," she whispered. "This country is being torn apart."

He wrapped his arms around her and held her to him tightly. "I wish we had more time," he whispered. They lingered like that — lost in each other — until two officers rushing against the stream of the main crowd collided with them. A lieutenant caught his foot on Falcon's bag, tripped and fell with his full weight onto Falcon's shoulder, his top cover flying onto Meg's lap. A captain hurrying behind the lieutenant — following too closely on the younger officer's heels — tangled himself in the lieutenant's contorted body and nose-dived — spread eagle — directly onto Falcon's duffle bag. The captain looked up and glared at the young lieutenant untangling himself from Falcon.

"I trust this is yours," Meg said meekly to the lieutenant as she passed him his hat.

"Please accept my apology ma'am," the lieutenant pleaded while straightening up. "Oh and sir..." he said, his face waxing crimson after seeing he had toppled onto a full bird colonel. The young officer then reached down to help the captain to his feet.

"What's your damn hurry lieutenant?" the captain asked angrily.

"I'm sorry sir," the lieutenant apologized. "I... I can't miss my transport."

"If you don't slow down you're never gonna make it to the transport alive!" the captain screamed, "Because if you don't get run over by one of the PODs you're gonna get somebody else mad enough to do the job!"

"Yes sir," the lieutenant said docilely. "Sorry sir." Falcon and Meg watched the captain dust himself off and walk away in the same direction as the younger officer. The lieutenant, a few steps ahead, skulked clumsily through the crowd, clearly forcing himself to take long slow steps. He looked as awkward as an ostrich picking its way through a glass knick-knack shop.

Meg leaned over and whispered to Falcon. "I hope that captain wasn't his Platoon leader or something!" Falcon laughed. It was a tension breaker and he welcomed the momentary diversion. As the excitement dissipated Falcon surveyed the ROC soldiers and U.N. peacekeeping troops hurriedly tromping through the deployment center; he wondered what the world would look like by Christmas. As he watched the crowd he was suddenly confused. He frowned.

"Shit," Falcon mumbled.

"What?" Meg asked.

"Well look... what the..." Falcon muttered, standing up to see over the heads of the hurrying troops. "What the hell is Rabbit doing here?"

Meg stood. "Where? I can't see anything over all these people."

"He's headed this way," Falcon said. He watched Rabbit — weighted down by a full duffle bag on his shoulder — pick his way through the crowded station.

"Colonel Colby," Rabbit yelled, from about fifty yards ahead. He waved and picked up his speed. Falcon followed Rabbit's movements as he weaved and ducked and sidestepped in and out of the sea of faces and in seconds he was standing next to them.

"Rabbit," Falcon said. "What are you doing here?"

Rabbit dropped his duffle bag and set his hands on his hips, his face was flushed and sweaty and distorted with obvious discomfort. He was gasping heavily, trying to catch his breath. "Missed the last POD... had to run all the way... from the office... it's like five miles... thought I was gonna miss..."

"You're going to have a heart attack!" Meg screeched. "Sit down!"

"Rabbit," Falcon said, latching onto Rabbit's shoulder. "Sit down before you drop dead — I don't have time to do the extra damn paperwork."

Rabbit laughed, plopping down on the bench. He nodded and exhaled slowly, "Better... better... yup, much better, thank you."

"Good," Falcon said. "Now what the hell is the big rush?"

"And what *are* you doing here?" Meg added.

"Your transport leaves," Rabbit took in three large breaths, "In like seconds..."

"Yup," Falcon agreed, nodding. "It does. That's why I'm standing here all dressed up with my duffle bag in hand and looking so damn thrilled. What I want to know is what you're doing here."

"Got transferred," Rabbit said, working hard to slow his breathing.

"That was fast," Meg noted. "I thought you still didn't know as of yesterday."

"Partly true ma'am," Rabbit agreed, sighing and leaning against the back of the bench. "I was pretty sure where I was going but didn't have orders in hand until this morning. Whoa!" Rabbit exclaimed, "There's your transport landing now sir. I just made it."

"Well I appreciate you killing yourself to get down here to say goodbye again but it wasn't necessary," Falcon said, picking up his duffle bag.

"Oh I didn't run down here to say goodbye sir," Rabbit said, popping to his feet and heaving his own duffle over his shoulder. "I have to... to catch a transport myself."

"Where are you headed?" Meg asked, sliding her arm into the crook of Falcon's elbow. Meg and Falcon waited while Rabbit took a few additional deep breaths. Then the three of them started walking toward the transport POD.

"Well you wouldn't believe it ma'am," Rabbit said, grinning. "Guess I'm going north... same place as the colonel; I have orders to Alaska."

"No shit!" Falcon said laughing, dropping his bag and slapping Rabbit's shoulder. Immediately he realized he may have been a little over exuberant for a full bird colonel and he reclaimed his poise. "I mean... that's great Rabbit." Falcon glimpsed Meg smiling at his enthusiasm and he felt his face reddening.

"*I* thought so too sir!" Rabbit proclaimed cheerily. "Here sir," Rabbit said, picking up Falcon's duffle. "Let me take that. I can get these squared away so you can uh... so you can say good bye." Rabbit moved closer to Meg. He set Falcon's bag down and reached out his hand to shake Meg's. "Major Winters ma'am, it's been a pleasure."

"I will miss you Rabbit," Meg told him. "Good luck!"

"Thank you ma'am," Rabbit nodded, picking up Falcon's bag and backing up; but he wasn't looking where he was going. Two MPs jumped out of his path to miss colliding with him. "I'll take good care of the colonel too," he added, grinning. With a quick wink he turned and headed to the transport. Falcon was tempted to protest Rabbit carrying both duffles but the lieutenant was already half way to the POD; one bag was slung across his shoulder, the other in his left hand. Falcon shrugged off the urge, shook his head and turned toward Meg. He held open his arms beckoning her to slip into his embrace. She moved to him and slid her arms around his waist, nestling her head against his chest. She squeezed him tightly and then looked up into his eyes.

"I'm sad about Rabbit," Meg said. "I was looking forward to an ally around the office. But at least I'll know you're not alone up there."

"You'll be up there with us soon. I'm sorry I have to... to leave like this," he told her.

"I know," Meg said, her eyes beginning to water.

"Meg?" Falcon muttered softly, his tone half questioning and half gently admonishing her to remember their pact.

"I know," she said, sniffling. I promised I would be strong and a promise is a promise. And you had damn well better keep your promise to get me to Alaska as soon as possible. Benton isn't going to let me do anything about it from this end."

"You know I will. Now that I have Rabbit," he

assured her, "It will be a breeze to get you a transfer. You know how amazing he is. He can accomplish anything faster than anyone I ever met."

Their gazes locked in silence, neither of them stirring. They kissed... more deeply and passionately than they probably should have but protocol was the furthest thing from Falcon's mind. They each tightened their grip around the other. Falcon closed his eyes for one final instant to allow Meg's full essence to seep into him. Then he felt Meg's arms loosen around his waist and he felt as if part of his soul were slipping away from his body along with her arms. Dammit! He cursed to himself. How could anything be as painful as this without killing him? How in hell can he leave? Goddamn army, he thought.

He had made her promise she would be strong without him while he was in Alaska and at this minute he wasn't sure he himself was strong enough to walk over to the POD without her. How could he let her go — just climb into that POD and leave? He tenderly guided Meg's chin upward with his finger, swallowed and worked desperately hard to steel himself. "Meg," he whispered, "I love you."

"I love you too Falcon," she said softly.

Falcon kissed her one last time and motioned toward the transport with his eyes. He forced a smile. "Looks like I'm holding up the show." Meg nodded and squeezed his hand. "I'll see you soon," he whispered into her ear. Then he turned and briskly walked toward the POD. No way in hell was he going to tell her good bye, he told himself. He wasn't going to say those damn words.

The waiting POD was a larger transport with eight rows of two seats on each side of the center aisle. When he climbed aboard he saw Rabbit sitting about six rows back. The POD was full except for the one vacant seat next to Rabbit. Before he reached that row Rabbit jumped up and entered the aisle, waiting to see if the colonel wanted to scoot across to the inside seat. Falcon did. He peered out the window as he was getting into his seat and saw Meg. He raised his left hand in a stationary wave and Meg returned the gesture. After Falcon buckled his harness he looked back toward the platform but Meg was gone. He searched up and down the walkway and managed a glimpse of her as she disappeared through an exit door. He felt as if there were a boulder dead center in the pit of his stomach, as if all of the blood had been drained from him, as if a soggy woolen blanket had been stuffed into his nose and trachea. He wasn't certain but the need to vomit crossed his mind. If this wasn't a sudden brutal case of influenza or bubonic plague brewing in his bloodstream then this sensation was the pain of longing... when you cared more about loving another person than whether you took your next breath or not. It sucked.

The POD lifted off, hovered for a moment and then accelerated, lurching forward into the steady stream of traffic. Falcon thrust his head back against the headrest and squeezed shut his eyes. He drew in a deep breath and let it pass his lips slowly.

"Hey Colonel," Rabbit whispered, "Before you go to sleep... all right if I ask you a question?"

"I'm only resting my eyes. I don't plan to be doing much sleeping," he answered, turning his head to face the lieutenant.

"Well I'm not sure if it's okay to talk to you about this..." Rabbit mumbled hesitantly.

"It sounds serious," Falcon said. "Look... whatever you say isn't going any further than right here; if that's what you're worried about."

"Great! Thank you sir," Rabbit sighed heavily. "I just

knew you were going to say that was the case."

"So fire away," Falcon smiled.

"Okay," Rabbit began, whispering as if General Hazkill were in the seat behind them taking notes. "Phase II is imminent, right?"

"As I understand it," Falcon said. "Why?"

"Well something's bothering me sir," Rabbit began, "And I haven't talked to anyone about it because of course we aren't supposed to... but since you don't mind me bringing it up, and I trust you, and we're whispering and no one else can hear us..."

"Rabbit," Falcon interrupted.

"Sir?" Rabbit frowned.

"I know we have four thousand miles ahead of us on this trip," Falcon told him. "But it would be really good to get to your question before we get to Alaska."

"Oh," Rabbit laughed. "Yes sir absolutely."

"So... you asked about Phase II..." Falcon reminded him.

"Oh right... you're absolutely right sir," Rabbit said, nodding. "Well Phase II could get... pretty bad, you know?" Rabbit began, peeking around the inside of the POD, alternately staring down at his hands and then back to Falcon. "I mean I have relatives all over the place you know?"

"What's bothering you Rabbit?" Falcon asked.

"I'm worried sir," he whispered. "What if I'm out on patrol in the U.S. of A somewhere and what if I... you know... have ROC orders to do something... but what if this 'something' is really bad? What if I have orders to ... to shoot somebody or Taser a woman or a child? What if I have orders to... to turn my gun on someone... someone I might know?"

"Are you afraid of weapons Rabbit?" Falcon asked.

"Oh no no no sir," Rabbit laughed. "I'm not worried

about the weapons... well not exactly... not unless you count who I'm pointing the weapon at as being worried about it."

"Okay... so go on," Falcon said.

"Well what if ROC gives me an order to shoot somebody and it's like... my brother or my uncle or a kid I went to school with or maybe just someone like me from a small town and... well... what if I think that maybe the ROC order is... uh... not exactly... right? Or I don't agree with it? Maybe I think it's even illegal or something; because you know it's not the same as fighting ten thousand miles away across an ocean or two. In a foreign country we would be all military... a brotherhood against the enemy... you know? But... this is *our country* we're talking about. Maybe the enemy is... well... not so easy to pick out. So what am I supposed to do? Shoot or Taser someone when I'm ordered or refuse and be shot myself for disobeying a direct order under enemy fire or something?"

Falcon laughed.

"You're laughing sir," Rabbit said, instantly straightening his torso, sitting stiffly in his seat, eyes wide... brow angled up sharply.

"I'm not laughing at you Rabbit. Please don't think that," Falcon explained. "It's just that someone asked me pretty much that same question verbatim two years ago."

"Who?" Rabbit asked.

"A damn wise man," Falcon answered, "My Uncle Caleb."

"And...?" Rabbit probed.

"Well," Falcon said. "In all honesty I have spent a lot of sleepless nights over this question — and a few other questions about ROC forces. On one hand as a military man you have vowed allegiance to the Commander In

Chief..."

"Right... my point exactly sir," Rabbit said.

"Then too... you have sworn to uphold the Constitution of the United States," Falcon continued.

"Yes sir," Rabbit nodded. "I surely did."

"But," Falcon continued. "On the other hand you have a duty to mankind... right? To God... you know... to do what's right."

"That's it exactly sir! Exactly," Rabbit agreed.

"So," Falcon went on, "You have to look into your heart and ask yourself what kind of man you are. Are you a man who lives by your oaths... a man who follows orders no matter what because you have sworn that oath? Or are you a man who tries to do the right thing... even though sometimes trying to do the right thing can get you killed?"

"Well but what if the right thing... isn't totally clear?" Rabbit whispered.

"That's the big dilemma maybe. Sometimes... sometimes something we think might be the right thing... maybe turns out to be something less than one hundred percent the right thing. I guess that's the bottom line Rabbit," Falcon told him.

"What's that sir?" Rabbit questioned. "The real bottom line I mean?"

"Whether morality and honor and integrity are... are a matter of degrees..." Falcon answered. "I have tried to think of it in terms of black, white and gray. Many times the answer to something is very clearly either black or white. I mean... we all know the Ten Commandments tell us not to lie yet show me a person who has not once told a little fib, or stretched the truth or omitted something they maybe shouldn't have. Yet this is one of the Ten Commandments and for those of us who are God fearing people we are supposed to follow

God's law. Yet would we burn in hell for committing an offense against that law? According to the Bible we wouldn't if we have accepted God's Son as our Savior. But I think the problem comes in for us if we try to go down paths in life that we have rationalized in gradations... paths that can't be understood in terms of degrees. What is a *little* kidnapping... or a *little* robbery... or... or a *little* murder? I think somewhere a line has to be drawn. We have to define the boundaries in our life; we have to know where shades of gray are actually okay... and where they're just plain wrong. I know this doesn't help much as far as answering your question," Falcon said solemnly.

"No I think it helps; it helps me to know I'm not alone in thinking about this stuff... that I'm not the only person who is maybe questioning... uh... right and wrong and duty and honor. But..." Rabbit hesitated.

"What?" Falcon asked.

"Well it's just... it's just... this Phase II... the way things are going to be... what is going to happen... how bad the country will get; I... I'm a little... well... I'm..." Rabbit stammered. Falcon looked squarely into Rabbit's eyes to see if he could read in them what Rabbit had on his mind. What Falcon saw there was no surprise. He had seen it before... in Meg's eyes only minutes ago... in his own eyes — lately more often than not — each time he glanced in the mirror.

He frowned and nodded to Rabbit before he spoke. "We're all... we're all scared Rabbit," Falcon told him. "We're all scared."

Reference Section

General Notes:

For reader convenience each book in the American Rage series incorporates a cumulative reference component comprised of General Notes, Text Notes, Character Notes, Definitions and Acronyms.

Text Notes:

Non-English words, sounds (including some thoughts or conversations occurring solely in a character's mind), newspaper quotations (real or fictitious), book titles, and presidential press conferences (fictitious) when quoted and not offset from the text, are generally italicized. When a character's accent is represented with a phonetic type spelling of English, these words are also italicized. Dashed lines are used to set off definitions of foreign words, to explain concepts or uses of words or to simply add clarification or emphasis to the word or phrase. Military hours are used in sections of the book where military hours would normally be used such as where action occurs in military facilities or in the scientific community. Those hours are expressed using the twenty-four hour clock. For purposes of pronunciation and punctuation they are expressed as follows: For morning hours, 0800 hours would be 'oh eight hundred hours'; 0830 hours would be 'oh eight thirty' hours, and so on. Note: PRESIDENTIAL ASSASSINATION: William McKinley was shot and mortally wounded on September 6, 1901 inside the Temple of Music on the grounds of the Pan-American Exposition in Buffalo, New York. Leon Czolgosz, an anarchist, walked up to the president in a receiving line and shot him with a handgun. President McKinley died on September 14 from a gangrenous wound. Note: The full text of the poem by Robert Service (1874-1958), *The Cremation of Sam McGee*, can be found on the Internet at the Poetry Foundation, www.poetryfoundation.org.

Characters Notes:

To assist in character identification throughout the American Rage series each book includes a cumulative list of characters grouped by family, affiliation and/or status from the first book onward. All characters — except well-known historical personalities such as President McKinley and his assassin — events and character actions are fictitious or are used in a fictitious manner.

Definitions:

Non-English words and their definitions appear in the reference section of each book in the series as applicable. Within the text most definitions are provided upon first usage of the word and set apart with dashes. Any longer definitions used in the text are attributable to Wikipedia for the most part and have been paraphrased. Links to pages can be found using keywords for Internet searches.

Acronyms:

The American Rage series contains numerous real and fictitious acronyms that are defined in each book in the series both in the body of the text on first usage and in the end reference section. Some acronym definitions of well-known terms were comprised from online and reference sources such as encyclopedias, dictionaries and other sources in the public domain. Most of these sources were not cited unless the source specifically required or requested attribution. No proprietary sources of information were used in acronyms or definitions unless specifically noted. Any omissions in citing sources are purely unintentional.

Characters

Falcon Colby: Major, ROC trainee, initially stationed at ROC Training Facility Marietta, Georgia and ROC Eastern Division Headquarters in Massachusetts. He grew up as an only child in Templeton, Massachusetts. He has one living aunt and great uncle at the start of ROC training.

Whitehawk: Major, ROC trainee, roommate of Falcon Colby during ROTC college years and through ROC training. He was born in Alaska and was like a brother to Falcon. Whitehawk was separated from Falcon at the ROC graduation ceremony.

Ilya Salko: Juneau, Alaska, Tlingit *ichta* — shaman — grandmother to Viktor Salko.

Five Running Rebels*:*

Viktor Salko: Juneau, Alaska, twenty-six year old scientist, founder of the FRR Corporation — (FRR), the Five Running Rebels. Viktor officially works at the SUA Research Facility Southeast in Southeast Alaska. He is an Aukwan Tlingit Native Alaskan, the youngest and last in a line of seven siblings..

Matthew (Matt) Cordwick: Scientist; original member of the Five Running Rebels (FRR), younger cousin of Dan Cordwick.

Anders (Andy) Borca: Scientist; original member of the Five Running Rebels (FRR).

Gilman (Gil) Pope: Private pilot and scientist; original member of the Five Running Rebels (FRR).

Grace Stonewoods: Scientist; original member of the Five Running Rebels (FRR).

Daniel (Dan) Cordwick: M.D. and general surgeon, older cousin to Matt Cordwick (FRR). Dan becomes an essential member of the FRR Research Corp.

Fizer Family:

Nick Fizer: Forty-five year old full Bird Colonel, twenty-two year career army officer assigned to Regional Operations Command (ROC) Training Center, Marietta, Georgia, Chief of Staff to General Pierce Tucker, in charge of the ROC training program. Nick is a West Virginia native who grew up on his parents' farm.

Stephanie (Stephy) Fizer: PhD in psychology, writer of fiction, Wife of Nick Fizer.

William Fizer: Father of Nick Fizer, resides with wife on Fizer farm in Shepherdstown, West Virginia.

Julia Fizer: Mother of Nick Fizer, Shepherdstown, West Virginia.

Goodriver Family:

Henry Ivan Goodriver: Deceased.

Miriam Goodriver: Takotna, Alaska, thirty-five year old widow, Native Tlingit originally of the Eagle Moiety in Southeast Alaska, lives alone with children, Kyle and Kenzie. Husband Henry Ivan Goodriver.

Kenzie Goodriver: Takotna, Alaska: Twelve-year-old daughter of Miriam and Henry Ivan Goodriver.

Kyle Goodriver: Takotna, Alaska: Nine-year-old son of Miriam and Henry Ivan Goodriver.

Malikov Family:

Pavel Aleksandrovich Malikov: Takotna, Alaska, forty-eight year old native Russian serving with U.N. Peacekeeping force in support of ROC forces, thirty year career military man in what is now the Russian Federation Army, attained the rank of *Senior Starshiná* — NATO equivalent of Chief Master-Sergeant. Stationed at the FOLT — Forward Operations Laboratory Tunnel — Takotna, Alaska.

Aleksi Malikov: Zolotaryovka, Russia, grandfather to Pavel Aleksandrovich Malikov, WWII veteran of the Soviet Army and a Russian peasant farmer in the *Chernozemnaya polosa* — Black Earth Belt, fought at the Battle of Stalingrad.

Irina Malikov (Babushka): grandmother to Pavel Aleksandrovich Malikov, the woman against whom all other women were measured by Malikov.

Other ROC Forces:

Sergei Nikulin: serves with Malikov in Russian Federation Army, equivalent to Tech Sergeant in U.S. Army and U.N., attached to the U.N. peacekeeping forces in Takotna, Alaska.

Yury Bugak: Tall, lanky, unpleasant Russian Federation Army sergeant attached to the U.N. peacekeeping forces in Takotna, Alaska.

Eric Booner: Staff Sergeant U.S. Army, ROC forces MP stationed in Takotna, Alaska.

Frank Benton: Major, ROC trainee, assigned Headquarters, Regional Operations Command (ROC), Eastern Division.

Pierce Tucker: Major General (two stars), Commander, Regional Operations Command (ROC), Training Facility, Marietta, Georgia.

'Rabbit' Packlander: First Lieutenant, Headquarters, Regional Operations Command (ROC), Eastern Division, aide to Falcon Colby.

H.B. Hazkill: Lieutenant General (three stars), Commander, Headquarters Regional Operations Command (ROC), Eastern Division.

Meagan Winters: Major, U.S. Army, ROC officer trainee, assigned to Headquarters, Regional Operations Command (ROC), Eastern Division, grew up in Portland, Oregon, only child of two only children.

Minor Characters

Kapitan Boris Natkorksky: An *advokat* — attorney — who meets with Malikov.

Nurse Elizabeth: Nurse Practitioner at the Takotna Medical Clinic.

Macey Kindings: Stephy Fizer's longtime friend.

Mr. Olani: Owner of the Takotna, Alaska General Store.

Definitions

English

Some English words are not often used in daily conversations. For reader convenience, occasional definitions of this type will be included in the reference sections of the American Rage series.

Adit: horizontal passage leading into a mine for access or drainage.

Aircraft boot: The boot of an aircraft is a system of atmospheric ice protection. Ice on an aircraft can cause the shape of airfoils and flight control surfaces to change which can lead to a complete loss of control. There are a number of boot types: pneumatic deicing boots, electric thermal, bleed air, electro-mechanical, weeping wing and passive.

Alaska State Trooper Hellcat 650C: A fictional single turboprop engine, fixed gear, upper winged, short hop Cavalcade Reptile with Sleakaire 9000 floats capable of touching down on land or water.

Cryptid: in cryptozoology and sometimes in cryptobotany, a cryptid creature or plant is one whose existence has been suggested but is not recognized by scientific consensus.

Cryptobotany: the study of various exotic plants which are not believed to exist by the scientific community, but which exist in myth, literature or unsubstantiated reports.

Cryptozoology: the search for and study of animals whose existence or survival is disputed or unsubstantiated such as the Loch Ness monster, yeti and chupacabra.

Malikov's Hippocampus – Hippocampus is an area with elongated ridges on the floor of each lateral ventricle of the brain, thought to be the center of emotion, memory, and autonomic nervous system. This is arguably the home of Malikov's best and worst contemplations.

Russian

Transliterations (the conversion of text from one script to another) and translations for the Russian language used in the AMERICAN RAGE Series the letters of a word or phrase are written by substituting English letters for Russian characters. Definitions and usage may vary from other renditions of the same word or phrase. However every attempt was made to use the most common and accepted translations, transliterations and definitions. Colloquial forms of the translation were used wherever possible.

Cardinal numbers used:

Raz — one.

Dva — two.

Tri — three.

Chetyre — four.

Pyat' — five.

Amerikanskaya tyuremnaya kamera — American prison cell.

Amerikanskaya tyur'ma — American prison.

Amerikanskiy duraki — American fools.

Amerikantsy — Americans.

Angel-khranitel — guardian angel.

Babushka — grandmother.

Beshenaya sobaka — mad/rabid dog.

Blyadskiy rod — Goddamned it.

Bog sprashivayet — please; imploring, God asks.

Bud'te spokoyno vso budet khorosho — be at peace, everything will be ok.

Chernozemnaya polosa — Black Earth Belt (zone) (Also known as the 'Breadbasket of Europe').

Da — yes.

Dacha — country home.

Da, *tochno* — yes, exactly.

Da, tovarishch — yes, comrade.

Da? Vy nichego ne znayete — you know nothing.

Derevenskiy magazine — the village shop.

Dobroye utra — good morning.

Glupyy Amerikanets — foolish Americans.

Govno sobach'ye — Dog shit!

Idi k chortu — go to hell.

Kakashka — piece of shit.

Kapitan — captain.

Krest'yan — peasants.

Krest'yanin — peasant.

Krest'yanka — peasant woman.

Khorosho — good.

Kolkhoz — collective farm.

Leytenant — lieutenant.

Lyudi uvazhali menya — people had respect for me.

Mayor — major.

Mir — a community which acted as a village cooperative government.

Mladshiy leytenanty — junior lieutenant.

Mne nado k dyadya Vane — I need the head (colloquial); literally, I have to go to uncle Vanya.

Moskovskaya militsiya — Moscow police (after 2011). In 2011, the Militsiya became the Politsiya as the Russian police reform initiated by President Dmitry Medvedev began to improve the efficiency of Russia's police forces (C.P.).

Moskovskiy politseyskiy shtab — Moscow police headquarters.

Moy dragotsennyy mal'chik — my precious little boy.

Moy khoroshiy drug — my good friend.

Moy malen'kiy vnuk — my little grandson.

Muzh — husband.

Muzhchina or chelovek — man.

Mycop — trash.

Neplokho — not bad.

Neudachnik — loser, lame duck, nonstarter.

NKVD — *Narodnyĭ Kommissariat Vnutrennikh Del* – the secret police agency in the former Soviet Union that absorbed the functions of the OGPU in 1934. It merged with the MVD in 1946; OGPU – *Gosudarstvennoye Politicheskoye upravleniye* (Joint State Political Directorate under the Council of People's Commissars of the USSR); MVD — *Ministerstvo vnutrennykh Del*-MVD (Ministry of Internal affairs).

Nuzhno kak v zhope zub — absolutely worthless, as worthless as tits on a boar hog.

Nyet — no.

Penza oblast — Penza region.

Politbyuro — Politburo.

Pozhaluysta! Bud'te dobry — please! Be so good.

Provodnik — conductor (as in *Provodnik poyezda* – train conductor).

Rodina — birth land; motherland.

Ryadovoy — private.

Samovar — a self-boiling urn.

(Senior) Starshiná — A senior Master-Sergeant in the Russian Federation Army, formerly the U.N. equivalent of Chief Master Sergeant.

Slushayte menya — listen to me.

Smert' — death.

Staryye voyennyye veterany — old military veterans.

Svin'ya — swine.

Svolotch — scum.

Tikho vso budet Khorosho — quiet, everything will be ok.

Tsvet obshchestva — cream of society.

Tpyc — coward.

Umer — dead.

Voyennaya militsiya — military police.

Voyna — war.

V zhopu p'yanyy dolboyob — drunk ass mother f*...!

Ya budu mochit'sya — I will urinate.

Ya budu vyssat'sya — I'll piss myself.

YA khotel bit' yego i v rot, i v sraku — I should kick his ass from hell to breakfast.

Ya tak dumal — I thought so.

Ya yebu — well, f*...!

Zalupa — dickhead.

Zalupa konskaya — ass-hole.

Zhigul' — a 1970s re-engineered version of the Fiat that ultimately exported as the Lada/Zhigul'.

German

Hitlerjugend — Hitler's youth movement.

Stielhandgranate — German M24 stick hand grenade.

Tlingit

Ichta — shaman.

Kanat'á — blueberry.

Kaneegwál' — salmon egg berry pudding.

Leelk'w — grandmother.

Tléikw — berry.

Tu kinajek — guardian spirit.

Tpyc — coward.

Was'x'aan Tléighu — salmon berry.

Acronyms

AP2R — Active Phase II Readiness; the phase of the Olympus Project where, by order of the President's National Security Directive 1-0078 and upon implementation of the Phase II order, domestic security falls under oversight and control of the Olympus Project. Within ninety days of AP2R, Regional Operations Commanders would receive the order to initiate implementation of Phase II of the OPSEIM Directive.

A-TEONIC — Artificial Tunnel-Enhanced Operational Nano Intellect Cell.

CO — Commanding Officer.

COMSEC — Communications Security; a system used in the Department of Defense to ensure the security of telecommunications confidentiality and integrity — two IA — Information Assurance — pillars. There are five COMSEC security types: 1) Cryptosecurity-encrypts data and renders it unreadable unless properly decrypted; 2) EMSEC-Emission Security prevents release of emanations from equipment such as cryptographic equipment thus preventing unauthorized interception of data; 3) Physical security-ensures safety of and prevents unauthorized access to cryptographic documents and equipment; 4) Traffic-Flow Security-hides messages and message characteristics flowing on a network and; 5) TRANSEC-protects transmissions from unauthorized access, preventing interruption and harm.

DARPA — Defense Advanced Research Projects Agency.

D-Grid — Destination Grid; Area directly surrounding a POD's programmed destination. Once a POD travelling in a tunnel nears the area within 500 yards of the programed destination, all vehicle ancillary systems automatically shut down (systems such as passenger VRD Streamcast Videos displayed on a VRD equipped helmet).

DHS — Department of Homeland Security.

DoD — Department of Defense.

ELF — Extreme Low Frequency; Electromagnetic radio waves emitted by H.A.A.R.P. systems. Said to cause atmospheric and environmental disturbances, disruption of brain wave activity, physical symptoms.

E-GPS — Enhanced Global Positioning System; Military enhancement of commercial global positioning system technology.

ENMOD — Environmental Modification Convention; A treaty signed and ratified by the United States, is an international agreement prohibiting military or other hostile use of environmental modification techniques having widespread, long-lasting or severe effects as the means of destruction, damage or injury.

EPA — Environmental Protection Agency.

FC — Field Commander; Regional Operations Command (ROC) designation.

FOLT — Forward Operations Laboratory Tunnels; Military facilities that are essentially self-supporting underground military cities protected from disclosure by high-level secrecy protocols. Plausible deniability — refusal to acknowledge the existence of these complex underground tunnel networks in America — is the present standard operating procedure in the *American Rage* series.

FRR Research Corp — Five Running Rebels; Viktor's corporation doing business as the FRR Research Corp. and consisting of Viktor Salko, Andy Borca, Matt Cordwick, Gil Pope and Grace Stonewoods. Dr. Dan Cordwick joined the group shortly after Viktor formed it. Members are all scientists with the exception of Dan who is a physician/surgeon.

G-ROC — Global Regional Operations Command; Sister agencies to the U.S. Regional Operations Command serving located worldwide.

H.A.A.R.P. — High Frequency Active Auroral Research Program; An ionospheric research project reportedly jointly funded by the U.S. Air

Force, U.S. Navy, the University of Alaska, and the Defense Advanced Research Projects Agency — DARPA — among others, located in Gakona, Alaska.

HQ — Headquarters.

IA — Information Assurance; Pillars of security used in Department of Defense computer networks (see COMSEC).

IAR — Inverse Anti-Rectenna; An element of Viktor's theoretical application to convert light into larger radio waves that can be conducted from the earth into the Ionosphere rather than from the Ionosphere to earth.

IRI — Ionospheric Research Instrument; A component used in research at the H.A.A.R.P. facility in Gakona, Alaska.

JPATS — (pronounced *Jaypats*) Justice Prisoner and Alien Transport, nicknamed Con Air; An agency of the federal government. Technically it is a revolving fund activity with total operating costs reimbursed by customer agencies. JPATS coordinates the movement of the majority of federal prisoners and detainees, including sentenced, pretrial and criminal aliens, in the custody of the U.S. Marshals Service and the Bureau of Prisons.

LMS – Little Man Syndrome; Stephy Fizer's descriptor for annoying, short, narcissistic men who try to monopolize every conversation, manipulate people and puff themselves up to compensate for perceived shortcomings and insecurities based on their own deep seated feelings of inadequacy.

MCCSLA — Mandatory Corporate Community Service League Act (pronounced *Miksla*); A mandatory obligation first implemented by executive order and later reaffirmed by congressional bill requiring two years full time unpaid 'volunteer' service for every American citizen.

MJTF — Multijurisdictional Task Forces; Foreign troops and vehicles amassing on U.S. soil for the stated purpose of training. The government explains MJTF as part of a global training exercise for preparing multijurisdictional special forces to fight terrorism and the world drug problem... and to render aide in times of calamity.

MODv-PODs — Military Operational Defense Vehicle PODs; PODs for short, are military hovercrafts or flying cars. POD is the common term for all types of hovercraft in the ROC military realm.

MRI — Magnetic Resonance Imaging.

NKVD — *Narodnyĭ Kommissariat Vnutrennikh Del*; The secret police agency in the former Soviet Union that absorbed the functions of the OGPU in 1934. It merged with the MVD in 1946; OGPU — *Gosudarstvennoye Politicheskoye upravleniye* (Joint State Political Directorate under the Council of People's Commissars of the USSR); MVD — *Ministerstvo vnutrennykh Del*-MVD (Ministry of Internal affairs).

NRA — National Rifle Association.

NQ Rating System — Non-Qualified rating system; new terminology developed by the government eighteen months prior to the ROC (Regional Operations Command) graduation ceremony, that replaces the old Selective Service method of categorizing an individual's fitness for induction into the armed services. Pronounced '1-Knock', the new system is based on a presumptive Non-Qualified baseline: 1-NQ, signifies you'll never get into the military no matter whether the country is at war or peace; 2-NQ signifies you have some chance of getting in if the country is at war and; 3-NQ signifies, the government wants you in peace time or we're at war and you will be immediately called up to serve.

OPSEIM Directive — Olympus Project Strategic Execution and Implementation Manifesto; initially signed in 1901 by parties not yet disclosed. It is the blueprint for the new global society that encompasses all New World Order objectives and other blueprints.

OTSSP — Olympus Top Secret Security Protocol; Brutal, absolute standards by which ROC forces must maintain secrecy when conducting business and when referencing elements of the Olympus Project and OPSEIM Directive. Punishment for infraction is harsh and will become harsher.

RFSN — Regional FOLT Systems Network; similar to a VPN, Virtual Private Network, and connects throughout the entire FOLT tunnel network grid system.

RIF— Reduction In Force; (pronounced 'riff' in government and military circles) and defined as a separation from employment due to lack of funds, lack of work, redesign or elimination of positions or reorganization with no likelihood or expectation that the employee will be recalled because the position is eliminated. The U.S. Office of Personnel Management (OPM) developed policy and provides guidance to federal agencies undergoing a RIF. Federal agencies are required to follow procedures outlined in Title 5 of the Code of Federal Regulations, Part 351, and must consider the following factors when releasing employees: 1) tenure of employment (type of appointment); 2) veteran's preference; 3) length of service and; 4) performance ratings.

ROC forces — Regional Operations Command; Branch of

Department of Defense, was created under Presidential Emergency Executive Order 1216606, *Immediate Order to Restructure All Military Branches*. Upon the occurrence of certain contingencies or as specifically ordered by the President of the United States, ROC forces would assume command of the United States FOLT T21— twenty-first century tunnel grid — consisting of a complex network of secret underground military bases, laboratories and research facilities across America. ROC forces serve as the instrument of implementation, execution and enforcement of all OPSEIM Directive components and mandates.

ROC-GPCS — Regional Operations Command (ROC) Global Point Community Site; a ROC Virtual Private Network (VPN).

ROC-LOCK — ctrl-alt-del-ROC-LOCK; an OTSSP (Olympus Top Secret Security Protocol) sequence for locking all components connected to the A-TEONIC server system.

SAP — Special Access Programs; Programs off the 'transparency grid,' not subject to congressional, audit or other oversight due to a national security component.

SCIF — Sensitive Compartmented Information Facility; (Pronounced 'skiff') is an enclosed area within a building or Tunnel Sector that is used to process Sensitive Compartmented Information (SCI) types of classified information.

SEEDS — No direct correlation of the letters to words as with other acronyms – used more as slang by the Five Running Rebels). The word represents rectennas that function under the principles of nanotechnology; multiple antennas invisible to the naked eye spread over a wide area to capture a greater area of signal or, in the case of Viktor's theoretical application, more energy.

SHIDS — Short Term In-FOLT Detainment Sector, pronounced 'shidz' — a detention area in all FOLT facilities for enlistees, and occasionally officers, committing minor or administrative offenses such as failure to report, disorderly conduct, malingering, brawling or for temporarily housing of more serious offenders during investigations or while awaiting assignment to long term detention sectors.

SIPRNet — Secret Internet Protocol Router Network — a system of interconnected computer networks used by the United States Department of Defense and the U.S. Department of State to transmit classified information (up to and including information classified SECRET by packet switching over the TCP/IP protocols in a completely secure environment).

SUARS — SUA Research Facility Southeast; A private independent research facility in the Juneau, Alaska, area with several satellite facilities throughout the state. Viktor Salko and the other members of the Five Running Rebels (FRR) are employed there as researchers (their day jobs). The FRR is the group's own research facility based in the Perseverance Mine, Juneau, Alaska.

TBM — Tunnel Boring Machine; These TBMs are usually comprised of a rotating cutting wheel, cutter head with a main bearing, a thrust system and support mechanisms. The type of TBM selected for drilling particular tunnels depends on the geology of the target area and ground water levels. Also called a Mole.

TSA — Transportation Security Administration; A federal agency under the Department of Homeland Security. In 2014 there were 55,600 employees ready to preserve the security of the public traveling domestically. There are several divisions: 1) The TSOs — Transportation Security Officers, carry no guns and are not permitted to use force. These are the screeners; 2) BDOs — Behavior Detection Officers — are TSOs who observe passengers going through checkpoints selecting suspicious passengers for extra screening and searching; 3) FAMs — Federal Air Marshal Service — carry weapons; 4) TSIs — Transportation Security Inspectors — inspect, and investigate passenger and cargo transportation systems to see how secure they are; 5) National Explosives Detection Caine Teams Program-the canine teams with dogs who can initiate warrantless searches based on signals from the dog; 6) VIPR teams — Visible Intermodal Prevention and Response Teams — controversially deployed to special events and train stations, ports, truck weigh stations and other places. They actively engage in approximately 8,000 operations per year. All sections of the TSA are issued badges resembling police badges and this has caused contention by bonafide police organizations. One TSA individual was killed at the L.A. airport in the 'line of duty'. A man wearing fatigues and carrying a bag containing a hand-written note that said he wanted to kill TSA and pigs shot a TSA in the airport. Little information about the 'gunman' was released. The GAO — General Accounting Office — issued a report noting there is no evidence that techniques like SPOT — Screening of Passengers by Observation Techniques, a behavioral detection program with an annual budget of hundreds of millions of dollars — are effective. The TSA was created following the 2001 'terrorist' acts.

UAS — University of Alaska Southeast; Is located in Juneau, Alaska. Viktor Salko and the original members of the Five Running Rebels' alma mater.

UAVs — Unmanned Aerial Vehicles.

USDA — United States Department of Agriculture.

UnWDMCC — Unique Weather Display & Manipulation Control Component; A system application whereby Malikov's laptop was programmed to manage, analyze and ferry data through to a mainframe control structure on the RFSN — Regional FOLT Systems Network.

VRD — Virtual Retina Display.

VTNs — Virtual Telecommunications Network Stations; A system allowing virtual computer interface within ROC, space satellites and the global tunnel grid. Most ROC PODs, other vehicles and mobilized field command systems are equipped with this technology.

Acknowledgments

❄❄❄❄❄

I am grateful to my family members for their unconditional support, their unwavering encouragement and their willingness to overlook my untimeliness with all of the important affairs of life. I also wish to thank Sandy, Rachael, Marty, John, Kathi and Fran for the many hours they so generously devoted to reviewing the manuscript. Thank you to Catherine for her poignant comments and her guidance with the nuances of Russian translation, transliteration and Russian colloquial expressions. Special thanks to John, B.B., who never once questioned my sanity... aloud anyway... and who ignited a new awareness of reality in me many years ago.

Photographs and Maps

Some photographs and maps contained within this text — while manipulated to reflect particular aspects of the story line or achieve certain effects — are copyrighted in their basic form. I am grateful to these artists for providing the following:

We the People Photo ID 957151 © R. Gino Santa Maria Dreamstime.com;

Gray Scale 3D Map of North America Photo ID 23009217 © Raya Dreamstime.com;

Pair of Bald Eagles ID 12281290 © Richard Lowthian Dreamstime.com.

About the Author

❄❄❄❄❄

N. A. Bottari, a U.S. Air Force veteran, grew up in New England and lives on Douglas Island in Southeast Alaska. The island is comprised of 199.243 square kilometers of mountains, glaciers, forest and shoreline and lies directly across the Gastineau Channel from Juneau. She was a Salt Lake City Olympic Torch Bearer for the 2002 Olympics and in 2005 traveled to Iceland to dog sled on the Langjokull Glacier. In addition to eagerly planning and awaiting the next visit with her family, the author has spent some of her free time contemplating the serenity of two particularly curious bald eagles that sit for hours every day on the light poles in the Gastineau Channel right next to the Juneau-Douglas Bridge.